The Loss of Heaven

Doubleday

NEW YORK · LONDON · TORONTO · SYDNEY · AUCKLAND

The Loss of Heaven

Ben Greer

Published by Doubleday, a division of
Bantam Doubleday Dell Publishing Group, Inc.
666 Fifth Avenue. New York, New York 10103

Doubleday and the portrayal of an anchor with a dolphin
are trademarks of Doubleday, a division of Bantam
Doubleday Dell Publishing Group, Inc.

Library of Congress Cataloging-in-Publication Data

Greer, Ben.
   The loss of heaven.

   I. Title.
PS3557.R399L67   1988   813'.54   88-14972

ISBN 0-385-23616-6

This book is for Benjamin Dunlap,
in whose class I first began to feel the possibility.

The Loss of Heaven

1

WICK LONGSTREET WAS SITTING
in the bell tower smoking a cigarette and looking at the stars. The night
sky was heavy with them and they shone through a mist which made
them look big and soft and yellow. Cicadas buzzed in the trees and
crickets and tree frogs cried in the willows, which the moon turned
silver and black by degrees. Was there a God or was there not? And if
there was—His existence raised more questions than it answered.
Where had evil come from? It seemed inescapable to him that God had
created evil. His Aunt Boykin told him that she found it comforting that
God had, because it meant that everything would turn out all right for
everyone. He considered this thought naive. How could he trust himself
to the creator of cancer, Adolf Hitler and hell even if He had also
created women, Saint Francis and heaven? At best, God was duplicitous
and at worst—and this truly frightened him—He was beyond good and
evil.

He knew he had these thoughts because his parents had been killed in a plane crash when he was young. He and his three brothers had gone to live with their grandmother in a great house far from the small one in which they had been raised. It had not been such a good life. People might envy him and say yeah but you were rich, and sure he was rich, but it had been a very difficult youth. He didn't miss it. He had struggled against his grandmother's iron will from the beginning. He could still recall their first argument. He was twelve years old, his mother and father had been dead a week, and Harper insisted that each boy sleep in a separate room. No lights were allowed after 8 P.M. At bedtime, Blackie and Ford cried, Starkey said nothing, but Wick spoke up.

"Grandmama . . ."

"I'm Harper. I'm not anybody's Grandmama or Gram or Nana. It's H-A-R-P-E-R to each and everyone of you."

"Harper, I don't think it's fair."

"What's not fair?"

"Not having night-lights."

"Why not?"

"Because we're all used to it. Ford and I had a night-light in the wall and Starkey and Blackie left a lamp on. It makes sense if you think about it. Starkey and Blackie are younger so they need more light and Ford and me are older, so we need less light, but all of us need a little help because we're growing up."

Harper had been irritated that she'd been appealed to in such a logical manner, but she allowed the night-lights, secretly admiring the boy's courage.

Wick felt grateful for the light, grateful for the home, grateful for the grandmother he could not call grandmother, and though he and Harper often argued in the years that followed, his sense of gratitude only deepened and eventually turned into love.

But the struggle between them continued—or rather the struggle among them, because his grandmother ran his brothers' lives just as carefully as she did his own and he often witnessed the fights that resulted from the clashing of powerful egos. When he was sixteen Harper engaged a fencing instructor during the summer to teach him and his brothers the fundamentals of the foil. The boys met with the master secretly and honed their skills in eager anticipation of beating Harper—always a delightful prospect for the boys. They competed at chess, bridge and even badminton. Matches were held in the great ballroom during the dead of winter.

Wick and his grandmother had battled most bitterly over religion. She was a Presbyterian with very little faith and she was suspicious of anyone who had a lot. Wick had become interested in long-distance running his freshman year and Starkey had introduced him to a trainer who was also a priest. The two of them spent a lot of time together and the priest produced acceptable answers to Wick's questions. As soon as Harper discovered that he was talking to a priest, she got angry and told him to learn to figure out life for himself—"you can't depend on someone else for the basics." She told him to stop seeing Father Ryan and find a nice Presbyterian minister to make him feel better about this life and the most possible lack of one in the hereafter.

Naturally Wick started going to Mass, where he fell in love with the traditions and liturgy of the Church. When he started taking instruction, Harper took away his car. A year later he made his first Communion and Harper cut off his allowance. It was all right, though, because the protracted struggle gave him an edge. It made him competitive.

Sometimes Wick believed he chose the Trappist order out of competitiveness as much as anything else. The day he told Harper he was thinking of becoming a priest, she was so shocked that she immediately tried to act nonchalant and started naming the various orders which he might consider.

"After all, if you're actually going through with this you should consider everything the church has to offer; there's Benedictines and Jesuits . . ."

"The Dominicans," Wick said.

"Franciscans."

"Trappists."

"Well, I don't think you could make it as a Trappist."

"Why not?"

"I don't think you could cut it. They don't drink. They don't bathe and they don't speak. They are the Anabaptists of the Catholic Church."

Wick was fascinated by the challenge. He located the nearest monastery and started spending his weekends there and during one of them something happened to him. He discovered stillness. He had been at the monastery for three days and on the last day during vigils at four-fifteen in the morning he suddenly began to experience a feeling of utter peace and joy and health. It was like a drug.

Three weeks later, in his senior year of college, he asked to enter the Monastery of Peace and he was accepted as a novice. That had been six years ago.

Below him a bell tolled two o'clock; it was time to wake the community.

He slipped down through the bell tower, opened a side door and entered the dark abbey. It was wonderful here at this hour of the morning. He stood at the back of the church and leaned against a wall. It was so dark and mystical in the middle of the night. Only two lights burned—the small sacristy lamp and the gold light behind the altar. The floor was black marble and the walls white limestone, the choir stall before the altar was oakwood. Seven arches supported the brown planks of the roof. Trappist architecture was simple and pure and he loved it. At first the arches had reminded him of the ribs of a whale and he had felt as if he were inside its belly, looking through great ribs toward the long backbone.

Wick walked down the aisle between the wooden choir stalls and knelt in the gold light of the altar and whispered, Oh Lord, help me to do my best. As he prayed an insidious thought crept from some corner of his mind, You don't believe.

Wick climbed to the second level of the dormitory, entered his cell and put on his habit. First came the white ankle-length alb and then the black cowl and finally his sandals and leather belt. He grabbed a box of three-foot beeswax candles. His cell was the first one on the hall. Beyond it lay nine cells on the left and ten on the right.

At each cell he pushed back the cloth curtain, stepped inside and touched a monk gently on the foot, whispering, "Brother, it's time." Usually the monks woke quickly, but now and again he had to shake a foot.

Wick woke forty men in the dormitory, giving each one a candle, then he left the main building of the monastery and walked toward the shops and barns. Another ten men slept here.

Everything was covered with dew and the air was cool and wet. Before him stood a clothesline. Several cowls hung from the wires, as well as white altar cloths and a host of white purificators. Dewdrops beaded the wires of the clothesline and the moonlight turned the drops into thousands of sparkles. Beyond the clothesline was smooth grass and this was covered with millions of points of light. Tall shops with angular roofs and black shingles stood here.

The Brothers who slept in the barns and shops were called characters. They were usually older men who wore white, long beards and brown skull caps and a sour odor which came from rarely taking showers. They were toothless, hairless and often joyless. Upon his arrival, Wick had been surprised when others said these men were saints. He had thought saints were happy.

Quietly, Wick entered the wood-working room. Brother Pius slept on a straw mat in the corner by the buzz saw. The old monk was lying on his back, wearing his black and white habit. A brown skullcap covered his eyes and the bridge of his large nose. Sawdust and woodchips were spattered across his white beard.

Wick touched the old man's sandal-clad foot and Brother Pius jolted and sprang awake, knocking the cap from his bald head and waving two fists which held two rosaries made of black beads.

"I was praying," the old monk said.

"Brother?"

"Don't you . . . how dare anyone disturb the . . . uh, deeply at my prayers . . ."

"Brother Pius, it's time for Father Abbot's . . ."

The old monk yawned a mouth of smooth pink gums, then rubbed his two bony thumbs into his sleep-swollen eyes. He looked at Wick suddenly.

"Who are you? Oh yes, I know, you're that young fella who's putting together . . . Why are you doing it though? It's very unusual. I don't know if I like it, in fact—I don't like it. I think it's worldly and a temptation—are you a devil?"

Wick laughed. "I think sometimes I am a devil—or at least have devilish traits. I wonder how long it will take me to get rid of them."

"Oh, all your life and then some. What's in the box?"

"Candles."

"I'll take one. This thing's not going to take long, is it?"

"No, Brother."

"Good 'cause I don't approve of it. Not at all, not in the least. I'm offering it up as penance. I have prayers . . ."

Wick helped Brother Pius find his way through the dark to the kitchen door of the monastery, then he went to wake the others in the shops and barns. One of the old men spat at him, several refused to wake. In the end, he only got three more monks to go.

Around three o'clock Wick had placed the forty monks into position. They stood in a semicircle around the lower part of the choir. In their black cowls they could hardly be seen. The abbey was very dark beyond the gold light of the altar.

Quickly Wick went to the kitchen, opened the cupboard door and picked up the coconut cake. It was two feet high and glistened with fresh coconut. Wick had learned to bake from Nathaniel at Waverly. He thought that this cake was probably the best one he had ever baked and that was fitting because today was the abbot's fiftieth year as a priest and also his birthday and he deserved the very best.

At precisely three-fifteen, Dom Lewis, abbot of the Monastery of Peace, made his way down the center aisle of the abbey as he had for the last thirty years. He was small and stooped and thin with gray hair and a clean-shaven face. He was blind in one eye and partially sighted in the other. He climbed the two steps into the wooden choir and opened his folding seat with his left hand. Behind him, as he opened the office, the first monk lit the first candle. Softly, in Gregorian chant, the forty men began to sing the abbot's favorite hymn—*Pange lingua gloriosi.*

The abbot turned and watched the invisible semicircle brighten with candles.

Wick was standing in the sacristy, just off the altar. He was holding the coconut cake, whose center candle was lit. He looked down into the dark church and the wooden choir. His brothers were singing the hymn softly and the candles were flickering white and blue flames and there was in the air the faint trace of old incense, and he thought to himself, This is the most beautiful place in the world tonight, the most pure and lovely and surely I belong here, surely I do.

When the monks finished the hymn, they immediately started singing *Happy Birthday* and Wick walked down the aisle holding the shining coconut cake before him. The abbot turned and smiled, clapped his hands and folded them over his chest.

Afterward there was cake and coffee and good cheer, but when Wick spoke to the abbot, the old man seemed cool and somehow weary.

"This was a lovely event," the abbot said. "It must have taken a lot of planning. You are very good at bringing all the men together. You have a real gift for organization, for—politics. You should not waste it." He set his coffee cup down and looked at the young man. "Your probation period is not over until next week, but I've reached an early decision. I'm sending Father Alered to speak to you." He paused again. "Nicodemos, you have so much talent, perhaps too much."

A half hour later, Wick waited in his cell. He felt sick. He wondered what he had done that was so wrong. It was true that he was not a quiet little monk. He was always looking at ways to improve the life of the monastery. As one of the cooks, he had started preparing tastier foods, adding basil to the boiled potatoes and bay leaf to the tomato stew. He had worked for two years to get permission to throw out the molding and ancient straw mattresses, replacing them with new ones made of cotton. He had lobbied the abbot tirelessly to allow the men to take a shower every day as opposed to once a week. He had done all these things and he had not prayed as often or as deeply as he should, but weren't actions prayers, too?

He heard a soft voice outside his cell. "May I come in?"

"Yes."

Father Alered stepped into the room. He was Wick's confessor and friend. He was bald and wore glasses and yellow false teeth which were continually slipping out of place. He had red cheekbones and broad shoulders and huge hands, the fingers always black and gritty with topsoil. He was a bonsai master and his greenhouses held over a thousand plants.

The old man sat down on Wick's bed. He held a brown paper bag. His hands were dirty. He was sad.

"I spoke to him last night. I would have told you, but I knew you wouldn't sleep. He said he likes you and thinks you're a nice young man with lots of potential, but—not for here."

Wick looked at Father Alered, then shifted his eyes out the small window toward the black morning. He sat down on the other end of the bed.

"When do I have to go?"

"Today."

"Today?"

"The abbot's ordered a cab for 2 P.M. He's already paid for your bus ticket."

In the abbey, Big Mike rang and called the community to Vigils.

"Can I visit on the weekends?"

"No."

"Once a month?"

"No."

Wick shook his head. "I've been here six years. I was ordained here. This is the only life I ever wanted, Padre. The only one. What did I do wrong, I mean how did I mess things up? I'll tell you something. I am Father Abbot's best friend. I think I really am. I understand him. I know what he wants before he wants it. I know exactly how to, how to . . ."

"Please him?"

"What's wrong with that? I really like him."

"We've talked about all this before."

"No we haven't. We haven't talked about it at all. I mean what is the problem? What is it? Why doesn't he think I belong here? I'm the first one to Vigils. I'm the first one to chapel. I don't eat meat—even on Holidays. I shovel out the cowsheds and the chicken coops and spend hours explaining the Immaculate Conception to Baptist tourists. Why don't I belong? What's wrong with me? In one word, just one word— why can't I stay?"

Alered started to speak, but his dentures slipped and nearly fell out of his mouth. He thumbed them back into place, took off his glasses and held them in his black hands. "Ambition."

He thought his confessor was going to say lack of faith, that he had too many doubts and uncertainties. It was said that Alered possessed the gift of discernment, the ability to see into a man's heart and identify a spiritual problem. Wick believed in his confessor's gift and so this charge of ambition baffled him. He was so surprised that he could not even argue.

Alered opened the bag and pulled out a plant which occupied a square vase. The plant had tiny leaves about the size and shape of clover. Several white blooms sat among the leaves. Each blossom had five petals and the center was a yellow five-pointed star. The heart of the star was indigo.

The old man held up the plant. "Do you remember what it is?"

Wick was studying the floor.

"Do you?"

He looked up. "Flowering hyssop."

"But I've done something new."

The brown trunk had been split so that it had grown into a fork. The fork had been tied into the shape of a heart and the leaves and white blossoms radiated from it.

"I thought I could sell them to young couples."

Wick was looking at the floor again.

"On Valentine's Day, and—you know, occasions like that."

"It's a good idea."

"Of course, it blossoms twice a year and it needs to be pruned right afterward. So in six months you bring this back to me."

"I can come back?"

"In six months."

"What do I do until then?"

"Well—you could work for your grandmother's newspaper. What was the name of it again?"

"I can't do that."

"Go home. Be patient. The abbot will write you a letter."

Father Alered offered the flowering hyssop.

Wick Longstreet took it and then put his head in his hands and wept.

It was August 3, 1964.

2

LATER IN THE DAY and five hundred miles to the north, Boykin Longstreet sipped English breakfast tea in her favorite room in Waverly—the trunk room. It lay on the second story of the house at the end of the east hallway. She liked the room because it was secure and cozy and no one bothered her here.

The trunk room had four stained glass windows which were six feet tall and two feet wide. The floor was made of thin planks of yellow fir which squeaked and popped when you stepped on them. Trunks stood everywhere. They were stacked to the ceiling on either side of the stained glass windows and they stood in bluffs in the center of the room and the corners held smaller suitcases and overnight cases, octagonal hatboxes, round fur boxes and long makeup kits. All the trunks and suitcases and fur boxes were leather. The most battered, worn leather, scarred and scratched and all the leathers ablaze with foreign stamps: pictures of kings and queens, birds, vehicles and dogs, blue triangles and red squares and green circles and the smell of the leather, the dusty, smooth smell of it lay on Boykin like a perfume making her feel soft and warm, a balm to soothe her jarred nerves: today Cat McGregor was coming to Waverly.

When Boykin set down her teacup, she saw the tremble in her hands and there was plenty of reason for it. If anything went wrong with Boykin's plan, the girl would not make it. There was real danger, and if Boykin had not thought clearly enough and Cat was discovered trying to escape, there would be pursuit, and maybe something worse.

The McGregor family lived in Cloudy Gap, North Carolina—the same mountainous hamlet where the Longstreets maintained their summer residence, a twenty-one-room stone villa called The Hills. The Longstreets had owned The Hills since 1851 when James Longstreet had come upon the small mountain (situated between two larger ones) while he was hunting black bear. Having just returned from a visit to Italy, where he had been impressed with Italian "grand simplicity," he contracted for a group of Florentine stone masons to come to America and build him a summer place. Twenty masons and their wives and children took the boat over. They had names like Giavelli, Tigoloresi, Bonachilo and Scazzagaloponichi. There were only four families living in the Cloudy Gap area when Longstreet bought the land. Their names were Smith, White, Jones and Hick. If there had been any more of these monosyllabic Pentecostals, they would have murdered the invading Italians, but since they were small in number, they retreated to snake handling and moonshine.

In two years, The Hills was complete. It was a Renaissance-style palazzo composed of four different marbles, seven native woods and the same style of green slate roof that Longstreet had put on his mansion in South Carolina.

Sixty years later, when Lackey McGregor first saw the mountain palace, he determined that one day he would own it. He found a local school marm named Mary Jones, married her, produced five children and, using ten years of hate and mining skill he had learned in West Virginia, he bought a tract of land and fought to build an empire of coal.

The McGregors were poor. They lived in a six-room shanty with no running water. There were four boys and one girl, and on the eighth birthday of each child, McGregor took it to a ridge that overlooked The Hills and said, "You see that house. I want it. You help me get it." After school, he worked them five hours a day in his coal mine. At night the children ate grits and cheese with a chunk of tasteless mountain tomato or a rind of yellow fatback. They rarely took baths and so the dark, oily soot of the mines stained their skin and stained their hair and stained the happy pastels of childhood.

Mary Jones was the children's only hope and respite. She had married Lackey McGregor because he was good-looking and young and she was thirty-seven and wanted children more than anything in the world. As soon as the couple had their first child, McGregor made Mary stop teaching and it broke her heart because she loved books; more particularly, she loved literature. Within a year, however, Mary found a way to mend her heart. From the earliest age possible she began to read to her children. She read to them before they went to work and after supper and before they went to sleep. She read them every book she could find in the library: *Great Expectations, The Scarlet Pimpernel, Prince Valiant, Robinson Crusoe, Eugenie Grandet* and in between these novels and many others she read "Thanatopsis" and "Elegy in a Country Church-yard" and a thousand other poems and essays.

Cat was her mother's star pupil. By the age of twelve, she was racing down the hills of Switzerland with Heidi, starving with Oliver Twist and later vacillating with Hamlet and shivering in bed awaiting the arrival of the tattooed harpooner called Queequeg.

All of these characters and images and words sheltered Cat from McGregor and the tyranny of the mines, at the same time laying an intellectual foundation which would support a future she could not then possibly imagine.

By 1960, after years of bondage to hammer and shovel and pick, the McGregors were still poor and Mary Jones was dead. McGregor still believed he could be rich and so he pushed his children harder than ever—and that's when the old man first started to notice it, the telltale sign—the pinkness.

McGregor did not hate his children and he would have taken Tom (his eldest and the one first afflicted with the skin discoloration) to the doctor, but he was too cheap. And so day by day, he watched Tom's energy and work decrease and the pink color, which had started on the back of his hands and his face, spread over most of his body.

McGregor worked his children in pairs. Each team was given a separate finger of the mine. He kept Cat, the youngest, with him. The others worked out of his sight for several hours a day. It was when Ian started showing the same symptoms as Tom that McGregor knew the disease was spreading. Ian and Tom were a team and before the disease their coal cart was the fullest. When Tom had taken sick, their coal production had dropped a third, and when Ian started showing the same lassitude, same pink hands and face, the coal went down even more.

Finally one morning when McGregor and Cat were hammering in shaft number six, he decided that he had to take the boys to the doctor. He left fourteen-year-old Cat with a lantern and started out for shaft three where Tom and Ian worked. It was a mile's walk in darkness. Only the small battery-powered lamp in his helmet gave light. He was looking at his watch (9:20 A.M.) when he first heard the sound. It was distant, a half a mile away, maybe more. He stopped to listen. The air of the mine was flat, stale and heavy. When he breathed, he could feel the coal dust coating the back of his throat and deeper. He waited a moment, then started to walk and he heard it again—something light and round, something alien.

He rushed toward the dark crack which formed the entrance to the shaft. He cupped his hands behind his ears and poked his head into the entrance.

It was a sound that he had never heard in the mine, a sound that was completely foreign here, a sound that for some reason made him angry and determined to end it—it was laughter.

Carefully, McGregor stepped through the entrance, took two or three twisting turns. He followed the laughter to a small cavern that he had never seen. He entered and his lamp revealed a shining wall of gorgeous coal. In the center of the coal from a wooden stake hung two new pairs of trousers, two white shirts. McGregor snapped off his lamp, felt his way around the corner and peeped into a room lit by a kerosene lantern.

Tom and Ian stood stripped to their underwear before a wooden tub. They were bathing and laughing and Tom was smoking a cigarette. Ian dipped a round sponge into the tub, lathered it with white soap and scrubbed his brother's back. Both of them were pink, their clean flesh so shiny and bright that it glinted in the glassy walls of black coal.

"What do you think she'll have me do today?" Tom asked, taking a long drag from the cigarette.

"You gotta learn to serve."

"Serve who?"

"Not who—what. You'll learn to serve roast beef, learn how to hold the tray just right, then tilt her forward a little bit so the red juice runs into the gravy pot. Oh, it's a fine job with a big ole fat sandwich for you when you're done."

Tom turned to look at his brother. "A roast beef sandwich?"

"This thick."

Tom shook his head.

"You've never had roast beef?"

"Nope."

"It's like nothing else in the whole world, Tommy. It's like something a fella shouldn't have till he gets to heaven."

The brothers looked at one another and laughed. They dried off, then stepped toward their clothes.

A few seconds later, they were moving down shaft three with their father quietly following them. Holding a lantern, they took a turn through another huge crack that McGregor had never explored and in a few minutes walked into the cool mountain sunlight.

McGregor followed them to the edge of the dark shaft. He watched them walk down a trail to the nearby road. They waited for a few minutes and then a bright new Ford truck pulled up. The truck bed was open and several other men stood in it. On the truck's door, in large silver letters, was written: The Hills.

The old man was enraged. He felt that his sons had betrayed him. When they returned to the mine later in the afternoon, he confronted them. He told them that they had to quit The Hills, and when Ian refused, he grew so angry that he struck the boy in the head. Ian raced from the tunnel with his father threatening to kill him if he went back to the Longstreets.

A month later, deep in the dead air of a mountain night, Ian returned to the McGregor hovel, crept inside with a basket of food and candy. He told his brothers and sister about his new job as a foreman for the Longstreet dairy and that he was making just over six thousand dollars a year.

There was a big fire in the small room and the children had wrapped themselves in ragged blankets. They had not been permitted a bath in over a week and there was a sour stench about them, though no one really smelled it but Cat, who sensed everything. Their blond hair was stringy and matted with black coal dust and their little necks had rings of soot and grime and sweat. They sat in a huddle around their big brother with his fluffy blond hair and shining green eyes. How beautiful Ian looked that night, Cat thought. He was wearing a gray suit and red tie and some kind of perfume which made him smell like a bowl of shaving soap.

"What's it like?" Cat asked.

"What's what like?"

"The Hills."

"Oh, The Hills," said Ian, and he smiled and reached out and touched her cheek with a warm hand. "It's the most beautiful place in the world. It's got floors slick as glass and silk curtains and soft rugs that you sink up to your ankles in. It's got a whole gleaming forest of hardwood furniture and water fountains . . ."

"Inside? It's got water fountains inside?" Cat asked.

"Yep, inside and it's got a room filled with purdy little birds and another room's got a glass tank filled with little fishes. Tee-ninsee little fishes every color you can think of, like somebody scattered a bucket of jewels in the water."

And Ian talked on and on about The Hills and the glow of the children's eyes filled the room as they devoured the fried chicken and boiled eggs and peanut brittle.

Finally, about dawn, old man McGregor stepped into the room with a shovel. The two men shouted at one another and then McGregor hit his son so hard in the side of the head that blood spurted from Ian's right eye and ear. The old man would have killed the boy, but the children subdued him and once more Ian escaped.

That was the night Cat stopped talking and three years later when she started secretly working at The Hills' dairy from which her brother had disappeared, she was still mute, so that when Boykin met Cat at the milking machine, she assumed that the girl had never spoken a word. They became friends.

Just after Cat's first month of work at the dairy, another servant told Boykin that old man McGregor had discovered Cat's secret and that he had beaten her badly. Marie went on to explain McGregor's whole story and it was then that Boykin decided to spirit the young girl away—if she wanted to go, and she did.

Marie also told Boykin that McGregor was very smart. She said if they were going to help Cat, it would have to be in a clever way.

Boykin thrilled to the challenge.

In one night, Boykin laid out the plan. Twice a week trucks picked up several hundred boxes of McGregor's domestic coal, drove them to the Charlotte train depot and shipped them south. Each box was stamped with the customer's name and address. Once the coal boxes reached the correct city, an independent delivery service took them to the proper address. Boykin told Cat to confide in one of her brothers about the escape so he could help. One of the boxes would be half filled with coal and stamped with: B.L., Waverly, South Carolina. Since Boykin would have to be at Waverly, she would have Marie receive the box at the Charlotte depot, free Cat and drive her south.

Two weeks before the escape, Boykin met with Cat and explained everything.

On the day of her departure, Cat McGregor was terrified. She felt somehow that her father was going to find out. She did not sleep all night and finally rose at 4 A.M., an hour before usual. She built a fire, threw oatmeal into boiling water for the family's breakfast. She looked at the dilapidation she had called a home: a plank floor covered in green linoleum, one naked light bulb dangling from a ceiling which was plastered in yellow newspapers and rotting burlap bags, the ravaged kitchen window whose broken panes had been replaced with dingy cardboard. In the center of the room sat the round table and twelve chairs that had been her mother's pride and joy. Before her mother died, she told Cat that the table and chairs were hers and now as the young woman looked at the scarred pine wood, at the black pot boiling on the yellowed stove, now she felt she didn't want to go. It was awful, all of it, but it was her home and all that she had ever known.

When her brother stepped into the kitchen, she cried. He gave her a hug and then whispered that she must be quiet. The old man had good ears.

She loved Mike, and of all the children, she would miss him the most. He was skinny and tall with a head of wild blond hair.

"You sure you want to do this?" he whispered.

Cat nodded yes, but she could not look at him.

"Well, when you get where you're going, you let me know." Mike gave her a quick squeeze, then reached into his pocket and pulled out a small box.

"I bought you something at the store. It ain't much."

Cat opened it and felt her eyes burn. It was a blue notebook and two red pencils.

"So you can write things. So you can let them Longstreets know you got brains like they never seen."

McGregor came into the kitchen. He was bald and had high cheekbones, a narrow red chin and green eyes.

Cat hid the notebook and pencils.

"What you hiding behind your back?"

"I just give her some paper," Mike said, his face flaming.

The old man put his hands into his pockets, rocked on his heels. "How come?"

"It's just a present," Mike said.

"Bring it here," said McGregor.

Cat dropped her sooty blond head and handed them over.

The old man threw the notebook into the woodbin and stuck the two pencils into his pocket.

"You don't need to be writing things down all the time. It's useless. Words is useless and anybody puts store in them is useless, too. Now get me my porridge."

It was the last time she handed the old man a bowl of oatmeal. Later, she retrieved her notebook.

At two-thirty in the afternoon, Cat crept outside the mine to the loading dock. She found the right box and slipped inside. She wrestled the heavy wooden lid into position and locked it down and all the light in the world left. The hard coal stuck into her back and pine resin from the box stuck in her hair and she could hear the scuttle and scrabble of the black coal bugs beneath her.

The truck would not come for an hour, but old man McGregor was looking for her in thirty minutes.

It was McGregor's custom to check on his children after break time. He reached out and touched them as if he did not trust his vision. Usually, he would grab them by the arm or the back of the neck, give them a sharp rattle and then, examining them minutely with his green eyes, he would say, "So, you're finally back at work, huh?"

McGregor trudged through the black mine, found that Cat was missing and went to Mike's station. He grabbed his son so fiercely that the boy's blond hair flew about his face.

"You back working?"

"Yes, sir."

McGregor squinted beneath the light of his helmet lantern. He examined his son's face and hands for any sign of pink skin—which he still regarded as a kind of disease.

"Where's Cat McGregor?"

"She'll be right along."

"I said, where's Cat McGregor?"

"She's probably in the toilet, Pa. Good grief."

"Yes, it's grief all right. It's grief to me. If all of you take this much time, we'll never find the mother lode. Never."

McGregor walked to the last shaft, which was ten minutes away. Tom was working hard, but when he returned to Mike, there was still no Cat.

He grabbed his son by the soft tissue beneath the boy's big Adam's apple and shoved him against a wall. "Where is she?"

"I don't know."

The old man laid his cold pickax beside Mike's face. "Where?"

Mike shut his eyes. The old man took the point of the sharp pick and placed it against the boy's temple.

"She's at the loading dock."

"Which one?"

"Number two."

By the time McGregor got to number two dock, number one had already been loaded and the truck was driving away. The second truck was just backing into position. Eighty boxes waited on the wooden platform.

"Which one?" McGregor asked.

Mike was broken. "B.L., Waverly, South Carolina."

Three truckers were moving toward a rusted overhead crane which sat at the end of the loading dock. McGregor waved at them and shouted. "Take a break, boys. I'm making a last-minute check."

The pine boxes, dirty with soot, were stacked three deep. McGregor leapt on top of the long rectangles and read each address until he found the box. He put his small red hands on top of the crate and leaned over it. He tapped one finger against the wood, then began to hum, and finally sing, "Oh my darlin', oh my darlin', oh my darlin' Clementine. You are lost and gone forever, dreadful sorry, Clementine."

He rocked back on his heels and laughed so hard and so silently that all the blood of his thin body rushed to his bald head and face, turning the nest of broken capillaries in the tip of his nose a brilliant lavender.

When he finished, he once more leaned over the crate and whispered, "Come out."

Mike sat at the end of the loading dock holding his face in his hands.

"Come out," I said.

The box was silent.

McGregor grabbed the pickax from his back pocket and wildly attacked the lid. Wood chips flew. When he had made a large hole, he dropped the pickax, rocked back on his heels, laughed and wiped sweat from his upper lip. Then suddenly he lunged and thrust both hands through the opening. He felt around in the box, his eyes wide and excited.

"Don't you hide now," said the squeaky voice. "Don't you pull away from the hands that fed yee."

He extended his hands and arms into the large crate as far as he could. Still feeling only coal, he screamed, grabbed the ragged lid and jerked. Several boards broke free in his hands, enough to allow him to see that the crate was empty—empty except for coal. Great, black, shining lumps of coal and nothing else.

At eighteen years of age, Catherine McGregor was bound for the Charlotte depot. Two days before the escape, Boykin had communicated to Cat through Marie that she must prepare and secrete herself into a second box and that she could not tell her brother. At first Cat refused to leave Mike out, but Marie finally convinced her. Now, sealed in the sooty coal crate, riding to Charlotte, she began to compose the letter she would write to her brother as soon as she reached the house called Waverly.

3

WEARING HIS BLACK SUIT and Roman collar, Wick was riding in a cab up the dirt road to Waverly. He rolled down the window and stuck out his head to inhale the air—it was the sweet smell of home, freshly cut hay and dry dust and pine resin. In the twilight through the gingko trees he could see the white columns of the house and the two magnolias which stood at the bottom of the marble steps.

It was while he was riding around to the back entrance that the feeling of defeat began to creep over him. Six years in the monastery, six whole years, and all the talking he had done about his vocation. Every time he visited home on Christmas and Easter, all his palaver about how well he was doing and how he was a leader in the monastery and how if he kept progressing he would be the youngest abbot in the Trappist order.

The thought stopped him. Had he said that? The youngest abbot? Well, maybe they're right then. Maybe I never had a vocation at all.

Maybe it was all just ambition. I didn't care about God and I didn't care about my brothers. Oh yeah, I went into the order with the idea of being a holy little monk and then when I got inside my true colors came out: I wanted power, not holiness. I should have joined a bank, not a monastery.

Wick was so deep in this self-recrimination that the cab driver had to shake him to pay the bill. He gave the driver a good tip, then lugged his suitcase toward the back steps.

Pear trees stood on either side of him, while against the back of the house grew four holly trees. Behind the green hollies lay the back porch. The floor was limestone and the walls were screen covered in strips of white lattice. Upon the lattice grew a host of green vines and the yellow and pink blossoms of morning glories.

Once on the porch, Wick took a left and opened a door into a small hallway which led into the den. It was a big room, twenty yards long and twenty yards wide. The family spent most of their time here.

Two sofas covered in aquamarine corduroy faced one another and below them sat two squat chairs, their arms and backs round and fat with goose down and the chairs covered in the same corduroy. Beside the chairs and at each end of the sofas were small wooden tables. Some of the tables had round tops and some square and two were triangular, having Indian peace symbols inlaid into their mahogany legs. Deeper into the room, just before a bay window, were more chairs, two brown muslin couches and several brass floor lamps. The walls were painted white and the floors were wide planks of oak.

In the right wall of the room stood a fireplace. It was six feet high. On either side of the brick fireplace were two fluted pillars whose summits were carved into acanthus leaves. Across the capitals of the columns sat a six-inch slab of brown pecan wood. To the left of the mantelpiece was an American-style buffet. Traditionally this table held snacks for the family. Today there was a silver bowl holding red apples and yellow pears, a small red bowl heaped in white and brown boiled eggs and a wooden tray stacked in the yellow faces of muffins freckled with blueberries.

When Wick walked a few feet into the room, he saw Blackie lying on the floor between a couch and a coffee table. His head was propped against a sofa and on his chest sat two red apples and two yellow pears in a straight line from his chin to his belt buckle. He was wearing blue jeans and a white T-shirt. His summer tan was dark and sleek.

"What're you doing home?" Blackie asked, and took a bite of apple.

Wick looked at his brother sprawled out on the floor. It irritated him. He was not in the mood for Blackie today. He went to the buffet and poured himself a cup of coffee. "I'm just taking a little break."

"I didn't know monks could take breaks."

"Sometimes they can."

"You never did it before."

"Where's Boykin?"

"I don't know, man."

Wick hated it when Blackie started saying *man*. It meant that he thought he was—to use another favorite word of his—cool. Wick's predominant feeling toward his younger brother was one of irritation. He thought he was spoiled and lazy and an embarrassment to the family. He took his coffee and sat down in a straight-back chair with a yellow cane seat. He popped off his white collar and sat it on his knee. He was pale and even the splash of brown freckles across his nose looked washed out. His blue eye was red and tired. His brown one was fresher.

"You ought to forget that coffee and grab you a beer and a ham sandwich. You look half starved, man."

"I'm doing just fine."

"Probably that damn diet y'all eat down there. Do you ever get any meat?"

Wick sipped his coffee.

"Well, I'm gonna tell Hannah to fatten you up. How long you home for?"

"Why are you asking me all these questions?"

"Hey, be cool, be cool. I'm just trying to find out the big picture."

"I'm going to be home a good while."

"Good," said Blackie. He crammed the remains of one pear into his mouth: stem, seeds and core. "We'll work out, lie in the sun, eat steak and drink beer. We've got to get some meat on you before you go back."

Wick wanted not to tell him that he had been sent from the monastery, but he couldn't hold it. One of the curses of his character was that he could not keep quiet about anything of importance. He had to let the world know every facet of his life.

"Not going back," he said quietly.

"What'd you say?"

"At least, not for a long time."

"Are you serious?"

"Yep."

"Man, that's great."

"Oh, yes. It's great, Blackie. I'm real happy about it."

"Why'd they throw you out?"

"They didn't throw me out."

"Why'd you have to go?"

"Look, I just don't want to talk about it now, okay?"

"You know what we got to do? We got to get you some leg."

The front doorbell rang.

"Leg is not the solution to everything, Blackie."

"You need to forget all that monk stuff and drown in a sea of titties."

Wick shook his head. It was also true that Blackie could make him laugh. He had always been able to make him laugh, particularly when Wick did not want to. Somehow it surprised him, too. Just when he thought that he had it firmly fixed in his mind how much he disliked his youngest brother, Blackie would make him laugh and he would start to feel softer toward him and it bothered him because he did not want to feel softer.

The doorbell rang again.

"I'm serious, man. Listen, if those skinny, bead-rattling dumb asses don't want you there—forget them. You're home and you're gonna stay home and I'm gonna find you a gal. A real, live, Southern wo-man. The kind you love."

Wick looked at his suntanned brother. "And what kind of wo-man is that?"

"Do you really want to know?"

Wick smiled. "I guess."

"Do you really want me to describe your future dreamboat, your sugar, your main squeeze?"

"Well, maybe not."

"She's about five foot one, ninety-two pounds, corn yellow hair and blue eyes and carrying two of the biggest boobs a fella's ever seen. I mean, these things are melons, man. Honeydews."

The doorbell rang and this time Wick rose to answer it. He was laughing.

"Come back here," Blackie yelled. "She's got legs, man. She's got legs like . . ."

Wick walked down the cool hallway toward the front of the house and he was still laughing and thinking: he's a good guy. Why do I give him such a hard time? I should take it easy on him. With a sense of weariness he felt a resolution coming on. He was continually making resolutions and here was another one. I'll try to be more understanding. What's wrong with that? I'll try to be more tolerant and understanding. He's a good fella, he really is—I guess.

He stood still at the lower end of the hallway. He liked the feel of it in the summer. It was cool and breezy and filled with the smell of pine trees and honeysuckle and the staleness of red dust from the dry fields. This end of the hall was quiet, but thirty yards down the oak floor, the foyer was a melee.

Wearing dark print dresses and ankle-length white aprons, the maids dashed from the east parlor across the hall to the west. They carried silver trays and copper bowls and stacks of crystal and china. Two young black girls with plaited hair dusted the panels of pecan wainscoting. In addition to the maids and the girls, five or six black men toted rolled carpets upon their shoulders or hauled large walnut tables or carried couches covered in purple satin or blue and gold striped silk. Two of the black men were old. Their hair was white and they were trim with narrow shoulders and long necks. They were brothers and they wore the old uniforms of Waverly: red jackets and blue pants and red bow ties. The jackets were patched and faded and the blue trousers were shiny in the seat and several of the jackets' brass buttons had been replaced with black plastic ones, but the old men refused not to wear them. Bub and Jebodiah had worked for the Longstreets longer than any of the other servants. They stayed with the family because the Longstreets paid the best money around. Bub had always worked for them and he loved them, but Jebodiah, the younger of the two, had once had a dream.

He had wanted to play baseball in the major leagues. He had been a good player as a boy and then went on to be a star in the black leagues, but he broke his leg on the road. Harper Longstreet went to Alabama and brought him home and took care of him until the leg healed, but

Jebodiah resented it. He really did not want to return to Waverly, but no one could say no to the old lady, so Jebodiah came back and he stayed because there wasn't any work anyplace else and he grew bitter and unhappy and he hid his unhappiness behind the biggest smile and the sunniest disposition that anyone had ever seen.

Those who had not been born into the Longstreet family might have been impressed with all this action, but Wick was not. He had seen the last-minute housecleaning before. Harper was due in the next day and Boykin and the help usually put off chores as long as they could. The last month of the summer was a time when Waverly could sink into a sleepy, humid deshabille, far from the blackness of Harper's eyes.

As Wick stepped onto the gray limestone porch, he could feel the heat of the stone columns. The sun had hit them for most of the day and so they held the white heat in themselves the way a radiator might hold scalding water.

He looked out from the porch and saw a truck from The Hills sitting in the gravel driveway. Marie came around from the west of the great house and stepped onto the white gravel. The sound of her feet crunching the gravel brought back a childish memory.

For years, until he was nearly seven years old, Wick had imagined the driveway was ice—a long sheet of ice which crunched and cracked and blazed in the sunlight—and once when Harper had run out of ice at a party, he had taken the ice bucket and filled it with gravel and presented it to Boykin, who became furious at his prank, would have spanked him if Harper had not taken the ice bucket filled with gravel, looked at it, placed her hand upon the stones and then—shivered, hitched her shoulders, pursed her lips and shivered as if she had touched the blue heart of an ice house. She smiled and kissed him and said, "Great men always have great imaginings."

Marie was thin. She wore her hair in a beehive and she was smoking a cigarette. She seemed agitated.

"Have you seen Miss Boykin?" she asked.

"I just got in."

"She's supposed to meet me."

"She's probably up in the trunk room. I'll go look."

Just then, through the darkening air, Boykin's car turned onto the dirt road that led to the house. It raced up the drive and stopped beside the truck.

"Marie?" Boykin asked.

"Yes, ma'am, it's okay." Marie glanced at Wick. "She's scooted down in the front."

"Let's go to the blue guest house."

Wick got in Boykin's car.

The red guest house was dark, but the blue one had all the lights burning. It was two stories, built on a white lattice foundation with a screen front porch, yellow shutters and brick chimneys.

Riding over, Boykin reached out and touched Wick's arm. "I need you to keep a secret."

"Okay."

"Nobody, but nobody, can find out."

"I'll keep it quiet."

Boykin quickly told him all about Cat McGregor.

At the guest house, Boykin left her car, then opened the front door of the truck. It was dark outside and the interior lights of the truck did not work. She leaned into the black seat well.

"Cat, honey? It's me. It's Boykin—are you okay?"

Bub turned on the front porch light and then descended the stairs.

Wick stepped a little closer.

Carefully, the young woman rose from the black well of the truck and stepped into the porch light.

Wick was so surprised by Cat's appearance that he made a sound. She had a dirty face, perhaps the dirtiest face that he had ever seen, the face so infested with grime that it seemed as if it had been singed by a flame. There was a sooty pug nose, sooty round cheeks, a wrinkled swatch of sooty hair and two long braids, each of which had been tied with a grimy tatter of red rag. Two small hands surfaced from the dark and they, too, were soiled and greasy. In the midst of this grime was the only hope for cleanliness—two green eyes whose shine and luster seemed completely out of place in their frame of soot.

"Oh, Cat," Boykin said. She reached out and touched her dark cheeks.

"This chile need something to eat," Bub said, and dashed up the steps into the house.

Boykin brushed back the girl's thick and potentially blond bangs. "Cat, are you all right, darlin'? Are you okay?"

The girl didn't move.

"You do remember me, don't you? You remember ole Boykin, don't you?"

The girl's dirty face looked at Boykin then glanced at Wick, who finally managed to speak.

"Hey, uh—Cat. How was your—trip?"

Cat blinked and smiled. Boykin put her arm around her and guided her into the house.

Bub entered the living room carrying a bamboo tray which held a white porcelain cup and saucer and a large porcelain plate. Each piece of china had a golden border on the outer edge. The cup held tea and the plate a tiny cucumber sandwich on crustless white bread. When Bub extended the tray to Cat she looked at the porcelain and gold and then the black man's face and she laughed silently.

Boykin took over. "Bub, you take that tray on now. I think she just needs to have a hot bath and a good rest. She can eat a little later."

With an arm still around Cat, Boykin directed her upstairs.

Wick was standing with his hands in his pockets, still not completely recovered from the surprise of it all. He looked at Bub. "How long do you think this is going to stay a secret?"

"Not too long, Mr. Wick."

"Not long at all."

Wick walked back to Waverly hoping that Harper would let Cat McGregor stay. What a great place this would be for her, he thought. If everything works out, if Harper allows her to stay. We should do this every year. We should bring someone who doesn't have a chance to Waverly. It's ridiculous to have four extra bedrooms with nobody in them. In fact, we could bring two people a year. Take care of them, see that they have a good job, give them a chance.

The great wealth of his family had troubled Wick all of his life. Though he could not remember it now, the guilt of that wealth had been one of the subtler reasons he had entered the monastery. He had thought it unfair that he had been blessed with an overabundance and so many others didn't even have the necessities. Once he sensed the stillness, he had wanted to give up his birthright and devote his life to prayer, hoping to please God, hoping that his sacrifice would bring blessings on all those who had so little.

It was a young man's reasoning and now he was not so young. Though Wick did not know it yet, the monastery was far behind him.

When he stepped into the den, Ford jumped from a chair. He held a wineglass and his big face was flushed and sweating. He wore a gray navy flight suit and a red ascot.

"Little brother!" Ford said, and rushed over and hugged Wick, giving him his usual kiss on the side of the cheek that to this day made Wick blush. "What are you doing home?"

"Fattening up."

"You can't imagine where I've been and what I've done. It was a-a-I'm so tired I can't think of the word. It was a—peregrination. Yes, exactly. It was an illuminating peregrination."

And Ford began to tell him about his adventure.

4

WHEN CAT MCGREGOR AWOKE in
the guest house, she was afraid. She lay in the sprawling canopy bed
and looked around the room. The two windows were covered in lavender curtains, behind them gauzy linens. The floor was yellow maple and
covered with a royal blue rug. However, it was the walls which caught
Cat's eyes. She had never seen walls like these. They were the lightest
color of April rose, and more than that, the walls seemed to emit a
radiance, a fuzzy pink light.

Rolling over beneath the white billow of satin canopy, she reached
out and touched the wall—it was cloth. It was some kind of smooth
pink cloth. She got out of bed, crouched along the maple wood base-
board and carefully put her cheek against the wall. It was the softest,
most wonderful wall she had ever felt. She pulled away, looked at the
delicious pink color and then once more put her face against it.

There was a tap at the door and she jumped back into bed.

Hannah came in. She was thin and wore a white hat which was

bordered in a band of hand-sewn daisies. Her long apron touched the top of her man's Sunday lace-ups. She was carrying a tray.

"You sleep good, chile?"

Cat was nervous. She had never seen a colored person dressed like this one.

"Oh, that's right—you dumb. You don't talk. That's all right. This family could use a lot less talking. A lot less, um-hum, I'm telling you that now."

Hannah walked over to the bed. "Sit yourself up."

Cat looked at the tray and the colored woman and then she understood: it was breakfast in bed. She had read about it in several books. It was the prettiest breakfast Cat had ever seen. It was a silver tray and etched in the center of the silver was a big house with a high roof and twelve columns. A yellow rose with three pretty green leaves sat in a sparkling vase. In the center of the tray was a brown egg sitting on a little gold stand. Cat thought the egg in the gold stand was funny. Beneath the egg was a white bowl with a lip of gold. Beside the bowl was a piece of toasted white bread and square of butter, a pink napkin and a glass with juice.

When Hannah set the tray in Cat's lap, the girl smiled.

Hannah stuffed the soft napkin around Cat's neck. She took a silver spoon and smacked the top of the brown egg.

Cat laughed.

When Cat laughed, so did Hannah. "You ain't seen a egg cup, huh? It's one of them things white people think up 'cause they ain't got nothing else to do." Hannah removed the top of the egg, stuck in the silver spoon, dug for a little white and yellow and then moved it toward Cat's mouth.

"Open up," she said.

Cat's green eyes looked at Hannah and then at the spoonful of egg.

"Look at them eyes," Hannah said. "I ain't never seen no eyes so big and so green as them eyes. Open up, going down the chute now. Let's open all the way up."

The egg tasted warm and sticky and yellow.

Hannah wiped the girl's mouth and then offered her a sip of juice.

Boykin Longstreet tapped on the door and then entered the room. For a moment she just stood and stared. It was one of the most beautiful sights she had ever seen—the girl's blond hair was pulled to either side of her head in careless pigtails, each gathering of wheaten hair fastened by a blue barrette. Her eyes were shining, the lightest, most delicate green, and her nose was small and round and shiny.

Boykin had never cared about marriage, but all of her life she had wanted a little girl of her own. She had badgered Harper for years to let her adopt one, but to no avail. She even asked Harper if she could be a foster parent, taking in a troubled girl once a year or so, but Harper refused and Boykin had given up. Then she met Cat and the situation presented itself and she acted instinctively. If she had any doubts about what she had done, once she saw the child's big smile, they vanished.

"Well, breakfast in bed. What a nice way to start the morning," Boykin said.

"She not eating right, Miss Boykin. She doing too much laughing and cutting up and not eating right."

"It's okay," Boykin said, and she sat down beside Cat. "I want you to finish your breakfast if you can and then Hannah is going to start you on your lessons. In six months' time, you'll be a real pip. Bona fide gentry. What are you working on first, Hannah?"

The perennial scowl which had so far been absent from the old black woman's face returned as she reached out, pulled back one of Cat's pigtails and looked behind an ear. "I still see some soot and some dirt and so we gonna start learning to take a bath and get all the cracks and crannies. Then we work on silver."

"It's important to know how to handle your silver, Cat. A lot of people around here don't have brains so they judge you on how you use a knife and fork." Boykin kissed her on the cheek and rose from the bed. "Now I won't see you until this evening because my sister— Harper, whom you will soon meet—is coming home today and there's always a big hoopla and a lot of bowing and scraping."

Hannah closed the door to Cat's room and then turned to Boykin. "When you gonna tell Miss Harper about this chile?"

"In a week or so."

"A week! Ain't nobody gonna keep no secret for a week around here. You better tell Miss Harper sooner no week."

"Cat needs a little time, Hannah," Boykin said. "We need to polish off the rough edges."

"You better get on to the hardware store then."

"Why?"

" 'Cause we gonna need a lot of sandpaper."

After the two women had left, Cat took the buttered toast and wrapped it in her napkin. She got out of bed, took the two jelly jars from the tray and the napkin and carefully hid them under her mattress. It was an old habit. She had been able to feed herself and two of her brothers when the rest of the family had run out of food. Beneath the canopy, beneath the warm covers, she felt safer having put something aside.

Just then, she heard a horn blow and then a second horn, and then the two horns beeping at the same time. She went to the window, pulled back the soft lavender and saw eight or nine colored people dash up the back steps and into the white house.

Harper Longstreet was home. She had stayed a week longer than usual in North Carolina and she was anxious about her sons as well as the everyday affairs at Waverly and whether or not there were any problems at the newspaper. As she rolled over the crunching gravel drive, she wondered if Starkey would be able to make it home for her birthday party and hoped that she had convinced him in her last letter to leave the army and run for public office. Was Wick eating the special diet— steak and liver and eggs and cheeses—which she had finally won from that silly abbot? Did Ford meet with the President? Had he agreed to write the story? And was Blackie still seeing that awful girl named Carol. Actually she was not a girl, she was a woman, and Harper did not like her one bit.

Harper knew that almost all of these questions could be answered as soon as she saw them. Each one would betray the truth on his face, in his skin color or his posture. Even though she knew she would have the answers quickly, she was terribly anxious to see them. Perhaps something had gone wrong that she had not thought of. Disasters, she said to herself. You're always worried about disasters, and just as quickly as she said this, she thought, The only people who do not worry about disasters are those to whom disasters have never come.

Harper looked for her sunglasses and masked her anxiety behind icy aloofness. Waiting for the driver to open the door, she thought that part of her apprehension could have come about because of the attack in the Gulf of Tonkin. For the last six months, she had followed events in

Vietnam carefully and she had anticipated that something was going to happen. War could change everything in her life, in her family. She had four sons. The thought of it made her shudder.

Wick was the first one to step down the left side of the double staircase which sat in the center of the house. Close behind was the shirtless Blackie. Ford was changing clothes. The teakwood staircase was the spine of the house. It was an immense structure which contained eighty-five steps on each side. The wood was dark and shiny and both set of steps were covered with a purple wool traveler whose outer borders were decorated in gold stars. In the large heart-shaped space between the two sets of stairs, a tapestry hung against the wall. It was woven wool, twenty feet wide and thirty feet tall. It was red and blue, beige and silver and depicted the young Alexander sitting upon his white horse at the summit of a mountain. The young man was clad in golden armor and beneath him sprawled an endless city. Into the bottom of the tapestry were woven these words: *Mundus tuus est.* The world is yours.

The black Cadillac had long tail fins and big whitewall tires. Harper opened a back door and got out before the driver came around. She wore a double-breasted, white linen suit, her neck muffled in black silk, her skirt swinging into panel pleats low on the hipbone.

She was surprised to see Wick and supposed that he must have come home for her birthday. She hugged Wick and Blackie, then glanced back at Wick and asked if something was wrong and he said he would talk to her later. The limestone porch was filling up. There was Bub and Jebodiah and Hannah, then Fuzz and Tee Tat and Vic Cash and his seven boys whose names and faces everyone (including Vic) confused and finally, the last one out, her thirty-two braids sticking straight out of her head, was Tadpole, who looked at Harper Longstreet and pronounced, "The lady of the house be home."

Harper waved at everyone, tucked at a loose strand of her black hair and said, "Let's get right inside. I have lots of presents."

When the small crowd on the front porch heard this news, there were handclaps and smiles, headshakes and whispers. It was Harper's custom once a year, when she returned from one of her long trips, to bring presents for her sons and for all who worked at Waverly. Even though the ritual had gone on for thirty years, it still produced the most childish kind of excitement. Everyone seemed to become lighter, as if suddenly filled with that magic gas helium, their movements effortless and airy, their smiles and the light of their eyes the same as those they bore on Christmas Day.

Harper swept into the house shaking hands and patting heads, giving an order here and remembering a sick relative there, asking questions about livestock and land, spotting a loose pine board that needed to be replaced, encouraging improved posture in Jebodiah, correcting a white layer of shoulder dandruff on Bub and silently enduring the inky Tadpole, who cleared her mistress's path by saying, "Outa the way. Outa the way. Get on, get on, get on."

Deep in her gaggle of servants and just before she entered the door, Harper turned and waved at her driver. "Bring the large leather traveler into the ballroom."

The young chauffeur tipped his cap. He wore a black suit and black bow tie and white shirt. He was one of the Cash boys. His name was Nathaniel. He was born at Waverly and had lived on the estate all his life. He had just turned twenty-one and only recently become Harper's driver. He had just taken an apartment in town. He was one of Blackie's best friends.

Nathaniel and Blackie walked to the black pickup truck which was parked behind the Cadillac. The leather traveler was six feet high and six feet wide. It sat among eight brown leather suitcases, two black leather trunks and several octagonal leather hat boxes. The air around the truck smelled like rawhide.

"I wonder how many cows it took to make this luggage," Nathaniel said.

"Probably a herd," Blackie said.

"This the one?"

"Yeah, the big one there."

They maneuvered the leather trunk out of the truck bed and onto the white gravel driveway. Even though it was still morning, the air was stuffy and thick. The two young men were sweating.

"You coming to that sit-in tonight?" Nathaniel asked.

"If your daddy finds out you're going to those things, he'll make you come back home."

"I just like to listen."

"Don't get yourself arrested."

"What you talking about?"

"Where's the sit-in at?"

"Woolworth lunch counter."

"Why in the world would you want to eat at the Woolworth lunch counter? Hell, the only people who go there are winos and Injuns."

"You gonna come with me or not?"

"I'll see."

Blackie loaded the leather crate on Nathaniel's back and the black man struggled into the house.

The ballroom was seventy-five feet long and fifty feet wide. The center of the pecan wood floor was covered by an enormous blue rug. It had been handmade by a village in Iran called Khoul, pronounced "cool." Blackie would often infuriate Harper by suggesting to awed guests that the rug was in fact "really Khoul." Above the rug, from a vaulted ceiling hung a crystal chandelier which had been especially designed at the Waterford crystal factory in Ireland. At the north end of the room stood a pink marble fireplace. The inside of the fireplace was six feet tall and ten feet wide. Two pink Corinthian columns supported a thick shelf of marble. The andirons were four feet tall and cast from bronze— reproductions of Revolutionary soldiers with three-cornered hats and presented muskets. On the left-hand corner of the mantel sat a clay tub holding an explosion of impatiens, pinks and whites.

Along one wall of the long room sat a line of forty rosewood chairs. Jebodiah took one chair and set it directly beneath the chandelier. Harper situated herself here as Nathaniel and Blackie set the leather traveler at her feet. The door was unbuckled and opened and the crowd of servants and children packed around. The older black women (Hannah's age) wore the ruffled white caps and the white aprons which came to the top of their black shoes. The younger women wore short white dresses, nylons and brown sandals.

Silver hair immaculate and thin, moustache freshly clipped, Bub retrieved presents from the leather traveler and handed them to Harper. The gifts were wrapped in gold or silver paper, having blue silk bows or pink lace ribbons. Harper had carefully attached a name to each package and slowly called them out. She had selected each gift herself and remembered exactly what she had bought—except, of course, for the Cash boys. She remembered what she had gotten for Nathaniel and Vic, even Tim and Tom, but after that, the gifts and the faces were a blur.

"Tee Tat Jones," Harper said.

"Yes, ma'am," said Tee Tat. Wearing her ruffled cap and apron, she stepped forward and extended a black hand which was missing two fingers—little and ring.

"You're still a church goer, I guess?"

"We having a healing this Sunday, Miss Harper."

"Who's being healed?"

"Rastus Dozier. He's got the goiter on his neck big as a hen's egg."

"Well, you may wear this to the healing of Rastus Dozier's goiter."

Harper had selected a pair of gold earclamps cast in the form of a cross for Tee Tat. They were not very expensive, but they were gold. The gift was not practical at all. None of the gifts were. Harper believed that presents should be fanciful and pretty and completely impractical.

When all the gifts had been passed out to the servants, Harper nodded and they opened them. There were sighs and squeals, squeaks and hallelujahs.

THE LOSS OF HEAVEN

5

AS SOON AS FORD embraced Harper,
she could see his growing disgust. Up until the last few years, he more
than anyone had loved this time of handing out presents. At thirty-one,
however, he had finally learned to see beneath the surface of things and
thought that he was the only one who did so. She looked at his round,
unhappy face and the way his plump chin pushed his bottom lip beneath his top and she became irritated at his confounded simplicity.

"Did you see the President?" Harper asked him.

The question pulled Ford from his silent condemnation. "Yes,
ma'am," he said. "He sent me to Vietnam."

"He what?"

"I interviewed some young pilots. They were terrific. I've about got
the article written."

"I want to see it."

Suddenly a young Cash child leapt from the crowd and dashed up to

Harper bearing a handful of goldenrod. She sat the little boy on her lap and saw Ford step back with his brothers, his face clouding up again.

"We've got to stop it," Ford whispered to Blackie. "We've simply got to put an end to this, this—feudalism."

Ford had black hair and blue eyes, a lavender birthmark in his cheek and wire-rim glasses. He was heavy and out of shape and sensitive about it. He was the only Longstreet who was fat and it set him apart from his brothers. Of course, other things set him apart as well. He was completely unathletic, bumbling, nearsighted and endowed with a ferocious intellect and a tender heart. As a child, he learned quickly and deeply, usually surpassing his teachers after only a few weeks of instruction. The problem was that after he mastered a particular subject he became completely bored with it, abandoning the discipline altogether and immersing himself in yet another one.

His mind was so quick and so intuitive that he could understand any point of view in any given situation. It all made sense to him, everyone's position, everyone's passion. As chairman of the debate team in college, he could argue as brilliantly for pacifism as he could against it, as tenaciously for communism as for capitalism, and these arguments were not idle, intellectual exercise, but rather felt convictions depending upon what point he was championing, what author he was reading.

Ford knew Harper bristled at this quality in him, this lack of center which allowed him to be a consummate egalitarian, but he didn't care. He thought this tradition should end.

Blackie patted his brother's back as Harper began calling out the names: Blackstone (on these occasions she did not use nicknames), Wickliff, Ransford, Starfield (even though he had not come home yet) and Boykin. The family's presents were no larger or more decorated than the servants', though they were more expensive.

Boykin began opening her present first. Beneath the pink paper, the box was thin, six inches long and sandalwood. She took off the box top and lifted out a royal blue sack. On the outside of the small poke was stitched a five-point star—a fastener whose center was embossed with a silver ball. Carefully, she unhooked the star and pulled back the outer flap.

Family and servants leaned forward to see the dazzle, as Boykin pulled the long crystal into the light. She read aloud an attached note. "Swizzle stick. Found it in Asheville. Harper."

The swizzle stick had six sides of crystal, a sparkling surface below which lay six golden filaments running into a pear-shaped bulb.

"Gee, I'm glad you stuck a note on it," Blackie said. "I thought it was a meat thermometer."

The servants giggled.

"Blackie, please," said Ford, momentarily lifted from his gloom. He gently took the piece from Boykin. "This is exquisite. I would say Cartier, circa 1925. Used to decorate champagne, probably."

Chin in the air, eyebrows raised, black eyes surveying her sons, Harper said nothing.

Blackie quickly eviscerated his present. He held up a china jackass. The animal wore a pair of trousers which had fallen down the hindquarters, exposing a very white, very human pair of buttocks.

"An ass," Boykin grinned.

"Oh, is that what it is, Boykin?" Blackie asked.

"How could you not have known," said Ford. "It's obviously a jackass. Look at it."

When it had been time for Ford to go to college, Harper had chosen the University of South Carolina and Ford chose Clemson. There was a fight, but he prevailed. It took him five years to slog through and the day after graduation he went to Ireland. He spent two years in the British Isles ending up as a gillie for wealthy American sportsmen who wanted to fish the black lakes of Killarney and the highlands of Scotland. His delinquency infuriated Harper, who finally went over and told him that he needed to come home and begin his career.

"I don't know what I want to do."

"Well, go to law school."

He was getting tired of guiding anyway, so he did what Harper suggested. His first semester he worked hard and stunned his law professors. At the end of the year he made Law Review and promptly slacked off. Harper told him that if he did not finish law school she would kick him out of Waverly, so he did that, too. Upon graduation, she insinuated him into the most prestigious law firm in the state. He won half a dozen unwinnable cases and then spent more and more time fishing and giving and attending parties at his various clubs. One day, a senior partner of the firm told him that he seemed distracted and that maybe he needed to take a sabbatical and he accepted, not realizing for a while that he had been fired.

The day Harper found out that he had been fired, she evicted him from Waverly. It was no great tragedy because he had come into his trust fund at twenty-six and there was plenty of money, but he loved Waverly and he hated to go. He fished for a year and a half and caroused with the younger members of his old law firm, enduring lectures from Wick, who told him that he was embarrassing the family.

At the age of twenty-eight, he finally overcame his shyness of women and started dating. Somehow he managed to fall in love with a nineteen-year-old redneck girl. Her name was Patti Russell. For the first time in his life, he became thin, learned how to two-step and paid attention to his wardrobe, wearing mostly blue jeans and Western shirts and narrow-heeled snakeskin boots. (Harper was ill.) Ford had never been in love before and so he opened all the doors in himself and the girl saw this and knew she had him and so she started seeing someone else. Ford was devastated. He talked endlessly about Patti Russell, calling Starkey at Fort Benning and Wick at the monastery at all hours, even seeking advice from Blackie (an inveterate womanizer by the age of seventeen), from whom he had always felt distant. His obsession became worse and worse until one night he was arrested in the bushes outside Patti Russell's house.

Harper took over. She gave the girl five thousand dollars to leave town and then brought Ford back to Waverly. She nursed him for three months, combining sedatives with long walks and bream fishing and the best food that Hannah could turn out.

Ford slowly recovered. For the last year, he had been writing a wild-life column for the family newspaper, the *Southern Chronicle*.

Ford received a tortoise shell fountain pen inlaid with lapis lazuli. Wick opened a box to reveal a Chinese black lacquer casket whose two front panels were decorated in red and gold butterflies. While the family and servants beamed over their gifts and plied Harper with questions, a figure stepped through the front door, walked down the hall and stood in one of the doorways to the ballroom. It was Starkey.

He wore his uniform. He had rolled the green beret and held it in a hand behind his back. His jacket and trousers were green and the tie and shirt khaki. On his left shoulder was a Special Forces patch: a blue arrowhead with the tip pointing toward his elbow. In the center of the arrowhead was a gold sword crossed by three lightning bolts. Above the arrowhead were two smaller patches. The first was Airborne and the second Ranger.

Harper saw him. "Oh," she said, rising, palms upon her heart as if she felt a pain.

The rest of them saw him then and the black women dropped their jaws and put their big hands to their faces almost to a one, saying "Aw, Lordie, Lordie." The black men set thumbs on hipbones, dangling their heads with shy smiles, saying little and if anything at all something like, "look out now, uh-huh, you better look out."

Starfield Longstreet was everyone's favorite. He had black hair and blue eyes and a dimple in his chin, high cheekbones and a square jaw. He had all that, but there was something else, something fetching about the way he smiled, the way he looked at you with his light blue eyes, then looked away and looked at you again as if he were slightly embarrassed by his handsomeness. Harper gave him a hug, his brothers clapped him on the back and grabbed his hand, Boykin reached out and pinched the base of his neck and was shocked when he turned and kissed her squarely on the lips. He grabbed Hannah and Bub in one big embrace and reached out with his hands to touch the others, calling everyone by name, including all seven Cash boys.

Jebodiah handed Starkey his present, and when he opened it, even he was surprised: a yellow rectangle of paper matted in navy blue, framed in sterling silver, the message upon the yellow paper written in a meticulous hand—*Dort-il toujours?* The signature which lay beneath the note was bold: Napoleon.

"Where did you find this?" Starkey asked.

"Actually I got it last summer in London. They say it was one of his last dispatches at Waterloo."

Wick pointed to a long decoration on Starkey's left breast pocket. "What's this?"

"C.I.B. Combat Infantry Badge. You're awarded it after you've been fired on."

"Did you really get shot at?" asked Blackie.

"Yep."

"Did you kill the bastard?"

"It's not the Wild West," said Ford.

"It kinda is the Wild West, Ford. You'd like it." Starkey smiled at his older brother.

"I would?"

"The Army needs people like you, too. They need guys who understand ideas."

Starkey always filled the room, Harper thought. The way he carried himself, his confidence, his buoyancy. How quickly he warmed an individual or a crowd. It was an ability that was completely wasted in the Army. Those people could never appreciate his sensitivity. She quietly determined to start pushing Starkey very hard to retire from the Army and run for office. He will be a statesman, she thought. A marvelous statesman.

"Well, why don't ya'll visit awhile. I'm going for a little nap. I'll see you for lunch," Harper said.

She waved at her sons and gave a few orders to a few servants.

Harper climbed the staircase and went to her office, filled with dread. It always happened to her when she returned home from a trip. She was afraid that something had gone wrong with the newspaper—problems with the presses or personnel problems or perhaps someone was threatening suit, and if the newspaper was quiet, then she worried about the peach farm or the chicken farm or whether there might have been a fire in the thirty thousand acres of pine and cypress trees that she owned. She had all of her mail sent to The Hills, of course, but she never felt entirely comfortable until she went over the in-box on her desk.

This time there were no problems. There was no mail at all from her foremen concerning the farms and only two letters from the *Southern Chronicle*. The first one was from an air-conditioning company wanting to put in a system in the office building and the second was from a young woman who was asking for a job as a fashion writer. Harper would do neither. Both would cost money. Satisfied all was well, she went to her room, pulling off her shoes on the way.

It was a large room with a four-poster bed made of mahogany. There were deep red curtains on the French doors which led out to a marble balcony. Below her bed was a dark blue Edwardian couch and two low Edwardian chairs. These were clustered about a rosewood table. The wall facing her bed was filled with black and white pictures in gold frames which detailed the building of Waverly in 1852. In the very center of the wall was a ten-foot portrait of her father, James Longstreet. Like her, he was short and thin with black hair and black eyes and high cheekbones.

Harper pulled off her stockings and found her bedroom slippers, which she had inadvertently left. They were blue cotton slip-ons and were ratty and gray and torn and she loved them, though Hannah did not, saying that they were trashy. She was always trying to throw them away. Just before she slipped her feet into the bedroom shoes, Harper glanced at her big toes. They looked awful. They were both red around the edges and the flesh beside the nail was yellow and dry and cracked. The corners of each toe where the top of the nail folded into the flesh were horny and yellow and it made her feel sick. She would call Minnie first thing in the morning.

She fluffed two pillows and picked up the morning edition of her newspaper which lay at the foot of the bed and settled down with a sigh.

As a child, Harper Longstreet had been shy and dreamy and gave no indication that she would turn into such a strong woman. She liked reading Mark Twain and H. G. Wells and Kipling. She wrote poetry and spent hours in the dark, green woods which surrounded Waverly. Everything in her world was quiet until about the age of ten, when things started going wrong. Several of the familial retainers had to be let go. Part of the vast forest which belonged to Waverly was sold, the big sycamores and oaks cut down. Even food began to change in the house. Gone were roast beef and lamb. Present were squirrel stews and lots of chicken. It was all the fault of her father. He was soft and funny with a supple mind and good looks. Everyone loved him. He could tell the best jokes and the most frightening stories. He was a good shot and a good dancer. He was also a terrible businessman. He paid no attention to details, let other people make his decisions, hunted and fished and told great stories while his businesses and his land slipped through his fingers.

By the time Harper was seventeen, the family was nearly ruined. She had watched her world dwindle. She loved her father, but she began to resent him for his weaknesses. Even at the age of seventeen, it seemed to her that he had been given everything in life and that he had wasted it all and that as a result of his wastefulness, the whole family was teetering on the edge of disaster. It was then that she decided she would never, ever take for granted what she had been given, but that she would work and strive and control and dominate and would not lose anything that was hers. She became ruthless.

Over the years, Harper's ruthlessness had shocked much of the populace, but there was one event in particular which was legendary. It was an incident so cruel and cold that even certain members of Harper's family blanched at her wielding of personal power.

A Northern union had infiltrated her newspaper. Two union organizers and eleven newspaper workers barricaded themselves into the *Southern Chronicle* building. The workers were so serious about the strike that the second night they snuck their entire families into the building, vowing to live there until Harper increased their pay.

Harper went directly to the governor. Within three days, the homes belonging to the workers were seized for delinquent back taxes. Harper herself went into each house and made a list of everything which could be sold. She started out with stoves and refrigerators, then sofas and dining room tables, then earrings and bracelets and combs, even putting on the list two pet turtles and a white cockatiel which whistled "Crown Him with Many Crowns."

When Harper had completed the lists, she had them delivered to the *Southern Chronicle* with a simple note:

Get out in an hour or I sell it all.

H.L.

They did not get out, and so by four o'clock on the same day, three of the houses and everything in them were auctioned off, including the whistling cockatiel, which was bought by the Presbyterian choir director.

The strikers left the next morning.

The worst event in her life had been the death of her daughter and son-in-law. They had gone down in a plane in Georgia. The shock was so great that at the funeral she had been calm and quiet with a commanding smile and no tears, spending the day comforting others and saying that there was a purpose to it all. A week later, it became real to her—Antonia's death—and she grieved for weeks, losing a great deal of weight and becoming addicted to sleeping pills. It took her seven months in a sanatarium to recover and when she got out she knew that there wasn't a purpose to anything unless she gave it a purpose.

She adopted her grandsons and began to mold their lives and never looked upon them as grandsons again. They were her sons.

She changed their last name to Longstreet.

She believed that there were only two things that really mattered in life—brains and ambition. Her sons had the first and she was determined to see to it that they produced the second.

6

THE BROTHERS GATHERED IN the den. Even though it was only eleven-thirty, the sun poured white heat through the bay window. They avoided the two brown couches and wingback chairs which sat in the sun, preferring to sprawl in the blue corduroy couches and the stuffed armchairs which lay in the shadows before the fireplace.

Starkey was exhausted from his plane flight, but the sights and smells of home were reviving him. A lot of times when he had been in the jungle with mud in his ears, jungle rot between his toes, having just discovered the second leech of the day attached to the back of his thigh, a lot of times he thought about this room, the way it smelled, the way it felt. His mind drifted through the last conversation he had had with the colonel. The old man had said that he must have a lot of pull to get to go home for a birthday party.

It was true. Starkey had pull all of his life, but he rarely used it. He believed that what he accomplished he had to do himself. He was quite certain that if he had used Harper's connections he could have been a major by now, but he had not used them and he was still a first lieutenant. He wanted to be the best officer in the United States Army. He had been first in his class at the Citadel and captain of the tennis team as well as editor of the newspaper. He was driven to be first, and when he did not make it, he went into a savage depression because in his heart he feared that he had little talent at all. He felt that he was a third-rater desperately trying to be first, and even when he made first, he believed that it was some kind of fluke and that it would never happen again.

Starkey was terrified of failure. He feared failure so much that on those rare occasions when he did fail, he made himself fail worse than anyone else. The last time had been a year ago. He was on a long run. When it was clear that he could not win the eighteen-mile course, he started making himself run slower and slower until he was at the last of the pack and his friends jeered at him and called him names and he told himself, Yeah, that's right, you are a fag, you are an old woman. You deserve to be laughed at. You're nothing. You're shit.

Hannah entered the den carrying a tray which held a bowl of potato chips and another bowl with a peach-colored dip. Everyone called this concoction "Hannah's Revenge." It consisted of a pound of cream cheese, two packages of dried onion soup, green capers and garlic. She set the tray on the sideboard with the pears and blueberry muffins.

Blackie hurled himself against the base of one of the couches, propped his head up with a pillow. He was still wearing cutoff blue jeans and a T-shirt. His tan was radiant and his Beatle haircut looked particularly wild and black.

Starkey sat on one side of the couch and Wick on the other. Ford loitered near the bar beside the fireplace. He had gained weight on his trip and his belly pushed out his white tennis shirt and hung over his belt.

There was tension in the room. The brothers had not been all together in a long time, and while they basically got along, there was always hesitancy and a little coolness and sometimes even exaggerated politeness among them when they first sat down. Though everyone was a bit edgy, most of the tension was between Starkey and Wick. They had fought since they were children. They had never agreed on anything and the competition between them had often been violent, like the time they both wanted to take the head cheerleader to the same party and Starkey had succeeded, only to have Wick come over later and bust him in the nose so violently that blood squirted all over his white dinner jacket and the cheerleader threw up in the Planter's Punch.

Wick went to the sideboard, grabbed the potato chips and dip, turned on the RCA TV and sat the dip on the coffee table. "I've been keeping up with Vietnam. Things sound like they're getting worse." He felt uncomfortable.

"Oh, they're about the same, I guess," Starkey said, not wanting to talk. He could tell Wick had been having a rough time about something. He was thin and his hands were shaking and it seemed to Starkey that he was exaggerating the shakes so that everyone would notice. It made Starkey look away and roll his eyes. Wick was a manipulator. He was always "going through something" and wanted everyone's sympathy and Starkey was determined not to show him any because he knew it was just manipulation and he had always thought that half of Wick's problems were in his head and that he spent far too much time worrying and little time doing.

"You know Ford just got back."

"I heard him say that."

Ford sat down in a chair. "I conducted a marvelous interview on the *Constellation.*"

Starkey perked up a little. "Isn't that the flattop where we launched the Tonkin Gulf strike?"

"Exactly. It was exquisite in a way—or maybe not exquisite—exotic, yeah. It was the most exotic kind of experience."

Hannah entered the room. "Mr. Ford, Miss Harper wants to speak to you."

"We were at ten thousand feet," Ford said on his way out.

"Pretty good view?"

"I'll tell you all about it. There was this horrible kind of beauty to it —like a ballet almost. In fact, exactly like a ballet." Ford pushed a finger to the bridge of his wire-rims, studying his own words, and then he followed Hannah from the room.

When Ford left, everyone became silent and Wick was more uncomfortable than before. He was very pale and very thin. There were dark circles under his eyes and his black clericals hung on his bones. He pulled out a package of cigarettes and lit one up. His right-hand fingers were yellow from sneaking them at the monastery. "What do you think we ought to do over there?" Wick asked.

"I don't know. Have we got any cold Cokes down here?"

"Hey, what's the matter with you?"

"I'm tired, goddammit."

"Oh, pardon me."

"I don't feel like arguing with you right now, Wick."

"It's called conversation."

"Okay, all right, fine. You want to argue. We'll argue. I think we ought to throw everything we've got against them and do it early."

"Or what?"

"Or the whole Southeast will fall."

"Oh, for God's sake."

Starkey sighed and loosened his khaki tie. Blackie was watching television.

"You know what your problem is? You have the typical American's viewpoint. Why don't you read a little Ho Chi Minh? Why don't you see what he thinks he's fighting for?" Wick said.

"All right, let's be objective, let's read and think and when we find out that the Viet Cong really are our enemies, then what should we do?" Starkey asked.

"That's begging the question," Wick said.

"Don't intellectualize it, just answer me."

"Oh, excuse me," Wick said. "I'll try to be more brainless—why, we should bomb the greasy little bastards."

Starkey threw up his hands, "What do you know about it anyway? You live with a bunch of fucking monks."

"Not anymore," Blackie said.

"What do you mean?"

"They threw him out."

"Not exactly," Wick said. "I don't know—the abbot says I need some time off."

"I'm gonna fatten him up, get him a little leg."

Wick looked at Blackie.

"I am," said Blackie. "I'm gonna work him out with weights, fill him up with beer and barbecue and then find him the prettiest little girl around here. Hey, you remember Becky Thompson?"

At the mention of her name Wick winced.

"I remember Becky Thompson," said Starkey. "Wasn't she Miss South Carolina Queen of Peaches?"

"Yeah. That's right," said Blackie, stuffing his mouth with dip—no potato chips, just four fingers of pure dip.

"No, she wasn't," Wick said.

"Miss Peaches," Blackie said, wiggling his eyebrows.

"She wasn't Miss Peaches," said Wick. "She was Miss Soybean," he said, almost inaudibly.

His brothers guffawed and then he laughed too and things relaxed a little. Starkey opened up some about Vietnam, talked about the jungle and life in Saigon, mentioned briefly that he was not seeing Eugenie anymore and that he had been going out with another girl named Lin, though he wasn't sure how long it would last. There was a moment of quiet among them then as they let down their guard and listened to the television.

Wick finished off his first cigarette and lit another and saw the headline of the morning paper: TODD SEEKS THIRD TERM.

"Hey, you ever think about politics anymore?" he asked Starkey.

"Not too much."

"I think Harper would love for one of us to end up as governor—or, I should say, start out as governor."

"It's a good job."

"Of course you could run for Pinky Smith's congressional seat. That election's only three months away."

Blackie jumped off the floor, launched into a hand stand and then flipped backward onto his feet. "I love it! I absolutely love it! You resigning your commission and coming back home and jumping into the last of ole Pinky's campaign and shaking hands and going to fish fries and stump meetings and coming from behind and just beating the hell outa that old crook!"

"Hey, just calm down, Blackie," Starkey said.

"Somebody should do it," Wick said. "Pinky Smith's such a racist. Do you realize that his organization makes colored people take a voting test? When they come down to the court house to register, Smith's boys give them a Chinese newspaper and they say, 'Here boy, read this. If you can't read this, you can't read the ballots and if you can't read the ballots you can't vote.' "

"Pinky Smith does that?" Starkey asked.

"Hell, yeah, Pinky Smith does that," Blackie said. "And worse."

"I think it's worth considering," Wick said.

Starkey folded his right hand over his left and popped his left knuckles one at a time. He knew it was what Harper wanted him to do. In the last few years she had been pushing him hard to leave the Army. He seemed to be forever struggling with her. He had won an appointment to West Point but Harper insisted he go to the Citadel. He had thought that upon graduation he would be his own man, but he wasn't. They had fought about his extended training. He wanted Special Forces, but Harper had argued for Armor because she said it was from Armor that most generals were chosen. He won out, but there was always a test of wills between them and the horrible truth was that he wanted to please her. In almost every case, he wanted to do what Harper suggested and it was only by the sheerest act of his will that he went contrary to her. This constant need to please her worried him.

"Maybe *I'll* think about running," Ford said, walking into the room.

"Oh come on, Ford," Blackie said.

"I don't think it's your cup of tea," said Wick.

"I think I'd make a good politician. I believe in the truth. I believe in the democratic proposition."

"Hey, man, take some advice from your younger brother—politics ain't you," Blackie said.

Blackie and Wick continued to construct Starkey's political future while Ford sank into a small gloom. I would make a good politician. You have to care about people—I care. You have to commit yourself to progress, I'm certainly for that. And you have to want it. You have to want to be elected. This thought stopped him. He wasn't quite sure if he wanted it or not. In order to want something you had to have a reason. This idea sent Ford off into a flurry of philosophical questions about motive—what was motive and was any motive pure? He was lost for forty-five minutes.

An hour later, Starkey lay in his bed with a big bowl of vanilla ice cream and chocolate syrup. He had not been home in a year and he let his eyes wander over his room. The right-hand wall held nearly fifty glass frames which contained his arrowhead collection. On the left wall, beside and between the two big windows stood cabinets holding his shotguns and rifles, the top shelves of each cabinet rife with fuzzy squirrel tails stuffed into red twenty-gauge shells. The wall immediately before him was an inlaid bookcase which contained his whole youth: the bottom level was cluttered with brown baseball mitts, cracked football helmets, silver cap pistols and white cowboy hats and a big fishbowl crammed with old baseballs, their skin yellow and frail. The next shelves held a collection of model ships—destroyers and flattops and subs.

He sat the bowl beside his bed and felt his ankle itch. There was a purple-black hole there and he knew better than to scratch it. It was the last leech bite and as he looked at it he wondered about the assassination. It was the colonel's idea, but it was political and politics was mire that he wanted to stay out of. Two of his friends in Special Operations Group had been involved in politics. They had infiltrated a coffee plantation in Laos. For seven hours they had buried themselves in a bin of black coffee beans, breathing out of the plastic IVs from their medical packs. At night they left the bin, crawled across to the French plantation house and slit the throats of a Vietcong leader and his three sons. Back in Da Nang, the SOG commander had put them in for a bronze star. This move invited an investigation and both men had been reprimanded and sent down to an infantry company.

But—if he did it and got away with it, he was sure to get a promotion. He needed something to push him up the ladder. He was stuck. Several of his classmates at the Citadel had already made captain. The question was whether or not assassination was murder. That's a terrible way to look at it, he thought. That's the way Ford would look at it—in the abstract, as if it were some kind of collegiate debate: Is assassination murder in a time of war? The point is it would be murder. And why would I be doing it? Well, you could say because it would help to shorten the war, but number one, you don't know if that's true, and number two, you do know that's not the real reason you would do it. You would do it to advance your career. Isn't that right? Yes or no?

Starkey slipped beneath the cool cotton sheets. A thunderstorm rumbled in the distance and a breeze blew white curtains into his room. The cicadas were churring in the oak trees and the storm wind was blowing through the hickory woods.

How could he even consider something like this, he thought. It was monstrous.

LATER THE SAME NIGHT, Blackie was laying out the nylon jumpsuits that Starkey had sent from Vietnam. They were perfect. They had many pockets and were lightweight and, most importantly, they were black as the night itself. Beside the jumpsuits, he arranged the tools: three shiny chisels with black plastic handles, a glass cutter, a small grappling hook and twenty yards of coiled nylon rope, a small hammer, pliers, wire cutters, two black suction cups with handles, a roll of black tape and fifteen rubber window wedges.

Something banged against his bedroom window and he jumped. He waited, then went toward the sound. Her blackened face appeared in a windowpane. He opened the window. It was raining.

"Carol, what are you doing?"

"This is not so hard."

"Get in here."

Blackie pulled her into the room. Below, against the side of the house, he saw a ladder.

"I thought I'd surprise you," Carol said. The black grease paint covered her face and hands. She wore blue jeans, a black sweatshirt and black ballet shoes laced about her ankles with pink ribbon. Around her neck she wore a gold chain and Blackie's college ring. She was soaked.

Carol was thirty years old and Blackie was twenty-two. She had taught him freshman biology. The course had lasted a long time after the class was over. Only recently had she discovered his obsession. Tonight was her first outing with him.

Blackie was wearing nothing but his jockey briefs. Like his brother Starkey, he worked out four days a week. Blackie was shorter than Starkey, but his shoulders were wider and his muscles more defined. The cuts under his pectorals were sharp and the ridge between them was deep and hard and suntanned.

When Carol looked at his green eyes and black hair, even after two years of dating, she felt her heart shudder. More than anything, she loved his stomach, the blocks of muscles there. She had always been attracted to younger men. She had had three young lovers at the university and she knew that this was abnormal, but she could not stop.

"We've got a problem," Blackie said, hanging his hands from narrow hips. "The dog's there."

"The doberman?"

"All hundred and thirty pounds."

"Sounds exciting."

"Oh, it'll be exciting all right."

"As exciting as you?"

With her index finger, Carol circled one of his dark nipples. Blackie moved toward the black jumpsuits.

"After I found out I went to the vet's and bought some stuff called Quiet." He picked up one of the red bottles. "Hit him right in the nose with this stuff and he'll go down."

"I hope so."

"You need to do something with that." He pointed at her blond hair.

It had been pulled straight from her face and at the back of her head separated into seven braided ponytails. Six of the small braids were bound at the end in tiny bows of yellow ribbon. The seventh had been looped into a figure eight and stitched to the side of her head by nine or ten brown bobby pins. This last braid was tied in a red ribbon.

"What's the matter with my hair?"

"Too many tails. They'll get caught in something."

While Carol fumed and began brushing out braids, Blackie picked up two dumbbells. He watched himself in a full-length mirror. He watched the veins pump and swell in his brown biceps. The blood expanded his chest and the rounds of his shoulders. He broke a sweat and his abdomen tensed and collected.

Carol watched him. When she had brushed out her long blond hair, she came from behind, pushed herself against his moist back and rubbed her hands across his working stomach muscles. Blackie did another complete set and then set down the weights.

He opened her jeans and they looked at one another in the mirror. "Do you think we oughta be doing this?" Carol asked.

"Naw, let's quit."

She held him. "Jenny Talbot told me girls whistle at you on the beach."

"Aw, that's not so."

"Yea, right. Look at that body." She pushed him away, sized him up. "I don't hear you whistling."

"Can I do something?"

"We need to go before the rain stops."

"Just let me do this."

Carol turned Blackie at an angle to the mirror. She bent over and stuck her tongue into his navel and when she did she watched his hard stomach contract. She swirled her tongue and then slowly drew it over the brown ridges of his stomach and watched his knees buckle and his head drop back upon his shoulders. She worked up to and across his chest and carefully avoided his nipples, which had gone hard, and her hands delicately touched his shorts until he said, "Do 'em for me."

"You don't want me to."

Blackie's hands rushed beneath her damp sweatshirt.

Carol slid her tongue up and down the ridge of his chest and still did not touch his nipples. She loved the power this gave her and loved seeing the brown boy plead with her.

"Come on, suck 'em for me, please."

"Did you say please?"

"Please, baby, yeah, do 'em."

She held him in her hands now and carefully licked her way around his left nipple until she heard him make a sound, a kind of gasp and shudder, and then she set her mouth on his nipple and sucked hard and he went down to the floor.

In a second he flipped her and they watched not one another, but the two images in the mirror—brown boy and blond girl with black face, teeth bared and hands interlocked and bodies in syncopation.

When it was finished, Blackie held her and felt the cool wind blow rain through the window. He loved the rain. It was important. He couldn't do anything without the rain.

Blackie had started breaking into houses because it was fun and thrilling and also because he hated being diligent like everyone else in the family. Harper and his brothers were always trying to be good at this and good at that and by the time he had reached fourteen they all made him sick. Everyone but Boykin.

He loved her because she wasn't constantly striving for something and because she let him do what he wanted and did not forever question his motives and his goals. She was so different from Harper that it was hard to believe they were sisters. He had talked to Boykin earlier in the day.

"I mean why can't you just have fun in life, Boykin? Why do you have to always want to get ahead?"

"I don't think you have to."

"I'm so tired of it. I remember last week I saw Ford down at the lake and his face was all pooched out and scowling and I said, 'Fordie, what's the problem, man?' And he said, 'I've only caught two bream today.' So I said, 'What's wrong with that,' and he said, 'I need to have five. If I don't get five, I've wasted the day.' Can you believe that? I mean it's just sick."

It was true that Blackie detested work and achievement and loved thrills and dares, but he had another problem. Unlike any of the other boys, he resented being a Longstreet, or at least resented being named Longstreet. He had learned at the age of ten that Harper had changed his and his brothers' name from Hartley to Longstreet and he never forgave her for it. It was as if Antonia and Charlie Hartley had never existed, as if Harper had wanted to destroy any memory of her daughter and son-in-law. It infuriated Blackie and made him perverse. If Wick scored two touchdowns during a high school game, Blackie would break out two streetlights the same night. If Ford boasted of the highest grades in his courses, Blackie would work to get the lowest. By the time he was sixteen, he had developed a completely perverse ambition: if his brothers were determined to be the best, he was hellbent to be the worst.

"Do you like it?" Blackie asked.

"Yeah."

"No, I mean the rain."

"I know what you mean."

"It hides everything, you know. Sounds, sights, smells. The rain's the best friend I've got."

"Is it really?"

"Well, almost."

Blackie stood, faked a stagger and sprawled on the bed beside the black suits. "Well, my legs are gone now."

Carol laughed.

"Couldn't climb a set of stairs, much less a wall."

"Sure you can."

"Just call me Jelly Legs."

"Blackie."

Carol lay down beside him and they held hands and Carol wondered about the secret room. It was somewhere in Waverly. Blackie kept everything there. She wanted to see it, not so much because of the stolen treasure (and surely it was a treasure now because Blackie had been doing this for three years), but because if he revealed the room, it would mean she was closer to him than anyone.

She loved the smell of his room. Not the smell of perfumes and hair conditioners and nail polish, but everything here smelling metallic: rusting metal barbells and the slick odor of linseed oil shining on the blue barrels of shotguns, old tennis shoes and tall green rubber boots still caked with mud from hunting, and in one smelly corner, mildewing tennis balls, dusty racquets, and handball gloves. The smell of men was splendid. Funky, rude, rich as if anything in the world could take root in only the smell of men and grow and grow.

Ten minutes later they were dressed in their black suits and stepping down a narrow servants' staircase and out one of the maids' entrances. It was just after 1 A.M.

As Blackie drove his jeep from the back of the house, he saw that Harper's light was on. If she saw him leaving she would worry about him and he liked it. He knew that she loved him. He had always known it. When he was a child she had fussed over him more than his brothers. She had spent a lot of time with him, constantly taking him to psychiatrists and psychologists trying to discover why he failed at his school work or why he got in so many fights. He saw her weakness for him early and it made him want to exploit her. When he was younger, he felt guilty about hurting her and sometimes tried to make up, but after the age of thirteen the guilt left him and he did everything he could to get back at her for loving him because he knew that he was not lovable, not in any way, and it was only a game and she was tricking him. So he tricked her back.

You don't love me and I don't love you, he would think. You play your game and I play mine. My brothers are all dopes and maybe they'll jump through your hoops, but I won't, because I know the great secret: if you love somebody, they will kill you. They will take your heart and crush it and kill you and I know that and I know all the tricks of it and I will never love anyone, particularly you, Harper Longstreet. I will never love you.

8

BY 3:30 A.M. THEY sat on Tradd Street in Charleston. Blackie parked the car in an abandoned lot which was overgrown with green milkweed and oleander and wild fig bushes. The house he wanted to crack sat five blocks away. It belonged to the Duprés, an ancient French Huguenot family that had made its wealth a hundred years earlier. Through social contacts, Blackie had discovered that the family kept some of their jewels in a third-floor linen closet. The Duprés had one daughter named Sally. Her boyfriend was a movie star.

Blackie touched up Carol's black face and her hands and then did his own.

They slid along the shadows of the street and approached the large house. It was four stories high and built of brick plastered in pink stucco. Ivy grew over the lower portion of the house, but stopped just beyond the second story. From the second story to the roof was stucco, here and there worn through to expose raw brick.

The air was thick and cool and salty. It smelled of the harbor and the persimmon tree which stood beside the driveway. Below the big tree, the ground was littered in amber persimmons, which made the ground squishy and sour. Closer to the house, Blackie stopped.

"Damn," he whispered.

"What?"

"The garage." Just inside the open garage sat a black Jag. "It's Bart's car. He was supposed to be out West." Blackie set his hands on his hips, sighed, grabbed his satchel.

Carol caught him. "Where're you going?"

"It's over."

"Why?"

"What do you mean why?"

"Bart White's here. Just imagine it. Bart White himself."

Blackie stepped down the driveway, dragging her along.

"It's exciting. It's incredibly, incredibly exciting."

Blackie turned, looked at her. Older women had guts. It's why he liked them. He looked at the house. All lights were out. Maybe it could work. "Usually the dog's on the first floor—usually. If we run into him, you let me handle it."

Carol followed Blackie to the right side of the house. Clashing palmetto trees made the darkness even deeper here. He gave her a penlight and opened his bag. Quickly he slipped into a leather belt which held an array of tools. From the bottom of the bag he pulled one of the small grappling hooks. The four prongs had been covered in black tape. The eye of the hook was attached to a black rope.

On the fourth throw, Blackie snagged the inside of an eave. He gave a trial tug, then turned to Carol.

"We're going to the bedroom on the third floor. The linen closet's down the hall and to the left. The safe's inside of it. I'll go up first, then you."

Quickly, Blackie was eight feet off the ground. Carol was amazed. He climbed the pink stucco as if he were going up some unseen ladder.

At the third-floor window, he stopped. He balanced on his legs and one hand and tried to raise the window. Carol moved farther from the house so she could see him. Carefully he brought his knees up and spread them. He used both hands now. The window did not move.

"Glass cutter," Blackie whispered.

Carol flashed her penlight into the black bag: pliers, wire cutters, hacksaws. "What's it look like?"

"Red handle."

She fished around in the bag, found it. "Ready?"

"Don't throw it. Use the line."

"What line?"

Blackie extended his hand below his belt.

Something spidery touched Carol's right cheek. She had not noticed it when he was climbing: a black nylon line from which dangled a metal clip. The line rose thirty feet above and connected into a swivel in Blackie's belt. She fastened the clip into a hook in the handle of the glass cutter.

"On?"

"Yes."

Still balancing on his knees, Blackie reeled up the tool. Carefully he worked the cutter into the windowpane. Carol heard a small splinter and pop, but she did not hear falling glass. Blackie slipped open the window, disappeared, then reappeared and told her to climb.

The first ten feet were easy.

"You're going too fast," Blackie whispered.

"It's fun."

"Slow down."

"Oh, hush."

The end of the cool ivy lay about a foot over her. She could feel the soft leaves against the back of her hands. She was pushing with the bottom of her feet, then pulling with her left hand and then the right.

At twenty feet Carol paused. She looked down Tradd Street. It was beautiful in the streetlamps of the black morning drizzle. Tall houses painted yellow and gray, blue and pink.

"Don't stop," Blackie said.

"It's beautiful up here."

Carol felt the pain then. It was in her palms. She tried to move more quickly. Ten feet below Blackie, she felt the pain spread into her fingers. Her grip was going and for the first time that night she was afraid.

"Got some problems," she said.

"I can't pull you."

The pain burned and her two middle fingers on both hands went numb. "Got some real problems here."

"Five feet more."

"Can't grip good."

"Five feet. I'll haul you the rest of the way."

Carol pushed with her feet, but there was a pain in her chest and she could not breathe. She drew up her left foot and shoved and suddenly lost balance and spun. With a dull whack her left side slapped the cool stucco and her left hand completely lost its grip.

She was falling.

When she hit the ground she saw a flash of lights and then everything went black.

Something cool on her face brought her back. Blackie was holding a damp cloth on her head. She was sitting in the back seat of his jeep.

"God, you scared me to death," Blackie said.

"I'm okay."

"We should go by the emergency room."

"No—really."

"Just let them take a look."

"Take me back home. If I don't feel right, then we can go."

Blackie kissed her and climbed into the front seat.

Driving home, he wondered what he was going to do about her. Lately, he had the feeling that she wanted some kind of commitment out of him and it made him feel sick. He didn't want to be committed to anyone or anything. And this was not his only problem. Harper was pushing him to make a decision about a career. The fact was he didn't want a career—unless it was burglary. He liked it. It was fun and different and he was always walking on the edge. I'll just tell Harper that, he thought. I'll say, Well, I finally have decided on a career and its burglary and I promise to be real good at it and never get caught. It made him laugh.

"What are you laughing at, bunny?"

It was her nickname for him and she had just recently started using it and it meant things were just getting too thick.

"Don't call me bunny."

"It's cute."

"I don't like it."

"It hurts my feelings when you talk to me like that."

He knew that he was going to have to do something about Carol soon —very soon.

9

MIRACULOUSLY, CAT MCGREGOR'S
presence at Waverly was kept secret during the next ten days. Boykin
came to see her primarily at night. She usually brought a surprise of
some kind and the girl seemed happy to see her. Boykin thought that so
far everything was going well, but she was afraid that once Cat had
been introduced to Harper, her sister would begin to work her spell and
Cat would fall beneath it. Everyone in the house always had. All the
boys and the servants and even the children of the servants regarded
Harper as the be-all and end-all and that nothing could be done without
her approval. Blackie was the only one who didn't kiss Harper's feet.
Boykin loved him and she knew he loved her and she wanted this same
kind of relationship with Cat, but she knew that Harper would try to
interfere. Whenever Boykin thought about this, she got worked up and
anxious and she felt that pain in her chest, that queer, sharp pain that
ran into her elbow. She decided that once Cat was settled, she would go
see Dr. Owens.

Though Cat loved Boykin's surprises, she was beginning to feel like a prisoner. She left the guest house only once. It was at night and she and Boykin rode in a car for about an hour down a country road.

On another night Boykin brought Cat a box of new outfits. There were dresses made from linen and cotton and silk. Shimmering yellow and white blouses and squeaky brown sandals and patent leather shoes and even a pair of red high heels. There were two pleated, blue cotton skirts, a light pink gabardine jacket and a saffron jacket.

Cat's days were spent with Bub and Hannah. The first few days, Bub was instructing her in cutlery.

"Take hold of your silver," Bub said.

Cat's blond hair was pulled into two pigtails which were bound by two carved giraffes made of white ivory. She wore a silk robe embroidered with pink rose buds. She looked up at Bub with her green eyes.

"Mmmmmmm, they gonna break some hearts now, mmmmmmm, I'm telling you them eyes gonna do that. All right now, pick up that silver like you was going to eat something."

Carefully, tentatively, shakily, Cat reached for the fork. She held it with her index finger and thumb. The black soot of the coal mine still lay beneath her fingernails. She held the thick silver with a limp wrist and looked at it as if it were something dead.

"You gonna eat like that?"

Slowly she circled a white fist around the back of the fork.

"Uh-huh, that's what I thought. You trying to choke the silver. Don't be chokin' it now. Look here . . ." With his large hands, Bub carefully shaped Cat's fingers into the right position. "Now, you see how that feel? You hole it just like that. You play like that fork's a—a little bird you holding. A little silver bird that's just picking at its food. You understand?"

Cat looked up at the black man and smiled.

"Now we gonna try your knife, and later this week we gonna get Minnie over here to do your fingernails. Ain't no way for a young lady to looks with them black fingernails."

A few days later, Minnie Johnson was escorted by Bub into the living room of the guest house. Minnie had tended to the Longstreet sisters' fingernails for eighteen years and their toenails for three. She had not started clipping and polishing the toenails until lately because, as she confided to her friends, "The Longstreets got the smelliest feet in the whole world. I mean to tell you they smell like something that's been dug up and left to bloat."

Minnie had only begun to work on the Longstreet feet when her adenoids had swollen to the size of figs and prevented any sense of smell whatever. She was thin with red hair and a nose which was long and bumpy and orange. On the inside of her left forearm she had a tattoo—a small pair of fingernail clippers and one word printed in blue beneath them: love.

"Now don't you dare mention one word of this to Miss Harper or Miss Boykin. It's our secret, but that chile got to have her nails looked at."

"Bub, I ain't gonna say no damn word to no damn body," Minnie said.

"Don't you be cussing before that chile neither."

"What's got into you?"

"The chile's special. She's a mute."

"She's a what?"

"A mute, she can't talk."

Minnie narrowed her brown eyes and wrinkled her nose. "Is her tongue split?"

"What you talking about, woman?"

"Mutes have split tongues. Some of them. I've heard tell that if they learn to talk, some of them can make one part of they tongue say hallelujah and the other say amen."

"Git on in there, Minnie," Bub said, and pushed her into the dining room, where Cat sat at the table.

When Cat saw the skinny woman with the orange nose, she didn't like her. She was a flat-chested woman and that was a sure sign that she was mean. All flat-chested women were mean or seemed to be. On top of being flat-chested, the woman carried a black leather bag that looked just like a doctor's bag and everybody knew that doctors' bags carried shots—needles and syringes. Cat stuck her chin out and raised it a little. I will not be afraid, she thought. I will not tremble or vacillate. She set her red hands on the table. The coal grime shone under her fingernails.

Minnie sat down beside the girl. She opened her bag and set out a tin bowl, several pairs of small scissors each with a leather grip, emery boards, files, several small bottles of oils and ointments, round tins which held emollients and salves, a cluster of black handles at the end of which were hooks and gouges and pointy-headed things and all these bound by a red ribbon.

Minnie smiled an incomplete set of teeth: some were black, some yellow and some red. She spoke loudly, moving her mouth a great deal to exaggerate the pronunciation of words. "Have you ha-ad your nay-ales done be-for-ore?"

Cat shook her head, no.

"It wi-ill be fu-un," Minnie said, saying the words very big and very loud.

She poured the contents of two bottles into the tin pan, swished it around then rudely took Cat's left hand and dunked it. Using a small brush, she scrubbed the girl's fingernails, dried them and oiled them, dried them again and rubbed in a salve and then, looking at Cat full in the face, blew across the nails until the salve had evaporated. She took one of the black-handled implements which had a triangular, razorblade head and held it before Cat's eyes.

"Now we gonna get at the goody."

Cat jerked away her hand and placed it under her arm.

"Gimme that paw, girl," Minnie said, baring her teeth.

Bub stepped in at this moment. "Minnie, don't be scaring her now. Look here, sugar, you just go ahead and let Minnie do it. It's not gonna hurt none."

With more coaxing from Bub, Cat delivered her hand. Minnie squinted one eye closed while the other studied the razor, then quickly she slipped the blade beneath the nail of Cat's little finger. She pared out a small black tail, her face rushing with blood, her face so seething with delight that you would think she was trimming out curlicues of gold.

In twenty minutes, both hands were done and Minnie gone and Cat back in her beautiful room with the lavender curtains and the white satin canopy. She looked at her fingernails. They were beautiful. They were shining and clear and clean. She had never known that fingernails could be so beautiful. They were—she remembered the word now and it made her smile—her fingernails were—pristine.

After a while, she got out of bed and crept toward a window. Crept because she felt so out of place here, so awkward. She felt almost guilty, as if she were stealing something. As if she were stealing joy. She looked at the back of Waverly. Just to see the house gave her goosebumps. It was so tall and so big and so white. Even in the daytime it was glistening, shining like a palace of ice. She wondered what was inside. Were books there? I bet there are, she thought. I bet there is a library with every book in the world. I bet they have all of William Shakespeare's books and Mark Twain's, especially that one about the boy on the raft and I know, I just know they have Kipling and e.e. cummings and that fella—oh, what's his name. That fella who wrote "Break, break break on thy cold gray stones, oh sea." And if they have him, they have to have all of Edgar Allan Poe's poems, though none of them could ever be as beautiful as "Annabel Lee."

Just the thought of "Annabel Lee" made tears come to her eyes and the house seemed to shine even more and that was when she decided that she was going to find a way inside.

There was a knock at the door and Bub stuck in his white head. "Come on back downstairs, we working on this silver every day till you get it right. After lunch Miss Boykin's taking you into town, too. Something 'bout a physical or something."

Bub closed the door and then Cat overheard a conversation that set her imagination clattering.

"Who you coming as?"

"Hannah, I done told you who I'm coming as."

"You can't come as yourself."

"Miss Boykin says we dress up like our favorite American character and my favorite American character is me. Now who you coming as?"

"Eartha Kitt."

"Eartha Kitt? Huh, you better think about coming as Buckwheat."

"Now look here, I don't have time to be fooling round with you, old man. You decide who you gonna be and what you wearing so I can get it decent. That party starts at eight o'clock and they'll be a hundred people in the Big House. I want to be through with you early."

"I told you I'm coming as . . ."

The argument descended the stairway.

Cat crawled into her satin bed and curled into a ball. A costume party. She had never been to one, but she remembered her mother reading to her about them. She frowned. She had hardly thought of her family since she had been here. She took the notebook and pencil from her nightstand and started writing a letter to Mike. She made a promise to herself that she would write her brothers twice a week.

In the middle of describing Waverly, she wondered if there was any way she could go to the costume party.

Harper's birthday was three days away. She would be seventy. Instead of the usual party she had decided to have a kind of costume ball. All the regulars of South Carolina society would be there: gentry and aristocracy, politicians and clergy and lawyers and *Southern Chronicle* employees.

Now in the first light of dawn, after her third cup of coffee, she sat at her walnut desk thinking about her sons, considering where they were at this point in their lives, planning where she wanted them to go. She knew she was lucky to have the boys home. She had used all of her political power to bring Starkey from Vietnam and she would have used her ecclesiastical connections to retrieve Wick, but she didn't have to. Though she was delighted that Abbot Lewis did not think Wick's vocation lay in the Trappist order, she was worried about the boy. He was too thin, and once he found out that the Abbot would not allow him back, she was afraid he might have a breakdown—not that breakdowns were all that bad; she had had several and she believed they allowed you time to rest and think—but Wick might not recover so quickly.

Of course she had been opposed to Wick's conversion to Catholicism and shocked when he told her about wanting to enter a monastery, but once he was ordained a priest, she knew that she must live with it. Now there was a break, however. Abbot Lewis had told her that he would propose to Wick that he should join the Diocese of Charleston and work for Monsignor LeConte. It was a welcome change in events because as a Diocesan priest Wick would be able to advance far in the church hierarchy, and Harper was planning to use all of her guile to make sure that he made up for those wasted years in the monastery. Ultimately she wanted him to work with Cardinal Spellman—a man whom she had interviewed several times and who counted on her donations to Catholic charities—but she knew that first Wick must spend a year or so working with LeConte—that senile old maid, Harper thought. How in God's name did he ever make monsignor. He should have joined a convent. It should be Mother LeConte, not Monsignor. But it's a good place for

Wick to start. If he plays his cards right he should make chancellor in one year or maybe even sooner if I can see a place to get my teeth into.

She was still working on Starkey to resign his commission but she thought she was cracking him and as for Ford—well she had printed his interview with the pilots on the front page of the *Southern Chronicle*, though she shouldn't have. It was awful. The writing was ponderous and the questions uneven—how could anyone as intelligent as Ford say, "Lieutenant, what's your favorite dessert?" She had hoped that by giving him the wildlife column she had piqued his interest in writing. Apparently not. Since working with Johnson had not brought out the best in him, she now wondered if anything would. What she really needed was for Ford to begin to run the newspaper, to take an interest in news and stories or even in the business end of it. He wouldn't, of course. She tapped her finger on the desk. Sooner or later I'll get you though. Sooner or later something will engage that marvelous intellect of yours and when it does you will outshine them all.

As for Blackie—the thought of him filled her with such despair that she opened the accounts receivable book for the chicken farm. An appropriate transition, she murmured—a bad egg if there ever was one.

10

BY SEVEN-THIRTY THE next morning, the whole first floor of Waverly was buzzing. Jebodiah and Bub were arranging chairs and tables. Hannah and Tee Tat were glazing ham and stirring shrimp gumbo (two jobs that they would not relinquish to anyone else) while overseeing the frying of chicken and baking of crown rib roast. Tadpole and Vic and the Cash boys and other assorted hands drawn in from the country polished silver and dusted pewter and began arranging the Brazilian rosewood table with eighteen legs which would lie beneath the dancing light of the ballroom chandelier.

The Longstreet brothers (except for Starkey, who rose at seven to run and survey two adjacent Longstreet farms) didn't begin to stir until ten o'clock. They were awakened the same way that they had been every morning at Waverly. There was a tap at the door, then a pause, another slightly louder tap, and then a soft voice: "Mister Ford, the sun's up and the birds is singing."

Then Bub or Jebodiah would enter carrying a silver tray, engraved with Waverly's twelve columns and triangular roof and on which lay the *Southern Chronicle* and pineapple juice in a crystal glass on a white porcelain saucer, the outer rim of which was decorated in hand-painted cardinals. There was also a yellow rose in a stem glass. (In years past, old man Longstreet had insisted that his rosebud should have morning dewdrops on its blossom and green leaves, so Bub would spray the bud with a little lilac water before he entered the master's bedroom. Unknown to the family, he persisted in this custom.)

Jebodiah tapped on Blackie's door first.

"Not this morning," Blackie said. He was already out of bed, curling two forty-five-pound dumbbells.

"I got your paper."

"I don't need the paper, Jeb."

"I got your juice."

"I don't want any juice, thank you, Jeb." Blackie winced when he said this. He found it hard to say no to the black people who waited on his family. He was close to them all and he was embarrassed when they fussed over him. He thought it wrong that they were servants. Nobody wanted to admit that in the family. Everyone called them "help" but the fact was they were servants and he tried to never call on them to help him because it made him feel guilty.

Carol turned and propped her head on one of Blackie's blue pillows. She was still sleepy: pink lips and brown eyes and a little girl's voice.

"Oh, let the poor ole thing in," she said. She had come over the evening before and then sneaked upstairs with Blackie.

He was standing in front of a mirror, shirtless and wearing a pair of blue jeans. The curls were swelling his arms. His brown stomach was contracting with each repetition.

"You have to pose," Carol said.

Blackie did his reps, then set down the weights.

"Just lean up against the door. You know how. Just look tough and mean."

Blackie shook his head, then relaxed, crossed one bare foot over another and leaned his brown weight against the door.

Carol sat up in bed. She pulled the covers across the top of her breasts, her right bare leg extending from the sheet.

"Tug your jeans down a little."

"Come on, Carol," Blackie said, trying to act bored, but he wasn't.

He liked it. He liked having her ogle him, having her stare at his body, the muscles and thin waist and the tan which he worked on so hard.

"Two inches. Pull them down two inches."

Blackie straightened up, then pulled the jeans below his navel. He resumed his pose.

Carol felt herself grow warm. She loved his body. She loved the long jaw and the young man's stubble looking more violet than brown, the wide shoulders and the way his nipples became round and soft when they were warm, though the muscles in his chest were sharp. She moved her hands across herself and studied the brown ridges of his stomach, the golden trail of hair below his navel and finally, his thick, brown feet, and she loved the way the faded jean cuffs just touched his ankles and the dusting of brown hair upon them.

Blackie saw a round bruise on Carol's thigh. He went over to the bed, sat down, gently touched the brown and green mark. "Did you do that at the Duprés'?"

"You know you're beautiful."

"Does it hurt?"

"Ouch."

"Sorry."

"Why do you steal things?" Carol asked. She touched the dimple in his chin, ran a finger up the stubbly jaw all the way to the lump of muscle in the hinge. She stared at each beautiful, black whisker and the brown flesh beneath the whiskers and the tiny ear which had a black mole on the lobe.

"I don't know."

"Sure you do."

"I do, huh?"

Carol ran a hand through his soft hair. "You steal for the same reason you wear your hair long. You're rebellious."

"I just don't want to be like everybody else in this family. I want to be different."

"You want to break the rules."

"Yeah, I want to break the rules. I want to break them all."

"Why?"

"Rules are like bars. They keep you in or keep you out. I hate them. I want to see what's on the other side."

Carol reached up and kissed him. She was thirty-two now. She had wanted to be a New York model once, but that dream had long since withered. She had done well in South Carolina, having been second runner-up in the Miss South Carolina pageant, Miss Darlington Five Hundred and Miss Pork. The titles were nice but they didn't pay the bills and so she taught freshman biology at the university. The boys made her feel young, made her feel beautiful. Blackie made her feel best of all. He made love hard and without inhibition and sometimes fiercely, even for the third time on the same night. She had become infected by his confidence and his humor. His optimism and nonchalance made her feel free and somehow successful. Carol was perfectly happy with Blackie—almost. There was one thing she wanted from him, just one thing she was dying to see: the secret room where he kept the stolen jewelry.

"You wanna fool around?" Carol asked.

"Not now."

"Why, baby?"

Blackie set her back against a pillow and tucked her into the sheets.

He pulled two straight-back chairs from a wall and set them side by side. "Need to do some push-ups, take a shower and get dressed." He set his left hand in one chair, right in the other, and put his brown feet upon the edge of the bed.

With a quick movement, Carol sprang from the sheets and squirmed under the two chairs beneath him. She was wearing one of his T-shirts. The white shirt bore a green crocodile under which another crocodile had been hand sewn. The green animals were—embracing.

"Carol?"

"Pay attention to me."

"I need to do some reps."

"I'll be your cheerleader," Carol said. She pulled the T-shirt up to her neck, exposing her panties and thin stomach and breasts. She looked at Blackie. He was beautiful and steamy and brown and hard.

He started doing the reps slowly. He did not go down deeply between the chairs. He did not touch her.

By the twelfth rep, he was breathing harder and dipping down deeper now, but still they were not touching until she reached out and pinched one of his dark nipples.

"Oh-h-h . . ." He quivered, threw back his head.

"I'm sorry."

"No, it's good."

"It's good?"

"It feels good."

She reached her left hand toward his other nipple, squeezed and he shut his round blue eyes and bared his teeth. The blood was rushing into his face and the veins swelled in his neck, and when he dipped down, when he fully extended himself between the chairs, she felt his hard chest touch her own, just barely touch and then pull away and just touch again and she dug her thumbs into him and watched his young neck throw his head backward—his hair, a black, soft shimmer and he pumped faster and his brown chest slapped her own as she ran her hands across the glistening muscles, deftly unfastening his jeans, exposing him so that when he was near, she pulled him from the chairs and down into herself and they made love quickly.

How marvelous it was to hold him: the soft hair upon her shoulders, big-knuckled fingers laced into her own, the round calluses at the base of his fingers scratching and hard in her palm and all the rest of him warm and moist and pressing.

She smoothed his hair. It was the kind of hair most women would kill to have, each follicle thick and lustrous and straight. She kissed the stubbly cheek.

"Time to get up," Carol said.

"Ugg."

"What's that mean?"

"No want move."

"What if Harper comes in?"

"Heap big trouble."

Carol laughed and he did, too. They squeezed one another.

Still lying between the two cane chairs, she looked toward a wall on which a poster hung. It was a picture of a large blue stone sitting on a velvet pillow. The caption read DIAMONDS ARE FOREVER.

"When're you going to show me?" Carol asked, weaving a finger into his hair.

"Oh now, don't start that."

"You promised."

"I'll show you."

"Maybe I'll find it myself."

Blackie snorted. "Not in a million years."

His derision was inflaming. Oh, I can't, huh? she thought. Well, we'll see about that. We'll just see.

The next afternoon, Starkey decided that he needed to see Harper. Over the years, he had brought his hardest decisions to her, even though he knew it invited her interference. Sometimes he worried that he was dependent upon her and wondered if he could make a tough decision on his own, but he told himself that he had made a lot of solitary decisions and that it was foolish not to consult someone who understood him so well. He knew that all of his brothers were dependent upon Harper, even Blackie in an odd way. He wondered if it was unnatural.

She was at the back steps of the house, below the screened porch which was covered with the puckered faces of the blue and pink and white morning glories. She wore a straw hat tied under her chin with a white bow. She was holding a red water can and tending to the portulacas.

They talked briefly about the newspaper and sales and a pending suit and then Starkey told her that he had a chance to score a solid promotion, but that he wasn't sure about it because it was a kind of op that he had never done and she asked what and he said an assassination and she continued sprinkling the plants.

"I feel like it's wrong. I feel like it's murder."

"What are the repercussions if you don't do it?"

"Well, the colonel said there would be none, but I'm not so sure."

"What's his name?"

"Now, Harper, you don't need to know his name. I have to work this out for myself. I just don't think I should do it. I think its completely immoral. I think it's murder plain and simple, but I'm in a goddamn rut over there. I'm not advancing. I'm not moving, I'm just stuck in that damnable intelligence unit, but if I did this, it'd get me out. It'd give me a chance at being a camp commander, which is the way you make lieutenant colonel."

"Is there any other way of becoming a camp commander?"

"I'd need to do something spectacular. I guess I need to work at it harder. I just don't want you to think that I'm over there doing nothing. I don't want you to think that I'm going to be a lieutenant forever."

Harper set down her water can and came over and hugged him. "Oh now you listen here, you just listen here. I have all the faith in the world in you. All the faith in the world. You are a very special young man, Starfield Longstreet. You keep listening to yourself and your own feelings and your own set of values and one day, one day very soon you will be one of the most successful commanders in Vietnam. I'm absolutely certain of it."

Later that night three of the brothers lounged in Starkey's room. They had drunk a few beers and had been getting along well, until Starkey said that he had been to Harper for a little advice and that he was amazed at how much better he felt.

"She's an amazing woman," Starkey said.

"Yeah, she's real amazing," Blackie said.

"Why are you always so hard on her?" Wick asked. His monastic haircut was beginning to grow out. He was wearing a pair of old red sweatpants and an old tennis shirt and he was smoking.

"How can you even ask that question, man? I mean the woman dominates your life and everybody else's. You can't scratch your ass around here until she approves it."

"I don't understand you, Blackie," Starkey said. He was wearing a pair of green, army issue briefs and a camouflage T-shirt. "She's done everything in the world for you."

"Yeah, and you know why? Because she wants to control me. She wants to make me into one of you and I'm not going to be one of you. I don't give a damn about a career and I never will and I'll tell you something else—I'm changing my name back to Hartley."

"Oh, God, you're not starting that again, are you?" Starkey asked.

"It doesn't bother you at all, does it? I mean the woman, or excuse me, Harper, took away your name and gave you her name and never asked you and it doesn't bother you a bit, does it?"

Blackie closed his eyes, sucked his lips between his front teeth and laid his tongue against them. This was what made him furious about Starkey, about them all. They were completely hypnotized by Harper. If she said jump, they said—how high? When he had controlled his temper, he opened his eyes and looked at Starkey. On his elder brother's right shoulder, he had a tattoo. It was new. It was a green parrot with yellow eyes and purple feet sitting on a branch. Somehow it made him even more angry, because he knew how his brother must regard it—it was an expression of independence, of defiance. God, how pathetic, Blackie thought. The only thing he can do on his own is get a lousy tattoo, but in a way it's perfect for him. A parrot. It's what he is. It's what all of them are—fucking parrots.

"What are you wearing to the party tomorrow?" Starkey asked.

"Don't brush me off like that."

"I'm not brushing you off. Go ahead and change your name if you want to. Now what are you wearing tomorrow?"

"I don't know and I don't care."

"I was thinking of wearing my clericals," Wick said.

"You're gonna burn up. Supposed to be ninety-five," Blackie said. He was sprawled on the floor, playing with a red-handled glass cutter he had used at the Dupré house. "Let's see, maybe I'll come as Jesse James or maybe John Dillinger."

"Sounds like you," Wick said.

"It is me."

"Harper's not wearing a costume," Starkey said.

"Now you see there—that's just like her," Blackie said. "She tells everybody else to wear costumes, has everybody looking like a fool and then she appears in a black satin gown or something. It's just a power game. Her whole life."

Above them, in the attic, there was a bump.

"Damn," Blackie said, looking at the ceiling.

"Old Bone Man's getting some weight on him," Starkey said.

"I almost forgot about him," said Wick.

"Y'all think it's funny, but I've seen him," Blackie said.

"Oh come on, Blackie, you've never seen Bone Man."

"The hell I haven't. I got up one night to get a drink of water and I saw him in the hall. It was like he was waiting for me. He was leaning against the wall with his head propped on his arm. He looked just like Hannah said: a skeleton in bib overalls and an old straw hat. It gives me shivers."

Another bump and then the sound of something dragged across the attic floor.

"Don't you have a heavy bag you work on up there?" Starkey asked.

"Sounds like somebody's dragging it across the floor," Wick said.

"Come on," Starkey said. "Let's find out what's going on."

"Y'all go on," Wick said.

"Okay, I'll go," Blackie said. "But I'm telling you he's real. I've seen him. There's something about the way he looks at you from under that straw hat. There's something about the way he turns his skull, like he's watching you watch him. He ain't funny—Bone Man. He ain't funny at all."

The brothers walked down the west hall of the great house. There were rugs on the red cedar floor. The white plaster walls were decorated with the heads of beasts that James Longstreet had killed just before the turn of the century. There were ten- and twelve-point bucks whose amber eyes were veiled with gray dust and the tawny heads of cougars across the yellow fangs of which spiders had woven intricate webs. There were black bears and brown bears, bobcats and at the very end of the hall the enormous head and shoulders of a black Russian boar that Longstreet had killed in Horry County. It had reportedly weighed six hundred pounds. The great snout and the head and neck were covered in black bristles and from either side of the mouth protruded two tusks that were an orange color and nine inches long. From the beast's gaping mouth hung the perfectly preserved tongue—a faint lavender.

At the end of the hall, they turned left, walked twenty yards and then took another left into a narrow and dark alcove. Blackie flipped on a light. The attic stairs sat between the two halls of the house. The alcove was dusty and dark and the air smelled stale and warm and dry. There was no decoration and the floors were gray cypress. There were only two pieces of furniture—two grandfather clocks, one standing on either side of the dark stairs which steeply ascended into the gloom. The clocks were running and their time was perfect. Harper insisted on it.

Blackie set his hand on the banister and leaned forward to look up the dark staircase.

"It's a spooky place," Blackie said.

"It's just an attic," Starkey said. "All attics are spooky."

Simultaneously, the two clocks struck nine-thirty. Blackie jumped and made a sound like someone had punched him in the stomach. Starkey didn't move. He looked at his brother and snorted and stepped up the narrow stairs, which popped and cracked. When both of them reached the gloomy landing, Blackie looked behind them. Dust completely covered the stairs except where he and his brother had stepped.

"Look at the stairs," Blackie said.

"What?"

"Nobody's been up here for days."

"Maybe we stepped on some footprints."

"No, I noticed. The steps were covered with dust."

Starkey turned the rusty handle of the small door and pushed. It wouldn't open. He put his shoulder against the door and shoved—nothing.

"Can you lock this from the inside?" Starkey asked.

"I don't think so."

Starkey bent down and pulled a key from a broken board. He inserted the key and opened the door to a dim world of dust and memory and, in the stale shadows not thirty yards away, an intruder.

11

THE ATTIC WAS VAST. A few ceiling lamps furnished some visibility. The place was crammed with the refuse and memorabilia of a hundred years: appliances and furniture, racks of clothes, stacks of tattered books, muskets, rusting swords and bayonets from the Civil War, a pyramid of cannon balls, a wooden Egyptian sarcophagus, a red and blue cliff of quilts, foot-worked sewing machines and spinning wheels and huge, wooden crates, stacks of bird cages and doghouses and aquariums and in the center of this distinguished dump sat the prince of it all—a beautiful, red and yellow, two-door, convertible, 1926 Rolls Royce. Even in the attic's perennial twilight its paint and whitewalls looked shiny and new, the famous hood ornament glistening beneath a ceiling light as if newly minted. It was Harper Longstreet's first car. When she had finished with it, she hired an English mechanic, had the car taken apart, hauled to the attic and then so perfectly reassembled that the first time she went upstairs and put her key into the ignition, the engine turned and purred.

The escarpment of treasure and junk towered above the two brothers. The air was rich in the smell of leather and oils, dust and ancient wood, rust and the smell of rotting silks and satins, flaxes and hemp.

The lights were ten feet above them. They stood in a dark canyon.

"We should have brought flashlights," Starkey said.

"I didn't remember it being this dark."

Somewhere before them, there was a creaking noise, like a door opening.

"Bone Man sounds like he's climbing back inside his coffin," Starkey said.

"Listen, there's something really up here," Blackie whispered.

Starkey pointed down a dark channel. He moved forward.

"Where you going?"

"Come on."

"Wait a minute."

Starkey moved quickly and soon both of them stepped into the deepest shadows of the attic.

"Kinda fun, isn't it?" Starkey whispered. "Like hunting."

"Yeah, I'm having a ball."

Starkey led the way through dim paths between walls of boxes and crates and pallets. When his brother stopped to figure his bearings, Blackie stepped close to an eye-level stack of mason jars. He put his face against the jars and then shuddered to see gold and black eyes staring back at him. Each mason jar held liquid and the small green and black body of a baby alligator. Starkey's collection, naturally.

Finally, they emerged from the boxes and stepped into an open space which was directly above the veranda. So far the thought had not occurred to Blackie, and then he saw—just beside the discarded rug that had covered it—the trap door to his secret room.

It was standing open.

Carol was sweating.

She crawled along a channel toward a pale light. The passageway was dusty. She could feel the dust on her hands. It was soft and smooth. The passageway smelled like the inside of a cedar closet. It was two feet wide and two feet high. She had entered the attic by climbing out Blackie's window. Using one of his grappling hooks, she had snagged a dormer window and pulled herself up and in. She started searching the attic on a hunch. The yellow light shining through the hinge of the trap door had given it away.

She paused and rested her calves. She was pushing herself along with her toes and the crawling was cramping the muscles in her calves. Looking at the pale light beyond, she felt mischievous and naughty and alive. Secretly exploring the house was delicious. She felt as if she were itching along the surface of her bones and suddenly she felt aroused—sexy and hot—and crawling again she began to smile at her arousal and smile at whatever waited in the light ahead. The thought that whatever was there had been stolen by Blackie, that he had taken it in the middle of the night and that no one had seen the secret room but him, made a shiver of sex run up her stomach.

She reached the end of the passage. The light was shining through a piece of gold fabric. She touched the fabric—silk. Carefully she pulled the silk away and for a moment she was blinded by the light.

Little by little, as she opened her eyes, the room glimmered, winked, blazed in gold and silver.

For a few moments, Carol lay in the dark passage, then she climbed down a wooden ladder and stood in the gleaming treasure light. Three long tables lay along the walls. Each table seemed to hold a different treasure. The first one held jewelry. There were five or six piles. Carol stepped toward the table stealthily, as if she were approaching something alive. The first few sparkling heaps were earrings, necklaces and pins. The earrings were the most elaborate and beautiful that Carol had ever seen. She reached into a small, sparkling mountain and picked up a set: a pair of turquoise nuggets sitting upon silver leaves. Each dazzling blue stone was as big as a thumbnail. From another pile she pulled cloisonné earrings. These were onyx balls decorated in opal flowers. The hearts of the opal flowers were made of star-shaped sapphires.

Reverently, Carol put the gems back and then set her long fingers to each side of her face. She opened her mouth and tried to breathe deeply to calm herself. Her heart was beating hard. She took her fingers from her flushed face and held out her arms as if to embrace the whole sparkling table.

Slowly her arms hugged herself and she rocked back and forth, a big smile upon her face. She looked again at the cloisonné earrings. She smiled, dipped her chin and batted her eyes at them as if they were a boy. In another second, she had them on. They were cold and heavy, incredibly heavy, so heavy that they stretched her earlobes. She glanced around the room, surveyed the other gleaming tables, suddenly angry. Here she was—bejeweled at last and there was not one mirror, not one.

Fuming, Carol stood with hands on her hips. She was a strange sight and lucky not to have found a mirror. Her blond hair was unruly and mottled by several dust balls and cobwebs. She was wearing her black ballet slippers tied with pink ribbons, black sweatpants, a black sweatshirt, and hanging from her now elongated, elfin ears were the pair of dazzling earrings.

Cupping her hands over her earrings just to feel their cool tickle, she moved to the next table. Here were rings. Every kind of ring imaginable. Wedding rings and signet rings, pinky rings and rings that were just big, fat, diamond-stuck-in-gold rings. Victorian engagement bands whose centers were diamonds or opals or rubies and these same centers surrounded by circles of white seed pearls; decatur rings made of gold and black enamel; a ring whose stone was a ten-carat blue diamond held by four horns of silver; a pinky ring composed of eight aquamarines each the size and shape of a grain of rice.

The table below the one holding the rings was shimmering in bunches of silverware, gold plates, platinum goblets and tiny stacks of gold toothpicks and puddles of silver salt wells. There were two smaller tables at the end of the room but Carol simply couldn't look at any more, and wrapping her arms about herself, smiling the biggest and longest smile she had ever smiled, she suddenly began to cry—great big smiling sobs in a room of silver and gold.

"What are you doing?"

Carol jumped.

Blackie was coming down the ladder. "This is my place. Mine. What are you doing here?" His eyes were boiling blue.

"I told you I'd find it."

"How?"

"Can I have these earrings?"

"You're really pissing me off, Carol. You really are." Blackie jammed his brown hands into his pants pockets.

The ladder wobbled and two feet appeared on the top rung.

"Who's that?" Carol asked.

"Starkey. He was with me. I had to bring him. I hope you're happy."

When Starkey got down the ladder, he stood and gaped.

"It took me about three years," Blackie said. "I worked real hard at it. I've been bitten by dogs, attacked by a raccoon. You wouldn't believe all I've been through to collect these things."

Starkey did not look at his brother or Carol. He stared at the jewels, finally walking over to the tables, picking up a piece here and a piece there. Satisfied that they were real, he walked back to the ladder, still did not look at Blackie and climbed two rungs before he finally said, "I think you and I need to have a talk."

The next evening Hannah was having problems. "No, you can't go," she said, arms pinned to her bony hips, white hat with the yellow daisy border down over her eyebrows. "You can't go. I ain't going to talk about it no more. I ain't fixing no costume and that's that."

And Hannah meant exactly what she said, all the way to the fourth step down the staircase. Then she heard Cat crying. Now Hannah was used to crying. She had raised four rambunctious boys and had listened to their squalls and wailing for thirty years, but Cat's sound was not like the boys'. It was soft and small and horribly tender. She stuck out her ledge of blue lip, went down two more steps and then heard it again: it was a mournful, cooing sound followed by silence and then the cooing sound again and then she realized where she had heard it—it was the sound of a mourning dove, soft and gentle and painfully sweet.

She nudged the white cap onto her forehead with a big black thumb. "You ain't worth spit, woman," she said to herself. "Not spit."

When Hannah found out who Cat wanted to be, she huffed and puffed and then trudged to the big house, slipped into Blackie's room and then Starkey's and finally Ford's.

Half an hour later, the old black woman pushed the young blond woman before a full-length mirror. Cat wore black boots, a pair of brown canvas pants, a brown leather motorcycle jacket, white scarf, goggles and even a leather aviator's cap.

"You could pass for Miss Amelia Earheart herself," Hannah said.

Cat whirled around and tried to give her a big kiss, but the old woman turned her face away, screwed up her eyes and batted at the girl like she was a fly.

"You just be home at ten o'clock. You understand me? You be home here at ten o'clock sharp and not one second later. And when you see

Miss Boykin Longstreet, you just sashay yourself to some other place. If she find out you over to the party, be both of us skinned alive."

Hannah reached and pulled up the goggles and looked fiercely into the green eyes. "And one more thing. You ain't going in through the front door neither. I'm going to take you straight to the west side door and that's where you getting in at."

Hannah directed Cat McGregor to one of the side doors on the west end of the house. The old woman hobbled up the steps, opened the door and pushed the girl inside.

"Go three doors and turn left. That's the main hall."

Cat nodded.

"You all right, girl?"

A smile from behind the goggles.

"Get yourself home at ten o'clock," Hannah whispered, and then closed the door.

Cat stood in the dark room, reached out, felt a light switch and turned it on.

She was surrounded by baskets of potatoes. There were stacks of them: brown and red and black potatoes. Well, she *could* get to the party this way, but wouldn't it be more exciting to go to the front of the house and walk through the front door?

It was the most beautiful sight Cat had ever seen—twelve tall columns, each one lit by a spotlight. In the middle of the columns, a white marble stairway descended to the gravel drive, and on either side of the stairway stood two tall, broad magnolias.

In the warm night, in a maze of boxwoods, she stood and let her eyes and her heart, let everything that was empty, fill.

Cars were slushing up the gravel driveway and stopping before the staircase. Vic and Nathaniel were wearing black ties and tails and greeting the guests. Some were Indians and some were cowboys. There were ballerinas and gangsters, a spaceman carrying a small silver box, Mickey Mouse, Pluto, Perry Mason and Della Street, and even the lanky form of Abraham Lincoln, complete with black cape and stovepipe hat.

At a lull in the traffic, Cat took a breath, left the boxwoods and crunched up the driveway. Her heart was fluttering and she could hear everything: the August locusts burring in the trees, a barn owl hooting, the hiss and rattle of sprinklers in the yard and wind clattering the big magnolia leaves.

When Cat got close enough for Vic and Nathaniel to see her, she pulled the goggles over her eyes. She walked straight toward them and stopped and put her hands behind her back. Her bottom lip was trembling so much she had to bite it.

Vic Cash looked at the aviator and then looked down the driveway behind her and then smiled. "Good evening, sir. Welcome to Waverly."

"For your convenience," said Nathaniel, "there's a bar on the veranda and one in the ballroom."

The two black men gave a small bow and then, at the same time, extended a white gloved hand toward the marble staircase.

Cat looked at the tall steps and the tall columns and started to climb.

Blackie was standing on the veranda. His hair was slicked back and parted in the middle, the scalp a ruddy pink. He wore a white dinner jacket and red bow tie and pearl studs: he was John Dillinger, and rather like the outlaw, tonight his own temper was getting hot.

He looked at his watch—eight-thirty. He was still angry with Carol and on top of everything else she was late. She was supposed to arrive early with a date for Wick—Becky Thompson, Wick's old girl—the Soybean Queen. He wanted the couple to have time to get acquainted before they had to mill around. Now that was impossible.

He walked to the edge of the stairs and watched a pilot slowly, almost painfully, take one step at a time. At the veranda, the pilot stopped and adjusted goggles at him.

Blackie winked. "Nice outfit. How long it take you to put it together?"

Cat couldn't breathe. He had the most beautiful black hair. She had never seen hair this long on a boy. His eyes were blue and his neck so thick that it looked like it was going to pop off the red bow tie.

Behind the pilot, Carol and Becky dashed up the steps.

Carol was dressed as a dance hall girl. She wore gold high heel shoes, a gauzy skirt and a low-cut blouse.

Becky was a bit more brash.

Blackie crossed his right arm over his chest and, using the middle finger of his left hand, rubbed beneath the corner of his eye. "Gee, who are you supposed to be, Becky?"

She had dyed her face, hands and arms a light green. Her hair was a cheap red, parted in the middle, each stringy wing of it tied around what looked like an actual bone. She wore a one-piece bathing suit with a single strap. It was painted to resemble a leopard skin.

"You can't guess?" Becky asked, sounding hurt.

"No, I really can't."

"Sheena, Queen of the Jungle."

"Great. That's just great. My brother's been in a monastery for six years, eating boiled wheat and rice, and his first date is with Sheena, Queen of the Jungle."

Becky crinkled her green nose. "Well, I just think he needs to get a little funky."

"Weren't you a debutante?"

"I was lots of things, man, until I got the beat."

"Becky just got back from the West Coast," Carol said.

"Oh, wonderful."

Still staring at the beautiful boy, Cat felt a light touch on her arm. "Ma'am, can I help you?"

It was Jebodiah, though Cat did not know his name. He looked beautiful in the black suit and long tails, the white vest and shirt and white bow tie. Even the pink arrowhead scar on the left of his chin looked dashing. Like he's been in the Zulu Wars, Cat thought. An African king.

She shook her head no, and quickly walked through the two wooden doors and stood in the biggest hall she had ever seen. The double staircase swept down like a river of wood and carpet. The floor was white and made out of squares. She stooped down and felt it: it was marble. She couldn't believe it. A floor made out of marble. She had always thought marble was only for statues. She just knelt there for a second, making small circles with the tips of her fingers. The white marble felt cool and smooth.

When she saw two Indians staring at her, she got up and clicked across the floor into a room on her left.

Hanging from the ceiling in the middle of the room, scattering blues and yellows and reds, the gas chandelier mesmerized her. It was narrow at the top and flared out at the bottom, having glass rectangles and triangles, spheres and squares and round dishes from which a hundred blue flames danced.

This is the meaning of the word *chandelier*, Cat thought. This is the word *chandelier* made flesh.

When Becky Thompson pounded on her chest and emitted a shrill scream, Wick moved backward into a corner of the ballroom. He was wearing his white collar and black clericals.

"Wow, are you really a priest?" Becky asked, following him, the green dye beginning to run down her forehead.

"Yes."

"I met some really hip priests in San Francisco. They smoke a lot of pot."

"Pot?"

"Marijuana," Blackie said.

"Oh, a drug, yeah," Wick said, having backed away as far as he could.

"A drug—a drug," Becky said, shaking her head, inserting green fingers into her red hair and scratching beneath the two turkey thigh bones. "I really dig the way you talk, you know. I mean—I dig your style, man. You've changed a lot since high school."

Becky drew a finger down Wick's jaw and Blackie finally interceded, moving her away and putting himself beside his brother.

"Who is that?" Wick whispered.

"The Soybean Queen."

"That's not Becky."

" 'Fraid so."

"What happened?"

"Drugs, man," Blackie cracked, and then turned to Becky. "Would you like some roast pig meat?"

A girl with short auburn hair wiggled a finger at Wick. He followed her out of the corner, through the crowded foyer and out onto the veranda.

"You looked like you needed a little break," the girl said. She extended a hand. "I'm Alice Grooms."

Wick gripped her small hand and then remembered the brown eyes and upturned nose. She had been a cheerleader at the university and he had dreamed about her for six months, daring to talk to her once and only long enough to find out that she was dating the captain of the tennis team.

"Oh, of course, I'm sorry, I . . ."

"Who is that girl anyway?"

"The Soybean Queen. Or at least, she was the Soybean Queen when I, uh—you know when I used to . . ."

"Date her?"

Wick turned scarlet. The black suit and Roman collar accentuated the blush.

"She must have been some girl," Alice said.

He laughed.

"Well, to coin a phrase—are you really a priest?"

He leaned against a pillar and stared out into the black yard. "I don't know what I am really. I spent some years in a monastery. At one time I wanted to be a monk. I wanted to be the best monk that ever lived."

"Better than Saint Augustine?"

Wick liked her saucy quality. A lot of people deferred to Longstreets because of their name. He liked the way she came at him. "I'll admit a couple of fellas did pretty good in the past."

"You could take them, though."

"Well, I'll tell you this, if I ever go back—and I may next year—but if I ever go back I'll be the best American Trappist who ever took the vow."

Alice dropped her head back and smiled. "Yes, I think you would."

Alice Grooms was from a wealthy Georgia family which had moved to New York. She was twenty-seven years old and for the last several years had been working as a press agent for her father's shipping line. Because she had been born with everything—everything but a conscience—she was a risk taker. She liked mountain climbing, skin diving, flying small planes and having affairs with men who belonged to someone else. Her last two lovers had been married, and when a friend of hers asked why she always dated married men, she said, "I don't know, just like to take a piss in other people's yards, I guess." She was bold and brazen and had a curious penchant for occasionally falling in love. The last time had been two years ago. He was married. It had started as a fling and then she had fallen for him and gotten burned and decided for the umpteenth time not to fall in love again.

"So what happened to the tennis captain with the year-round tan?" Wick asked.

"I married him."

Wick's face dropped.

"You know how he kept that tan?"

"No."

"Sunshine in a bottle. You know, a tanning liquid? He rubbed it on every night. During the day when he was playing tennis he had on a triple coat of sun blocker. He was terrified of wrinkles."

"A tennis player?"

"He left me for a ball boy."

Still wearing her flight goggles and aviator cap even though the room temperature must have been eighty-five degrees, Cat stood gawking at a long table of food. In the middle of the table, on a pedestal of watercress and surrounded by a steaming moat of ketchup-based barbecue sauce, sat an entire barbecued pig. Its skin was the color of a baked apple. Below the pig lay a semicircle of baked quail, each bird separated from the others by yellow slices of pineapple and strawberries. On a level below the roasted quail were a brown roast beef and a pink ham glazed in mustard sauce and three crisp legs of lamb. Behind the table stood ten servants ready to help.

On either side of the main dishes lay large silver tureens. Cat looked in each one. Some things she could identify and some she could not. There was a white oyster stew, a deep red gumbo with okra and bay leaf, yellow cream corn, buttery grits, a silver cauldron of fried chicken, fried catfish and hush puppies and liver pudding and stacks of sparkling pork chops whose tender centers were slightly pooched out just begging to be taken.

And Cat did. Without noticing that she was going to the head of a line, she grabbed a plate, bowl, spoon, and got two pork chops, two pieces of fried chicken, a slice of ham, roast beef, lamb, and into her large bowl gestured for the servants to ladle a spoonful of oyster stew, cream corn, red gumbo, liver pudding and, crowning the concoction (to the utter astonishment of one black waiter), two green olives and a crisp barbecued pork skin into the fatty curl of which she insisted that a pink boiled shrimp be placed.

For some reason the word *sybarite* floated into her mind.

12

ACROSS THE ROOM, BESIDE the
fireplace, Ford stirred his gin and tonic with the tip of his little finger.
The birthmark on his right cheek was flushed red. His black hair was
shiny and slick, his eyes an innocent and beguiling blue. He was
dressed as John C. Calhoun: black frock coat, ruffled shirt and boots.
The outfit made him look bigger and fatter than ever. This morning he
had weighed two sixty-two.

Boykin walked toward him. She was wearing a Girl Scout uniform.
She seemed nervous.

"Selling cookies?" Ford smiled.

"You haven't seen anyone—out of place, have you?"

"Out of place?"

"Well, you know, someone who doesn't belong here," Boykin said.
She had discovered that Cat was missing.

At that moment, Starkey stepped into the ballroom wearing the elegant gray uniform of a Confederate officer. (It was a costume he had

worn in a college play.) The crowd under the incandescent chandelier whispered.

"You know, everyone just loves him to death. He has a kind of charisma," Ford said.

"Yes, yes—charisma. It's a wonderful gift. Just wonderful," Boykin said, carefully scanning the ballroom.

Congressman Pinky Smith was one of the first to walk over and shake Starkey's hand. He wore a pink suit and pink tie and pink kid shoes and told his friends that he was coming as Pinky Lee. He was enormously fat. He had white hair and huge red jowls which cascaded over his shirt collar, almost obscuring his bow tie.

"Well, well, well, Starkey. I'm so glad you could come home for this here party," Pinky said. He detested the Longstreet family. He had detested them for years. They had been born into silver and gold. He hated their good looks, their good clothes, their good manners, he hated the very smell of them, which even now he thought he could detect: it was bay rum and talc and it made him suddenly understand the old expression *putting on airs.*

Blackie saw Pinky and made a bee line for him. Ford walked over just to make sure that his younger brother didn't cause a scene.

"Hey, Pinky," Blackie said.

"Hey there, boy. Why, ain't you spiffy tonight. I just told Starkey here, we were so glad he could come home from the war to honor his— well, to honor Miss Harper. How did you manage to do that, Starkey?"

"I had a little help," Starkey said.

"Pinky, I hear nobody's even declared against you this year," Blackie said.

"Well, you know there ain't no use for them to."

"You never know. You might be surprised one day," Ford said.

Pinky turned and smiled. "Well, lordie, lordie, lordie—the clan's collecting."

"It could be a big surprise," Blackie said. "Somebody you'd never expect."

"Like who?"

"Like one of us," Blackie said.

"Aw, now, you Longstreet boys don't want to mess around with Congress. Y'all was made for big things. Governor and senator, things like that."

"You got to start somewhere," Blackie said.

Pinky Smith's huge face of flesh became smooth and soft and viciously sweet. "Well, it'd be the bluebloods against the common folk. It'd make a good race, fellas—a damn good one. And you know something?" He leaned forward and laid his two huge arms across the shoulders of Ford and Starkey. "It's a race I've looked forward to a long time —a long, long time."

Pinky Smith squeezed their necks and then waddled off into the crowd.

"One of us ought to declare against that sonofabitch tomorrow," Blackie said.

"I think I could do it," Ford said. "I think I could beat him."

Starkey looked at him. "I think you could, too. The question is—do you want to?"

"I do. I think I really do."

"You've only got two months," Blackie said.

"It makes it a challenge," said Starkey. "Ford, you should announce next week."

"And I'll be your campaign manager, man," Blackie said.

"Do you think we could really win?" Ford asked.

"We were born to win," said Blackie. "We were born to race and run and win everything—everything in the whole damn world."

Ford looked at his two brothers. "Gentlemen, start your engines."

The kitchen of Waverly was white. The floor and walls were composed of hexagonal white tiles. The center of each tile was inlaid with a pink rose bud and two green leaves. Five windows looked into the backyard. Beneath the windows sat three stainless steel sinks. In the center of the room, beneath a hanging rack which held scores of copper pots, pans, broilers and steamers, lay a twenty-foot-long oak table, the top of which had been covered in a sheet of blazing brass.

Dressed in their long white aprons and black shoes, sweat gleaming on their black faces, four women toiled: Tee Tat split open fresh oysters, Hannah doctored bayou bisque with chicory, Ernestine peeled orange sweet potatoes and Tadpole chopped garlic for deviled crab.

Harper Longstreet's birthday cake sat on the table. It was Waverly, a perfect replica of the house with ten cinnamon chimneys, a roof made of sliced green melon, twelve sugar columns, a yellow veranda of glazed egg cream, the front doors made of fresh pecans with handles of crystal rock candy and, lying before the house, a driveway composed of white raisins dusted in powdered sugar. It was the creation of Nathaniel Cash, who was the "sweets" cook as well as Harper's driver.

Starkey and Ford entered the kitchen. "Tee Tat, where's the cake?" Starkey asked.

"If it was a snake . . ." Tee Tat said.

"Oh, I see it. Good lord, this thing is beautiful. Who did it?"

"Nathaniel," Ford said. "I told him he should open his own shop."

Starkey took one side of the platter and Ford the other.

Wick and Blackie came in. "I think Harper's coming down," Blackie said.

Starkey looked at him coolly. Blackie had disappeared during the day and Starkey had not been able to talk to him.

From the foyer, there was light applause and the beginning of "Happy Birthday."

Harper Longstreet stood on the landing of the double staircase. She wore a black brocade dinner dress with a crepe blouse, red velvet satin sash and black high heel patent leathers.

When she began walking down the right-hand sweep of stairs, her sons pushed the cart into the foyer. Several choruses of "Happy Birthday" were sung until Harper reached the cake and blew out the candles. There was big applause this time, punctuated by a few "bravos" and rebel yells.

When the costumed crowd settled down, Harper addressed them in a ragged though commanding voice, a voice of style and grace, a voice which by its very timbre, regardless of the words, compelled you to listen.

"Well, I suppose you all want to know what I wished."

Cheers and applause.

"As you may know, I never make one wish. I regard one wish as a failure of imagination. I have made four wishes, one for each of my sons. I suppose it would be asking a bit much of the goodwill of this country to have the President, Vice President, Speaker and Majority Leader all named Longstreet—though it has crossed my mind."

The crowd guffawed and hooted.

She raised a hand at them and then turned, accepted a silver knife from Blackie and made a cut into the cake. Bub and Hannah appeared. Tadpole teetered from the kitchen carrying a stack of dessert saucers.

Harper dissolved into the crowd, shaking hands and smiling, remembering everyone by name and not only the people she was greeting but their husbands and wives and children. Her jewelry was spectacular. Her earrings were designed in the shape of the quarter moon. The border of each moon was green emerald and the interior filled with red rubies and blue diamonds. On her neck lay a necklace which consisted of two strands of white opals. Just as Harper was shaking the hands of three state senators who were dressed as the Three Stooges, Mary Andrews touched her on the elbow and drew her aside.

Mary was a tall woman with narrow shoulders and blond hair. She fancied herself the most knowledgeable person about jewelry in the state. She also was determined to ferret out acquisitions of new jewels by her friends, so that she could immediately add to her own formidable collection. Tonight Mary had elected to wear gold. Her neck and the top of her bosom shone with a six-inch-wide filigree of gold scallops which had been fashioned to resemble an Egyptian necklace. She had seen Harper's opals from thirty yards away and she was furious. She knew that everyone had to be hypnotized by them. She decided the only thing to do was to confront Harper and thus indicate that she was not ashamed of her own rather plain selection.

Perhaps Mary Andrews thought her jewelry was plain, but Blackie Longstreet did not. He had never seen a gold necklace so ornate. As Mary was drawn toward Harper, so Blackie was drawn toward Mary.

"I must know where you got it," Mary said, looking at the necklace.

"I think it was made in Santiago," said Harper, well aware of the reasons for Mary's interest.

"It's gorgeous, perfectly gorgeous."

"But not as gorgeous as yours," Blackie said.

Mary was taken aback by the young man's boldness. "Well, Blackie, I . . ."

"Oh, he's had a fascination with baubles for years. I have guests waiting, so I'll leave you two to discuss Fabergé."

Blackie's blue eyes were bright with the gold.

"Blackie, you must tell me about those new opals."

"I'd be happy too. By the way, are you still living in Savannah?"

"Still in Savannah? Oh Blackie, you knew that. One thirty-two East Bay. The big yellow house. You must come see me."

"I may pop up when you least expect it."

As Harper moved through the house, she recorded bits of conversation, smatterings of gossip. The women talked primarily of the fall fashions: they were shocked about the new see-through blouse that was appearing in New York, pleased with the advent of mid-calf boots, particularly the ones with zippers, and even more pleased that hats were finally and definitely out. The men talked of politics: it's about time we got tough with these North Vietnamese Commies and they were fools to attack us with torpedo boats and if they want a war we'll give them a war and I heard or read someplace that their leader or chairman or whatever you call him was once a short-order cook in New York City, can you believe that?

Cat had discovered the library, though she did not know it. Having eaten more food than she had probably eaten in her entire life, she left the ballroom in an attempt to see as much of the house as she could. She had been counting and so far had been through ten rooms. Never had she imagined that one house could have so many lamps, rugs, tables, pictures, chairs, even doorknobs. And what wonderful door-knobs they were: some octagonal and made from brass, some pure crystal, having turned the faintest violet from years of sunlight. There were white porcelain doorknobs and intricately carved wooden door-knobs and doorknobs made of sleek silver and polished copper and even smooth, worn, pink marble doorknobs.

And now she was turning one more. This one was hexagonal and made from black marble. The door was oak and eight feet high. She pushed open the door and stepped into the dark room. She raised her goggles. She found the light switch, and when a room full of lamps cut on, she saw them—books—three complete walls of them, walls that were twenty feet high and thirty yards long and the walls packed, stacked, teeming with books. There were red books and black books, brown books and gray books, yellow and green and gold. Some were tall and some short, some fat and some thin, some with smooth backs and others with knobs.

To Cat McGregor it was an entire world of books and she was stunned, thinking of all the characters that she had never met, all the descriptions that she had never read, all the words that she had never encountered. And somehow her confidence, that magical part of herself which had propelled her through so many dark times, her confidence began to quake. Before the books, before row on row of them she suddenly felt so small, so terribly, awfully small, as if she were no more than some insignificant piece of punctuation.

I'm just a comma, she thought. Just a crummy ole comma.

She reached out to the wall nearest her and ran her fingers across twenty dusty spines. They were leather. She had never felt a real leather book before.

On the other side of the room, a phone rang, and reacting, Cat grabbed the nearest book and sprang from the library into the hall, stumbling through a half-open door and colliding with Harper Long-street, who, black eyes flashing in discernment, leaned toward the young woman and said, "Who are you?"

Cat clutched the leather book to her stomach.

Boykin stepped from the crowd of people. "She's a friend of mine."

"Oh?" Harper said, setting her hands upon the shimmering hips of her black evening gown.

"Her name's Catherine McGregor and she's my—guest."

"Well, I'm so glad you invited her."

Harper addressed the crowd. "Now I must cut up the rest of that cake. Everyone must have a piece."

Just as Harper was leaving the room, she turned and looked at Boykin. Her chin rose into the air. She touched her black hair, her right index finger caressing an emerald and diamond earring.

"A guest?" Harper asked.

Boykin took Cat back to the blue house. She said little to the girl. She did not rant or rave or threaten. Her tone of voice was even and her sentences long and soft. Once Boykin had tucked Cat into bed, she picked up the book that the girl had taken from the library.

"Bartleby the Scrivener," Boykin said. She looked at the big green eyes and the wheaten hair that she had pulled into two pigtails. "Do you like Herman Melville?"

Cat shrugged.

"Tomorrow you and I will have to see Harper. It's earlier than I wanted, but it has to be done. I don't know how things will end. I wish I could say I did, but I don't."

Boykin kissed Cat on the cheek. She pulled the yellow cotton sheet to the girl's neck and then turned off the bedside lamp. She sat on Cat's bed smoothing the girl's hair and then she stopped and she did not move at all and then she said, "If you go to a party again, I'd like to know about it in advance."

Cat felt ghastly, just ghastly. How could she have done that to Boykin? It was selfish, completely selfish, and now she had to face Harper. Cat sat up in bed and snapped on the lamp. Well, that meeting was going to take place anyway. The day had to come, there was no running from it. Besides, I'm not afraid of Harper Longstreet. I'm not afraid at all. I know words and all my words will come to my defense. She picked up her notebook from the bedside table and wrote: adamant, trenchant, vociferous and harridan.

Just looking at the words made her feel better. She wrote four more: optimistic, ebullient, sanguinary and Pollyanna. After all, what was the worst that Harper Longstreet could do? What was the most awful, the meanest thing that she could do? The McGregor hovel jumped into Cat's mind. The ceilings plastered with newspaper and the broken windowpanes and the greasy soot that permeated everything and everyone. Surely that couldn't happen, could it? Surely Boykin would not have brought her here if that were a possibility?

Cat picked up *Bartleby the Scrivener* and started to read. She used the words to build a wall. The more she read, the thicker and taller the wall became until she was safely behind it. She read until the present world with its present difficulties left her. She was captivated by Bartleby and by his refusal. His refusal to work, his refusal to kowtow, his refusal to leave the place that he had come to love.

At two o'clock in the morning she finally went to sleep, *Bartleby the Scrivener* upon her breast, and somewhere in her mind she still heard the clerk's refusal to be vanquished. A refusal composed of five words which to Cat seemed so sharp and clear and—adamantine: I would prefer not to.

13

BY TWO-THIRTY, THE last guest had left and Starkey collared Blackie and led him into the trophy room. Surrounded by Cape buffalo and the golden heads of dusty lions and cheetahs, they sat down on either side of a leather couch. Starkey was still astounded by what he had seen in the attic and he was not quite sure what to do about it. He started out quietly.

"Where in the world did you get all that stuff?" He was wearing his gray Confederate pants, though he had taken off his tunic and sat in a long-sleeved white shirt.

Blackie unfastened his tie and shed the tuxedo jacket. "Mostly they were friends of Harper."

"Are you kidding?"

"Nope."

"How long have you been doing it?"

"I told you, three years."

Blackie recounted the first break-in, which was innocent enough. He and a friend were hunting. A storm had risen. They came across what they thought was an abandoned cabin in the middle of the Congaree swamp. Upon entering, however, they found that the seemingly dilapidated cabin was in fact a trysting place for someone, having polished cypress floors, antique furniture, china and delicate crystal. Blackie had returned to the cabin time after time, on each occasion discovering something else in the house: a drawer full of silver, a secretary whose hideaway drawer contained ancient coins.

"I've never felt more alive than when I was in that house. Sneaking around, discovering beautiful things, knowing that I shouldn't be there. Look, I'm just not like you and Ford and Wick. You want to be the best at something—well, that's fine, that's good, but I like being bad. I like lying and cheating and stealing and fooling around with lots of girls. It's great, man. It's the best thing going."

After his first encounters with the cabin in the swamp, Blackie said it was easy and even more fun to break into occupied houses.

Starkey sat and looked at his brother. "What are you going to do?"

"What do you mean?"

"You're a criminal, Blackie."

"I'm not a fucking criminal."

"Yes, you are."

"All right, fine. I'm a criminal. So call the fuzz, lock me up."

"You've got to get rid of that stuff in the attic."

"What if I don't want to get rid of it?"

"I wanna tell you something, buddy. You're in a lot of trouble here. A lot of goddamned trouble and you better damn well cool it."

Blackie sighed and shut his eyes.

"Now you got to get that stuff out of the house. That's the first thing." Starkey stood up. "I don't know what to do after that. Maybe go see Harper."

"Oh, great."

"You need help, Blackie. Have you got any idea how much time you could do for this? Probably your whole life." Starkey pushed the back of his hands into his eyes and blew some air out of his mouth. "I don't know. We'll just have to think about it, and do me a favor—don't break into any more houses, okay?"

"Sure."

"Blackie?"

"Yeah, yeah, yeah. Okay, fine."

Blackie left the room just as all the clocks in the house struck 3 A.M.

Harper was still awake. She was standing on her balcony on the east wing of Waverly. The August night was thick and steamy. It sounded like some kind of insect symphony. The steadiest rhythm was that of the crickets, their music bright and cheerful in the deep grass, while in the trees above them the cicadas burred and rattled, and on the highest branches of the trees, just below the silver light of stars, the katydids were singing.

Below Harper the hundred-year-old boxwoods hugged the house and dewy grass stretched out to the distant forms of willow trees, and moonlight poured over the willows making them silver on the outside, though inside, between the long, loose branches they were black and silent.

Harper was pleased with the party. It had gone well. She was particularly happy that all of her sons had been able to come. Mary Andrews had told her about Blackie and Ford challenging Pinky Smith. She thought that it could have been handled more correctly, but she was proud of Ford nonetheless. It was true that she wanted him to work for the paper, but the main thing was to get him started doing something.

She felt more content tonight than she had in a long time. It finally seemed that everyone was moving forward: Starkey would head back to Vietnam with confidence, Wick would enter the Diocese, Ford was edging into politics, and somehow she even felt that things might begin to work for Blackie, that he might be caught up in the current of his brothers' ambition and soon find his own career.

Boykin stood outside her sister's door. She was nervous. All her plans of a slow and careful introduction had been destroyed and Cat's presence at Waverly had come as a rude slap, rather than a sensitive revelation. Boykin knew that she had to be very careful now because Harper might be angry and it was her habit to shoot from the hip when she was provoked. In most of her dealings with Harper, Boykin was more or less of a straightforward person, but now and again, she had to dissemble. Tonight was one of those times. She wasn't quite sure which air she should affect when she entered the room: should I be dizzy and cheerful or cowed and repentant? And for a moment her temper flared. Why do I have to be either? Why can't I just be concerned and worried about Cat? Why do I always have to cater to Harper?

These thoughts made Boykin smile. Now's not the time to reform. Accept what is. There will be other days. Accept what is. Boykin tapped on the door.

"Yes?"

"It's me."

"And who is me?"

Harper always made you identify yourself when it was late at night and she did not want to be disturbed. "It's Boykin, Harper, why my goodness I'd think you'd know my voice by now," she said, entering the room.

Boykin was able to tell a lot by the way Harper held her chin and the position of her eyebrows. If chin and eyebrows were held high, the conversation was going to be difficult. If the chin was low, she had a chance.

Harper was wearing black pajamas and silver slippers and her chin was low.

"I just couldn't sleep a bit and decided I'd come and see if you were awake," Boykin said, in a dizzy and cheerful voice.

It was a voice which Harper knew well. It meant: I'm sorry that I made a mistake and you know silly ole me and how I just get everything all balled up. The voice of helplessness was one of Boykin's most skillful tools.

"Well, I haven't been able to sleep either," Harper said.

"It's this heat," Boykin said, sitting down in an armchair. "It's this awful ole heat. Why sometimes I feel like I can't even catch my breath."

"Maybe I should put in air-conditioning."

"Oh, that's a sweet thought, but that would cost a fortune and I think I'll be fine. September's right around the corner and you know how my spirits pick up in the fall."

Harper raised an eyebrow. "Now Boykin, all this beating around the bush is not doing anybody any good."

Boykin's red hair was curly and shining. She sat very erect, folded her small, red hands in her lap, tilted her head and batted her eyes. "I guess I should just come right out and tell you about Catherine McGregor."

"About who?"

"The girl at the party who bumped into you?"

"Oh, yes. Well?"

"She's been living here for a week."

Harper's black eyebrows floated to her hairline.

Boykin cleared her voice and told Cat's whole story, including the abuse by her father and the fact that she could not speak.

". . . so I brought her to Waverly and started taking care of her, or rather all of us started taking care . . . I mean Bub and Hannah and Wick and all of us and . . ."

"Just calm down now. Take it easy," Harper said. She sat down on the couch and squeezed her sister's hand. She hated to see her get flustered because after the fluster came tears and Harper couldn't bear tears tonight. "You should have told me."

"But I was planning to," Boykin said, and all of her guile and affectation disappeared. "I had everything all planned out and she was going to stay awhile and I was going to rub off the rough edges and then present her, but I didn't get a chance to," Boykin said, and the tears streaked mascara down her face.

Harper raised her eyes toward the ceiling and hugged her sister. "It's okay. I understand. It's all right, honey."

"Will you let her stay?"

"Oh, Boykin."

"She's so helpless."

Harper laughed. "You know what this reminds me of? It reminds me of that time when we were walking home from high school and you found that baby gray squirrel in the ivy. My Lord, you would have thought it was made out of gold the way you were cooing and fussing over it. 'Please let me keep it, Harper. Won't you please let me keep the little baby.' "

"And you did let me keep it."

"Yes, I did and you fed it pecans and almonds and cake till the thing weighed almost eight pounds."

"He did get pretty big."

"Pretty big? The damned thing looked like a dog. You spoil things, Boykin. You spoil everyone in this house—including me. You need to learn to be tougher."

"Maybe she could just stay for a little while."

"We've got four boys already."

"Will you think about it? Will you just think about it?"

Harper looked out her tall windows toward the bright moon, thinking, There is no one in the whole world less capable of raising a child than you, Boykin. No one at all. She will turn out spoiled and sweet and giddy—it's the last thing the world needs, one more giddy girl.

She led her sister to the door and told her that she would consider it carefully. "By the way, are you sure the girl can't speak?"

"Oh, I don't think she's ever said a word in her whole life. A cleft palate or something."

"Are you sure?"

"Well, no."

"In that case, I think she should be tried. I think we should talk to her and challenge her."

"Oh, Harper, I don't—"

"I'll take care of it—good night."

"Good night."

She let her out and came back to one of two small desks that sat in a corner of her room. On one of the desks sat three Greek lexicons and then several vertical piles of Greek books. Mostly the books were works of the pre-Socratic philosophers: Heraclitus, Melissus and Empedocles. On her other desk sat Latin dictionaries and Latin books. The works of Virgil and Catullus, Lucretius and Caesar. In college, Harper had studied both languages and now, even at the age of seventy, she translated and worked at them on a regular, if not fanatical, schedule.

She scheduled herself at everything. Her days were planned and rarely varied. A typical day was as follows:

6:00—rise and exercise
7:00—breakfast
7:30—translate Greek or Latin
8:00—office at home
8:30—go to paper and work
12:30—lunch
1:00—nap
2:00—practice guitar, learn one new piece a month
3:00—return to paper
6:00—two drinks, exactly one ounce each

7:00—supper
8:00—correspondence with sons
11:00—bed

Harper followed this routine carefully, and if she happened not to practice her classical guitar or did not finish a poem of Catullus, she hated herself for the rest of the day because Harper believed that once something was learned or possessed, it must never be let go, to let something slip away from you was an indication that you were losing control and Harper was terrified of that and so she worked fanatically to keep all that was hers.

She looked at the line of Greek she had translated that morning. It had been very difficult and she had grown so angry at the obscure forms of the verbs that she had thrown the book against the wall before she had worked it out:

Alas, that the pitiless day did not first destroy me before I contrived with my lips the terrible deed of eating flesh.

It was Empedocles and it made her feel full and content and healthy to read it because it meant that she had not lost it. She climbed into her bed and went to sleep.

At eight o'clock in the morning, on the second story of Waverly, Cat McGregor was trembling before the double doors which led into Harper's study.

Behind her fretted Hannah and Bub and Tadpole.

"Now just be yourself," Boykin said in her airy voice. She was wearing khaki pants, a white shirt and loafers which held new pennies. "I explained the whole situation to her late last night."

Hannah was wearing her crumpled hat and the long apron. "You just sashay yourself right in there and be yourself, chile. Don't you be 'shamed of nothing."

"Sashay," said Tadpole with her pigtails sticking straight out of her plaited scalp.

Bub just stood there in his red jacket and blue pants. His black face was long and sad. He didn't have much hope for the white girl who couldn't talk. Miss Harper's heart could be cold—Lordy, it could be cold—and he didn't give Cat much of a chance.

Cat was wearing a blue skirt and blue sailor's blouse. Her blond hair had been combed and lay down her back. Boykin had touched her cheeks with blush and clipped on her ears a pair of blue and gold earrings.

She brushed a golden hair from the girl's green eyes. "Ready?"

Cat nodded and then held out her arms and everyone—Bub, Hannah, Tadpole and Boykin—everyone hugged her in a single crush.

She stuck out her chin, squared her shoulders, opened one of the mahogany doors and stepped inside.

This room was Harper's sphere and Harper's style. Everything was elaborate. There was a French crystal chandelier whose low light glinted off walls of pale vanilla. On the floor lay a wool rug of red roses on a black background. There were four Empire armchairs and one sofa. The furniture's wooden scrolls and crowns and dentils were gilded. The right-hand wall was books, hundreds of them.

As soon as Cat saw the books, her trembling left her. These are my friends, she thought. They will not forsake me. They will not suffer me to stumble.

Behind a desk whose front panels were decorated in gilded swords and shields and spears sat Harper Longstreet. Her black hair was bunned and severe. She wore a black cotton suit, a black high-necked blouse and an emerald brooch. She finished writing a note, raised her chin and her thin black eyebrows. She put her right elbow on the desk and gently rubbed her thumb against her white index finger. Her nails were bloody red.

"I've spoken to Boykin. She told me your whole story and I have a few things to say to you because I don't think you're going to be here very long. Your life has been an appalling one and you are to be pitied, but life is unfair—and that you will find is nobody's fault but God's. If you have any backbone or sense at all you will learn to depend upon yourself and when you feel self-pity—which we all occasionally feel—you will turn the self-pity to anger. Anger is much better than sorrow. Always choose anger over any of the emotions. It is healthier than anxiety, safer than despair and infinitely more dependable than joy. Never trust yourself to joy. It is rare, evanescent, disorienting—and it always leaves you craving for more. The unhappiest people I have met in my life are those people who are continually searching for joy. Stay away from them and stay away from it."

Harper stood, walked from behind her desk, her hands folded behind her back so that the two little fingers interlocked and turned purple.

Behind Cat, her four friends were peeping through a crack between the two doors.

"As you no doubt have gathered, Boykin wants you to stay here at Waverly. I've thought about it. Maybe if you had—arrived—somewhat younger, it would have been possible. Now it would be difficult. I think you're too old." She paused. "How old are you?"

Cat's lips opened a bit.

"I said—how old are you?"

Cat looked at the wall of books on her right and she said in her heart a prayer to the God whom Harper did not trust. It was a simple prayer —Oh Lord, please help some of those words come to me. Not many, just a few.

"Well, it's no matter really. I have four sons and I assure you they keep me very busy and I'm afraid that I shall have to send you back home, unless—unless you can think of a reason why you shouldn't go back home. Can you?"

Cat's lips were trembling again and she felt tears fill her eyes.

"I wish that girl could say something," Tadpole whispered.

"Hush," said Hannah.

"Yes, well," Harper said. "If you can't think of a reason why you shouldn't be sent back . . ."

"I wou-wou-would . . ." Cat stammered.

Harper looked at her. "Yes?"

"She said something," Tadpole whispered.

"Naw," said Bub.

"I would . . ."

"Yes, she did, too," Tadpole said. "She did say something."

They pressed forward.

"Why shouldn't you be sent home?" Harper asked.

And in a soft voice, a gentle mountain accent, Cat said the words slowly and clearly: "I . . . would . . . prefer . . . not to."

With that sentence Tadpole, who had been leaning forward so desperately, lost her grip on the doorjamb, fell forward, bashing her head into the door and sprawling into the study. "My Lord, the dumb done spoke," she said.

The three others rushed into the room and hugged Cat while Harper looked on with arched eyebrows and the blackest of black eyes.

14

FOR THE NEXT FEW days, Cat was dizzy. She was moved into the big house and given an end room on the second floor. Her two windows overlooked the backyard and the two guest houses in the distance. Cat asked if she could have the lavender curtains and the white satin canopy bed which had been in the guest house and Boykin agreed. She was also going to ask if she could have the walls of her new room covered in the same kind of pink material, but she thought that it was asking too much. Her first night in her new room, she wrote a long letter to Mike and told him all about everything.

One afternoon Boykin took Cat through the guest houses and helped her pick out pieces of furniture for her room. Cat chose black cherrywood: a small vanity with an oval mirror and an oval stool braided in new cane; two chests of drawers with brass handles; a seven-foot-tall chiffarobe, the doors of which were inlaid with pearwood; a lady's chair and a gentleman's chair both carved from black cherry, the soft seats covered in pink silk.

Bub and Jebodiah rearranged the room four different times and still Cat was not satisfied, but she felt guilty about asking the colored men to do any more work.

Earlier, Cat had been introduced to the rest of the staff, and finally the Longstreet sons. Wick had been true to his word and had not mentioned the girl to his brothers and he was pleased when Harper revealed that Cat was staying with the family—temporarily.

Three of the brothers had been standing in Harper's grand study (which they called the throne room) when Harper brought Cat in.

"This is Cat McMurphy," Harper said.

"McGregor," Cat corrected in her new, gentle voice.

"Quite right—McGregor. Now she is to be our guest for a while. During this time of trial and—evaluation, all of you will treat her with kindness and help her find her way about. Cat, I think that, generally speaking, my sons are nice young men, although sometimes they tend to be a bit sly and rather brash. At any rate, starting from the left to right we have: Blackstone, Wickliff and Ransford. There is another who is not present—Starfield. He received a telegram in the middle of the night and returned to Southeast Asia. So, now, there we are. I'm sure you'll be the best of friends."

Cat didn't hear much of Harper's speech after the introduction of Blackie. She recognized him as the beautiful boy she had seen on the veranda the night of the party. On this second meeting, he wore white pleated trousers, white buck shoes and a pale blue shirt that made his blue eyes shine. When he smiled at her, she smiled back and flushed and immediately looked at the floor.

After the introduction, the boys invited her out. They told her about Ford's campaign.

"We're setting up our headquarters in the blue guest house," Wick said. "Didn't you stay there?"

"Maybe Cat could be the appointments secretary," said Ford.

"Naw, she looks like the press secretary to me," Blackie said, and winked at her.

Cat's knees felt weak.

The brothers positioned Cat in their midst and walked over to the guest house. Ford showed her where he planned to have his office and Wick talked about the importance of having a large phone bank and

Blackie propped his feet on the diningroom table and said that he would be in charge of the proper locks on doors and windows.

Over the next few weeks, the only time Cat was left alone was when she went to sleep at night. During the day one or more of the Longstreets was showing her a new room in Waverly or driving her through the lands and farms and forests surrounding the house or involving her in the first stages of Ford's late campaign to unseat Pinky Smith.

Like the rest of the family, she was awakened every morning by a soft knock on her bedroom door and Bub or Jebodiah saying, "Miss Cat the sun's up and the birds is singing." Then a silver tray would be brought in with fresh pineapple juice and the *Southern Chronicle.* On one of these mornings, Wick was right behind Bub as he sat the silver tray in Cat's lap.

"When you finish your juice, let's take a look at the farms," Wick said. He had just had his first haircut since he had left the monastery. The black hair was parted on the left side. The Longstreet ruddiness had returned to his skin and his splash of freckles had been darkened by the sun and he had gained ten pounds. He was smoking a cigarette.

"Farms? You mean there is more than one farm?"

"There is three or four farms on Waverly," Bub said.

"And we've got to get moving if we're going to see them all in one day," Wick said.

In ten minutes, Cat and Wick were driving down the road in a 1954 black Chevy truck.

On either side of them lay the forest. Close to the road were bushy cedar trees and sprawling chinaberries and a few silver-trunked wild plums and then beyond these roadside trees towered the great hardwoods of the upcountry: vast American sycamores with the gray bark of the trunks peeling to reveal whiteness and ancient English oaks with hollow knotholes any one of which could contain a gallon of rainwater and a black cloud of tadpoles or a wiggling host of mosquito larvae. There were sweetgums and live oaks, gingkos and pecans and poplars and shady sugarberry trees which the local people called ironwood because the finish of the bark was polished and gray and smooth, though termites loved these trees, and on a summer day, in the winds of a coming black storm it was not unusual to see a silver cloud of winged termites stream from the rotten trunks.

While they were riding along, Wick occasionally glanced at Cat, watched her face light with wonder at something along the roadside or deep in the dim woods. Even though he had grown up in the center of the hardwoods, he himself was fascinated by them. When he saw a beautiful tree or a lovely tract of land it was his natural inclination to say thank you, God, for this beauty. Lately, however, as soon as his heart said thank you, his mind said, Why are you always saying thank you God for this and praise to you Father for that? When you see something ghastly—a dog smashed and swollen or an old man hobbling on one leg with a swarm of yellow deer flies stinging his poor old face, what do you say to God then? You say nothing. You pretend that the beauties of the world are God's and the horrors are not. If we praise God for the beautiful things, shouldn't we be free to castigate or at least question him about the ugly? Be truthful with yourself, his mind said. Be honest with yourself and your God.

This division between Wick's heart and mind was serious and disturbing. His heart was generous and soft and childlike, but his mind was that of a skeptic: cool and manipulative. It also had the ability to be objective. It could analyze its own strengths and weaknesses as well as those of the heart—it could assess Wick Longstreet the human being. More and more his mind was saying, You need to forget the monastery and go into the structure of the Church. You should work for the Diocese. A sweet, childlike heart and a skeptical mind are a marvelous foundation for a career in the Church. What you could not accomplish through guile, you could acquire through goodness.

This thought made Wick grimace. Sometimes he wished his mind was not so perceptive.

Abruptly, the forest ended. The land was level and planted in thousands of peach trees. The average tree stood six feet high, though many of them were smaller. They were hardy trees, the bark consisting of folds and wrinkles and smooth black spots where old limbs had been pruned. In the center of the orchard sat one of several peach sheds. It had a silver tin roof and brown studs all the way around with no walls. The workers beneath the roof could look directly into the blazing light of the orchard.

"Want to go to the shed?" Wick asked.

"I'd love to," said Cat.

"Have you ever worked peaches?"

"We have mostly apples in North Carolina."

"When we were kids, Harper made us work every summer. We could have our choice. We could either work on the dairy farm or the peach farm or the tobacco land."

"What a wonderful choice."

"It was hard work."

Cat smiled to herself. Did he know what hard work was? "Well I know it must have been, but—just think what you could learn. If I had been you, I would have worked a full summer on each farm and made notes on everything so I'd never forget."

"Never forget what?"

"The experience of it. I mean what the peach shed smells like, what it feels like. Did you ever pick peaches?"

"Well, we hire migrant laborers to do the picking."

"Oh, I would love to pick a peach tree. Grab a sack and climb a ladder and work all day long in green leaves near the blue sky, and at the end of the day return to the earth—weary, aching, but holding on my shoulders a sack of rosy peaches that I had gleaned myself."

"You can pick a tree in about seven minutes."

"Oh."

Wick parked the truck in the shadow of the shed. The September sun was still furious and yellow even at eight-thirty in the morning. Under the silver roof of the shed thirty fans were whirling. The shed was fifty yards long and twenty-five yards wide. At the north end, thousands of wooden boxes were stacked to the rafters. The older boxes were a bleached gray and the new ones a light pink or yellow. Each box was stamped with the triangular roof and twelve columns of Waverly. Beyond the wooden boxes lay a concrete loading dock, brown pallets and two tractor trailer trucks.

At the south end of the shed, the field trucks emptied loads of peaches into metal bins which automatically dumped them onto conveyor belts. The belts took the fruit to long and narrow tables which lay beneath a blaze of blue lights. These were the culling tables. Eight cullers stood on either side of them. Immediately over the moving flood of yellow peaches lay long lamps which made the blue light that allowed the cullers to spot bruises and insect bites and otherwise damaged fruit. The cullers were usually older women who wore print dresses and silver or black-rimmed spectacles and sandals or high-topped tennis shoes and white socks.

After the peaches were culled, they were sprayed with water and then carefully packed in the wooden boxes and set on pallets. The tow trucks stacked them in the tractor trailers.

As Cat stood under the south end of the peach shed, the feel of the place captivated her. It was dark and noisy and hot. The huge electric motors that powered the conveyor belts roared and clacked while the conveyor belts themselves yipped and squeaked and sometimes screamed when one became stuck. The shed seemed alive to her. Things were humming and vibrating, jostling and shaking so that the very air itself had a feel—it was fuzzy, hairy. Cat stuck out her hands, wiggled her fingers. Yes, there was no doubt—the air was hairy, just like a peach, and then she began to feel, first on her bare arms and then on her face and neck—an itch, a stinging, and she started rubbing her arms and face.

Wick laughed.

"What is it?" Cat asked.

"Peach fuzz."

"It makes you itch."

"You have to get used to it."

"Can we stay awhile?"

Cat was determined to work in every area that she could. Fortunately, she had worn dungarees and a short-sleeve cotton blouse. Early on, she separated her blond hair into two braided pigtails and then pinned these in two golden loops to the back of her head. Introduced by Wick, she culled peaches beneath the blue light with the old ladies, boxed peaches with ten black men and learned how to repair busted peach crates with old John White, who had made and repaired boxes for thirty years. Eating only raw peaches for lunch, she and Wick set out into the sweltering orchard. Stubs Taylor, the head of the migrant gang, lent her a red ladder and a brown burlap bag and showed her how to twist and not pull a peach from its stem. With Wick and Stubs looking on, Cat spent the rest of the afternoon in the orchard. The sun hammered her head and the peach leaves sawed her skin. The burlap bag became so heavy at one point that it pulled her from the ladder and she sprawled onto the ground. Wick rushed to her, but she was unhurt, and started picking again.

By five o'clock in the afternoon, she had picked a hundred pounds of peaches. She was sunburned and stinging from peach fuzz, peach resin and the cuts of peach leaves. When she finally stepped back beneath the shed, the noisy darkness felt cool, though it wasn't. While Wick fetched her a mason jar of artesian spring water, she studied the shed. Never had she seen a place of work that held so much life: there were brown sparrows and black starlings in the rafters, yellowjackets and red wasps and fat, golden honeybees whizzed through the air, green chameleons climbed the brown studs and currents of black gnats sang above the peach bins. Even beside the bins in the brown dirt sat the telltale funnels of ant lions, which now and again swirled as the doodlebugs searched for prey.

Peach shed, Cat thought as she was riding home, drifting to sleep. You wonderful, hot, noisy ole peach shed. How have I ever lived without you.

When she walked onto the back porch, Hannah immediately grabbed and hauled her upstairs. The old colored woman drew a cool bath and set out a pile of white towels, the whole time fussing about too much heat and too much work and not enough sense. She scrubbed Cat's back, helped to wash her blond hair. Cat dried off and Hannah painted Merthiolate on five or six of the worst cuts and smeared cold cream on the sunburned nose, face and arms.

"Out there doing field niggers' work," Hannah huffed. She had taken off her white cap and her hair was silver and plaited like Tadpole's though there were only six or seven pigtails. Her starchy white apron was damp. Her nose was flattened, her face scowling and her bottom lip so blue and swollen that it looked as if it had been frozen.

"And you with the most tenderest white skin—don't you do nothing like that again. That's why the field nigger be the blackest nigger in the whole world 'cause he's the one doing the work, you hear me? Now supper's at seven o'clock sharp and don't you make me come up these stairs to get you neither."

Cat set her clock for six forty-five and slept for an hour.

When the alarm went off, she quickly rose, went into her pink and white tile bath and wet a cotton washcloth. She wiped her face and then put on a violet linen dress that Boykin had given her. She put a white leather belt around her waist, slipped on her new loafers and brushed out her blond hair.

As she descended the right-hand side of the double staircase, she went down slowly, taking in the beauty of the house: the glassy, teak handrail and the carpeted steps and the cool smell of the stone floor in the foyer. Once she reached the foyer, she stopped to watch the evening sunlight flash through the leaded glass fan window which sat above the front doors. A clock in the hall struck seven. She passed by the ball-room and eight doors down took a left. It was a small room the family called the baby room. It was painted white with an oval carpet and along the walls stood white pine cupboards which held bronzed baby shoes and bronzed rattlers, silver spoons and tiny gold cups and the other minutiae of those who had passed through infancy at Waverly.

Even though Ford had given her a tour of the house, Cat was lost and just about to go through a door at the end of the room when Blackie appeared. He was wearing blue jeans and a short-sleeve knit shirt which showed off the muscles in his chest and arms. His hair was freshly washed and dried. He wiggled his finger at her and she followed without saying anything, though that simple gesture of his—his coolness and lack of words—made her stomach draw, made her want to run behind him and throw her arms around his narrow waist.

The Longstreets ate supper in what they called the little dining room. It was a smaller version of the formal dining room. Behind the little dining room lay a large butler's pantry and the kitchen. The dining room table sat in the middle of the room. It was made from walnut as were the ten chairs. Along opposite walls sat two buffets, each one holding elaborate silver punch bowls, the edges of which were escalloped and the soft, gleaming bellies of the bowls sitting atop the outstretched wings of silver eagles. There were silver pitchers, trays and cups.

When Cat stepped into the room, most of the family was already there. Harper sat at the head of the table, Boykin at the foot. The brothers sat on either side. To the right of Boykin was Cat's place. The room was noisy with laughter and debate. When Cat sat down, Harper nodded, Wick offered a short prayer and the Longstreet brothers started passing bowls of food. The bowls were big and white and thick, having around their middle or the edge a band of blue or yellow or red. They held country food, which was the primary diet of the Longstreet family.

Tonight there was fried chicken with rice and gravy, green beans, fried okra, cantaloupe and blackberry cobbler for dessert. Tee Tat had prepared the meal. Her fried chicken was supposed to be the best for miles around. She prepared it the same way she had for years: a cut-up, fresh fryer was dipped into a bowl holding two egg yolks whipped into a cup of milk. After a short soak, she placed the orange chicken into a brown bag containing a blend of yellow corn meal and white plain flour and garlic salt and pepper. She shook the bag and then put the coated chicken, one piece at a time, into a black iron frying pan half full of hot oil. The chicken was browned quickly and then left to fry gently for twenty minutes. In the end, the crust was brown and crisp and the meat itself luscious with juice.

While everyone might love Tee Tat's fried chicken, probably only people brought up in the country would appreciate her vegetables. Everything was cooked with either salt pork or bacon drippings. Green beans and crowder peas, even creamed corn was boiled until soft. Country people hated crispy vegetables. Crispiness was for salads. Before butter beans or squash or any vegetable was boiled, wedges of smoked salt pork or several pieces of bacon were fried in the bottom of a black iron pot. (Black iron was essential to every country meal, the metal holding seasonings and a special taste.) After the pork or bacon was browned, the vegetable was added along with cold water. The boiling was hard and long.

Cat took a small taste of everything. She was exhausted. She ladled a spoonful of brown gravy onto fluffy rice, adding to her plate soft green beans shiny with bacon drippings and several pieces of cut-up okra (fried in yellow corn meal) and a long orange quarter of cantaloupe. Her favorite piece of chicken was the wing and she got one.

The Longstreet brothers were joking about Pinky Smith, making plans for the campaign, asking Harper about methods of attack and whether certain powerful country preachers and judges and businessmen would support them. While the brothers argued and laughed and piled their white plates with brown chicken and mounds of rice and gravy, Harper sat quietly answering questions and musing: Pinky Smith had neglected his district. He had taken his supporters for granted and spent all his time cavorting in Washington. If that weakness was exploited, his opponent had a chance to win. She looked at Ford's high cheekbones and the lavender birthmark. How much he looked like his father, she thought. And for some reason, right at that moment, while the boys were arguing about the last two pieces of chicken, she could see that Ford had luck. It was around him like a light and so strong that she sat back in her chair to observe the light of luck which seemed to radiate from his ruddy face. He'll win, she thought. If he persists, he will win.

After supper the brothers took their blackberry cobbler out onto the veranda. They sat in green cane rockers and ate the bittersweet cobbler and planned out Ford's announcement speech, which was to be made at the courthouse at ten o'clock the next morning.

Even though it was early, Cat went to bed. She climbed beneath her white canopy and slipped under a sheet. In the backyard, she could hear Boykin giving last instructions to Hannah and Tee Tat, Bub and Jebodiah. There were farewells and then she heard the wagons jingling in the soft summer night. The colored people still used them. The wheels crunched across the gravel as the wagons pulled toward the front of the house. Someone began playing a harmonica and the wagons were jingling in the dark until they finally dissolved into the melody of the harmonica and then this, too, faded away into the soft sound of crickets and tree frogs and the whisper of wind through the green trees of the night.

15

AT TEN O'CLOCK IN the morning, Ford stood before the red brick courthouse and gave his announcement speech.

Harper had orchestrated the entire event. There were two brass bands, banners and balloons. She had dismissed the one hundred and fifty employees of the *Southern Chronicle* for the morning and bussed them to the courthouse, making sure that each of them had a Longstreet for Congress hat. She and Ford had hurriedly put together his platform, which paralleled Pinky Smith's, calling for increased defense spending, an end to imported textiles and more money to be raised for state highways. In Ford's announcement speech, he attacked Pinky on only one issue—his attendance record. Pinky had the worst attendance in the entire Congress, missing nearly seventy percent of the votes. This lack of diligence became the thrust of Ford's entire campaign and was summed up in his slogan—Longstreet for Congress: He will be there.

During the next few weeks, the whole family came together. Blackie took charge of the technical side of things; he had eight phone lines installed in the blue guest house, had maps hung on the walls which pinpointed concentrations of voters, such as mills, factories, schools, churches and hospitals. He printed up handbills, posters and two hundred thousand small cards which read—Longstreet: He will be there. Wick worked up the issues and ideas as well as contacting the major power holders in the district, like Reverend Leroy Orange, pastor of the largest black church in the upstate and Judge Bill "Hang the Bastards" Epps, who had run the toughest court in South Carolina for thirty years. Harper would make the initial phone calls to the power brokers and then Wick would go to see them, completely disarming everyone with his easygoing style and humor and his unfailing interest in everyone's problems and needs and aspirations. Boykin put together ten coffee and tea receptions a week, as well as organizing almost two hundred high school students who handed out literature door to door.

Harper probed Pinky Smith's rural underworld of crooked sheriffs and payoff men and redneck thugs. One of the most powerful allies of Smith was the Ku Klux Klan and Harper herself took the job of undercutting their power. The head of the Klan in the upstate was named Jacob Gibbs, and Harper was one of two or three who knew a secret about Gibbs which, if discovered, would dethrone the grand dragon and might even cause him to be murdered: Jacob Gibbs was a Jew. Around nine o'clock on a hot night, Harper went to Jacob Gibbs' house bearing a cold watermelon. She told Gibbs about the family's high hopes for Ford. She and Gibbs sat on the back porch. They split open the melon and picked the cold, pink meat and Harper with delicacy and great care revealed that she knew Gibbs' secret, and that several people were pushing her to publish a story about it, but she was resisting. The small man with the sagging ears smiled then, and said, "How can I help Ford's campaign?"

"Just tell your boys not to get involved."

"Hell, it ain't any of their business anyway, is it?"

They shook hands. By neutralizing the Klan, Harper had cut Smith's power by fifty percent.

One day in the middle of October, Wick received a letter from Brother Alered. It was gentle and warm and brief, as usual written on the inside and back of a Japanese card. It contained several greetings from Wick's brothers at the monastery and a few sentences about how beautiful the summer had been and that the rain was gentle and the sun soft and that everything growing was green and healthy, and reading the words, Wick felt the old ache in his heart that he had not felt in a while. It was like the pain of hearing about an old lover, someone you're not quite over, someone you really never wanted to leave, though you had to.

In the midst of campaign headquarters, surrounded by twenty volunteers and jangling phones, Wick set the letter down and looked out into the stillness of the green yard. What am I doing here, he thought. How did I end up in the middle of all this? And for a moment he remembered the beauty of stepping into the tall cavern of the abbey at 3 A.M. How quiet and soft and dark and fresh it was. How beautiful were the morning psalms and how simple and good he felt to be speaking to God when most of his brothers were still sleeping, when most of America itself was sleeping, and he felt like a guardian, a protector, his morning prayers covering all, beseeching for all, blessing all.

Brother Alered wrote that he missed Wick and so did many others and that the cooking had become completely bland, consisting mainly of turnip soup and boiled potatoes. He told Wick not to worry about his vocation, that God would provide. He told him to read Psalm 139 every day.

At the bottom of the card was a different handwriting: a precise printing of black ink.

Dear Brother,
Hope you are well. Go to Monsignor LeConte. Work for him.
Dom Lewis

Wick smiled. How typical of the abbot. Cold, brutal simplicity. Any affection was seen as weakness. Wick stuck the letter in his back pocket. Did he really want to be a diocesan priest?

One night in the third week of October, the family decided to take the evening off—no campaigning. The fall had finally come to South Carolina. Now the temperature rose to only eighty during the day and dropped to forty-five at night. There had been one frost and the leaves of the hardwoods were beginning to turn red and yellow.

About half past eight in the evening, a gentle rain began. Blackie was in his room when the rain started. The sound of it and the smell of it awakened his predatory instincts. His heart sped up. He could feel a tingling in his hands and fingers, even his nostrils dilated with expectation. For a while, he simply lay on his bed and enjoyed this arousal, wondering how other people could live without excitement in their lives, particularly his brothers. They were all so diligent, so serious about life, their careers. Why couldn't they just relax and have fun and enjoy things? They don't have ecstasy, he said aloud. They have lots of brains and lots of ambition but none of them, not one, has ecstasy in his life. It's the one thing I have that they don't: the ability to appreciate ecstasy, to be able to identify it and to go after it and, once I have it, to really taste ecstasy, to eat it and drink it and, once it's finished, to forget it completely, so the next time it's new, completely new.

For a moment, Blackie's inferiority was banished and he laughed and picked up his bedside phone and called Carol.

"Is it raining where you are?" he asked.

"I thought about you as soon as it started."

"Wanna take a little trip to Savannah?"

"Who are we going to visit?"

"Mary Andrews."

"That woman at the party?"

"I want that gold necklace."

Mary Andrews' house sat on a promontory of land which overlooked a tidal marsh. It was a Victorian house consisting of ten rooms. She had retained the house when she had divorced her husband two years previously. Knowing Mary's penchant for collecting jewels, Blackie had cased the house several times. Through conversations with mutual acquaintances, he had learned two important points: the house was equipped with an alarm system and the jewels were kept in a safe. Where the safe was located, Blackie did not know.

He drove his camouflaged jeep a quarter of a mile down an abandoned logging road. The road went through a pine forest which ran up to the backyard of Mary Andrews' house. Tonight he and Carol wore the black nylon suits, though they had not bothered with the black greasepaint. Carrying two bags of tools, they walked down the logging road to within fifty feet of the backyard.

They stepped to the edge of the woods and looked at the large house. The rain was heavy and the woods were noisy with the falling of it.

Mary Andrews' place was dark and so were the two houses on either side.

"It's too dark," Blackie said.

"What's too dark?"

"The houses. All of them. They're way too dark."

"Well, it's three o'clock in the morning."

"The yard lamps are out. So are the lights under the doorbell buttons." He turned and looked at her. "That's real good."

"Let's see—the storm knocked out the power?"

"You got it."

"Piece of cake."

"Not quite."

"Why not?"

"She's got birds."

"Birds?"

"Toucans. Two of them. They're great watchdogs. We've got to avoid them, then find the safe and hope it's not too complicated."

"You know how to open safes?"

Blackie took a breath and looked up at the house. "I hope she's asleep like a good little girl."

But she wasn't. Mary Andrews had not been able to sleep, so she had taken a hot bath and gone downstairs to make herself a drink. She was deep into the second gin and tonic when the lights had gone off, and now wearing only a silk robe, she sat in the den fantasizing about a bag boy at Winn Dixie. He was sixteen or so and had big, ruddy hands and fluffy hair and broad shoulders and the smallest waist she had ever seen on a boy. He always smiled at her and never called her ma'am. At forty-eight years of age, Mary was bored with bald heads and beer guts and salesmen. She wanted a little excitement.

Blackie cut a neat oval into a dining room window, attached a suction cup and pressed. The oval of glass popped free and he handed it to Carol. He reached a hand inside, unfastened the lock and pushed the window open.

Once inside he said to Carol, "Make sure you shut the window behind you in case the power comes on."

He took a penlight from his nylon suit and carefully flashed it along the floors of the room, avoiding the windows. No wooden floors, he thought. Just carpet. He relaxed and turned off the penlight and allowed himself to enjoy the house, to eat up the feeling that he was here and no one knew. What would he find? What would he see? The joy of the break-in gave him goosebumps and shivers and made him feel incredibly sexy—as if he could do it all night.

When Mary saw the first flash of light in the dining room, she barely noticed, thinking it was lightning or her imagination. But the second time she saw the beam of light her heart jumped. She sat in her chair and could not move. A shadow crept into the door of the den. The small light flicked on again. It was low at first, then slowly rose. Held close to the body, the light revealed a black suit and part of a face, and then as the light rose over the head and explored the room, it illumined most of a face and she almost gasped when she saw that it was Blackie Longstreet.

She watched him cross from the den into the kitchen. As she recovered her breath, she became fascinated by his movement: the silence and confidence and elasticity of it. When Blackie once more crept through the den and back into the dining room, she gulped the last of her gin and carefully got up to follow him.

Blackie pulled Carol into the dining room. Her heart was beating fast and she was shaking. Somehow this time was not quite as fun as the first. She felt as if she couldn't breathe, as if she wasn't getting enough air.

"I don't feel too good," Carol said.

"Just come on. You'll be okay."

"Blackie, I really . . ."

He took her hand and pulled her behind him.

Silently they explored the living room, which held a beautiful chandelier made of rose crystal, and then a den, which contained two Remington sculptures of bronze cowboys and bucking horses. They went through a parlor and a billiard room and then began to climb a set of stairs.

"Put your foot on the part of the step closest to the wall," Blackie said.

"Why?"

"It won't pop as much."

* * *

Mary Andrews was furious that he had brought a woman. She had considered going to the phone and calling the police when she saw that girl creeping around her house, but she decided to wait awhile just to see what happened.

By the time Carol had reached the top of the stairs, she was out of breath, but she felt a little more calm. Some of the fun was returning.

As Blackie stole down the hall, he inhaled the scents of the upstairs: there was the smell of new soap and old porcelain from the bathroom, the white, dry odor of mothballs from a hall closet, one spare bedroom smelled of dust and the other had in it, just barely, the scent of something dead, like a rat in a wall, and farther down there were two other bedrooms and then a dressing room. Blackie paused here and let his penlight flash through the room. It was a good room for the safe.

There was an elaborate vanity with a pink silk stool and gold lame mirrors. The top of the vanity was cluttered with scores of nail polish bottles, their thin and translucent tops sparkling with light while the bottles themselves held thick reds, lavenders, pinks, purples and mauves. There were canisters of powder and golden phials of perfume and philters of emerald essences. Blackie luxuriated in the aromas. They thrilled him. It was as if he had never used his sense of smell before.

"Isn't it incredible?" he said to Carol.

She looked at him and saw his face shining, his blue eyes filled with a luster that she had never seen in them before. It made her want to make love with him.

"You stay here," Blackie said.

"Why?"

"I got a funny feeling."

"I don't want—"

Blackie put a finger on her lips.

He stepped down the hall and opened a door to a small sitting room. His light searched it and he crossed to the door on the other side and peeped into a bedroom: a pink wool rug and pink floor-length curtains, a large four-poster bed and beside the bed—the safe. Blackie smiled. He put his bag of tools under his arm and went to the safe and knelt down beside it.

"Old, aren't you, boy?" he said to the safe. "Yea, you an old one and you gonna pop open like a ripe pecan." He took a small bottle of gasoline from his bag and doused his fingers, then wiped them dry. The gasoline made his fingertips feel more sensitive. He laid his ear against the cold metal of the safe and began turning the lock.

When Mary touched him on the back, he hunched his shoulders and made a sound. She had come up the back staircase which led directly to her room.

Blackie turned and the penlight hit her directly in the chest. She wore a red robe. Her curly brown hair was perfectly brushed and her brown eyes were sparkling.

"What do you want?" she asked.

"I, uh . . . somebody said, one of your neighbors said, because they saw me, I was jogging and they said they thought somebody was in the house . . ."

"Pretty good line."

"Well, it's not . . . I mean I was up here to help, it's not a line at all."

"Why were you fiddling with the safe?"

"Just to make sure it was okay, make sure nothing was stolen."

"Do you usually jog with a suitful of hardware?"

Blackie sat down on the floor and the power turned back on. The bedside lamp lit. He shrugged, raised his hands. "So—what now?"

Mary crossed her arms, put a finger to her lips. "Oh, I think we could work this out. I just want a little compensation. You take care of my compensation and I'll never say a little word." She swept a hand through his hair.

"There's somebody with me."

"You don't have to stay long. I just want a flash, you know? I just want a real flash. Send her outside or something. All I need is twenty minutes. You can give me that, can't you?"

Carol was frightened. She had seen the light from the bedroom. She grabbed Blackie as soon as he came back.

"You've got to go," he said.

"Did you find the safe?"

"Yea, it's there, but I want you to go back. The lights are on. It's too dangerous."

It made sense to Carol, but he looked funny. "Are you okay?"

"Sure."

"You don't look okay."

"The lights surprised me."

"How long will it take?"

"I don't know—twenty minutes."

"Do you think you can get it that quick?"

He looked at her. "Yeah."

Blackie helped her through the dining room window, thought about making a run for it and then went back upstairs.

Mary's mind was racing. She found four of her ex-husband's ties and tore off the covers from the bed. She wanted this to be wild. She knew she'd probably never have anything this sexy again. She wanted it wild, wild, wild.

When Blackie walked into her bedroom, Mary picked up the last of her neat gin and sipped it.

"Take off your suit," she said.

Blackie stood with his hands on his hips.

"I said—take it off."

He did as he was told and stood before her in cutoff blue jeans and a T-shirt.

"Now the shirt," Mary said. She drank the rest of the gin and felt it burn her throat.

He pulled off the shirt and balled it up and threw it at her.

"You think you're tough, don't you?" Mary said.

Blackie snorted and his eyelids half veiled his blue eyes.

"Well, that's fine, because I want you to be tough with me." She threw the ties at him. "Do you know how to tie a knot, Mr. Cool? Do you?"

"Yeah," Blackie said.

16

SUDDENLY, IT WAS election day.
Harper and Boykin had decorated the house for the victory party.
Red, white and blue bunting hung on the twelve columns of Waverly.
The east drawing room, the hall and the ballroom were covered with
Ford Longstreet posters, Longstreet balloons and signs and slogans.

The family ate breakfast at six o'clock. There were grits and brown
link sausage and mounds of yellow scrambled eggs, pink wedges of
sugar-cured ham, stacks of buttery English muffins, jars of peach, pear
and blackberry preserves. Hannah and Bub and Tee Tat bustled around
the dining room filling coffee cups and clearing dishes. At the table
everyone was talking at the same time. Harper and Boykin were worried about Buster Jones "turning boxes" down at Greene's Ferry and
Wick said that he should have hired another fifty callers to get out the
vote and Ford worried aloud that he had not challenged Pinky to a
debate and Blackie loaded his second plate with grits, eggs and four
more sausage links, saying through a mouth crammed with the remains

of his first helping, "It's gone too easy, it's gone way too easy, and I'll tell y'all something—that fella's got a trick or two, you wait and see. You just wait."

In the midst of this cacophony, Cat started thinking about writing. Wouldn't this scene make a great story in a newspaper—the Longstreets on election day. What the most famous family in the state ate for breakfast. What their conversation was. The more Cat thought about the idea, the more excited she became, until she finally called out to Harper, "It would make a terrific story."

Harper's chin and black eyebrows raised. Her face was smooth and white, and since it was without makeup, a five-pointed pink birthmark was visible.

"What would make a terrific story?" Harper asked.

"Election day at the Longstreets'," Cat said. "What they did, what they felt, what they wore. All the—the accoutrements."

"I think it's a good idea," Ford said. He was dressed in a dark suit— navy blue linen with wide lapels, stuffed shoulders, a blue tie and white shirt with French cuffs sporting octagonal gold cufflinks.

"You do?" Harper asked.

"Yes, don't you?"

"I want this story to come alive, Ford," Cat said. "I want to fill it with all the minutiae of Waverly so that fifty years from now if some- body reads my story they will know exactly what it was like when Ford Longstreet was elected to Congress."

"Use the first person," Ford said.

Cat set a small hand over her mouth, her middle fingers touching beneath the tip of her nose and stroking the spot of down. What person to use had never occurred to her.

"As you know, the rule is to use third person to be objective and distant, but you have an original way of speaking. Maybe it will trans- late. Use the first. I'd love to have a look at it when you're finished."

Cat was radiant.

After breakfast the Longstreet household prepared to go to the polls. Teeth were brushed, baths and showers taken. Harper supervised who would ride with whom and what vehicle they would ride in. She knew the press would be taking a lot of pictures and she wanted the right impression of the family conveyed: wealthy, yes, but also practical and simple. Bub, Hannah and the other help would ride in pickup trucks; Boykin, Ford and herself in the Cadillac limousine; Cat, Wick and Blackie in the 1963 black Ford coupe.

The vehicles were drawn up in the white gravel driveway before the front of the house. The Cadillac first, then the black Ford and the two blue pickup trucks. As Harper and Boykin and the rest of the family were walking toward their cars, Wick pulled his grandmother aside and asked whether it was a good idea to drive to the polls in a motorcade. Wick thought that such an arrival would make a bad impression, something like—"Ah, the aristocracy arrives." Harper was irritated with him. Yes, the Longstreets were aristocrats, but more importantly, they were a family and they had voted as a family since long before her father's death. It would be complete hypocrisy to drive to the polls piecemeal.

"You don't have to flaunt your wealth, Wick," Harper said. "But you must never be ashamed of it. You must never try to hide it. If you do, people will see straight through you and brand you as duplicitous. You cannot make a silk purse into a sow's ear."

The motorcade arrived at the Boiling Springs Elementary School. Several reporters took the family's picture as they emerged from their cars. Everyone in the Longstreet clan (including the servants) voted the Democratic ticket and each stuck his or her paper ballot into a wooden box. Afterward, Ford shook a few hands, posed for a family snapshot and then returned to Waverly.

At seven o'clock in the evening the polls closed. There had been no rain in the state for over a month and everything was dry. The fan-shaped leaves of the gingkos were curling and soft. The grass had turned a light brown and even the thick leaves of the two magnolias were brown at the edges, the boughs scattering dead leaves that were crunchy and dry and elliptical. The whole countryside creaked and rattled in the wind. Everything was dry and brittle, even the blue beetles and the yellow moths of the evening clattering and rasping in their flight.

In the great house, the family was listening to the seven o'clock news. Boykin, Harper, Cat and the brothers sat in the den watching the television, while Bub, Hannah, Vic, Jebodiah, Tee Tat, Tadpole and others listened to the big wooden radio in the kitchen. The news wasn't good. The turnout had been low. A low voter turnout always favored the incumbent. In order to win, Ford had to carry his home county, Greenville County, with a huge majority. Greenville County had the largest population in the upstate. If Pinky Smith were going to try to do anything funny, he would try it here. Harper had hired private poll watchers in all the major wards of the county. If anything looked suspicious, she would know it quickly. Blackie did not sit with the family, but rather waited by the phones in Ford's office in the guest house, where two hundred and fifty supporters watched the television.

Ford sat in a green leather wingback chair by the bay window. The rest of his family was at the other end of the room by the television. He listened to their small talk and jokes, heard Cat asking every question imaginable about what they felt, what they thought, "right at this very moment." His mind wandered. Ford was not the same person at the end of the campaign as he had been at the beginning. Two months ago he had started campaigning out of a sense of outrage as well as the feeling that now was as good a time as any to begin some kind of career. His speeches had been glib paragraphs about the need for a congressman to respond to his constituents and that Pinky Smith spent too much time playing and not enough working. About the middle of the campaign in a black church in Ware Shoals, he quoted a line from Shakespeare, one of his favorites: "There is a tide in the affairs of men which taken at the flood leads on to Fortune, omitted all the voyages of their lives are left to shallows and misery." The church came alive.

He had never seen it before—the look in their eyes, the look on their faces. It was the look of hope—that they could have their dreams, that they could actually change their destinies. He used the quote at several other rallies: mills, high schools, homecomings, barbecues and the line became familiar and powerful to the crowd: there is a tide in the affairs of men. When he said it, the people would erupt in applause and "Amens" and "You say it, now" and "All right, *all right*, Ford." And he knew that the applause was not for him, the enthusiasm was not for him, the joy he saw in their faces was not for him—it was for the idea, the idea that they mattered and that they deserved the best in their lives and that they could have the best, they could do the best if only they would try, if only they would believe in tnemselves and in the ineffable importance of hope.

Blackie stepped into the room quietly. "Ford, could I see you a minute?"

The rest of the family did not notice their departure as they left the den and went to stand on the limestone floor of the back porch.

Ford crossed his right arm over his chest, set his left arm across it and ran his fingers down his long nose and crushed the bulb tip purple.

"Buster Jones is turning boxes. I just got the call," Blackie said.

"Greenville County?"

"Precinct three."

"Doesn't mess around, does he?"

"Let's not mention this to Harper yet. I'll get Wick. You get a truck. Should we take Nathaniel?"

"What are you talking about? I'll call Democratic headquarters. We'll challenge and impound the boxes."

"Bullshit," Blackie said. "We're going to take those boxes back."

"Do you know what you're talking about?"

"Yeah," Blackie smiled. "I'm talking about a fight."

Blackie drove the forty miles to Greenville in twenty minutes. Nathaniel and Ford sat in the front of the pickup truck. Wick was alone in the back. Nathaniel was wearing a dark purple suit. He had a new haircut. His gourd-shaped head had only black fuzz on the blackest of skin. He was going to a sit-in at the City Bus Company when Blackie grabbed him.

"I should have made you come with me," Nathaniel said.

"This is real important, Nathaniel. We need you," Ford said.

Nathaniel pointed a finger over his head. His nails were thick and yellow. "But I need you to help me too. I know this election's important. I know Pinky's a racist, but y'all need to come and help me sometimes on the other end of this thing."

Blackie pumped the brakes, began stopping the truck.

"What are you doing?" Nathaniel asked.

"I wasn't thinking. I'll take you back."

Nathaniel gently kicked Blackie's foot off the brake. "Let's go, let's go. Just help me when I need *you*. Just try to be with me some."

When they arrived at Summit Drive Elementary School, Blackie went into the building alone. The school was dark except for the cafeteria and a small room beside it. Inside the cafeteria, stacks of extra ballots sat on the green formica tables. There were four voting booths. Their short brown curtains were open. The voting boxes were absent. Blackie went to a door which connected to the smaller room. He pushed, but the door was locked. Now he wished he hadn't come alone. He thought about going to get his brothers, then took a breath and pounded on the door.

A sweating red face and bourbon breath opened the door six inches. "We're counting ballots."

Blackie tried to act nonchalant. "You seen Buster Jones?"

"Hey, ain't you a Longstreet?"

"I really need to find Buster."

"I bet you do."

The door slammed shut.

"Too late," Blackie said. "He already turned them."

"Let's get to Six and Seven," Ford said.

"It's over. He's got the biggest precinct in the district."

"If we win in Six and Seven, if we can keep it honest there, we still got a chance."

In five minutes they arrived at Parker High. Blackie shut off the lights of the truck and pulled beside the lighted gymnasium. Beside the double doors of the gym idled a large truck. On the silver cab was printed JONES'S MEATS. Wick, Blackie, Ford and Nathaniel slipped into the dark and looked through the windows of the gym. Four white men were pulling the wooden voting boxes from the booths and replacing them with four other boxes stashed in the middle of the floor. The two poll watchers sat at a table with a bottle of liquor and two glasses between them.

From a back room, Buster Jones stepped into the gymnasium and walked towards the polling booths. He gave a few orders, then stood with his hands in his pockets, cigarette in his mouth. Buster Jones was typical of many of the men who lived and worked in the cotton mills of the upstate. He had a long, bony nose and tiny eyes which were brown and dry and mean. He had a fourth-grade education and had never read a book. His joys were simple: a new Ford every year, fried porkchops and an infinite supply of Camel cigarettes. He didn't like women and he didn't like liquor, but he would lie and cheat and maybe kill for the rest of it.

When he saw Blackie step into the room and head straight for him, he took a drag off the cigarette, then cupped it in his bony hand and stuck the hand on the back of his bony hip. "Well, shit," he said.

"Hey, Buster," Blackie said.

"Hey there, boy," he said, and smiled yellow and black teeth.

"What you boys doing?"

"Oh, we turning these here boxes, Blackie."

"You wouldn't steal this election from my brother, would you, Buster?"

"Naw, I wouldn't do that."

"Looks like you are."

The four white men set their boxes down and looked at Buster. One of them broke and ran.

"Listen here, Blackie, you oughten to be here. We getting ready to count. It's illegal."

"It's also illegal to steal votes."

Buster stepped close to Blackie and took a puff from his cigarette. He smelled like tobacco and sweat and rotting teeth.

"You accusing me of something?"

"Stealing."

With a quick, light move, Buster reached into his back pocket, slipped into a pair of brass knuckles and swung.

The punch hit Blackie just below his left eye and knocked him back. Buster followed him quickly. "Why I'll kill you, you sonofa—"

But Blackie threw himself to the floor, tripped him and sent him sprawling.

The three white men rushed Blackie, and Nathaniel and Ford raced across the room and jumped in. The fight was fast. A big guy swung at Nathaniel, who ducked and remembered a kind of hip throw which halfway worked, though both of them ended up on the floor, where Nathaniel punched the man as hard as he could right in the nose. Blood spurted and the man covered his face and rolled away. Ford was hit in the stomach and knocked breathless, though he managed a solid right which struck his opponent to the side of his Adam's apple, stunning him for a moment. Blackie had pinned Buster to the floor.

"Are you tough now?" Blackie shouted in his ear. "Are you tough?"

Four city policemen rushed into the room with Wick behind them.

They had their clubs drawn and started pulling the men apart. One of them grabbed Blackie and he swung at the cop, missed and then the cop swung a nightstick at him and missed. The cop was preparing to try again when Ford shouted, "It's over! All right now. It's over!"

17

THE LONGSTREETS AND Nathaniel had to accompany the police downtown. Ford insisted that the ballot boxes be taken along. At the police station, Ford charged Buster Jones with vote tampering. Two hours later everyone returned to Waverly.

As soon as Blackie walked into the den, there was consternation over his injury. Harper sent Tadpole and Tee Tat scurrying for iodine and compresses and bandages and when she and Boykin learned of the fight and the various blows traded, she insisted that Ford and Nathaniel take off their shirts so that they could be inspected for bruises. Cat asked to take care of Blackie, but she was not allowed to get close. In an hour or so, after Nathaniel and Ford had been carefully gone over and Blackie had been patched up with iodine and gauze, the household settled down to listen to the incoming returns.

At eleven-fifteen, Ford Longstreet was declared the winner and he was immediately engulfed by hugs and kisses and cheers from his family. Tee Tat rolled in a cart holding two silver canisters and two bottles of champagne. There were toasts and more toasts and the champagne was quickly drunk and then everyone, except Harper, went down to the headquarters, where the campaign workers and volunteers were in a pandemonium of joy. Ford read his victory speech. Three bars were opened up and the party lasted until 4 A.M.

After the brothers had bid good night to the staff and the volunteers, they took a bottle of champagne and glasses and sat on the front porch in three green rocking chairs which they pulled close together. The night was chilly. They could see their breath. The two magnolia trees which stood before the porch were covered by a light frost. The big leaves were still and the light of the house shone on the leaves and made them look silver against the black trunks of the trees. The air smelled of wood smoke and the sweet aroma of fallen apples rotting in the orchard and the night was still and dark and the only sound was the sound of the cane rockers, tittering and popping.

"Well, what do I do now?" Ford asked.

"Hire a good staff," Wick said. He reached for the champagne bottle and filled Ford's glass and then his own. He looked at Blackie, who was slumped in his chair half asleep, the black eye swelling beyound the edge of orange iodine.

Ford sipped his wine, then set the glass beside his chair. It was the only alcohol he had drunk tonight. He wanted to remember every moment of this night, every nuance. "Did I tell you the President called?"

"President Johnson?"

"He called about two and said—you know how he talks when he's very serious, his voice gets terribly low and preachy—and he says, 'Now, Ford, the American people have put a lot of faith in you tonight. We are at a crossroads. We need leaders. We need warriors. The times are calling for decisive men and decisive actions. Will you help me on my watch?' "

"What do you think he meant by all that?"

"I'm not sure. And then out of the blue he said—'Goldwater was right!' "

"What?"

"Yea, he said that Goldwater was right and that extremism in the defense of liberty *is* no vice. Can you imagine that? Agreeing with the very essence of your opponent's campaign? I don't know. He's an amazing man, but his mind is incredibly abstreuse. At the end he sounded like a little boy. He said, 'Ford, if ole Goldwater gets more than two states it'll break my heart. I'll just bawl like a baby.' "

"He must've had a few."

"He's a redneck," Blackie said, stirring. "God, my eye hurts."

"Blackie, he's the President of the United States," Ford said.

"So? He's a redneck."

"Well, sounds like he wants you with him," Wick said.

"Yes, it does," said Ford, musing.

At five o'clock in the morning everyone in the Longstreet household was finally abed, though many were not asleep.

Ford was teeming with ideas and plans and hopes. He lay on his bed still dressed, wearing his wire-rim glasses, scrawling notes and thinking, I want to be the very best of congressmen. Once a week I want to be home in my district to see and listen to the people who elected me. I want to know their names and the names of their children and I want to know all their troubles and all their dreams and—he suddenly saw his stomach. I've got to get rid of this weight and stop drinking, too. I must set a good example, but the most important thing, the most important thing of all—he furiously began writing—is to be accessible, even in my Washington office. I know—I'll take the door off. Exactly! I'll take the door right off the hinges so the people won't even have to knock. In fact—I won't have any doors in my office at all. That's it! There are no doors in Longstreet's office. Everyone is welcome!

Three rooms down from Ford, Cat lay in the dark, hurting as she had never hurt before. She had met Carol Simpson at the victory celebration, and an hour later when she had stepped out onto the porch she saw the blond woman kissing Blackie in a way she had seen no one kiss before. She must be thirty, Cat thought. How could she kiss Blackie like that? Didn't she have any morals at all? Blackie is a boy my age. *My* age, not her age, and why doesn't she go find somebody old to kiss? When Cat saw the image of Carol pushing Blackie against the column and running her fingers through his hair, it made her heart pound and her stomach hurt. He's not yours, she thought. He's the sweetest, handsomest boy in the world and I know he was made for me and not for you. Cat grabbed a pillow and slammed it up against her headboard and addressed it: He's mine, not yours, and I won't surrender and I won't give up and one day it will be me kissing him and touching his hair. Me and not you.

While Ford was making notes and Cat was fuming, Wick kneeled beside his bed with his Bible open to Psalm 139. Tonight he decided he would no longer doubt the existence of God. It was over—all the questioning and all the insecurity—finished. It was a new beginning, perhaps inspired by his older brother's victory. When he was young, he read Nietzsche and Schopenhauer, Buber and Kant and Tillich, Kierkegaard, Heidegger and St. Augustine. He had read these and a hundred other philosophers and theologians in an effort to be philosophically honest. He could not just throw himself blindly into the arms of God— no matter what Kierkegaard said. He had wanted to doubt to the limits of his being, to face the possibility that there was no God at all and, having faced that gloomy prospect, then retire comfortably to a simple faith. The problem was that he had doubted and probed for so many years that now it was difficult to believe at all. No, Wick corrected himself. It's not hard to believe, it's hard to know. I do not *know* there is a God, but I believe there is. As of tonight, no more questions, no more ponderings. I choose to believe in God, whether he is there or not.

The very last person awake was Boykin. She had felt the pain in her chest and elbow twice during the day and it had been hurting so much tonight that she had made herself a cup of tea and gone to sit in her chair in the trunk room. She was wearing a pair of blue pajamas and a blue robe, and even though her arm was hurting, she had managed to put her red hair in rollers. She sat drinking her tea and the pain was less and she thought about Cat and how well she was doing.

There are so many things I want her to do, to see, Boykin thought. She needs to go to Charleston and spend some time there and then maybe up to New York to see an opera. Oh she would love that, she would just be transported by an opera, and as Boykin was thinking these things, she gradually became aware of her mother's voice. It was soft and gentle and it was saying something very quietly, but persistently, and as she became aware that it really was her mother, she felt dizzy, but she wanted to know what her mama was doing home. What did you say, Mama? What?

Hannah found her in her chair, in the trunk room, around ten o'clock in the morning.

The entire family was shocked. Boykin had never been sick in her life, literally never, not even the chicken pox as a child. The funeral was held three days later. Wick gave the eulogy. Ford was there. Starkey sent flowers and a long letter from Vietnam. Blackie did not come to the funeral, but rather stayed in his room for a week and grieved for the only one who he thought really loved him. Harper was smitten with guilt, thinking that she should have seen some sign of the illness, thinking, How could she die and I not know it, not sense it? Why, I should have sat straight up in bed. I should have felt it. I should have felt something. Cat was so distraught that she could not eat for several days. She woke up each night thinking that there was no one here to help her now, no one to buffer her from Harper and that Harper could throw her out anytime she wanted. She was alone now, alone in a world that she loved and wanted, but a world she did not understand, a world that every day after Boykin's death felt more and more like a world of glass.

Two weeks later Wick Longstreet carried his suitcase down a brick walk which led to Monsignor LeConte's house. It was three stories with yellow stucco walls and a black slate roof. It sat in the center of town, surrounded by a ten-foot-high wrought iron fence which was covered with ivy. He pushed the doorbell, which was bronze and cast into the form of a lamb. It was so worn that the lamb's head had almost disappeared.

A black woman answered. "Yes?"

"My name's Father Longstreet. I'm supposed to start working here. Is the monsignor in?"

The black woman was warm and took his bag, saying that the monsignor was expecting him. She led Wick through the mansion. There were chandeliers and parquet floors, a white marble staircase and hallways cluttered with antique bronzes.

The housekeeper tapped on a door: "Come."

Wick stepped into a room which had one barred window and no furniture, other than a large table which was littered with hundreds of pieces of sparkling silverware.

The Monsignor turned and smiled, both hands holding gleaming teaspoons. "Wick—Welcome, welcome, welcome. You came just in time to

see my new silver—Italian Renaissance. Oh, I've had to put up with the
most awful cutlery over the years. Shabby, just shabby."

The monsignor was a small man whose bald head sat in a hedge of
red curly hair. His eyes were brown and his skin wrinkleless and red.
He wore a purple cassock with red piping.

"Don't you think it's elegant?" the monsignor asked, holding out the
teaspoons.

"It's beautiful," Wick said. He picked up a heavy fork and studied it.
He wanted the monsignor to know that he really wasn't just being
polite. He was genuinely interested in his silver. "I like all the carving
on the handle."

"Scrollwork. Yes, yes. It's just lovely isn't it? Of course I'm sure you
were surrounded by elegance at Waverly. How's your grandmother, that
dear, dear—that sweet woman?"

"She said to tell you hello and sent her best regards."

The monsignor hurriedly set down his teaspoons. "Oh, I can't wait
for you to see your boudoir. I've just redone it." He cupped a delicate
pink hand over his mouth and raised a shoulder. "Why, if anyone in
this Diocese knew how much money I spent on this old house, they'd
run me out of town on a rail."

The room was lavish. The furniture was made of red teak, the windows covered in a red damask, the floor by a blue carpet. There were
three brass lamps and on the mahogany mantelpiece an ivory crucifix.

"What do you think?" Monsignor LeConte asked.

"It's very nice."

"Fit for a Longstreet. That's what I said to myself. Why this is
absolutely fit for a Longstreet." The monsignor pulled a typed piece of
paper from his purple cassock. "Now here's a list of the hours we keep
here: breakfast, lunch and dinner. Oh, it's not on the list, but we always
dress for dinner. Do you wear French cuffs?"

"I don't usually, but I can."

"Please do. I just think it looks so nice to have my priests wearing
French cuffs and some very nice cufflinks at dinner. At ten o'clock
tomorrow morning I want you to report to my office and I will give you a
list of your parish duties, but I can tell you right now that I don't plan
to waste you—oh no, no indeed. Mostly you will be concerned with
social matters—social, oh yes. But that's tomorrow. Why don't you take
a nap until supper."

Wick walked the monsignor into the hall and watched him descend the stairs, straightening pictures as he went. As Wick was returning to his room, a large man stepped out of a doorway. He had black hair and a day's growth of beard and looked as if he weighed two hundred and fifty pounds.

"Can you believe that guy? Can you believe him? It's no wonder kids don't want to be priests. Who would want to end up like him? Name's Ed Shaughnessy. Been here two years and ten days and I'm going nuts dealing with this bird."

Wick introduced himself. The big man leaned toward him. He wore a T-shirt beneath which his big stomach bulged, a black pair of pants and black suspenders and a pair of sandals. "Do you like to eat?" He reared back and gave Wick an appraisal. "Hell, you're skinny as a rail. But if you like food, you're in trouble in this house. The monsignor eats all this fancy stuff—sauces and crepes and all that stuff—and damn little of it. A big spoonful and that's it. Listen, you want to eat, you see me. Come here."

Father Shaughnessy threw a hairy arm around Wick and directed him into his room.

It was a bare room in terms of furniture. An iron bed and chest of drawers and cracked mirror, but the place was crammed with food. Over the curtainless window hung three red salamis, two brown bolognas and a cluster of pink sausages. A bookcase held cans of beans, soups and several varieties of canned spaghetti and meat balls. A small refrigerator sat in the corner. A hot plate rested on top of it and on the hot plate an aluminum pot steamed and clattered its lid.

"You really do like to eat, don't you?" Wick said.

"You like deli stuff?"

"Well, I like pastrami—particularly hot pastrami."

The priest's rough face fell. "I ain't got any of that." His nose was large and round and looked as if it had been squashed.

"But I like, uh—bologna, too."

"Hey, I got some German bologna that'll knock your socks off." Father Shaughnessy threw open a drawer, grabbed two slices of rye bread from a bag, slapped on mustard then whipped down a fat, brown bologna and cut off six thin slices. "You just don't have delis down here. I have to bus this stuff down from the city, you know?"

He presented the sandwich to Wick with a big smile. "You got to cut the bologna paper thin, otherwise you can't appreciate the delicateness of it. Lot of people don't know it, but bologna—good bologna—is a delicate thing."

Wick took a bite.

"What do ya think?"

"It's good."

"Not too spicy?"

"No, it's real—good. What's in the pot?"

"Hey, come have a look."

Shaughnessy took off the lid. Wick looked inside: potatoes and carrots with chunks of meat in a brown, bubbling gravy.

"Lamb stew," Shaughnessy said with a delighted face.

"Never had it."

"Oh, now, then listen, laddy. Let me do something for you," Shaughnessy said. He took Wick's sandwich and dunked a corner into the stew, then handed it back to him.

Wick bit off the dunked part. He looked at Shaughnessy and rubbed his stomach. The big Irishman smiled.

18

DINNER WAS AT seven-fifteen, an hour after Wick had eaten two bowls of stew and another sandwich, as well as samplings of polska kielbasa, Italian sausage and braunschweiger, which Father Shaughnessy had insisted he try. When Wick walked into the ornate dining room, he was stuffed. There were three other priests, to whom he introduced himself. Everyone wore French cuffs and cufflinks. Father Shaughnessy had decided not to attend. The room had a Hepplewhite dining room table, carved chairs, a Hepplewhite sideboard and two china cases filled with gleaming silver.

The Monsignor was the last one to come to the table. His face was red with two glasses of claret and his cufflinks gleamed with two oval rubies. He made sure that everyone had met Father Longstreet, then said the blessing in Latin. When he finished he rang a small bell and the black housekeeper entered the room carrying a silver tureen of she-crab soup.

St. Mark's was a society parish. Most of the parishioners were wealthy Northerners who had come to retire. They owned horses and vast farms. They played polo and golf and tennis and did little else. St. Mark's was one of the richest parishes in the state and Wick was surprised to learn the next morning that it was in debt.

"Oh, yes, it's just awful. I suppose I'm responsible," Monsignor LeConte said. He was standing behind his large desk, while a young nun knelt at his feet, adjusting a new gold chasuble. "But I was never good at figures—are you?"

"I seem to do all right with figures. I helped keep the books at the monastery."

The monsignor glanced down at the elaborate stitching of his golden pleats. "That's too short," he said to the pale young nun. "I hate short chasubles." He extended his arms to his side in the form of a cross. "What do you think, Wick?"

"It could be a little longer."

"And that's from someone who knows all there is to know about society, Sister. So drop the hem, please."

The little nun did as she was told. Wick felt sorry for her.

"Now, Wick, I want you to be in charge of my dinners and my teas. I have two teas a week—one high, one low. The high is on Wednesdays at four-thirty and the low on Sundays at three. I always have a Friday dinner—black tie. Lately, people have been turning down my invitations. I don't know why, but I do know that no one turns down Monsignor Halbert's. His mother was a Guignard, as you know. One of the great families of the state—but certainly not any more prestigious than yours. Anyway, can you help with the invitation list? I've been so disappointed lately."

"I'd be happy to," Wick said. "Monsignor, I hope this isn't too bold, but do you know how much we run in the red per month?"

"Oh heavens, I couldn't even guess. Maybe one or two thousand dollars. Would you like to see the books?"

Wick spent the afternoon going over the figures and was stunned to find that St. Mark's ran four thousand dollars a month in the red. When he returned the books to the monsignor and asked if he could help to retire some of the debt, the monsignor told him that he could have complete control of parish finances, "except for the purchase of food and wine. That responsibility I will bear myself. As for everything else, it is in your hands. Do what you will."

One of Wick's gifts was the ability to see waste and correct it. It was odd that the son of such a wealthy family could pinch pennies so successfully, but Wick was a master at it. He was also extremely quick at basic arithmetic. He had done poorly at trigonometry and physics in college, but at multiplication and division he was fast.

For one week, Wick made detailed lists of the expenditures for heating, electricity, water, laundry, office supplies and other necessities. The next week he began to cut off, turn down and turn out. Laundry was curtailed, lights extinguished and part-time secretaries were sent packing.

A few days into the cutbacks, he went to bed early one night. He lay in the light of his bedside lamp and, looking at a list of further cuts, noticed how much his handwriting resembled Boykin's and that even the way he made the list was the way she had made them—straight columns, each item a letter, not a number. Was she really alive, he wondered. Was there a place where she was bright and happy and at peace? It seemed so impossible—the idea of heaven. It seemed like an idea that a child would invent. He closed his eyes and said a prayer for his great aunt, whether she existed or not, and then a little dark voice said to him—even this you do for yourself and not for her. All virtue is selfish. The reason you do good things is because it makes you feel better.

Two weeks later, when all the bills came in, Monsignor LeConte was shocked to see a three-thousand-dollar drop in expenditures. In addition to this good news, Wick had packed the monsignor's teas and dinners for the next three months with some of the oldest and finest families in the state: McMasters and Debordes, Hamptons and DeSaussures. The monsignor twittered with happiness and made Wick associate pastor, promoting him above the three other priests.

During the process of belt tightening, Wick discovered his goal. He was one of those persons who had to have a goal—something that he could work toward every waking hour. As long as Wick had a goal to fret over and work at and worry about, he did not ask all those ghastly questions about the nature of good and evil and whether or not God was a caring god. What Wick wanted to do, what he was icily determined to do, was to completely rid St. Mark's of debt and, not only that, but to have the parish finish each month with a profit.

"Oh, that's impossible," Monsignor LeConte said, polishing a new set of silver salt wells, then handing them to Wick for a final buff.

"No, it's not. I think we could end up with eight to ten thousand dollars of profit a month. All we have to do is build a shopping center."

"How in the world can we build a shopping center?"

"All you need is land and location," Wick said. He walked over to a window, drew back the drapes and extended a hand. "We have both."

Out the window and across the highway laid ninety-three acres of woods and ravines which St. Mark's had owned for fifty years.

The monsignor smiled and that very afternoon Wick set to work. His first call was to Ford.

"I want to build a shopping center."

"I thought you wanted to be a priest."

"Are you and Hookey Simms still buddies?"

"Ate lunch with him yesterday. Never get that chicken salad at Brennan's."

"Can you get me an appointment?"

"Yes. When you coming home?"

"Soon."

They hung up without goodbyes.

Hookey Simms was wild about the idea. It turned out that he had been besieging the monsignor for years to develop the land for apartments, but he liked the shopping center idea even more.

One day just after Wick had returned from a luncheon with the architects for St. Mark's Plaza and was preparing for his regular afternoon nap, an idiosyncracy of the Longstreet family, Ethel tapped on his door and told him he had a visitor.

Alice Grooms sat in the small parlor of the rectory. She wore a white cashmere dress, a string of black pearls and white pumps. She was nervous. She was thinking, He's a priest. This is a bit much—even for you, Alice.

All of Wick's irritation vanished when he saw her. There was a radiance to her face, a kind of light around her golden eyes and auburn hair. He extended his hands and took hers and he felt it in his stomach. Alice talked a bit about her cousin in Charleston and the lovely view from her bedroom and that she was planning to stay a month or so.

Wick looked at her hands. They fascinated him—the hands of women. If they were too big or too fat or too veiny he was bothered, but if they were small and delicate, if they had unpainted nails, he immediately thought of how it would be to hold them.

Alice Grooms' hands were perfect.

Over the next few days, they saw each other several times, always for lunch. Alice liked him. He was handsome and intelligent and he possessed the sensitivity of an artist. She could feel herself getting ready to fall for him and she tried to pull back, saying; This is what always happens to you Alice. You leave one relationship smarting, fatigued, cynical, determined never again to become vulnerable and then you see —the profile—pug nose and blue eyes and a certain tint to hair and off you go again. You must stop this. Why not let him fall in love with you? Why not try a little gamesmanship? You're a bright woman. Of course you don't believe that—but you *are* a terribly bright and attractive— yes, attractive—woman. You don't have to fall in love first. Let him fall for you. Come on!

So Alice Grooms worked at not falling in love with Wick, and she thought she was doing awfully well at it until one Saturday afternoon in December.

It was a winter day on Pawleys Island. The sky was blue and clear, the light—gentle and warm. They had walked on the beach for a couple hours, then sat down on the sand to rest and drink some white wine. The sea was blue and the sand was light brown and big swells of it made dunes beyond the long reach of the sea, which at the end of reaching was only a thin wing of water sweeping the edge of the dunes and then falling back, gliding across the sand toward clear tidal pools and then the froth and bubbles of the waves. Big green palmettos sat in the midst of the dunes and below them grew brown cattails and here and there a sea oak, the trunk gnarled and brown and twisted.

"Is it always so warm?" Alice asked.

"The winters are pretty warm, yea."

"New York right now is frigid."

"I love New York."

"Do you?"

"I really do."

"Maybe you can visit sometime."

They looked at one another with wide unblinking eyes, not noticing eyelashes or eyebrows or any other part of the face, but rather concentrating only upon the eyes and it was then that Alice felt the emptiness, the big emptiness she had tried not to feel, and the more she looked at his eyes, the bigger the emptiness became until she said to herself, Stop it, stop it this minute, and she looked away from him, shutting the door to the emptiness.

"Still want to go crabbing?" Wick asked.

"Yes."

"In the right mood?"

"I'm fine," she snapped. How dare he be so flippant when she was so much in peril. "Are *you* in the right mood?"

Walking back to the car, Wick wondered what he had done wrong. When they got inside, Alice reached over and took his hand and whispered, "I'm sorry." He held her hand, saying nothing, only holding and feeling the warmth and smoothness of it, and thinking, It's the most important thing. Touching is the most important thing, we are not whole without it, we are not alive. We are not. *I* am not.

Half an hour later, wearing their rolled blue jeans and T-shirts, they stood up to their calves in a black tidal creek. They had stopped at a store and purchased two crab lines with big lead weights and a pound of chicken necks.

Wick opened the white butcher's paper and showed the blue and yellow necks to Alice.

"How awful."

"The crabs love them. Now the way you do this is to tie on a chicken neck and then reel off about twenty feet of twine. Let it fall at your feet . . ." Wick was demonstrating as he spoke. ". . . twirl the weight in your hand like a lariat, aim for a pool and then just let it go."

The chicken neck, weight and line shot in a curve right into the heart of a black pool.

"You let it sit there for five minutes or so, then pull the line back in. If you're lucky, a crab will be clamped onto the chicken."

"There's no hook of any kind?"

"No hook."

"Why does the crab allow itself to be reeled in?"

"What a crazy question."

"No, it's not."

"All the years I've been crabbing I never thought about it. I don't know—maybe they're just greedy."

Alice picked up her line and Wick tied a chicken neck on the end. She reeled off the proper amount, then twirled the line with the lead weight and the chicken neck and let it go. It missed the tidal pool by twenty feet. After two more tries, she made it. They waited a few minutes and started pulling in Alice's line first. At the end of it lay a big blue crab.

"Oh look, it's a monster," Alice said.

"He's pretty big."

"What do I do?"

"Keep pulling him in."

She pulled the crab through the black water until it reached the bank of the creek. The shell of the crab was blue and the big claws were orange except at the tip, where they were black with small white teeth.

"Now what?" Alice said.

"You grab him with your thumb and index finger from the back," Wick said. As soon as he touched the crab, it released the chicken and slowly waved its orange claws in the air. Wick tossed it into a tin pail.

They fished for two more hours, until the sun began to go down and the marsh grass turned brown and gray and violet with the last of the light. They caught six big blue crabs and put them in the tin pail, and when they were riding toward Charleston and drinking cold beer, feeling the sunburn stinging their faces and hands, they could hear the crabs scuttling and scraping in the tin bucket.

At Alice's cousin's house, Wick jumped out of the car and yelled; "Knife! I need a knife!"

"Is it murder or suicide?"

"It's crab cakes. I'm going to make crab cakes. Haven't done it since I went into the monastery."

They threw their arms around each other's waist and dashed into the old Victorian house. Alice situated Wick in the kitchen, then went to build a fire in the living room. Wick found a shining copper pot, filled it with water and sat it on the gas stove to boil. He opened the refrigerator, got a bottle of red wine and poured two glasses.

The beer and the wine made Wick feel warm and rosy and he sat down in a kitchen chair and called out what he needed: two eggs, whipping cream, mustard, onion . . . As he did this, he looked at

Alice—she was so beautiful. The sunburn had brought out a few lines in her face and emphasized the sharp planes of her cheeks. Her hair was windblown and her small hands looked red and chafed and inviting. It was a lovely feeling—the warmth of alcohol and the warmth of the boiling pot and the warmth of the pretty girl setting out the ingredients for supper. It feels so natural, Wick thought. It feels so good and right.

"There," Alice said. "Do you need anything else?"

"Maybe just a little assistance."

"Righto."

Deftly, Wick opened the eggs and then beat them in a small mixing bowl. He minced some onion and tossed it in a frying pan with butter. Into the frothy eggs, he put one half a cup of cream, one half a cup of bread crumbs, all the flaky crab meat, one-half teaspoon of chopped parsley, salt and dry mustard and paprika and the sautéed onions. He folded the mixture together, shaped it into cakes, dusted it with flour and quickly fried it in a little butter and a hint of garlic.

While the cakes were frying, Alice put together a simple salad and set the kitchen table.

The crab cakes were brown on the outside and white on the inside. Alice put her fork into the first one and a clear juice ran out of the cake and a sweet aroma filled the room. When she tasted it, she lifted her shoulders and rolled her golden eyes.

There were six crab cakes and Alice ate four.

After supper the sunburn was stinging them, but they sat before the big fire anyway drinking hot tea with orange honey and cream and Alice reminisced about college.

They talked late into the evening until the fire was reduced to chunks of glowing ash and the second pot of tea was finished and they were so tired from the fresh air and the fishing that their bodies were weak. Wick had propped his head against a blue couch and so had Alice and she lay only a few inches from him, and while he looked at an avalanche of coals which sizzled and sent up a puff of spitting fire, Alice studied his black hair, the ends of which were touched with red, and his tiny ears and she looked at the long curves of his eyelashes and at his brown eye and the blue one and she reached out and took his hand.

It made him ache—her touch. It made him feel things that he thought were gone. He held her cold hand and pulled her beside him.

Her face, hot with sunburn, nestled against his own and he could smell the salt of the marsh and her perfume. You are a priest forever, according to the order of Melchisedec—Psalm 92.

"We shouldn't be doing this," Wick said.

"Shouldn't be doing what?"

"You know what I mean."

"Shouldn't be holding one another?"

"None of it."

"We can stop."

"Can we?"

Wick held her awhile more and then decided he must leave. Driving back to the rectory, the two voices in his mind started debating and before the debate became too intent he wondered—are these two voices the expression of the brain's bicameral activity? The language of two hemispheres communicating with one another, or is it—is the debate of conscience—a stubborn proof of God? Is one voice that of God and the other your own or even the voice of the evil one?

He could not answer the questions and so he prayed in his heart, Oh Lord help me to keep your commandments, yet he knew the prayer was futile, because his desire to be with Alice was greater than his prayer.

Wick saw her only occasionally. He met her in restaurants and at movies, trying to stay away from the house in Charleston. He worked hard on St. Mark's Plaza, using many of his family contacts. Within a month, the architects had finished their drawings and built a model of the plaza and a week later Wick rented eighteen of the plaza's twenty-four stores. From these eighteen stores alone the parish would receive an income of seventeen thousand dollars a month. The story of how Wick Longstreet took the most debt-ridden parish of the Diocese and turned it into a gold mine in two and one half months reached the bishop. He summoned Wick to Charleston, reviewed the parish books carefully, studied the plaza contracts scrupulously and then told Wick he wanted him to work in the Chancellory, and that if he succeeded as brilliantly at that job as he had done at St. Mark's, he would be the youngest Monsignor in the history of the Catholic Church in South Carolina.

Wick accepted the job and moved to Charleston. The bishop's house sat two blocks from Alice's.

19

OVER THE PAST MONTHS, Cat Mc-
Gregor had been completely embraced by the Longstreet family. They
had accepted her enthusiastically and included her in all the family
outings and discussions. The only one who dealt with her somewhat
coolly was Harper, and Cat had determined that sooner or later she
would pierce the grande dame's exterior and make her way into the old
lady's sunny heart—for Cat believed that within Harper Longstreet
there was a warm and lovely place, a kind of secret garden, and that no
matter how Harper tried to disguise it, it was there and ready to be
loved by anyone brave and patient enough to enter.

By the first of February, 1965, the countryside had fallen into deep
winter. The sprawling English oaks had lost their leaves, as well as the
hickories and pecans. The sycamores were the most beautiful trees in
winter. Without their green leaves you could see the winter trunks. The
bases were thick and the outer bark brown and light gray until the bark
split open, revealing whiteness and then a splotch of green or a plane of

violet and these colors continuing all the way up the trunk and over most of the sycamore's limbs until you reached that one limb which had no bark at all, a limb that was completely white and shining against the blue sky.

One evening after supper, the family sat in the den watching television. Ford was going over some work that he would carry to Washington the next day and Wick (who had come home for the weekend) was studying some papers from the Chancellory.

Suddenly Blackie burst into the room. He was wearing a pair of black corduroy trousers, a blue sweatshirt and white tennis shoes. His hair was tousled and unkempt and he had not shaved that day. When Cat saw him she thought the violet stubble on his jaw made him look rough and cool. Even after living for months at Waverly and seeing Blackie almost every day, Cat's heart still sped up when he first walked into a room.

"Okay, everybody up," Blackie said. "I've got a surprise."

"Too full to move," Ford said.

"Up! Everybody up!" Blackie said. He grabbed Ford by the arm and pulled him. "Particularly you, Congressman."

"We need to digest Tee Tat's porkchops," Ford said.

"Well, you're just going to have to digest on the move," Blackie said. "Now—up, up, up!"

There was groaning and complaining, but finally Wick, Ford and Cat walked through the cold hall and out onto the veranda.

The air was cold. It was twenty degrees, so far the coldest night of the year. Waiting in the gravel drive were two wagons, each pulled by a brown horse. Nathaniel drove one and Vic the other. When the family stepped out onto the porch, Vic pulled off his brown fedora and waved. Nathaniel did not move, only thought to himself, Serving them—that's what this is. There is a difference between working for people and serving them. This is serving them. This is exactly the problem. Someday, somebody's got to show them the difference between working and serving.

Each wagon was loaded with yellow hay and a supply of red and blue quilts.

"Hayride!" Blackie yelled.

"I think I'm just too full," Ford said.

"We haven't been on a hayride in years," Wick said.

Blackie grabbed Cat by the hand and started pulling her down the white marble steps. "Come on now," he shouted. "Let's go. Everybody. Move it."

Five minutes later the two wagons were jingling down the dirt road between the two rows of gingko trees. Some of the gold leaves were still attached and beneath the light of the bright moon the leaves were glistening. Ford and Wick ended up in Vic's wagon, Blackie and Cat in Nathaniel's. The wagons creaked and jingled as they hit the tar-and-gravel road, then became quieter when they left the hard road for a soft one, which was covered with brown pine needles and ran in a circle around the fields and pastures of Waverly.

Actually Wheel Road was made of pine needles. It was fifty years old and the needles were four feet deep and the road looked like a brown bank running through the woods of the plantation. The light of the moon was so bright that the bare oaks and the tall cedars cast shadows across the edges of a rye field which had just been mown. The air was nippy and hard and bright. As the young people huddled beneath their blankets and yellow straw, they looked toward the freshly cut field and a thousand bales of green rye. The cold air was sweet with the cutting and the green bales were covered in frost so that beneath the light of the moon they sparkled and glimmered across the field of yellow stubble.

Cat was lying on her back looking at the stars in the black sky. Blackie sat beside her, hands upon his knees.

"I feel heavenly," Cat said. "Have you ever felt that way? Have you ever felt that everything in a certain moment is just perfect?"

She looked at Blackie. He seemed so peaceful. His black hair was barely moving in the breeze and he had turned up his shirt collar around his big neck. In the darkness his blue eyes seemed black. "I mean, I think that there are very few moments in life that are really heavenly."

"Naw, there're a lot of them," Blackie said, turning to look at her, he saw her for the first time. She lay half covered with straw, a blue blanket pulled about her shoulders and the top of her blond head. Her nose was red and her blond bangs framed green eyes that in the moonlight seemed wet and sparkling. For the first time since she had arrived, he wanted to be near her.

"I think everybody has lots of special moments—I do anyway. I remember last week I took an afternoon off and went fishing. Didn't stay long, maybe two hours. I caught three little bass and on the way home stopped and got a beer and some crackers and I turned on the radio and there was my favorite song and I was drinking my favorite beer and eating my favorite crackers and I said, This is it, you know. This is heaven."

"You must have more of those moments than I do. Mine are rare. I used to think the reason those moments came so infrequently was because they really were glimpses of heaven and God wanted us to just barely sense them—just barely get a taste of them. That way the real heaven would be wonderfully new."

"*Now* is the real heaven," Blackie said.

Cat felt a little hurt by this statement. She had somehow hoped that maybe they shared the same kind of spirituality, the same wistfulness.

"Come here," Blackie said. He gave her his hand and pulled her into a sitting position beside him.

The wagons had passed through the rye field now and they were just moving into a dark tunnel of cedar trees. Even though the pine needle road was soft, the wagons were jingling and ringing and the horses' hooves made a soft clopping.

Cat sat beside Blackie. She could feel her heart beating in the tips of her fingers, which he had pressed into the palm of his hand. She could smell him. It was musky and sweet and there was another smell too, which she had never sensed on a man before—a salty, biting odor.

"Now look at all that," Blackie said. He waved toward the land that lay behind them.

There was the last of the stubble field and the green rye bales covered with frost and the moonlight glittering upon them and beside the field the brown pine needle road and it was sparkling too except for the center of the road where the horses and wagons had left round hoofprints and brown lines through the glittering frost.

"That's heaven. Right there. And if you don't treat it like heaven, if you don't enjoy it for all it's worth, then you really haven't lived. You got to be happy now. You can't wait to be happy in the future. If you're not happy right now, if you don't take it, you'll never be happy in the future. No matter how high you go or how much you get—if you're not happy in the present, you'll never be happy in the future. You have to seize happiness by the throat. You have to throttle it until you get all it has to offer."

While he was still holding her hand, Blackie turned her face to him and kissed her gently—once, twice and then the third kiss was not gentle, but deep, and he heard her make a sound in her throat. He took her warm chin in his thumb and index finger and looked at her face. He wondered how in the world he had not seen how beautiful she was. You shouldn't be doing this, he thought. She should be like your sister. But this notion only made him want her more. The idea that he shouldn't be making out with her made the whole thing thrilling. He kissed her neck and then took her earlobe in his teeth and slowly ran his tongue around and finally into her ear and he felt her shudder.

Carefully, Blackie worked his hand inside her windbreaker and then reached under her sweater, finally unbuttoning her blouse and touching her.

Cat pushed him away.

He looked at her and laughed, then jumped up and sprang beside Nathaniel in the front seat. "Let's race."

"Pretty dark to be racing," Nathaniel said. His skin was deep black.

"Hell, it's light as day," Blackie said. He grabbed the reins from Nathaniel, snapped them across the horse's flanks and the wagon jolted forward.

Cat was mad or hurt or maybe both. How could Blackie act like that? Everything was beautiful until he had made it common. It was an insensitive thing to do, completely insensitive. For a moment, she crossed her arms and raised her chin and sat back in the hay, not even facing in his direction. Then something told her that if she was going to get Blackie, if she was to have him as her very own, she could not act pouty and spoiled. I need to act as if I don't care, she thought. I need to act as if I was not offended at all.

With this thought, she crawled behind him.

"What are we doing?" she asked.

"Racing," said Blackie.

"Why?"

"Because it's moonlight and we got a fast horse."

"And he's crazy," Nathaniel said.

"And I'm crazy," Blackie said. "Hold on."

Blackie popped the brown stallion once more, pulled the reins to the right and the wagon screeched and bounded off the built-up, pine needle road, racing across the flat ground until it pulled parallel with Vic.

"Let's race back to the house," Blackie said.

Vic pulled his brown fedora over his nose. "Not gonna be no racing."

"Aw, come on, Vic."

"I'll take him on," Wick said.

"It's too dark," said Ford.

"The hell it is," Wick said. He pulled the reins from Vic's hands. The old man scrambled back into the hay.

Wick was standing in the front of the wagon, holding the reins, looking over his shoulder at Blackie. He began counting. "One, two, three . . . go!" He snapped the reins and the wagons lurched forward.

For the first few minutes, the two wagons were neck and neck. Ford raced along the pine needle road while Blackie kept to the flat field. The gentle jingling of the wagons had turned into a shrieking and grinding of wood and iron. Everyone was hollering and holding on. The horses pounded across the white frost and the breath of the animals filled the cold air with clouds of steam. The moon was shining and below the cold light lay the black forest and the brown road and the flat, green field, everything covered in frost, everything white and shining and still and the two young men were standing in their wagons, their knees bent, their black hair blowing, faces full of laughter and flashing eyes as each driver popped the reins and shouted to his horse, "Come on boy" and "You can do it" and "Fly, fly! Fly like the wind!"

Up ahead lay a dark stand of cedar trees and a wooden bridge across a black stream. Wick pulled back on the reins to slow his wagon down and Blackie, sensing this was the place to take his brother, screamed out a rebel yell and whipped the leather across the flanks of his horse. When Blackie's wagon splashed into the rocky stream, water flew over everyone and Cat yelled and Nathaniel cursed and Blackie laughed and drove the horse up the bank through the black shadows beneath the cedar trees and onto level ground which lay before a field of unharvested corn. Wick thundered across the bridge and saw his brother take the lead. He knew Blackie could win now if he wanted to. All Blackie needed to do was cut back onto the road. There were corn fields and woods on either side of the road all the way back to Waverly and once Blackie got ahead there was no place to overtake him. But Wick knew his brother, knew he couldn't resist the chance to plow right through the middle of the corn.

"You better get back on that road," Nathaniel yelled.

"Look at all that corn!"

"That's what I mean."

"Going through!" yelled Blackie. "Going straight on through!"

Blackie lashed the horse, and the wagon blasted through the center of the cornfield. The old ears thumped and thudded against the wagon, and cornsilk and yellow kernels and bits of brown corn leaf spewed into the air. Blackie's speed was diminished by a third and by the time the light-filled windows of Waverly came into view, Wick was well ahead.

When Blackie arrived at the back of the house, his older brother had a beer waiting. He stopped the horse and jumped down from the wagon. Nathaniel and Cat were right behind him. They were covered with corn: they had corn tassles in their hair and corn kernels in their ears and bits of leaves and sticky corn juice all over their faces.

Wick handed his brother a beer. "Harper's going to kill you."

"Gimme that cold brew."

"You know you could have won."

Blackie drained the beer in three gulps and then took another one. His face was red and sweating and the black hair plastered to his head with corn juice.

He belched outrageously, then gurgled a few liquid burps, finally squeezing from his throat several last yips. "Did you see all that corn? Did you see it? Who in the world would want to win when you could do something like that?" He grabbed his brother by the neck. "God meant us to have fun, Wick. Can't you see that? You don't have to win all the time. Not even most of the time. We were made to have a good time. Why am I the only one who sees that? With all the damn, rotten, stinking brains in this family, why am I the only one who sees the real truth about it all? You make me sick. Sometimes you—all of you—you just make me wanna puke."

Blackie finished the beer, hurled the can at the wagon and ran up the back steps into the house.

Cat wanted to run after him, to put her arm around his waist and hug him and say, "It's all right. I understand you. Nobody else does, but I do." She wanted to wet a cloth and put it to his scalding forehead and say soothing words and whisper him to sleep. But she knew it was too soon to attempt any of these things.

Ford took out a handkerchief and daubed at his face. The birthmark on his cheek was a bright lavender. His face was huge and swollen and his belly bigger than ever.

"Lawlessness. It's just an untamable lawlessness in that boy."

"Why would you want to tame it?" Cat asked.

"Oh, I don't. I love it. I think it's one of the best quirks in this quirky family, but it will hurt him someday. I love him and I want him to be exactly the way he is—but I know that it will catch up to him. It will. It always does. Society does not tolerate anarchists. It never has—it never will."

The word troubled Cat all night long: anarchist. Was Blackie really an anarchist? She had thought that those were people who threw bombs and waved black flags in the midst of civil unrest. Blackie was not one of them. How could Ford say such a thing? Blackie was wild and untamed. He was like some kind of wild creature and he didn't want to be broken and that was a good way to be. She sat straight up in bed saying to the invisible Ford, You must make a distinction, Ford Long-street, you're so fond of philosophy. You must make a distinction between wildness and anarchy. One is pure and the other is not.

Having made what she thought was a stunning point, Cat said "Ha!," turned over and went to sleep.

Later in the evening Wick decided to tell Harper about Alice. He had been thinking of the appropriate time for some weeks now. It had never occurred to him not to tell her. He and his brothers told Harper every detail of their lives: sins, virtues, vices, hopes, fears. The brothers told Harper everything and none of them, except Blackie, none of them could imagine holding something back from her. It seemed wrong.

She was sitting in the library on a rosewood chair, her left foot upon a small footstand, left arm upon the raised knee, holding her guitar as she methodically played the scale. She wore a white skirt and a black cashmere turtleneck.

She saw Wick come in, but played for a full ten minutes more, infuriated that one more person was trying to prevent her from complet-ing the task. When she finished, she slapped the guitar and tossed her head and said, "There. Done, by God, in spite of everyone."

"You didn't practice earlier?" Wick asked. He was wearing black pants and a blue sweater.

"Couldn't." She set the guitar in its stand. Her black hair had been freshly curled and her cheeks had a little too much rouge. "How's the Chancellory?"

"I like it. It's very busy, lots to do."

"Are you learning O'Hara's eccentricities? How he likes his coffee, what his favorite liquor is, what music he likes? You need to get all of that down and make yourself indispensable. It's not enough to do your own work well, you have to make yourself a very, very important part of his life."

"I know that."

"And you're doing it?"

"Well, I think I could be doing it a little better, but something's come up, something I need to talk to you about."

These were the words which drew her full attention. She nodded and listened.

Wick told her about meeting Alice Grooms at the party and that they had gone to college together. He told her that they were seeing each other often and that he was afraid he was falling in love with the girl and that he couldn't help himself.

"Oh, that's ridiculous," Harper said. "Of course you can help yourself, just stop it."

"I don't want to stop it."

"So what are you going to do?"

"I don't know."

"Are you going to leave the priesthood?"

"God, no."

"Then you better get rid of this woman. It will ruin your career. It's one thing the Church won't put up with. You can be a drunk or a psycho or even a homosexual and they will look the other way, but they will not tolerate an affair."

"I know all that. It's just that I've never felt this way about a woman."

Harper picked up her guitar and set it in her lap. She wiped down the wood with a yellow cloth. "Love is the most powerful feeling in the world. There's no doubt about it, but you're going to have to choose between love and your career. It's too bad, but that's the situation you put yourself in and you've got no one to blame but yourself. The only thing I can say is that you better decide soon or it will get harder and harder and harder. Whatever you decide is fine with me, but you need to go ahead and do it. Do you understand?"

"Well . . ."

"Good. Now I want you to take a look at several different markers I'm considering for Boykin. I've got the catalog right here."

Harper had brushed him off because she did not want him to see how much this was affecting her. As she lay in bed thinking about it, she felt as if she was going to cry. Why did he have to become a priest? She had fought it with everything she had. In college he had girls constantly after him. Why couldn't he and Alice Grooms have hit it off then instead of now? It made her feel sick.

She got up and went to the bathroom and took a sleeping pill.

Twenty minutes later, just on the edge of sleep, the idea came to her. Maybe this could turn out well, if she played her cards right. He could still be married and have a career and a family and children—if she moved quickly. Maybe this whole thing is a dark blessing, she thought. It made her smile.

Earlier than usual, Cat heard the gentle knock on her bedroom door. She opened her eyes to see that it was still dark. The door opened widely, washing the room in the bright light of the hallway as Harper swept in carrying the morning tray.

"Good morning, good morning," Harper sang. "I've decided we all need to get up a good forty-five minutes earlier. We're wasting too much time lounging around in bed."

Balancing the silver tray in one hand, Harper used the other to cut on Cat's bedside lamp. She sat down on the edge of the young woman's bed, extended the silver legs and set the tray across Cat's midsection. "There now, I'll tell you a great secret or at least a great practicality: if you get up early enough you can do anything in the world—anything at all. What do you think of that?"

"Yes ma'am," Cat said. She was still half asleep.

"Yes ma'am? Well, yes ma'am is not an answer. It's a mannerism. What do you think about rising early?"

"I think it's a, a good idea."

"Good, because if you're working for the *Southern Chronicle* you have to get up very early indeed."

"You mean, I'm going to work for the newspaper?"

"You are."

Cat reached out to hug Harper, who withdrew herself from the enthusiasm of the girl, then slightly extended her cheek. She was wearing a dark purple business suit, pleated white blouse and an antique pin of carved white ivory. Her black hair was brittle with hair spray and her black eyes without the faintest indication of the early hour.

Cat kissed the old lady's cheek, feeling a layer of pink compound stick to her lips, smelling hair spray and Harper's own odor, which despite her formality and harshness was sweet.

"You need to subdue some of your enthusiasm, Cat. It indicates the need to be—coddled."

"I think enthusiasm is good."

"The correct form of enthusiasm is good."

"What's the correct form?"

"Optimism."

"Well, I think there's a difference between optimism and enthusiasm."

"Young lady, do you always have to debate me?"

Cat dropped her big green eyes and took a sip of her pineapple juice.

"Now, starting tomorrow morning, you will rise promptly at four."

Cat almost choked. "Four A.M.?"

"You need to rise at four so you can get a good, hot breakfast—I've already instructed Hannah to have oatmeal and raisins and skim milk waiting—and jump in the car. The paper should be out and you should be home by eight o'clock. Now this morning, you need to learn how to fold and how to wrap the papers in plastic in case of rain. Our customers hate soggy newspapers . . ."

"Miss Harper—are you saying I'm going to be a newspaper boy?"

"Woman—or girl. Yes, it's the place for you to start out. Every one of my sons had a newspaper route by the age of thirteen. Admittedly, you're starting a bit late, but there's nothing that can be done about your unfortunate upbringing."

Cat sank back into her pillows and felt all of her joy fade. Eighteen years old and a newspaper boy? How terrible.

At four-thirty the next morning, full of Hannah's gluey oatmeal and raisins, the old black woman's kiss still wet on her forehead, Cat stepped down the back steps of Waverly, staring at a map of her newspaper route.

She walked through the back garden. The air was sharp and bitter and the stars were bright. She wore a pair of red long johns, a sweater, a flannel shirt and wool socks which Hannah had snatched from Starkey's room, along with a camouflaged hat and black leather gloves. The grass of the yard crunched beneath her feet, and as she moved beyond the garden toward a shed where Blackie's old bike was waiting, she saw the mud puddles had frozen in the driveway and the floodlights of the house made the pools and rivulets of ice blaze and flash. Beyond the ice, dark frost made the brown grass stand straight up.

Just as Cat rounded the house, she saw a black Ford truck in the driveway. The motor was running and a cloud of gas streamed from the tailpipe. As she approached the truck, the front window rolled down and there in the freezing blackness of early morning shone the sleepy face of Blackie. "Hey, kid. Want a ride?"

Cat laughed, dashed through the white beams of the headlights and jumped into the front seat.

They drove to the *Southern Chronicle* building and picked up over one hundred newspapers. In a loading dock, Blackie taught her about folding a paper.

"Now there are three styles. You can roll the paper like this, so it's kind of like a bat." He was demonstrating as he lectured. "Or you can do the three-fold technique. Or—if you're really ambitious—you can make a triangle like"—this particular style took a bit more time— "yea, just like—this."

Cat was enchanted watching him. His big, red fingers worked nimbly in the freezing air and she loved the way he now and again brushed the back of his hands at his blue eyes, which were running because of the cold. And the entire time he was talking and folding and taking her small hands into his big, warm ones, she thought, He's mine, he's mine. Right now, nobody else in the whole world is as close to him as I am, and realizing this, Cat did not want the moment to end. It could have gone on forever for her—Blackie's fingers pressing her own along a crease in a newspaper and his blue eyes shining and his voice softly instructing her in the pure, black morning air that had now turned as warm as spring.

Around seven-thirty, they pulled into the backyard of Waverly, having folded and thrown a hundred newspapers. Blackie stopped the car and pointed to several cardinals which sat in a pecan tree. The birds were glistening red and the tree was bare, the limbs black and brown in the rose light of morning.

"Isn't that pretty?" Blackie asked.

"Oh—yes."

"You see something like that and you wish you were an artist or something so you could find a way to keep it, to hold it."

Cat was thrilled that he could think these kinds of thoughts, say these kinds of things. It meant they were similar. It meant there was hope. While she was looking at the cardinals, Blackie leaned forward and kissed her. The kiss was wonderful enough, but then for some reason he laid his head against her throat. He just laid it there, his soft hair against her chin and mouth and she could smell the fresh soap of his early morning shower and she felt light and high and floaty and then the strangest thought came to her: that now was the time to die. Now—not any other time, but right now—and for a second she almost prayed, Lord let it come right this very second, but Blackie raised his head just in time.

"Do you like adventures?" Blackie asked, and suddenly his face went nose to nose with hers. "God, you've got pretty eyelashes. I love the way they curve. *Do you* like adventures?"

"Sure I do."

"Well, so do I. They just make life fun, you know? They make life— alive. Lately most of my adventures have been at night. They're different, kinda dangerous. Would you like to come with me sometime?"

Cat was so excited, she could only peep, "Yes."

20

WHEN STARKEY HAD FIRST re-
turned to Saigon, he took a few more days to think about the mission
and then he turned it down. The colonel was furious and told him he
would never advance in the military. A week later, the colonel's plan of
assassination was discovered and he was arrested. Starkey was still in
his old job of intelligence and propaganda. Still spinning his wheels.
Still not advancing.

He was sitting at a table in front of a small café on the Rue Van
Duyet. It was ninety degrees in Saigon. The air was heavy with humidity. He was drinking his first aperitif of the evening and watching the
crowds pass along the wide boulevard. Many of the Vietnamese girls
still wore ao dais and the silk material let you see their petite outlines
easily. Across the boulevard an old man wearing a white suit walked
down the steps of a villa and waved at a crowd of Chinese. Out of the
midst of them darted another old man pulling a cyclo. The old man in

the white suit climbed aboard and then yelled as if for the benefit of the crowds, *"Allez! Vite! Vite!"*

Starkey sipped his cognac and soda. He was sitting outside the wrought iron enclosure which protected the front of the café. MACV had warned against any unnecessary exposure, but there had been no attacks against Americans in a while. Besides there was a breeze here and the delicate scent of ginger floating from an herb stand on the corner. The Rue Van Duyet was busy today. Many Americans were moving in the crowd. The Americans stood out because they were so tall and their skin and coloring often so fair and today most of them were women and children, though there were a few MPs and several Special Forces officers wearing their green berets pulled low over their eyes. The crowd was full of Chinese who wore black pants and white shirts and a few Buddhist priests dressed in golden gowns. The faces of the Americans were white and smiling, generally oohing and ahhing over something, the blond-banged children sticking pink fingers into the bamboo cages of animal vendors. These vendors were usually Vietnamese and wore yellow straw hats and black trousers and shirts and sold tiny yellow parrots or green lizards, once in a while a young monkey. The faces of the Orientals had no expression at all. They were smooth and yellow, seemingly detached and distant from the bustle around them.

A young boy approached Starkey. He was dark brown and barefoot. Behind him he pulled a wooden wagon which held several pineapples and a handful of yellow bamboo sticks.

"You want?" he asked.

"Is it fresh?"

The boy smiled hugely. "As pie."

Starkey held up one finger. The boy took a large pocket knife from his shorts and opened the blade. Starkey was just able to make out USMC on the knife's handle. He didn't think about it. The boy cut a wedge of pineapple, trimmed off the bark and stuck it on a bamboo stick.

"How much?"

"Ten p."

"Too, too much."

"Five p."

Starkey laughed and gave the boy fifty piasters. It was probably more than he made in a week of work. The boy's black eyes widened and then beamed. Pointing his hands beneath his sharp, brown chin, he bowed.

Eugénie walked up out of the crowd then. She was wearing a yellow cotton sheath and green belt. She had black hair. Starkey had been waiting on her for half an hour, as usual.

"You shouldn't do that," she said.

"I know."

"He'll tell all his little buddies and they'll hound you to death."

"Is this a drinking day or a nondrinking day?"

"It was nondrinking, but—what the hell."

A waiter came over and Starkey ordered her a gin neat with a sliver of lemon. He could tell that she liked his being able to recall the drink. He had run into Eugénie a week after his return to Saigon but it had taken them this long to get together. Their affair had lasted six months during the previous year and then they split up, just after Starkey had killed his first tiger with her father on a hunt in Kontum. There was a tortured attempt at reconciliation and then she went back to the States and finished her degree at Radcliffe.

The waiter brought over the drink and Eugénie pressed the thinnest of pink lips to her glass and swallowed. "So is it off or is it on?"

"I think you know what I want it to be."

"You're such an ass. I'm talking about your assassination plot."

He felt like he was going to blush.

"Don't," Eugénie said. "It makes you look so childish."

"They say when two people are really close that's what they do—know what the other's thinking or doing."

"Yes, that's what they say."

He sipped his cognac. The fizz had gone out of the soda. He looked down the boulevard and saw the green pepper trees bend in the wind. He wondered if he could go through this again.

Eugénie Villeneuve was a member of the elite in Saigon. Her father was a French planter and her mother had been Vietnamese. She had grown up in a world of exotic privilege, having been accustomed to a household of twenty servants, tiger hunts conducted from the backs of her father's elephants, steamy tropical evenings spent with potentates and chieftains like the aging Vietnamese Emperor Bao Dai, who told her stories about the tiger of Lang Tri whom he believed to be his great-grandfather. At fourteen she had been sent to the most fashionable girls' prep school in Saigon—the Marie Curie Lycée. At eighteen she went to the United States and spent a year studying art history at Radcliffe, then took a two-year jaunt around the world, ending up in Paris for eighteen months before she managed to return to the United States and two more years of books and affairs with blondish Harvard boys. Now, at twenty-seven, she had a cool face, cool hazel eyes and an occasional part in an Indian movie.

"How's your father?" Starkey asked.

"He misses you. He really does. The son he always wanted and all that. He wants you to come to dinner tonight."

"Does he still say his prayers standing on his head?"

"You remember the funniest things."

Starkey looked into her smoky eyes. He had avoided doing it until now. Things had not been warm enough. The bitchiness was always her first gesture because it put you on the defensive and allowed her to see how you were. She used the bitchiness with everyone at first—everyone except her father—and if she saw she was all right with you, she settled down a bit.

When Eugénie saw him offer her his eyes, she looked down a moment and then looked back up and accepted them. They finished their drinks and then got up and paid the waiter and walked in the direction of her father's villa. The sun was going down and the air was becoming slightly cooler. They left the center of town and moved along the Rue Marshall where the residential section began. These villas were not the nicest in town but they were very pretty with their walled gardens and the villas standing behind the walls usually two stories and the stucco a fading yellow or light pink or blue. The air here was humid and sweet with the smell of jasmine and papaya. From one of the villas came the sound of a piano. The music was soft and sorrowful.

"Chopin," Starkey said.

"Which one?"

They stopped to listen.

"Thirty-three, or maybe . . . No, it's thirty-three."

"You're right," Eugénie said, and reached out and took his hand. It felt so big to her that she glanced down to see it. No one else's hands were this big. His hands had always made her feel safe, though sometimes they had made her feel weak. She wondered if men used their hands, the size of their hands, to make women feel powerless.

Walking ahead of them was an old French Grande Dame. She was wearing a high-fashion French suit—violet linen and ivory buttons and a blue high-necked blouse. Her white hair was arranged in a tall coif and above it, supported by a long handle, was a golden parasol which was carried by a tiny Vietnamese girl who walked a step behind and to the side of the old lady.

Eugénie squeezed Starkey's hand then went ahead of him.

"Bonsoir, Madame Corbet. Quelle belle soirée, n'est-ce pas?"

"Oh, Eugénie . . . Oui, en effet, une des plus belles. Et l'air est tout embaumé. C'est la papaye. Vous la sentez?"

Starkey caught up with them. Eugénie grabbed his hand and pulled him close to her. *"Madame Corbet, je vous présente le lieutenant Long-street."*

The old lady's white powdered face wrinkled and the rouged lips opened to reveal a brace of yellow and black teeth. "Oh, you wear the green beret, young man. Do you know its history? The way it came to be that you Americans wear it?"

Starkey did not interrupt her.

"The partisans wore them in the war. It was their badge of honor, and when your OSS began to help, they too wore them and so this badge of honor comes down to you. Did you know?"

"I knew some of it," Starkey said. He glanced at the Vietnamese girl who stood holding the long handle of the golden parasol. She was straining to keep it aloft and her tiny arm was shaking. Starkey had a sudden compulsion to help her.

"Would you care to join us for supper?" Eugénie asked.

"Thank you, but on Saturdays I always go to the Cercle Sportif for the lamb. It comes from France by air. Isn't that astounding? By air."

They bid Madame Corbet a good evening. She and the Vietnamese girl crossed the street. The old lady with the stand of white hair teetered on yellow spike heels beneath a parasol of gold and the arms of the dark-skinned girl shivered with the weight of the umbrella.

"What's the situation between them?" Starkey asked.

"I think you already know."

"You mean that little girl's *congaie?* In 1965? I can't believe it."

"How long did it take for slavery to die out in the South?"

"It ended a hundred years ago."

"Did it?"

They walked past a park and turned left on Cong Ly Street. This was one of the most fashionable streets in Saigon and the villas here were the biggest and the best. The French *colons* had built these houses in the early twenties from the profits they made from their rubber and tea and coffee plantations. Life in the jungle was too hard for them so they visited there rarely, preferring to spend their time in the palaces of the city. In 1925 there had been two thousand colon families in Saigon. Now there were only a hundred or so left. Most of them lived on Cong Ly Street. They had survived Dien Bien Phu and the fall of the French government and the corruptions of President Diem. The colons were hopeful. They believed the Vietcong would pass away, too.

Starkey and Eugénie walked beneath the green elms on Cong Ly Street until they reached the Villeneuve house. It was surrounded by a pink stucco wall which was covered with jungle jasmine. Within the wall were tamarind trees and palms and a front yard of green grass. In the middle of the grass lay a black lily pond. The lilies were white and yellow. The villa was a gold stucco with black steps. It had thirty rooms.

When they met Monsieur Villeneuve in the front hall he was so enthusiastic that he hugged Starkey, kissed him on both cheeks, shook his hand and then kissed him again. Eugénie rolled her eyes. The old man was bald except for a fringe of white hair. He wore a square white mustache and dressed in a three-piece white linen suit. He ushered the two young people into a parlor which was paneled in glistening rosewood. With gentle condescension, he ordered drinks and hors d'oeuvres from two servants.

"Now tell me, Starkey, how is your lovely grandmama and Waverly and pecan pie? Does your cook still make pecan pie? Oh, how I remember that confection. *Ah oui, merveilleusement sucré, ça. C'est le meilleur dessert en dehors de ce qu'on fait en France.*"

Starkey laughed and filled in the old man on all that was going on at Waverly, which Monsieur Villeneuve had visited in the fall of 1963. They had three rounds of gin and tonic along with Dalat strawberries, a shrimp pâté and brie.

Dinner was held in a formal dining room which had polished teak floors and a vaulted ceiling composed of a blue ceramic tile. Each tile had a tiny five-pointed star and as the entrée was being served a servant flipped a switch and the stars twinkled.

It was steak two inches thick and a foot long, a huge, brown baked potato and asparagus out of a Green Giant can.

Monsieur Villeneuve raised his hands. "What do you think of my meal?"

"Papa!" Eugénie said.

"It's great. Looks like a meal out of an American steak house."

"The PX," Villeneuve said. "Before Lodge left he gave me my card and a TN license plate. Now I am a rich man, no?"

For the rest of the meal, Eugénie talked about Paris and the society of Vietnamese expatriates and the cavorting of His Royal Highness Bao Dai.

"I went out with him a couple of times," Eugénie said.

"With the Emperor?"

"Yes."

"God, I'm impressed."

"Are you?"

"What does he think about the war?"

Eugénie sipped some champagne. "Which war?"

Coffee was served in a parlor of glittering French antiques. Monsieur Villeneuve talked about his rubber plantation to the north and that it was difficult to make a decent profit these days. Things had been so bad last year that he had sold five thousand acres to Michelin. He still had thirty thousand acres left but there were so many expenses. He paid the government a land tax, there was a tax on the profits and then the sharecroppers took their part, which was the only loss he did not regret.

"I feel sorry for the jaunes," Villeneuve said.

"Papa, you shouldn't use that word anymore," Eugénie said. "The Vietnamese hate it."

Villeneuve raised his white eyebrows and his white mustache and went right ahead. "The situation is impossible for them. It's no wonder I can't find a stable labor force. If they work for me they must pay the government a high tax, they cannot own their land and they must put up with my managers—a number of whom are beasts. If they work for the Vietcong, they are given title to their land, but they must pay 90 percent of their profits to Ho Chi Minh. What are they to do?"

Starkey did not answer—though he knew what he would do. He would forget about the land, put together an army that was independent of Saigon and America and Ho Chi Minh and then he would fight until the land was free. For a moment, in the specious clarity of alcohol, he thought he had found the solution to all of it. How simple it seemed. Just refuse to serve any power—neither the Communists, nor the Americans, nor the Saigon crowd. Denounce everyone but the peasants and fight until everything foreign was obliterated.

Monsieur Villeneuve stood up to say goodnight. "Starkey, spend the night with us."

"I need to get back—but thanks."

"Oh, nonsense. You're drunk. Stay."

"I am?" He looked at Eugénie.

"Very."

"Well, I don't think very," Starkey said.

"No, no, no—not very, but a little. Look, tomorrow I'm going to Annam to view some new trees. Spend the night and we will go early in the morning."

"Am I very?" Starkey asked Eugénie.

"Well, perhaps not."

"Oh, well, then—if I'm not very, then I'll stay, but I need to call the BOQ."

Eugénie grabbed him by the arm and pulled him toward a telephone. Monsieur Villeneuve waved goodnight.

"I've got the solution," Starkey said.

"I see."

"No, I do. I have the solution to the whole war. It's incredibly simple. Incredibly."

"Is it?" Eugénie placed a telephone in his hands.

"Whom am I calling?"

"Ho Chi Minh."

21

WHEN THE KNOCK CAME at his door and the first light peeped through the opening crack, Starkey roused, thinking it was Jebodiah and Waverly. He grabbed the sides of the bed.

"It's just me," Eugénie said.

He rubbed his hands across his face, through his hair.

"Would you like breakfast?"

"What time is it?"

"Seven forty-five, I think. We've melon balls, pineapple cubes and grits."

"Grits?"

"I think they're called Uncle Ben's. I've never eaten them. Come on. Papa wants to leave in thirty minutes. It will be a hundred degrees by eleven."

It was a hundred and two degrees by eleven as they drove down a dirt road eighty miles northwest of Saigon. Starkey cradled a bottle of

Scotch under his left arm. Beneath a jacket lay his .357 and a hand grenade. He was not in uniform and he knew it was not safe in this area, though Monsieur Villeneuve insisted his jaunes were loyal.

They were riding through the midst of the Villeneuve plantation now. The earth was ruddy and on either side of the old Buick stood rubber trees. They were tall and dark and straight and the trunks had been scored so that the latex would ooze out and fill the white porcelain cups which hung on the trees. They rode through twenty-five miles of nothing but the straight trees with their savage cuts and the porcelain cups flashing in the sun and occasionally a band of peasants wearing straw hats which were doffed as the Buick sped by and the old man waved and the trees and the peasants bled and bled beneath the hardest sun that ever was.

Finally Villeneuve's driver slowed down and turned onto a cement driveway which ran a mile through a row of tall sandalwood trees. At the end of the road stood the plantation house. It was anything but grand, just a long, single-story structure with a veranda which ran around the house. There were big windows and light blue shutters and electric fans on the long porches which were turning in the heat.

The inside of the house was simple: sandalwood floors and wicker furniture. Starkey was introduced to Monsieur Vuillard, who was the manager of the plantation. He was a tall man, thin and missing a chunk of his left ear. Starkey glanced at the deformity, then quickly looked away and Vuillard saw him and laughed.

"It's quite all right. I would stare too. It's a hideous wound. Tell me what do you think did it?"

Starkey was embarrassed, but Monsieur Villeneuve winked at him as if to say—it's okay, Vuillard loves to talk about it.

"It was a chimpanzee. A big male chimpanzee."

"I didn't know they had chimps here," Starkey said.

"Oh, no, it wasn't here. It was at the Tuileries," Vuillard said.

"It was the name of our place in the Congo," said Eugénie.

"You had a place there, too?"

"Villeneuve Enterprises," she said. "From continent to continent, enslaving the world. I wonder why everyone puts up with us. I certainly wouldn't."

"*Est-ce que Dalai a préparé un de ses repas somptueux?*" Monsieur Villeneuve asked, silencing his daughter.

It was served on a split bamboo table with white linen place mats and bone china engraved on the outer edges with tiny blue elephants.

They had their drinks at the table, Starkey taking a straight Scotch while the others had pineapple juice and rum with *glace pilée*. The lunch was French—*poularde à la broche, soufflé Rothschild, Friandises* and *petits fours*.

After the lunch there was a siesta and everyone went to separate bedrooms. Starkey's room was at the back of the house. It had a double brass bed which was surrounded from floor to ceiling by a violet mosquito net. There was a ceiling fan turning in the room. Lying on the bed, Starkey could barely feel the moving air, though he could feel the heat pushing down on him from the ceiling of the room. He had laid the green grenade and the pistol on the pillow beside him and he was sweating and thinking about the absurdity of the heat, and to stop thinking about it, which was making him mad and hotter, he thought about home, about Waverly. It would be cold there now, with a big, clear, cold blue sky and frosty nights and fires. He pulled out of his back pocket the newest batch of letters from Harper. He had received three or four a week ever since he had come to Vietnam. He was amazed that she could write so much and still have interesting things to say. Some of it was news—Wick is seeing a woman and I heartily approve; some of it was advice—be careful, be prudent, but also take a certain amount of risk or you will not advance; some of it was revelation—of course, I do miss Boykin, but to be quite honest (and I feel I can with you, son) I also feel a sense of freedom, a sense of finally being able to run my own house. He shook his head. No one could accuse her of not being honest.

Eugénie tapped on his door and then came into his room. She stood for a second and looked at him and did not move. Starkey could see sweat shining on her cheeks. She was smoking a cigarette and walked over to his bed and sat down, not bothering to push back the mosquito net. She drew the cigarette smoke from the left side of her mouth and her left front tooth had a yellow spot on it.

Starkey knew she wanted him to speak first, to ask what was the matter or something. It was her little drama and he refused. He just sat in bed and looked at her hazel eyes and her short black hair with the auburn highlights running through it.

"What do you think?" Eugénie asked.

"What do I think about what?"

"The plantation."

"Looks like a lot of work."

"Do you think it will last?"

"The work?"

"Starkey."

"Nope."

"Not at all? I mean—you don't think any of it will last?"

"I think all you colons are in for a big surprise."

"Am I in for a big surprise?"

"You're a colon, aren't you?"

"I mean, you know, am I in for a big surprise about you?"

"I'm not the problem."

"Oh, I see, I'm the problem. Me."

"Yep, you."

"You're not part of the problem?"

"Very damn little."

Eugénie drew off her cigarette from the left side of her mouth and it bothered him. In his mind, he saw the yellow spot get bigger. He didn't like her smoking.

"What if I told you you're right and I'm the problem and you're not, but I've changed."

"I guess it depends how you've changed."

"Maybe I don't know how, you know? Maybe I just have and I really don't know how. Can I get in there with you?"

Starkey pulled back the mosquito net. Eugénie halfway climbed in, then saw the grenade and the pistol. She grabbed them as if they were potatoes, as if they weren't dangerous at all and tossed them to the foot of the bed. It was the way she could be sometimes and Starkey liked it.

"How would you want me to change if things were going to be okay between thee and me."

When Eugénie started saying thee and me it meant that she was sincere and without her drama.

"Well, for starters, it would help a lot if you didn't run off to Paris with a Chinese fashion designer and I didn't see you for months."

"What about a Swiss fashion designer?"

"Now that would be fine. That wouldn't bother me at all."

They laughed and Eugénie brushed back his black hair. She could smell the Eau du Pinaud cologne that he always wore and it made her a little dizzy. She loved it when his bangs framed his blue eyes. It made him look like such a little boy. She realized that in the past she had not treated him well and now she wanted to, but she wasn't sure if she could. Can I treat anyone well, she thought. For some reason with those people who really loved her she would be very good for a while—sweet, almost too sweet, and then, when she sensed that their guard was down, she would do something dreadful to them, something truly despicable.

"I really have changed though," Eugénie said.

"Not about everything though."

"Well, I'm hoping to."

"Not everything though," Starkey said, and traced a finger down her full throat and just inside her blouse.

"Well, that's true," Eugénie said. "There are some things I still do."

Later in the afternoon, Starkey was walking with Monsieur Villeneuve. Even though it was four o'clock, the sun was still throbbing in the blue sky and the heat was white and pressing. They were walking beside a large rice paddy that Villeneuve had made by damming a creek. The rice paddy was a brown soup of water and mud and green plants grew out of the soup and slogging through the bright green plants were many peasants wearing gray britches rolled to their knees and black shirts and yellow straw hats with black leather thongs tied under their chins.

On the dirt road which ran through the center of the rice paddy stood a water buffalo and a cart and a peasant. The water buffalo was a big one, six feet high at the shoulder. His hide was muddy brown and big black flies swarmed above his back. His horns were six feet wide from tip to tip and they were so dark, even under the sun, so dark they seemed purple, a smooth purple sharpness. When the peasant went to hitch up the water buffalo to the cart, the animal suddenly swirled his head and the purple sharpness of horns to the right and the peasant jumped and spun out of the way, at the same time smacking the big animal between his horns with a bamboo cane. The water buffalo flicked its ears and slowly turned its head back around and slapped its heavy tail against its flanks as if to say, Okay, hitch me up, but just remember what I could do if I wanted to do it, peasant.

And after the peasant swatted the water buffalo, he shouted and threw his hat in the air and laughed and did a little dance.

Starkey had never seen the dance before. "What was that all about?"

Monsieur Villeneuve took out a blue silk handkerchief and wiped the sweat from his white mustache. "I'm surprised you haven't run into it. The young man just killed his *ma-qui*, his bad ma-qui. He has two—a good ma-qui and a bad ma-qui. He believes—like most of the other peasants around here—he believes that his ma-qui live in his shadow. The good one brings him good things like health and boy children and the bad one brings him bad things or tempts him to do bad things. If a peasant just misses death himself and his shadow is struck, then the bad ma-qui is killed until Tet when he will be given another one. It's lovely, isn't it? I envy them."

A breeze blew the old man's handkerchief from his hand. Starkey went to pick it up and the grenade fell from the clip on his belt beneath his shirt. Starkey had assumed that Villeneuve had seen the grenade and the pistol, even though he had kept them covered. He went ahead and picked up the handkerchief. When Starkey handed it to the old man, he did not take it, but rather pointed at the grenade.

"What is that?" Villeneuve asked.

"I think you know what it is."

"Bring it to me."

Starkey set his hands on his hips and looked at the grenade, then dropped his head and grabbed it and gave it to him.

With surprising energy, Villeneuve tossed the grenade into the heart of the deep canal that ran beside the rice paddy.

"This is what you Americans do. You bring these things, these dangers to this country. You invite the peasants to murder by the presence of these things. I told you there is no danger here. My peasants have a simple heart. I treat them simply and they work simply. When you put these things before their eyes you make them think they are something they are not. You bring out their bad ma-qui. You should be ashamed. All of you."

Around six in the evening, several servants finished loading the car and Starkey and the Villeneuves prepared to go. The heat was letting up a bit and the air was filled with the sweet smell of the sandalwood trees. The old man was not talking to anyone since the grenade inci-

dent. Starkey and Eugénie were walking toward the Buick. The driver
was standing beside the car holding a back door open for them.

"What happened to you two?" Eugénie asked.

"I'll tell you about it later."

"Tell me about it right now."

"No."

"God, you piss me off sometimes."

She made a kind of growl and then jumped into the back of the car.
Starkey didn't follow her, but rather paused and looked toward the
shimmering green of the jungle as if he were interested in something,
though he was not. After Eugénie's little outburst, he didn't want to
scamper into the car behind her like a little dog. He stood by the car,
one hand in his pocket, the other playing with the hammer of his .357
Smith and Wesson, which he now wore openly on his belt.

Monsieur Villeneuve stepped out onto the veranda of the plantation
house. He shook hands with Vuillard, settled his brown pith helmet
atop his head and spoke to a few servants waiting at the bottom of the
steps. As he was walking to the car, seven or eight more servants came
out of the house, waving and saying, "Adieu, Papa."

As he got in the front seat of the car and the driver closed the door,
one small, gray-haired servant ran from the house with a basket of
bright yellow orchids. Villeneuve saw him coming and smiled and
rolled down the window. Two feet from the car, the old Vietnamese man
bowed, then reached his hand into the basket and threw something
through the open window and into the car. It bounced across the dash-
board and Starkey saw it and leaped from the backseat, just as it fell to
the floorboard.

He threw himself into the front, a knee hitting the old man in the
face, yelling "Get out! Get out!" and jamming his hands under the seat
feeling for it.

Eugénie had seen the grenade, too. She was trying to pull her father
from the car.

"What is it? What's the matter?" Villeneuve asked.

Starkey felt the grenade and grabbed it, knowing it was too late, so
he pulled it to his chest and closed his eyes.

Nothing. He waited awhile longer, then opened his hands and looked
at it. The pin was missing. Carefully he got out of the car, still holding
the grenade to his chest. He walked a hundred yards to the edge of the

jungle. The grenade was wet and cold, and before he set it down, he held it out from him and turned it upside down and a line of water ran out of the pin hole. He set the grenade on a brown stump.

Villeneuve came up behind him. "He's worked for me for twenty-five years. He's a good old jaune."

The two men stood and looked at the green grenade sitting on the brown stump.

"It's mine," Starkey said. "The one you threw in the canal."

"He's always been good. A good man, an honest man, a man who was always trustworthy."

The twilight was deepening now and the cicadas were crying in the jungle and the air was turning a dark lavender and somewhere far and deep in the jungle the men heard the deep howl of a tiger. Starkey had heard this sound only twice before and it made him shiver.

"It can't be," Villeneuve said, lifting his head and turning his ear towards the sound. "It's too far south. They never come this far south."

"They do now," Starkey said. "They do now."

22

HARPER WAS SHOCKED. IT was
eight-thirty on a Saturday morning. She was sitting at the kitchen table
with Cat at her right when she opened the paper and saw the headline:
ALL TWENTY-ONE DEFENDANTS RELEASED.

"How can they do this!" Harper said. "Has everyone in Mississippi
lost their mind? I can't believe it."

Cat was sorting through a wooden box filled with gloves. There were
leather gloves, black rubber gloves, cotton gloves, wool ones, even a
clear pair of plastic surgical gloves. She was daydreaming a little bit.
The mail had come and Mike had sent her a letter in which he said that
they had found a strong vein of coal and there would be more money. It
made Cat feel less guilty for leaving.

"Cat, did you see this?" Harper asked.

"I don't think we're going to have enough gloves for everyone."

"I just don't see how you cannot pay attention," Harper said, thump-
ing the paper down on the table.

Cat picked it up and read the headlines. "What happened?"

"I don't think you care."

"Yes, I do. I'm sorry."

"Well, you know the story, don't you? I mean, you know what happened last June?"

"There was a lynching in Mississippi."

"*A* lynching—there were three. The Ku Klux Klan grabbed three of those civil rights workers and took them out into a swamp and put a cold, hard, rough noose around their necks and hanged them. All three of them. And while those poor men were swinging from that oak tree with their faces turning black, with their purple tongues wagging from their mouths . . ."

"Harper."

"Well, it's true. A lynching is not a pretty sight. It's ghastly and there are even worse contortions that a strangling body goes through."

"How do you know?"

"I've read about them in detail."

"Lynchings?"

"Capital punishments of various kinds, which I'm completely against, and if you're going to take a position, a strong position on political matters, you have to read some sordid reportage, which I have. But the point is—the FBI arraigned twenty-one men, took them before a U.S. commissioner—a woman, mind you—and she let them go. After all that work by the FBI, Miss U.S. Commissioner, Miss Esther Carter, let them off scot-free."

"Why?"

"Oh, something about not being able to accept the testimony of a confession that the FBI extracted from one of the men."

"Well, the FBI are smart fellas and I'm sure they'll find a way to bring those hooligans to trial."

"I suppose," Harper said.

"Do you think everybody will need to wear gloves?" Cat asked.

"Everyone, not everybody. Yes, the woods are full of stickers."

Harper glanced at the letter from Alice Grooms. She had written the girl and invited her to spend the weekend "greening" with Wick and the family. (In the depths of winter, it was the custom of the Longstreet family to gather greens to freshen up the house until the first of spring.)

It had been a bold move, but she wanted to meet the girl, and if she liked her, she could begin pushing Wick in her direction.

By one-thirty, everyone had arrived and collected in the den. Wick introduced Alice Grooms as a parish benefactor. Ford returned from Washington, where he had spent the week putting the finishing touches on his congressional office—touches which included dismantling every door in his suite, including the one leading from the main corridor to the reception room. The last to arrive were Blackie and Carol. As soon as Cat saw Carol enter the den, she was crushed. She had never expected that Blackie would include Carol on a family outing. She was so overcome that she could hardly speak.

"Does everyone have gloves?" Cat asked.

"I don't," Blackie said. He had been lying under a sunlamp and his face was radiant with a February tan.

Cat reached into the wooden box and pulled out two remaining pair: the surgical gloves and a pair of pink wool mittens. She held them up.

"I'll take the pink ones," Blackie said.

"No, you won't," said Carol, playfully slapping his hands as he reached out for them.

Cat closed her eyes and turned her back.

Alice Grooms looked at Wick. The colder weather had brought out two red spheres in his cheeks and there were the beginnings of crow's-feet at his eyes, which she thought made him look distinguished. They glanced at one another and smiled, both of them immediately looking away.

With a flourish, Harper threw open the double doors of the den. She was decked out in rustic clothes: a leather coat, yellow canvas pants, brown leather boots, her black hair pinned with ivory combs in a stylish bun and a red silk scarf tied about her neck. "Is everyone ready? We need to get on the road. Last year we didn't retrieve nearly enough greens. This house was bare as a cupboard."

Two cars and a truck were taken and the family drove down the narrow country roads for thirty minutes before they reached that section of their lands where greening was customarily done. Usually there were four separate places to stop, each valley or hillside yielding its own particular form of evergreen: holly, similax, cedar and mistletoe. The first stop was at Miss Simmons' house, an abandoned wooden structure where the postmistress had lived for sixty years until her death. It was the place for holly.

Holly was Harper's favorite green. She directed the family to the black pickup truck which Vic Cash was driving. "You need to use saws and loppers. I want lots of holly. So work up a sweat."

Harper quickly chose the newest and best pair of loppers for herself. She did so because she knew she would work harder than anyone at the holly with the possible exception of Blackie—"Who can climb trees like an orangutan," Harper said aloud.

"What did you say?" Wick asked. He was wearing a royal blue overcoat. His roman collar was visible.

"Oh, nothing. Just talking to myself. Probably means I'm going crazy."

"They say you're going crazy when you answer yourself," Alice Grooms said.

Harper had talked to her riding over and she liked her, she liked her very much.

"You know—now that I think of it—I disagree with both ideas," Harper said. "I think you're beginning to get a bit off when you answer yourself in public—when you start asking yourself questions and answering them while sitting at the dinner table, then I think there's reason for suspicion."

Alice Grooms laughed and so did Wick and once again they looked at one another and this time Harper saw them and she was pleased. Time to get things moving along, Harper thought. She knew exactly what she wanted to do. She gripped her loppers and moved into the woods.

There were seven holly trees behind Miss Simmons' gray and disheveled house. The trees were tall and they had gray bark and straight trunks and the leaves were glossy green and the berries the brightest of red. The family moved into the holly grove and began working.

Blackie sized up the tallest of the trees, walked backward about twenty yards and then raced toward the tree and ten feet from the trunk hurled himself into the air, saw in hand. He crashed through a canopy of green leaves and sprayed a torrent of red berries across the brown leaves of the woods. Harper applauded and Wick whistled. Blackie climbed the smooth trunk, edged out onto a limb and began sawing a branch.

Normally, Blackie's acrobatics would have excited Cat, but today they only increased her depression. She stood beneath a tree and hacked at a low limb. She watched Carol gathering the bright branches of holly which the handsomest boy in the world was throwing down to her. I wonder if he is as beautiful to her as he is to me, she thought, and then looked up at him. His hair was curling over his collar and she could see his perfect profile: the small nose and tall cheekbones, a red color creeping into the muscles of his jaw as he worked. She wanted to hate Carol, but she couldn't; she envied her. She completely envied her. Hate's a better thing, Cat thought. Hate's a positive, active thing. You can use hate. You can get even, but envy—envy just eats up the envier. It sits in you like a pot of acid. It dissolves.

"Hey Cat!"

His voice shook her from her thoughts.

"Give me a hand."

Cat tried not to race toward his tree. She looked over her shoulder and saw Carol putting an armful of holly into the truck. Blackie put his back against the trunk, propped his foot on a limb and smiled at her. "How do you like greening?"

"Oh, it's wonderful."

"It's a blast, isn't it?"

"It certainly is."

"God," Blackie said, and put a hand over his eyes and shook his head.

"You're not dizzy, are you?"

"I think I might be."

"What? What did you say?"

"You know, I'm up here in this tree. Cutting a little holly, climbing, and I turn around and see this girl and she's just—well, a knockout. No wonder I'm dizzy. Who could blame me." He cupped his hands to his mouth and whispered loudly, "You are gorgeous, gorgeous, gor-gee-uus!"

In an hour the family had gathered all the holly they needed and moved on to the next stop, which was pine. Along the way they passed land that had taken on the barrenness of winter. Stands of black hickory trees were leafless, the long limbs holding squirrel nests which were balls of brown and gray leaves. In the middle of the black hickory were blue cedar trees and sinewy plums and they were rooted in clay which was covered by the fallen leaves of autumn. The smell of these decaying leaves, the black and gray and dark yellow floor of the woods, was sweet.

Beyond the hardwood trees and standing on a hill were the pines. They were tall and straight and their green needles were glistening. Ford was the first one out of the car. He had mixed feelings about greening. He loved to be out with the family, loved the exercise and the fresh air, but he felt somewhat guilty about savaging the woods. Yes, savaging, he said to himself. He could hear his brothers making fun of the word, but savaging was precisely what they were doing, particularly here. It was in the pine stand that the axes were used. Whole trees were felled to satisfy Harper's need for greens. Ghastly, Ford said to himself.

He went to the truck and pointedly picked out a small saw.

"You're not starting all that again, are you?" Blackie asked.

"We don't need axes."

"Oh God, here he goes."

"Blackie, has it ever occurred to you that you may be wrong?"

"Ford, trees do not have feelings."

"How do you know?"

Wick and Alice Grooms and Harper walked to the truck and sorted through the tools.

"Ford's talking about the trees having feelings again," Blackie said.

"It's not impossible," said Alice. "They've done some studies about it."

"Ah-hah!" Ford said.

"For Lord's sake don't encourage him," Harper said. "The next thing you know he'll be running around putting bandages on them."

Blackie brandished a new ax. "I'm going to hack and cut. I'm going to lay waste to the woods. I'm going to—savage them." He ran into the pine trees swinging the ax over his head.

"You're not funny," Ford yelled after him.

"Savage them!"

"Use your brain once in a while."

"Savage the whole bunch!"

"Well, I think the idea that other life than we might have feeling is—noble," Alice said.

"Thank you," said Ford.

"But don't tell your constituents, Congressman," Wick smiled. "They might think you're a little loony."

"You shouldn't underestimate the people's ability to embrace new ideas," Ford said.

Wick held up his hands, then grabbed a small set of shears and walked off with Alice into the pines.

Two hours were spent here. Harper put herself in charge of Blackie. He cut down four small trees and Wick helped him drag them beside the cars, where Vic took an ax and skinned the green branches from the trunk. This was the hardest work of the day and everyone was sweating and pulling off their coats and scarves. Harper and Wick and Blackie took turns skinning the trees and the others loaded the branches into the truck and the back of the station wagon. The air was sweet with the smell of pine resin and green needles and a light, cold wind was blowing, turning everyone's face red and the pine needles and brown wood chips and sawdust glistened in their hair and across bare, ruddy arms and their hands were sticky and pungent.

After the work in the pine stand was finished, the family drove farther down the road, stopping to pull down long vines of similax, then moving on to a cornfield and gathering a bundle of bright yellow stalks. At the very end of the cornfield stood seven or eight English oaks. Their trunks were enormous and the gray bark was a riot of knots and lumps and bumps, of holes and fissures and wrinkles. In the canopy of limbs which crowned the trees grew mistletoe. Each tree contained fifteen or twenty balls and the mistletoe was apple green.

Bub and Jebodiah carried the guns upon their shoulders and Harper ordered them to bring her one. This was her favorite part of greening. She was a good shot, having learned her craft as a child on autumn dove hunts with her father. She also liked the shooting because she always knocked down more mistletoe than Blackie, who imagined that he was a good shot, though he wasn't. The trick of knocking down the mistletoe was to hit the green stalk where the plant attached itself into the tree limb. Blackie was not very good at sighting the one green tab, but Harper was. She had good eyesight and she also understood the mistletoe, knowing where it would most likely attach itself to a limb.

Today, Harper was particularly eager to compete with her son. For the last couple of weeks, he had been acting more obnoxious than usual and she was ready to give him a little humility.

"Harper, I hope you told Bub to put fewer pellets in these shells. That bird shot we used last year just wasn't cool. Or at least, I don't think it was cool. We got too much, too easy," Blackie said.

"I got too much, Blackie. All you did was blast mistletoe all over the woods."

"Spoiling for a fight today, aren't you?" Blackie said. He loved baiting her. He knew exactly what he was doing. The way to beat her was much more subtle than just outshooting her, which he could do but he didn't. What he did was to pull his shots and miss and this troubled Harper much more than simply outshooting her. It implied all kinds of things about himself, most of which he was not sure of, but he was sure of the effect: it made Harper brood. Challenging her and then failing, just drove her nuts and it was the real way for him to win. He tucked his shotgun into his shoulder, laid his cheek against the shining wood stock and shot twice quickly. A blur of green leaves and white berries blew from the tree. The left side of his mouth drew into a perplexed dimple. "The sight must be off on this gun."

Harper snapped the gun to her shoulder and shot quickly and two green balls of mistletoe fell neatly to the earth.

"Did you have Bub sight your gun before we came out? You must have."

"Why do you have to blame your failures on someone or something else? You just missed, Blackie. You aimed at the mistletoe and shot and missed and it's that simple."

Blackie broke open the shotgun, which tossed out the two smoking shells. "Give me two more," he said to Bub. He was smiling.

In the next twenty minutes, Blackie fired twenty shots, completely leveling the tops of two oak trees. He got only two balls of mistletoe.

Harper shot five times and got five balls. She was pleased. She enjoyed beating him tremendously. She wondered if it was wrong to feel this way, but Blackie was begging for it. The thought worried her. Blackie's personality invited people to go after him. He was cocky and often insulting and this made you want to compete with him. The problem is he doesn't do well in the competition. Oh, he's very good at provoking you, but once you get in it with him, you beat him easily. That's a terrible way to be, Harper thought. How did he end up like that? Did I do that? How do I teach him the way to win? Oh God.

* * *

An hour later, as the last of twilight turned to dark, the family walked
up the steps to the back porch carrying armfuls of holly, similax, pine,
mistletoe, corn stalks and a box of rich fatwood. Even with Bub and
Jebodiah helping, it took twenty-five minutes to unload. The back porch
was crammed to the ceiling, and over the next few days, the entire
house would come to smell of the evergreens.

Everyone took off their gloves and hung them on the porch and when
they entered the den there was a blazing fire and the sideboard was
holding a baked ham and fresh, homemade bread and homemade mayonnaise and waiting by the sideboard were Tee Tat and Hannah in their
long white aprons. Ford went to the bar and took orders for drinks.
Harper made sure that Hannah had baked an extra ham for herself and
the others and then walked Bub and Tee Tat and the rest outside where
the mules and wagons were waiting.

The air was cold and brilliant black and the mules were biting the
steel bits in their mouths, knowing that they had been kept overtime,
their long ears flat upon their heads and their yellow teeth grinding the
bits.

"Why don't you come in an hour later, tomorrow?" Harper asked.

"No, ma'am, that's okay," Hannah said. "We'll be here on time."

"I really think you should come in later tomorrow. It's been a long
day."

"Nome," Bub said. "We be here plenty early in the morning."

Hannah and Bub were smiling, but they were looking down. Harper
knew what this meant—when they smiled and didn't look at you. They
were mad and she couldn't blame them at all, though sometimes she
wished they would simply stand on their hind legs and tell her so. This
smiling silence had always made her feel dreadful.

Half an hour later everyone was well into their second drink. The
color television was on and Huntley and Brinkley were reading the
news. Alice and Wick sat in two stuffed chairs before the yellow fire.
Wick had popped off his Roman collar and opened several buttons of
his vest. The Scotch made him look at Alice longer and more openly
now and he wanted to reach out and hold her hand. Carol and Cat stood
at the big bay window with Blackie in between them. He was telling
them about a letter he had received the day before from Starkey. Cat's
eyes were completely fixed upon Blackie's face and Carol was watching

her carefully. She had known for some time that Cat was infatuated with Blackie, but today she sensed that he might feel something for her as well. Harper was sitting close to the color television and listening to the news from Vietnam. The Buddhists were causing trouble again, running amok in Saigon. It made her nervous. She had thought that Saigon was the safest place in Vietnam. Ford was sitting in a chair beside her.

"The Buddhists are probably Vietcong," Harper said.

"No, not according to what I've been reading," Ford said.

"Well, why are they causing this ruckus?"

"They're an independent power. Always have been."

"I think they need to be put in their place. They can't be allowed to terrorize the capital city. You tell the President that when you see him. When do you see him?"

"The twenty-second. He wants me to come to the ranch. I've never been there. What's it like?"

23

THE LBJ RANCH SAT in the rolling, brown, dry land of the Texas hill country. The ranch house was a white box with two stories. The only evidence of presidential grandeur was the immense runway which lay behind the house. It was three thousand feet long and equipped with navigation lights and radar. Air Force One landed there with ease. Late in the afternoon, when Ford arrived at the ranch, the President stuck a bourbon and Coke in his hand and pushed him out the door and into a white Lincoln. The President drove eighty-five miles an hour drinking a beer and talking about the Secret Service which was desperately trying to catch up.

"Think we can lose them?" the President asked. "How's that drink? That's the Southerner's drink there, Ford. People talk about bourbon and branch water, but that's bullshit. We like bourbon and Coke. We're just scared to admit it because it sounds unsophisticated. You think we could lose them boys behind us?"

"It probably wouldn't be a good idea."

"Yes, it would. It'd be a damn good idea. I just don't have time tonight. You like to kill things?"

"Sir?"

Johnson's face smiled. The bottoms of his big, brown ears jiggled with the bumpy road. "Deer. I'm talking about deer, Ford. I can't wait for you to see my stand. I just redid the whole thing. Put new paneling in, new pine floors. Hell, even built an elevator. Imagine that—an elevator in a deer stand."

It was much more than a stand. It was a tower—forty feet high with a balcony, sliding glass doors and three large rooms, a bar and color televisions.

When Ford and the President walked into the front room two black servants snapped into view. "Hey boy, get us a drink. I want Cutty Sark on the rocks and this young man will have bourbon and Coke."

"I'd prefer a Scotch."

Johnson looped a great arm around Ford and pulled him close. "I know what you want. There ain't nobody to impress here. I know what all of you want." He snapped his fingers at the older servant. "Roosevelt, get me some of that calamine lotion. My hands are eating me up. Look, here, Ford. Look at what I have to put up with."

The President extended his big hands. Across the back of each was a red rash. The skin was splotched and swollen. Roosevelt handed the President a small bottle. Johnson lathered the brown liquid in his palms and then spread the brown froth over the back of his hands. "Nerves, the doctors say. They're always saying things like that. Hell, I haven't got a nerve in my body." Johnson walked out the glass doors onto the balcony. Below him lay a large soybean field. On four sides around the field stood pine trees. He took a pack of indigestion tablets from his pocket, tossed three into his mouth, chewed and swallowed, then grabbed a plastic inhaler from the same pocket, inserted it into his mouth, relaxed and shot a round down his throat. He shivered.

Ford sipped his appallingly sweet bourbon and Coke and stepped out onto the balcony. The President was rubbing the backs of his hands. He slumped over the railing. He was wearing blue cotton trousers and brown cowboy boots and a white Western-style jacket. Ford set his elbows on the redwood railing and looked down into the green soybean field. It was cold and the darkness was coming.

"You know the ones who get remembered, Ford? Do you know the ones who get the best shake from history? The fellas who win the wars. That's right. The fellas who just beat the shit out of somebody. They're the ones who history deems great. You think about it: Lincoln, Teddy Roosevelt and Franklin Roosevelt, Truman, even ole George Washington himself. Everybody says they were great men, great statesmen. Why do you think that is? 'Cause they were smarter than everybody else or gooder than everybody else? Hell, no. It's 'cause they won the war. They won their war—the one History gave them. Let me ask you something—do you think they would have built that goddamned shrine to Lincoln if he'd lost? Do you?"

Ford looked at Johnson, then stared into the black heart of his sweet drink. There was a quality about Johnson that frightened Ford. He could feel it now. It was something which emanated from him. It gave Ford the feeling that Johnson might do anything and so Ford just stared into his drink and tried not to look frightened, feeling that if he made the wrong move, Johnson might grab him by the throat, or something worse. He looked deeper into the black bourbon and suddenly he felt the dangerous part of Johnson turn off, as if the man had flipped some switch inside himself and the invisible, unsettling field around him immediately dissipated.

There was a quietness as the two men sipped on their drinks and then Ford began to feel angry. Why does he do that, he thought. He's a family friend. He doesn't have to intimidate me and I don't have to endure this behavior. For a moment, Ford felt like engaging Johnson, making him turn back on the danger and then pushing him, saying, All right, go ahead, you want to fight me—let's go, let's fight.

"What do you think about McNamara?" the President asked.

Ford did not answer immediately, by the pause registering his irritation. Then he said, "Smart."

"Rusk."

"Smarter."

" 'Cause he's one of us?"

" 'Cause he's smarter."

Johnson scrambled phlegm deep in his throat, clamped a thumb over one nostril and blew the line of phlegm through the other toward the soybeans. "Everyone else got Europe, you know? They were duking it out with Germany or Italy. That's real war. That's something to crow about. And what do I get—a chicken shit rice paddy. Hell, it ain't a war over there. I don't know what it is. But it ain't a war." The President took out the inhaler and shot it down his throat again. "Westmoreland seems pretty smart."

"Yes, sir. Westmoreland's good."

Below, three cars swished up the pine needle driveway. Eight secret service men jumped out of two cars. Some of them ran toward the tower. From another car two men got out. They wore white Stetsons and moved slowly.

"Starkey's back over there, I guess?"

"We got a call from him last week."

"Getting a lot of that Oriental stuff?"

"I reckon so."

"You let me know if I can do anything for him."

Ford and the President looked toward the set of stairs which led from below. They could feel the Secret Service racing up the steps. Johnson caught Ford by his right elbow and pulled him close. "You know I could have lost those fellas if I had wanted to, don't you?"

"Yes sir, I know."

The Secret Service burst onto the balcony. Several of them went straight inside the glass doors and began a search. The leader of the detail politely and windlessly told the President that he was making life very difficult for the team. The President sighed and smiled and apologized.

The two state senators with the white Stetsons stepped off the elevator and Johnson rushed them and threw his arms around them. The younger of the black waiters wheeled out a small bar and there were drinks all around, except for the Secret Service.

Johnson sipped his new drink, made a face and spit out a mouthful. "Good God almighty. What'd you put in this?" He pointed a finger at the young black man.

"Cutty Sark and water, sir."

"Well, you don't put water in my drink, boy. Do you understand that?"

The young black man said nothing. The older one rushed out to see about the noise.

"Roosevelt, who hired this nigger?"

"I did, Mr. President."

"You did? Well, you better teach him how to make my goddamned drink. What's his name? What's your name, boy?"

"Alfonso," he said in a tiny voice.

"Al-what?"

". . . fonso," he whispered.

Johnson slapped his thigh and stamped his foot and violently hugged one of the state senators. "Ain't that like them. Ain't that just like all of them. They got these names—Roosevelt, Al-fon-zo—all of them got these names so you know what they are just by their names. When's the last time you boys heard one called Chip or Jack or Ted. Tell me, when's the last time?"

The state senators hollered and started a round of jokes.

Ford couldn't bear to look at the young black man's face as Roosevelt helped him wheel the bar back inside. He had never seen Johnson act this way and was so stunned by the President's outburst that he sat and stared, mouth open, face completely without expression. When the President glanced at him, he blinked and composed himself.

An hour later the men sat inside around a wooden table. In the middle of the table lay a rack of barbecued beef ribs. The ribs were eight inches long and the meat was fat on them. The tip end of each rib was white and dry except for the hole which held the black marrow. To the left of the ribs was a bowl containing cole slaw which had been shredded very fine and the shreds of cabbage were green and white with the white sauce of sugar and mayonnaise and sour cream and white vinegar holding the cole slaw together and making it wet and tangy, the white sauce being the secret of it, tasting sweet and sour and cold. There were homemade rolls and hush puppies, brown and crisp on the outside and yellow and moist inside having a hint of onion and sage and black pepper. Three icy pitchers of beer sat beside the rack of ribs.

This was the President's favorite meal. He kept a pitcher of beer for himself beside his plate. He ate handfuls of hush puppies and serving spoon mouthfuls of slaw. When he grabbed a rib, he attacked it and did not pause or set it down until he had cleaned the meat down to the baked, gray bone, cracked open the rib and sucked out the soft marrow. He ate eighteen ribs at this one sitting, and when he had sucked the last one dry, he tossed it down on his plate, gulped several swallows of beer, belched and said:

"I'll tell you something, Ford. You can always tell how a fella's been raised by how he leaves his ribs. If they're like yours—still hanging meat—then you know he was born a rich boy with no worry about food. But if his ribs look like mine, then you know he was born poor and worried about every mouthful so there ain't nothing left but the dry and the cracked. Hell, when I get finished with ribs, even the dogs don't want it."

Everyone laughed, including the Secret Service, who were standing along the walls and out on the balcony. The plates were cleared away and Johnson told some hunting stories and the men drank a couple more pitchers of beer. When someone else started a tale, the President swept a hand through his thin black hair, picked up his pitcher and drank the beer in long swallows. His face was full of fissures and cracks and the soft flesh beneath his eyes was purple. He got up from the table and walked out on the high balcony and passing by a Secret Service agent he lifted the pitcher to him, at the same time raising his face and eyebrows as if to say, "Want some," but the agent shook his head, no.

When the President came back in, he was on tiptoe, his face full of surprise. "They're here," he whispered.

"Naw," said a state senator, his own face flushed with beer. "Can't be. It's too early."

"I saw them," whispered Johnson. "I saw three or four. Roosevelt, get the guns. Get the rifles."

"We can't use rifles. Where are your shotguns?"

"We're using what I say we're using," the President said.

Quickly, the two black servants laid out six .306 Browning rifles on the floor. Each rifle had a black scope. The wooden stocks were shiny and slick and smelled of linseed oil.

Johnson grabbed the arm of a Secret Service agent in charge of the detail. "Jack you gotta take a couple shots."

"It's against regulations, Mr. President."

"Aw, the hell with the regulations. I'm Commander in Chief and I'm giving you an order."

The Secret Service man smiled. "Yes sir."

"Ford, pick you out a gun," Johnson said.

"I don't hunt," Ford said.

"You ain't hunting. You're standing and shooting and I'm tired of everybody bucking me, now pick out a rifle."

A few minutes later the two state senators, the Secret Service agent,

**YOU'RE
INVITED!**

Enjoy a full year of

**GOOD
HOUSEKEEPING**

and

Woman's Day

for only $14.97

**HURRY!
THIS IS A
LIMITED-TIME
OFFER.**

BETTER TOGETHER

GET

GOOD HOUSEKEEPING

and

Woman'sDay

FOR ONLY $14.97

SUBSCRIBE TODAY!

Get BOTH for just **$14.97**

YES! Send me one year of GOOD HOUSEKEEPING and one year of WOMAN'S DAY for a total of just **$14.97** — a combined savings of **80% OFF** the newsstand price.

| 1 year of Good Housekeeping – ~~$47.88~~ | 1 year of Woman's Day – ~~$27.90~~ |

NAME _____
(PLEASE PRINT)

ADDRESS _____ APT. _____

CITY/STATE/ZIP _____

☐ Payment enclosed.   ☐ Bill me.

Ford and the President were standing out on the balcony. There was a cold breeze blowing and the stars were blinking and the breeze picked up a little and hissed through the pine trees which stood around the soybean field.

"Is everybody ready?" Johnson asked.

"We can't see shit out here, Lyndon," a state senator said.

"And He said," Johnson whispered. "And He said in his awesome majesty, Let there be light!"

The President pulled a lever beneath the railing of the balcony and the green soybean field exploded with light, a light so intense, so brilliant and powerful that the deer—twenty-five or thirty of them—the deer with their soft brown eyes and brown skins and white tails, the deer were frozen, completely without movement, only the white breath steaming from their mouths giving any indication that they were real, and then the firing began. The shots ringing out at once, then bolts sliding back, cocking and another fusillade and another and another and the deer falling down two and three at a time, some running, but most not running, only standing in the brilliant lights which completely ringed the field, standing without motion, without fear, their white breath streaming and the guns firing and cocking and firing until there were none left standing, though many writhed in the green field, silently screaming, thrusting horns and hooves into the dirt and blood of their thundering death.

When it was finished, the balcony was thick with blue gunsmoke and the powder so heavy in the air that the men could taste it. They held the hot guns in their arms and looked down into the leafy field where the deer lay, most of them still struggling beneath the imperishable light above.

"Anybody got a knife," someone said.

"Lyndon's got one somewhere."

"We need to git on down there and slit their throats."

Ford had not fired. The smoke of the guns was burning his eyes and he stepped back from the blue bank of smoke and walked around the side of the balcony, where he saw the President hanging halfway from the railing. He was throwing up. There were two agents near him. One of them had a hand on the back of Johnson's belt. The other stood in the shadows holding a small oxygen bottle and a clear mask.

When Johnson finished, he pulled a handkerchief from his back pocket and wiped his mouth and then dropped it. He straightened up and saw Ford and took another handkerchief from his other pocket, and when he opened it, a white powder flew into the air. He wiped his forehead and face.

"My uncle was a gentleman," the President said. "Much more of a gentleman than my daddy and he always said that you should carry two handkerchiefs. One for yourself and one for a lady. The one for the lady should always be doused with a little talcum powder, just a little biddy bit of sweetness. At least I've managed to do that." He dabbed at a few drops of sweat and looked at Ford.

"Is it over?"

"Yes sir."

"Did they kill all of them?"

"I think they did. Somebody said they need a knife."

"God damn," the President said. "God damn, Ford."

The President stood up and motioned for the agent standing in the shadows. He came forward and Johnson put the plastic mask over his nose and mouth and the agent turned a valve and the President breathed.

Two hours later the deer and the state senators were gone and Johnson was lying on a bed in his room and Ford sitting in a chair near him. Roosevelt came into the room carrying a small tray which held a glass of water and two red and black capsules. The President took the two pills and swallowed some water.

"Mr. President, I just want to apologize for Alfonso. His mama's been real sick. She been in the hospital two months now and that boy's been running back and forth trying to work and trying to see to her and he's bone tired."

"What's she sick with?"

"Something with her heart."

"Where's my calamine lotion?"

Roosevelt pulled the bottle from his pocket and handed it to the President and he began rubbing it into his hands. "First thing tomorrow morning I want you to call the hospital and find out what her bill is. Make sure you get everything now. Don't do a half-assed job. Get her food and her surgeon and her prescription bill—get all of it and call

Dick Jones and tell him the amount. I want to sign the check in two days. Now where's this boy living now? Is he at the ranch?"

"Yes sir, he's at the Hiccam place."

"The Hiccam place? Good God, nobody can live in that pig sty. Is he married?"

"Got two little babies, too."

"Who in the world put him in the Hiccam place?"

"Miss Lady Bird. She says it was empty and needs to be full."

Johnson glanced at Ford. "Ole Bird would squeeze blood out of a turnip." He reached into his pocket and took a hit from the inhaler.

"What committee you want to be on?"

"Oh—well, I'd love to be on the Foreign Relations Committee."

"Uh-huh. I bet you would." Johnson turned back to Roosevelt. "Fix it up. I want a new roof, new floor and new furniture. I want that place to be a nigger Taj Mahal. And lots of shag carpet—and a stereo set too, you put a stereo set, a big one in there."

"Mr. President, it's mighty kind of you, but that's the fourth colored house you fixed up this year now."

Johnson dropped his eyes to the floor and said, very quietly, "I wish there was a million of them, Roosevelt. I wish there was a goddamn million."

The President decided to spend the night in the tower and asked Ford to stay with him. The two men shared the same room. An hour after he had taken his sleeping pills, he was still awake, still fidgety. He wore blue silk pajamas with the presidential seal on the left pocket. Beneath the reading lamp over his bed, his black hair was shining and the rash on the backs of his hands was red. He had turned on everything in the room which was electric and emitted either light or sound or heat. His electric blanket worked at full capacity, two televisions, a radio, a tape recorder and a small weather radio yammered and crackled and hissed news and information, while he thumbed through handfuls of reports from the CIA and the Joint Chiefs, still munching digestive pills and taking a blast of his inhaler or tilting back his head for a spattering of eyedrops.

"How many men do you think it'd take to win?" Johnson asked.

It was two-thirty in the morning and Ford was fighting sleep. "Sir?"

"In Vietnam. How many men do you think we'd need to beat them?"

"I have no idea."

"Why the hell not? You want to be on the Foreign Relations Committee, don't you?"

"I haven't read any reports."

"Aw, who needs reports. Reports just confuse the issue—which is very simple: we must win. You can read all the reports in the world, but if you don't know it in your gut, there's no amount of information that can help. Now how many men?"

"Fifty thousand."

"McNamara says a hundred thousand for two years and we got it."

"I think a hundred thousand United States soldiers can do anything in the world."

Johnson whooped and pounded the bed. "Do you really?"

"I do."

"So do I. That's exactly what I think. Except they got to be Marines. I think a hundred thousand Marines can do anything in the world, don't you? I mean just think about it—a hundred thousand of my boys over there. Why there's nobody that could stop them, nobody on the face of this earth. But there has to be provocation. They have to go after us. We can't just send my boys in there. We need a reason. A sense of righteousness. Yeah, righteous indignation. That's what we need. Righteousness." With one switch, Johnson cut off everything in the room— all lights, radios and televisions though he kept talking about the boys and what they could do and why were certain people worried when the solution was so simple. He would mumble and doze, rouse and shuffle papers, and then say into the darkness around him, "Ford? Ford? You still here?"

"Yes, sir. I'm here."

And Johnson would slip away again, giving orders, laughing over some dreaming scheme, gliding briefly into a sonorous snore, only to rise and say, "Ford! You still here, aren't you?"

"Go to sleep, Mr. President," Ford said, completely awake and sitting on the edge of his bed. "I'm here. I'm not going anyplace. Go to sleep now."

For the rest of the night, Ford sat up in bed and watched the twitches and mumbles and contortions of Lyndon Johnson. For some reason, he felt protective of the man. He felt that he needed to stay near him and not to sleep himself so that he could reassure this incredibly troubled human being. He marveled at himself. Earlier, Johnson had frightened him, made him want to run and hide like a child, and then he wanted to beat him, fight him, prove to him that he was a man. Now, as he sat by his bed and answered again—"Yes sir, I'm here. It's four-fifteen about, everything's fine"—now he felt that he must not let anything harm Lyndon Johnson, that he must make the night comfortable and safe for him.

How is he able to do it, Ford wondered. How in the world is he able to bring out all these different emotions in me. And if he can do it with me, he obviously can do it with others. How incredible. He's a conjurer. He can summon up any feeling in you he wants. Ford slipped into a gloom. It was the mark of a great leader, no doubt—the ability to conjure. I can't do it, Ford mumbled to himself. I can't even get close to doing it. I'll never amount to anything, never.

24

IT WAS RAINING. CAT was sitting in Blackie's jeep and he was driving. When Blackie had told Cat exactly what his adventures entailed, she was crushed, then angry, then sad and finally determined—no matter what—to go. She felt miserable.

"You're sure they won't come back early?" Cat asked. Blackie had smeared her face and hands with black greasepaint. She wore Carol's black jumpsuit.

"No, I'm not sure, but I know that they usually stay out late on Fridays."

"What do we do if they come home early?" Cat asked.

"We run," Blackie said.

The Bosworths' house was only twenty miles from Waverly. It was the closest burglary that Blackie had ever tried. He had known that Mrs. Bosworth possessed one of the finest collections of diamonds in the state, but he had never attempted her house because of its proximity to his own. There was another reason, too: Mrs. Bosworth had been his Sunday school teacher for five years at the First Presbyterian Church.

"I got seventeen gold stars one year," Blackie said.

"What does that mean?"

"Well, you get a star every time you come to Sunday school. For the first third of the year you get bronze stars, the next third silver and the final third gold. Only two or three other people have gotten as many gold stars as I did."

Cat was flabbergasted. "Well, I think this is completely scurrilous. Breaking into the house of your Sunday school teacher. It's awful."

"Nah, it's okay," Blackie said. "You see, Mr. and Mrs. Bosworth are not such nice people. If you make a mistake in either one of their classes you get paddled. Let's say you didn't learn the books of the Old Testament—you couldn't repeat them. Mrs. Bosworth took you to see Mr. Bosworth and he paddled you hard while his wife took a picture."

"Mrs. Bosworth was taking pictures of it?"

"Yeah, she took a lot of pictures of a lot of children. Harper got word of it and had the sheriff pay her a visit. They had a room plastered with pictures of kids being paddled. There were other pictures, too. Really nasty. Kids in bed with kids. Stuff like that."

"Sunday school teachers?" Cat said. "I can't believe Sunday school teachers would do those kinds of things."

"Believe it."

Cat was not quite sure she did believe it, and even if she did, she did not think it made housebreaking any more moral. The two of them were standing outside the Bosworths' house. Cat had pinned her blond hair into a bun. Blackie wore greasepaint and a black pullover hat. He held his satchel of tools. Around his waist was a belt holding still other implements. The Bosworth place was a new, ranch-style house. Blackie had learned some years ago that they kept the diamonds in a solarium. Mr. Bosworth was a biology teacher. The solarium was full of his collection of wild flowers and shrubs.

"Just do what I tell you," Blackie said. "Take small steps. Keep your hands close to your body."

"I still don't think this is right."

"I know you don't. Now come on."

Cat followed him along the side of the house behind some boxwoods.

He stopped at a small window and pushed and nothing happened. He looked at the window a moment, then picked up his satchel and moved to another window about the same size. He pushed again and this time it opened. Quickly, he slid inside and then helped Cat.

At first Cat followed him closely. She stuck a hand into one of his back pockets and let him pull her along.

At the other end of the den there was a door. Blackie took a long, flat piece of metal and ran it along the inside of the door jamb.

"It's okay."

"What'd you do?"

"Good place for an alarm."

Gently, he turned the handle. The door opened and they stepped into a dark room. The air felt wet and heavy and warm. Blackie closed the door and switched on a flashlight.

The tunnel of light lit a brick floor and just beyond it four large philodendra, their brown stems three inches thick and the long green leaves shimmering. Behind the philodendra sat two witch hazel plants in large clay pots. They were four feet high and their yellow flowers were blooming. There were over a hundred plants here: the yellow blooms of evening primrose and purple meadow beauties and the shy, white faces of mountain silverbells and teaberry and wild geraniums.

Every step Cat took into the moist dark brought another sweetness: one was the heavy and deep perfume of rhododendron, another light and quick like the smell of flowering strawberry, and yet another so heavy that Cat could feel the yellow pollen of tea olive settling on her face.

She touched Blackie. "Why would they keep the safe in here?"

"Hard to find."

"Do you know where it is?"

"Second dwarf magnolia to the left of the cutleaf toothwort."

"Are you serious?"

"Follow me."

Silently they moved between the shelves and tables and bleachers of plants and woody shrubs and clumps and clusters of wild flowers and still they had not heard them, of course had not seen them.

As soon as the door had been opened, the amber eyes sensed the humans. The light hurt. It made their vertical pupils collapse, fall into the fierceness of their dry pits. They had not been fed in a month and so now in their hour, in the black night which was their day, they scoured the cool brick floors. They stole between the clay pots and tried to climb the bigger trees looking for food. And if they could think, perhaps they might be thinking:

"Why here? Why do you come here? In this huge structure, this mountain you call a house. You could have gone anywhere and you come to us. We who are hungry. We who wait. Why?"

Blackie brushed against a pot and knocked it to the floor. To the humans the sound was not so bad, a dull plop as the pot splashed dirt upon the floor. But to them, it was a shock, almost electric, something which caused them first to retreat, to streak toward deepest dark. Then because of hunger, because the sound could be something to ease the pain of their long bellies, they moved forward. Both of them. Easing toward the sound which had stung them.

"I thought you were a cat burglar," Cat said.

"I am a cat burglar."

"I think you're a moose burglar."

Cat reached down and scooped up the red fragments of the pot.

It sensed the heat. Another time, in some other place it would have fled, but not now. Not so hungry. Not at night.

"Just leave it," Blackie said.

"They'll know somebody's been here."

"Cat, we're robbing the place, remember?"

It was when she straightened up that Cat heard it. At first she thought it was Blackie fiddling with something in his belt, making a kind of burr, a rattle.

"Be still," he whispered.

"What is it?"

"Snake."

"Don't tease me."

"Hush."

Blackie had not heard one in a long time. He was shocked that the Bosworths used them. Usually only wily gas station owners set them loose in their stores at night. Or redneck pharmacists who sold mostly SSS Tonic and Geritol, or dime store proprietors who specialized in leather belts stamped with the wearer's name. Only these country people set rattlesnakes loose in their businesses at night—or so he had thought.

The burring was a low pitch. It meant the snake was a good distance away.

For the first time tonight Cat was scared. She had caught snakes as a kid, but only garters and kings and chicken snakes. She had seen a rattlesnake only once. She remembered that day now. It was eight feet long, its dry hide decorated in large black diamonds and the jaws were open as it shoveled and crammed the black-eyed rabbit into its gut and she remembered how the snake's jaws worked: side to side, showing pink wet gums and blue mouth tissue and the wild, liquid black eyes of the rabbit bulging.

"I'm moving back to you," Blackie said.

"Be careful."

"You hear it rattling?"

"I hear it."

"If it gets faster, real fast, it means he's close. It means he's real close."

Blackie did not turn, but rather moved backward. He looked over his shoulder, shining the light before he stepped. Only bricks were below him. Bricks and a few brown leaves, traces of soil. He moved smoothly.

Suddenly the burring increased. Higher pitch. He stopped. It was behind him. It was near Cat.

"Blackie?"

"Just don't do anything."

"Did you bring a gun?"

"Use the light."

"The light?"

"Shine the light into its eyes. They get stunned, paralyzed."

Carefully, Blackie handed the flashlight over his shoulder.

Cat could feel the sweat on his hand and just when she grasped the flashlight's handle the beam hit her eyes. She grabbed, missed. The light crashed below.

The rattling was frenzied.

"Blackie," Cat yelled.

"Don't reach."

"We got to have it."

"Don't reach, goddamnit. Don't move."

It went on for a while, the frantic burring.

Suddenly, it stopped. Not a sound. Black silence.

The light had fallen into a pot. Its harsh, yellow beam illumined a small sign—SNAKEROOT.

"You wouldn't believe where the light landed," Cat said.

"Don't squat down. Just bend and use your arm."

She did as he directed, keeping her legs straight, bending with her back, extending her arm, her hand—frail and white—extending into the dark. She got the light and clasped it to her chest.

"You okay?"

Cat felt her heart beating through her breastbone, knocking against the flashlight.

"Hey."

"Just tell me what to do."

"Look for it."

"What?"

"You have to. It's close. Aim the light at your feet and slowly work it forward. Hit it in the eyes."

"How do I know when I've got the eyes?"

"They'll glitter."

"Oh wonderful."

Cat aimed the light at her feet and moved the beam back and forth horizontally. Brown bricks and the old mortar in between them, dried leaves, pink petals and red petals and the lumpy yellow heart of a daisy and beyond this a gray shell—it moved.

She brought the light back to the dirty white shell and saw a vibration and then the burring started. She stepped to her left to see around the pot and the beam glittered along the gleaming body of the snake. It was three feet away, but moving toward her, gliding behind the pots and trays of boxwood and jasmine.

"I got it."

"Where?"

"Right up front. Right there."

"You got its eyes?"

"Can't find them. It's moving."

"Hit it in the eyes. Hit it."

Cat flicked the flashlight along the thick body, saw the muscles contract and release and then as the snake slid between two pots she saw the big, triangular head: it glistened and the head seemed golden, as if dipped in gold, flashing and angular and the split tongue black and then the head disappeared behind the long trays of plants closest to her. The rattling was electric.

"Is it paralyzed?"

"No."

"Do it."

"I can't."

The snake had completely disappeared and Cat was throwing the light everywhere before her. Then she saw it, a foot away. It was moving fast, right toward her. She shot the light low and suddenly two piercing lights radiated. The burring stopped.

"You got him?"

Cat looked at the bright eyes. The fat triangle of head poised six inches off the floor and the tip of the split black tongue lay flat against the golden snout.

"Cat?"

"He's . . . here."

Blackie made his way to her, gently held her hands which held the flashlight.

"He's huge," Cat said. Her stomach had shriveled.

"Seven foot at least."

"What do we do now?"

"Keep the light on him. Ease back out of here. Let me hold it."

Blackie took the light. The rattlesnake was perfectly paralyzed, only the black diamonds on the brown back rose and fell in slow breathing. Somehow the long jaw had cracked, revealing an inch of mouth tissue and the faint, sharp glitter of a fang webbed in pink membrane.

Slowly Blackie stepped backward, pushing the girl behind him. He kept the light on the reptile's triangular head and the open jaws. Cat bumped into the door and there was the rattling, the burring—immediately over them. She screamed. Blackie spun around and saw the other snake spring from the vines above the door. He blocked his face, felt the heavy, cool body hit his head and slap his back and then the stab into his neck, he screamed, threw it to the floor.

Cat pulled him into the hall, the light, slammed the door. The wound was bleeding just under his ear.

"Oh no," she said.

"Is it bad?"

"It's bleeding."

"We got to go straight to the hospital." Blackie grabbed a handkerchief from his back pocket, clamped it over the snakebite. He was fairly calm, but even now he was seeing things—flashes and black spots.

25

IN THE EMERGENCY ROOM, Blackie's neck was bloated and blue and black. One black vein distended and bulged all the way to his temple. Cat was holding his hand. It was cold and heavy and his blue eyes were half veiled with puffy lids.

"Sorry things got so messed up," Blackie said.

"Shush. Don't talk," Cat said.

"You're pretty cool, you know. You dealt with them snakes pretty cool."

Cat could barely look at him. Even his face was turning black.

Two orderlies swept Blackie through wooden doors and out of Cat's sight. When they took him away, she felt as if they had taken her breath. She couldn't breathe at all and made herself sit down.

He was wheeled into a small room and put under a great light. A nurse grabbed a pair of scissors and cut off his pants. There were three or four people around him, but he was not able to distinguish features. His throat was full of mucous and his eyes were swollen almost completely shut. He could hear himself breathing and feel his heart beating and with every beat it felt as though it was becoming bigger and rounder and more full of blood and for the first time in his life Blackie wondered if he was going to die.

Is this it, he thought. Is this the way I'm going? He tried to open his eyes, to see the people who were shouting orders and sticking him with things, but he couldn't. But he did feel his body—doing something, or perhaps not doing something. He wanted to yell to the people working on him, "Hey! Be quiet! Something's happening to me more than you think. Things are shutting off or cutting on. Be quiet! Leave me alone. Let me see what this is." And having said that, he felt as if the cells of his body, the tiny, invisible blocks which composed him, were snapping off the lights, each cell going from the brightness of a star to the darkness of an empty bulb and the last thing Blackie heard was, "Get the paddles."

"Should we hit him with more antivenin?"

"Stand clear. Just stand clear. Ready? Hit it."

Blackie felt the rush of something cold, something that made him stiff, and he could see the nurses and doctors again and hear his own ragged, thick, raucous breath and then suddenly they were gone again and he felt as if he were floating in a warm pool. Never had he felt so warm and safe and surrounded as now. In an instant he stood before a grid of light. A voice said, "Do you know where you are?"

He felt as if he knew the voice, though he knew he did not.

"You've had all kinds of questions about things."

"Well . . . yeah . . . sorta."

"Suffering?"

It felt easy to talk to the voice. "Yeah, why everyone goes through such misery in the world. My brothers think I never consider things like that, but I always have. I always knew we had it better than everybody and then I'd see some kid who was crippled and poor in the first place have something ghastly happen to him and I would wonder why is he having to go through this? He didn't have a chance in the first place and now this is happening to him. It's just not fair or at least it doesn't seem fair to me."

"Look down to your left."

Blackie was still standing before the grid of light and it was not so comfortable standing before it. The transition which directed him to the light was wonderful, but having to face the light itself felt neither bad nor good and if there was a feeling at all it was that the light shone through him completely and had knowledge of him completely and maybe there was one other feeling—awe. Absolute and complete awe at the vastness of the light.

"Are you looking down there?"

"Yep."

Blackie saw the earth. The beautiful blue, soft blue earth with brown continents and orange deserts and as he looked more deeply at the earth he saw an image of a book and then thousands of pages turning, millions of pages turning, a light yellow blaze of pages flipping through the image of the earth and suddenly he knew how everything connected, why good things and terrible things and mediocre things happened: he saw—communion, and all of his questions, his worries, his fears had no meaning. And the knowledge that he was given was a peculiar kind of knowledge. It did not answer his questions, but rather made the questions insignificant because the communion was so complete and profound and good that the questions dissolved before the vast, living beauty of it.

"I see it!" Blackie shouted at the light. "I see it all. It's incredible. I see how it all works, how everything, every little tiny thing works."

"Now there's something else," the voice said.

"I don't need anything else."

"Nevertheless, there is something else: I feel your pain."

"Well, that's not such a startling idea," Blackie thought, and in thinking it he knew that the voice understood what he was thinking, but still it seemed one thing to think and quite another to say.

"Now, so that you will know that I feel your pain, something is going to happen. In just a second the doctor is going to slip with a scalpel and you're going to hurt."

"Oh, that's okay. I really don't need to know anything else. I'm fine. I've got a whole head full of things."

And suddenly Blackie was away from the light and down in his body, lying on the operating table, and he felt as if lying beside him, close beside him, as close as a lover, was someone else. There was a pain in his jaw and he jumped and as he did he felt whatever was lying beside him recoil with his own pain. He felt his pain pass from his body and knock hard whatever was beside him and he sensed that the pain did not stop there but went on and on, reverberating into the universe, far out into black space toward the swirling, rippled light of the stars.

And then he was before the light again. "You felt it!" he shouted. "You felt my pain. I felt you feel it. It's amazing. It's true. You really do feel our pain."

"There's one thing you need to remember more than anything else. We are one. Everything is one. You and I and the earth and everything that has existence is one. Can you remember it?"

"No problem, no problem. I mean—it's true. I felt it."

"When you tell people about this—experience—you can say that it was the drugs they gave you while you were on the table. Or it was an hallucination or maybe hypoxia. Or you can tell them that maybe it was a vision. Let them make their own choice. They'll probably accept the drug theory. Everyone believes in drugs. But whatever you say just remember we are one. Everything is one."

"I will, I'll say that to whoever I tell. I'll—"

But before Blackie could say anything more he began to descend, to fall away from the light and as he saw it pull away from him he heard another voice, one very similar to the voice he was talking to.

"Well, how did it go?" the new voice asked.

"Okay, I guess," said the old.

"Did you tell him about things?"

"Well, I tried, but—you know their brains are so pitifully small."

And the last thing Blackie heard before he returned to the operating table was a deep, long and somehow physically cool—sigh.

Cat called Harper and she got to the hospital in twenty minutes and demanded to know the name of the doctor who was attending Blackie and when she found out he was not the best she caused a ruckus until a more suitable doctor was produced. In forty-five minutes both doctors came out to report. They were quiet and grave and said that Blackie was at a crisis point. They said that they had used the paddles eight times.

"What does that mean?" Harper asked. "What are the paddles?"

"Defibrillators," said one doctor.

"His heart stopped," said the other.

Cat reached out and held Harper's hand.

"It stopped?" Harper asked.

"Eight separate times, I'm afraid he has some very bad burns on his chest, but we're not worried about them right now. His heart is still not stable, but we're hoping to get it stable."

Harper pulled the collar of her red cashmere coat tightly about her neck. Her black hair was a mess of tangled curls and behind her ear there was still one pink roller which she had missed. She had put on no makeup and her face was smooth and white and cold. Her pink birthmark was showing. "Is he about to die?" she asked.

"He's very critical," the tall doctor said.

"Does that mean he's about to die?" Harper asked.

"It means he could, yes ma'am."

"How long?"

"Beg pardon?"

"How long will it be before we know if he's going to get better or not?"

"I think if he can make it through the next two hours he's got a real good chance."

Blackie lived and three days later returned to Waverly afraid to tell anyone about his vision.

Harper allowed him another two days of recuperation and then early one morning went into his room to ask him how he had come to be bitten by a rattlesnake in the dead of winter.

Blackie's neck was still swollen. A purple bruise spread from under the bandage. He had lost weight. When Harper asked him how it had happened, he told her straight and without hesitation.

"I was breaking into a house."

Harper, who was a master at masking emotion, sat down on his bed and asked him to explain and Blackie told her that he had broken into a number of houses and that he did it for fun and also because in a way he wanted to get caught because if he did he knew it would hurt and embarrass her, and that he was sick and tired of her running his life, trying to make him and all of his brothers into her image.

She straightened some wrinkles in his bedcovers and looked at him and said, "How did we end up like this?"

She left him in his room and went to her own and cried. She stayed there a good two hours wondering what she had done to turn him against her so. I know I'm bossy, she thought. I give everyone too many orders and I meddle in everyone's life and I try to make all of them excell, but I did it so that they would be good men, competent men, men who would amount to something, but maybe I was wrong. Dreadfully, dreadfully wrong.

For three or four days, Harper was depressed. She had her dinner alone, spoke to no one, tried to see no one, certainly not Blackie because the terrible truth was that Blackie was her favorite. This difficult, rebellious boy had always been her favorite of all of them and the thought that he hated her cut straight into her heart.

On the fourth day, she began to recover. She began thinking about the break in and if there was any way that the Bosworths might be able to trace it. She went to a trusted lawyer and told him to talk to the doctors and all who treated Blackie to make sure that they would keep quiet. She tried to cover his tracks as best she could and then she tried to turn her grief into anger. It was her old trick for surviving. Better to be mad than sad.

Okay, you little bastard. I've been meddling in your life, have I? Well, fine. Do what you want. I will never again give you advice or direction, and I will never again cover for your mistakes. Oh and by the way—she looked into her dressing mirror, putting on the makeup that she had not worn for five days—I am right to help your brothers. They need me. They need my advice and they need my direction and they have prospered from it all their lives. Maybe I was too hard on you, but I was not and I am not too hard on them and I will never let go of them just to please you. Never, ever and that's the end of it.

During her depression, Harper had not followed her daily schedule of exercise, translation and guitar and so she returned to it frantically. The first few days she read nearly a page of Empedocles and five pages of Livy, whom she hated, walking three miles a day instead of one and forcing herself to learn an entire Bach étude.

Having to deal with three sons instead of four seemed to focus her will and attention. In the evening, she started writing a letter a day, sometimes two to Starkey, asking if he was well, how was the morale of the troops, was he trying to move forward and that she had heard that his friend Robert Curtis had just made Major at thirty years of age. She began calling Ford once a day to make sure that he was working on getting direct access to the President and that the best way to do this was to involve himself in speech writing and she called and set him up an appointment with Bill Moyers. She wrote chatty little notes to Alice

Grooms, and finding out that Wick was scheduled to go back to the monastery for a retreat, she told Alice that she thought it would be a nice surprise if she went to pick him up and had a bit of champagne waiting.

And in the midst of this new burst of manipulation and advice and concern and relentless ambition, her mind returned to Blackie and she thought, Don't you see, if I don't do this, if I don't take charge of everything and everyone, it will all collapse, everything will start to run down and decay and then it will all just dissolve the way it did with Daddy. Sure, after the war he had a hard time, it was difficult, I know that, but the point is he was given everything—education, good looks, wit, intellect and land and a great house and businesses and he lost almost all of it, he squandered his birthright because he wasn't diligent, he was not diligent. He just smiled and hunted and dreamed of the way things were and he lost almost everything. Can't you see that, Blackie? Can't any of you see that? You must never let go of things. You must never cease to be diligent because if you do, there will be chaos. Horrible, horrible chaos and you will lose yourself, you will lose yourself, forever.

26

WICK SLIPPED INTO THE late after-
noon dimness of the chapel of the Monastery of Peace. As soon as he
walked through the doors, he stopped and let the chapel surround him.
It smelled of floor wax and damp stone and beeswax candles and, on top
of everything, the sharp, thrilling, spicy aroma of incense. The dark
granite floors were polished and the gray granite walls were shined. He
looked at the firwood ceiling. He had always thought that the ceiling,
more than the altar, was the heart of the chapel. The brown firwood
planks looked so out of place above all the cold granite. The ceiling
seemed so warm and vulnerable and he wondered now as he had so
many times before, Was this really the way God was? Somehow always
oddly out of place—even in the Church. Somehow soft and warm and
more vulnerable than anyone knew?

He genuflected and then went to one of the two or three rickety
wooden chairs sitting beside the pillars which supported the vault of the
ceiling. The wooden chairs made him smile. They, too, seemed out of

place in the severe grandeur of the chapel. The monks brought them here so they could sit in the shadows and fix their eyes on the altar and the sacrament and pray. Wick sat in the chair and looked at the golden tabernacle and said, "Please help this to be a good retreat. Please help me to know what to do about Alice. I know I should stop seeing her. I know it." And then he forced himself to quit before he got in too deeply too early and said, "Thank you for taking care of Blackie, for not letting him die, and thanks for Cat—she's working out fine and a real addition, and please look out for Starkey in Vietnam and Ford in Washington and help Harper and Blackie to mend their fences." Then he pressed his thumbs to his forehead and squeezed his eyes shut tightly, as if this would make his prayers go higher, saying, "Please, please, please give me the wisdom and courage to do what is right."

Wick left the chapel, grabbed his suitcase and went to his guest room. Sometimes when monks returned to the monastery they were allowed to stay in one of the cells of the dormitory, but Wick had decided not to put anyone to the test. He had booked himself a room like any other visitor. Other than the guest master—an ancient monk whom he had never really liked—he had seen none of his brothers. He washed his face and hands and walked down through the guest house and out into the yard of the monastery toward the greenhouses.

It was four-thirty and he knew Brother Alered would just be finishing up his work. As he drew near the greenhouse, he began to feel more and more guilty. Not because of Alice, but because he felt that he had somehow failed Brother Alered, failed all of his brothers. He had written Alered only occasionally and had not written any of the others, except Brother Pat, whom he had sent a postcard to. But beyond not writing to them, he felt guilty because he had left them. The ones he had prayed for every day and eaten with and worked with every day for six years—he had left them and given them little thought.

Am I that cold, he wondered. Am I that callous? Maybe that's the whole problem with Alice. If I really loved her I would either end this affair right now, this very instant, or I would leave the priesthood and marry her. Maybe I just can't love. That's it. I just don't have the capacity for loving.

Feeling depressed, he opened a wooden gate and walked into a side yard. The two greenhouses were made of white brick and glass. At the entrance to the nearest one, he paused feeling horribly shy and guilty. He hardened himself and entered.

The sun was flooding through the glass roof. The air inside was warm and rich and wet. This building housed Brother Alered's bonsai collection. There were three hundred trees, many of them over a hundred years old. There were tiny maple trees only nine inches high and miniature boxwoods and small cedar trees whose tiny needles were a shiny blue, the branches even bearing the smallest and most delicate of brown pine cones. Each tree sat in a clay pot or tray which was less than a foot square.

Wick saw the old man sitting behind a worktable at the far end of the greenhouse. On top of the worktable was a cluster of shelves on which sat twenty or thirty bonsai. Wick took a few steps forward and just watched him for a while, feeling his heart beat very quickly, feeling his eyes straining to catch every nuance and gesture of the old monk. He wished he did not have to speak at all. He wished he could just stand and watch and greedily absorb everything about Alered, because Wick knew that the old man was a saint and he knew that one day fairly soon he would be dead and he wanted as many memories of him as he could store.

Brother Alered sat on a wooden stool. He wore the black cowl and white surplice and worn leather belt of the Trappist order. He was carefully clipping a green boxwood, his bald head red and his glasses a bit cloudy with the humidity of the room.

"Brother Alered?" Wick said softly.

The old monk continued clipping.

"Brother Alered, it's Nicodemus."

The old man turned and squinted. He smiled and his rack of yellow false teeth suddenly shot halfway from his mouth. He plugged them back in with a big, dirty thumb and said, "Nicky," and opened his arms and Wick went over and hugged him and the old man didn't let go for a while.

Wick pulled up a stool and talked unstintingly. He talked about his first job with LeConte and how he had put together the shopping center, then chattered about his new post with the bishop and that the work in the Chancellory Office was hard but he loved meeting all the different priests of the Diocese and loved working on all the problems they brought him. Wick talked for twenty minutes straight and then finally

allowed the old man to speak. Alered told him that the abbot was as
difficult as ever and that Brother Bonaventure had left the monastery,
after having been a monk for forty years, because he no longer believed
in the reality of the Eucharist.

"How old is Bonaventure?" Wick asked.

"Eighty-three."

"Eighty-three?"

Alered clucked his tongue and pulled off his glasses and rubbed his
long, bumpy and slightly purple nose that was straight out of Dostoyev-
sky.

"We're worried about him."

"Where did he go?"

"Haiti. Yep, he went down to Haiti to build houses for the poor.
There're some Maryknolls down there who're supposed to look after
him."

Wick blew out some air, making a half whistle noise, and scratched
an eyebrow. He glanced at the old man's eyes, looked at them deeply
for the first time today. The monk's eyes always surprised him for they
were not the big, round eyes of an innocent, nor the dark eyes of a
mystic—they were worldly eyes, even the eyes of a sensualist, or one
who had once been a sensualist. They were green and slow and cold and
half hooded by sallow lids which had forgotten long ago how to be
surprised or ecstatic.

Alered smiled, but he did not let the boy see it. He missed the boy a
lot and it hurt him to see that all the insecurities in Wick had only
become stronger, more pronounced. Not that they weren't evident when
he was here, he thought, because they were. But so much less could
happen to him here. He was protected here, not so much from the world
as from himself. Why doesn't he realize what a wonderful person he is?
He's bright, he's funny, he's attractive and caring and enthusiastic
about everything he undertakes. Why can't he see that such people are
so rare and so valuable. Why can't he see himself?

"The bishop says I've got a shot at being chancellor," Wick finally
said.

"For the Diocese?"

"Yes."

"It's a very difficult job. Everyone will come to you with their com-
plaints. In some ways it's a harder job than being bishop."

"I really want it. Do you think that's wrong? To want to be chancellor?"

"Why do you want it?"

"Oh, I can tell you think it's wrong. I can tell by the way you're asking."

"Don't try to read my mind. Why do you want to be chancellor?"

"Well, to be straightforward—chancellor is one step below bishop and that's what I'm really after. I'm not going to lie to you, Padre. I want to be bishop more than anything."

"Like you wanted to be abbot here?"

"I still don't think I wanted to be abbot. Maybe you're right, but I don't think so."

A bell tolled the end of the last work period of the day.

"You're going to eat in the refectory, aren't you?" Alered asked.

The refectory was the last place Wick wanted to go. Everyone would see him there. After supper they would all come up and speak to him and it would make him feel awful because he felt as if he had betrayed them.

"Sure, I'll go."

"Good. A lot of the fellas have been asking about you."

The refectory was a long room with twelve tall windows which overlooked the green pasture and gray barns of the monastery. Eight stone beams supported the ceiling and on each beam was carved a line of scripture: MAN DOES NOT LIVE BY BREAD ALONE, or TASTE AND SEE HOW GOOD THE LORD IS, and others. In the center of the room sat three rows of long wooden tables. Beside the tables were backless benches. Once a monk was given his place at a table, he stayed there until he either died or left the monastery. At each place setting was a tin plate, bowl, spoon and metal cup.

When the supper bell rang, Wick and Alered filed into the refectory with the others. Almost everyone wore the black cowl though some of the men wore their work clothes—blue cotton trousers and light blue shirts and brown work boots. The work clothes had been introduced in 1963 as part of Vatican Two. Before 1963 the monks had worked in the fields and dairy and bakery wearing their long blue robes with the heavy hoods pulled over their heads. Each monk stood by his place. The abbot said a prayer and they sat down. Young novices wearing white cowls soundlessly delivered the evening meal. They carried steaming buckets and ladled the carrot and potato stew onto the plates or into bowls. Another three or four gave each man two slices of brown bread and the last set of novices poured the water. Wick was fasting and so accepted only the water. At a lectern in the corner of the room, a monk started reading a chapter from *The Imitation of Christ.* No speaking was allowed during supper.

On either side of Wick sat Brother Matthew and Brother John. Matthew was bald and wore a huge plastic hearing aid. He bathed only once or twice a year, usually Christmas and Easter. He was a cold man whom Wick had never liked and he gave no indication that he had seen Wick. Brother John was completely different. He had a head of white hair and blue eyes and tiny hands covered with blue liver spots. As soon as everyone sat down, he reached over and pinched Wick's cheek, saying in Trappist sign language: I miss you, Brother. You look good. I miss you very much. Wick signaled back that he missed him, too. The two brothers on either side of Alered signaled Hello and Thank goodness you're back and we need you to cook and you look big and fat and that is good.

Wick answered them in the simple Trappist sign language which he had picked up easily here. When their signing had stopped, Alered flashed him a simple one—Not so bad, huh?

After supper, in the small garden which separated the chapel from the refectory, over thirty of the monks crowded around Wick. Because the rule of the Trappists stated that there was to be no speaking during the Great Silence, which ran from five-thirty in the evening until four-thirty in the morning, not one monk said a word by mouth. But all of them said many words through sign language and touches and embraces and big smiles so that as Wick stood in the garden completely surrounded by his brothers the only sound was that of sandals sliding over the grass or the rustle of cowls or an occasional wheeze of delight or sigh of longing. Wick signaled how much he missed them too and yes I've got ten more pounds on and no I don't think I'm coming back now and Michael you've gotten two inches taller, and he signaled so many things so fast that he got his signs and fingers tangled up so that he just stopped and smiled or shook his head, feeling the warm press of them and thinking, Why did I leave? My place is here. This is the life I was made for—simple and pure and good. I never really wanted to be in the Chancellory Office. I never wanted to be great, I wanted to be small.

Suddenly, in the midst of them, Wick remembered one of his earliest goals upon entering the monastery—he wanted to say a billion prayers. He had been so serious about this goal that for the first three years he had kept a list of all the people he was praying for and all the countries and all the causes. In addition, just before he went to bed each night, he made another shorthand list of all the little prayers he had said during the day: Thank you for this pretty yellow daisy and please help me not to gossip and don't let the cake fall because it would ruin Brother Peter's birthday and please, please, please oh Lord of Hosts, help me not to get a sore throat so I won't have to miss choir again.

That was a wonderful thing to want—to say a billion prayers. Now that is the kind of goal that a good man should have, he thought. A billion prayers could change the world. Not because I said them, but simply because they were said. What happened to that idea? Why did I abandon it?

Finally Alered waded into the crowd of monks and waved goodnight to everyone and escorted Wick to the guesthouse. Though Alered had been given permission to speak, he was more interested in listening to Wick. He could tell that something was seething in the young man.

"I remembered it when I was out in the garden—that I wanted to say a billion prayers as a monk. A billion. I wanted to say more prayers than any monk who had ever lived. And I got pretty far along, too. Over a hundred thousand I think. The list is at home, but I'm sure it was way over a hundred thousand. Don't you think a billion prayers could change the world? A billion!"

Alered sat down in a chair in Wick's room. He took off his glasses and rubbed his violet nose. He sat back in the chair and interlaced his fingers, which after a good scrubbing were dark red though black topsoil was still under the nails. The skin of his bald head was glossy and red and his green eyes sat deep in their sockets.

"I don't know how I lost all of that. I don't know where it all went," Wick said.

"Where what went?"

"Zeal. Where all my zeal went. It's gone, disappeared."

"Maybe you have a different kind of zeal."

"I need to be honest with you, Padre. This is really going to upset you, but I need to be perfectly truthful about something—I'm having an affair."

"With a girl, I hope."

"Of course with a girl. What do you mean, you hope?"

"Well, I hope it's a girl rather than a boy."

"It's been going on a couple months. I didn't mean for it to happen, but now I'm all involved and I really care about her."

"What's her name?"

"Alice."

"I've always liked that name—Alice. It's so sweet, so pure."

"There's nothing pure about her. I don't mean that in a bad way. She's a perfectly lovely girl and smart and likes me, maybe loves me, but forget about purity. Who needs that anyway."

"You do."

"I know—I know I need it, but I don't know if I want it. Why are things so confusing? I'm almost thirty years old and the older I get the more confusing things are. I come here and decide I can't face my brothers, then I do face them and I feel better than I've felt in months. I get a job in the Chancellory Office and I really love it and I have a chance at becoming chancellor and then I come here and suddenly start thinking about prayer again."

"Chancellors can pray too."

"I want Alice and I don't want her. Things were so simple once, so clear, so—unmistakable. I don't know what to do. I know I took a vow of celibacy, I swore to be chaste and pure and now I've lost it and I don't know how to get it back or even if I want it back."

"Pray for it."

"Pray for what?"

"For purity."

"But I don't know if I really want it. Part of me wants it and part doesn't."

The old man put his thick hands on his knees, pushed his glasses back on his nose, leaned toward Wick and looked at him and smiled and his yellow false teeth came loose. He stuck them back against his gums and got up.

"Well, it's nine o'clock and past my bedtime. Come speak to me before you go tomorrow."

"Wait a minute. You have to tell me what to do."

"You know what to do."

"Oh, I see. You're just brushing me off. You don't want to sully yourself with all this sin. You just think I should drop her. Just snap my fingers and forget her and that's that, right?"

"No."

"Well, what?"

"Ask God."

27

AFTER ALERED LEFT, WICK took a
shower and went to bed, but not to sleep. He rolled and shifted for four
hours, then finally rose at 1 A.M. and went down to the night chapel.

How still the huge chapel was at this deep hour of the night. There
was only the altar lamp burning and the light just behind the tabernacle. The chapel felt as if it contained fathom upon fathom of darkness
and everything in the darkness was still, incredibly still and deep and
black and the tabernacle was the only light and it was gold and shining
beneath the fathoms of darkness. Wick kneeled on the cold stone floor
beside a pillar. He prayed hotly, furiously: Help me to want to give her
up because I don't want to. Or help me decide to give up the priesthood.
Probably that's what I need to be praying. Yes. I probably need to just
leave the priesthood. Give it up altogether. Is that what you want? Fine,
that's what I'll do then. I'll just quit. There—it's yours.

But he stayed on his knees two more hours—fighting and arguing
and feeling his heart beat against his ribs every time he even thought

the words *Help me to want to leave her.* Around three o'clock when he had hurled every question he could at the darkness, when he could threaten and argue no more, the stillness came and surrounded him and it made his shoulders and back relax and his gritted teeth unfasten and his squinted eyes half open and the stillness entered him and it was smooth and cool and very deep and he could not feel the hard floor against his knees anymore, but rather felt as if he were kneeling upon stillness and that stillness was holding him and covering him and somehow inside of him, the stillness sealing all the cracks and fissures, all the things which were rent.

At 4 A.M. the squeaks and scuffs of sandals brought him back. The monks were filing into the choir for Vigils. Stiffly, Wick got up and went back to his room and slept. He went downstairs about nine o'clock and called a cab to take him to the airport. He had not eaten now in two days and he was a little light-headed. He packed his suitcase and walked down to the chapel and found Brother Alered kneeling in his stall and saying his rosary.

Wick felt peaceful. He had made no decision and he did not have an answer, he just felt whole and utterly rested. He approached Brother Alered and looked at him a moment and then reached out and touched the old man's hands, which held the brown rosary and supported the red, bald head which was facedown on the hands. Alered's face rose. He smiled and winked and in sign language said, "Write me."

"I will," Wick signed back.

"Are you okay?"

"I'm good."

"Yes."

As Wick was walking back through the guest house, Brother Matthew stopped him. "You've a phone call."

It was Alice.

"How are you, darling? God, I've missed you."

"I'm fine."

"I've got a surprise."

"Oh?"

"Dear, dear, dear. You don't sound too happy. Are you all right?"

"Yes. What's the surprise?"

"I've borrowed my cousin's driver and car and I'm coming to pick you up."

"I'll just take the plane."

"Oh please, darling. I'm half an hour away and I've missed you terribly. You won't let me down, will you?"

Wick canceled the cab and walked down to the end of the long drive which led to the monastery. Twenty minutes later the black Cadillac limousine arrived and Alice popped out. She was wearing a rose linen suit and black high heels and her auburn hair shimmered in the sunlight.

"Wick, you look awfully pale."

"I've been fasting."

"How marvelous. I want to do that someday. I really do. It sounds so —disciplined. God, how I'd like to be disciplined."

They got into the car, and as the driver pulled away, Wick looked back at the tall spire of the monastery and the dark bodies of the bells hanging in the spire and he felt sad to leave.

"Now, look at this," Alice said. She opened her hand toward a white tablecloth which covered the small bar which was let down from the back of a seat. Beneath the tablecloth was a large hump and two or three smaller ones. Carefully Alice pulled the cloth back and revealed a small ham, a plate of biscuits, two motes of butter and honey. The ham was freshly prepared and the meat was red and covered by a light, brown sugar glaze. The biscuits were fresh and they were brown and a little yellow on the sides.

Wick looked at the food and felt slightly sick.

Beneath the bar and the food, a bottle of champagne sat in a silver cooler. It was already open. Alice filled a glass for herself and one for Wick.

"This will go straight to my head," Wick said.

"I want it to. Desperately."

Wick touched her glass with his own and he tried to smile, though he was uncomfortable. She was taking away his peace. With the first sip of champagne, he could feel it begin to leave him, and for a moment, he hated her for it.

They drank three glasses of champagne each and then Wick ate four biscuits, each one heavy with a slab of red ham and a dollop of yellow butter, and his humor returned and he laughed and joked and put his arm around the beautiful girl with the yellow eyes.

"But what I want to know is—why did you bring all this? What's the celebration for?" Wick asked.

"Do you know, when you drink, your nose—that cute little nose—turns the most astonishing cherry red."

"Does it?"

"Oh, terribly red."

"Rudolph the red-nosed Longstreet . . . has a very shiny nose, and if he drinks more champagne, you could even say it glows."

"Good nose, but lousy voice."

"But why? Why did you do this?"

Alice split the last of the champagne between them. "Well, it's a kind of celebration. I've known for about ten days, but I couldn't think of exactly how to approach it."

"Approach what?"

"Soon there will be another Longstreet striding about the face of the earth."

Wick looked at her. "That's not very funny."

"I don't think it's funny, but I do think it could be—fun."

"Alice, are you serious?"

"Yeah."

Wick closed his eyes and sat back in the seat.

"Oh now darling, it's not as bad as all that. We can find a way." She caught his hand and wove her fingers into his own. "I've made a lot of plans. I have a lot of ideas."

"I'm against an abortion."

"Oh, so am I."

"I'm totally and completely against an abortion and it is not because I'm a priest, I'm just—I think it's wrong."

"Ditto."

"The wages of sin is death," Wick said very quietly.

She took her hand away from him. "Don't start quoting Scripture."

"If I'd been quoting Scripture earlier we wouldn't be in this jam."

"Is it a jam?"

"Oh no. No, no, no. It's not a jam. This is wonderful. It's a wonderful thing to have happen. I'm so excited about it."

"I think you should be."

"I am. I'm just pleased all the way to my bones."

"Don't be hateful, Wick. I can't stand hatefulness."

"Why, I'm not being hateful at all. I'm just thinking of all the joy ahead of us."

"There could be joy."

"If what? Don't say it. I know. If I left the Church everything would be just peachy, right? Renounce my vows, say bye-bye to the bishop and go home to Waverly. Why, I could go to work for the newspaper. Now there's an idea. I could write a Dear Wick column. 'How to Handle Chastity,' by Wick Longstreet—ex-monk, ex-priest, ex-chancellor. Why, it would be a triple-ex column."

Alice put her hands to her face. "I didn't know you could act this way."

"You didn't?"

"Look." She reached and caught both of his hands. "I want to keep the child, darling. No matter what happens, I want to keep it."

Wick let her hold his hands a few moments, then he took them away and pushed them into his pockets.

They rode back to Charleston.

During the next week, he buried himself in the work of the Diocese. He met with a dozen disgruntled priests who believed the bishop was treating them badly. He spent hours going over the books of the Diocese Development Fund and attended five luncheons and six dinners and assisted the bishop around the state at three separate confirmation ceremonies, and in addition to all these things, he worked his regular nine hours a day as the bishop's right-hand man, screening all appointments for him and sitting in on meetings between the bishop and Catholic school principals or contractors, nuns, seminarians and prominent Catholic businessmen, all of whom wanted something. In a short time, Bishop O'Hara had become very dependent upon Wick and his insights into almost every problem that arose in the Diocese.

Around eight on a Saturday night, after having put in fourteen hours on his day off, Wick closed a folder which contained a petition for the annulment of a fifteen-year-old marriage. He knew husband and wife, knew that the marriage was a miserable one and also he knew that the bishop would not grant the divorce. He looked at his office. It exuded power and conservatism: walnut paneling and a dark red carpet, purple curtains and a leather couch and leather chairs and seeping in from the kitchen the smell of Mrs. Callahan's pot roast and mashed potatoes—a dish that had just as much to do with power as the office itself, since Mrs. Callahan's family had cooked for every Bishop of Charleston since 1840.

He had not spoken to Alice during the whole week. She had called once and Wick had told the secretary to say that he was on another line and that he would call her back. She had not tried him again. Because she's so smart, Wick thought. She knows I'm avoiding her and she's letting me get away with it because she's smart and kind. A baby. Alice is going to have a—my baby. What am I going to do? What am I going to say?

Wick had said Mass every morning at six as usual, but he had not prayed at any of them. He was angry at God for letting this happen and when he was angry with God he usually said nothing to Him at all, thinking, Okay, since He doesn't give a damn about me, since He doesn't watch out for me at all, let Him stew in His own juices. I'm not saying one word. He can come to me.

There was a tap at his door, then it opened. Bishop O'Hara strode into the room, his golf bag and clubs upon his shoulder.

"Wick, are you still here?"

Wick sprang from the chair. "I was just looking at a few files."

"What—the annulment files? For Lord's sake, Wick, take a break. Have a drink." The bishop zipped open a pocket in his golf bag and pulled out a bottle of Scotch and two plastic cups. He was a small man with thin bones and a trim face. He had black eyes and black eyebrows and white hair. His face was red and his teeth brown from pipe smoking. He poured a stout drink in each cup and handed one to Wick.

"Is Mrs. Callahan putting some kind of spice in her pot roast?" the bishop asked.

"Pardon?"

"It tasted very different. She gets on these kicks, you know. She thinks the old taste is boring and she gets on these kicks and wants to change everything. Why can't she just leave everything the way it is? Next thing you know she'll put coriander seeds in the corned beef and cabbage."

Wick smiled and sipped his Scotch. He was pale. He pulled out a package of cigarettes and lit one. His fingers were dark yellow.

"Have you eaten yet?"

"I'm not very hungry."

"That's not what I asked you. Have you had your supper?"

"No."

"You can't keep doing this. You're putting in too many hours and you're not eating." The bishop drained his cup of Scotch. "Come on. Let's go, right now. You're going to have some pot roast. Maybe you can tell me if she's changed the recipe."

A few minutes later, the two men were sitting at the kitchen table above two big bowls of steaming pot roast. Wick had just taken his first bite.

"It's bay leaf."

The bishop banged the table. "I knew it. I knew she changed it."

"I think it tastes good."

"I want it the way it was. First thing tomorrow morning you write a note to Mrs. Callahan." He pushed his bowl of stew toward Wick and then walked to the door of the kitchen. "Tell her to return to the old recipe and stop this, this—heresy. And sign the note Monsignor Longstreet."

Wick was writing down the bishop's words in a small notebook. He looked up at him. "Sir?"

"And if you want to doubly impress her, you might add Chancellor of the Diocese of Charleston."

Wick rose from the chair.

"Sit down, sit down, sit down. Your bay leaf stew's getting cold. And from now on, you will not work on Saturdays. Got it?"

"Yes sir."

"Oh, yeah, another thing. Abbot Lewis tells me you're a pretty good cook yourself."

"I do all right."

"Can you cook lamb?"

"I can."

"Marvelous. I want roast leg of lamb every Friday night and I don't want it seasoned with anything but salt and pepper and I'll tell you something, Monsignor—if you can fix a good roast lamb and keep the peace between me and the priest senate as well as the parish councils, I think you may go higher than you ever expected in the Church. Higher than you ever dreamed."

28

WAVERLY IN THE LAST of winter.
The fields surrounding the house were brown and dark yellow and the
pecans and gingkos and English oaks were bare and sleek. Only the two
magnolias which stood beside the front steps held leaves and they were
thick and green and lustrous. The woods surrounding the fields were
full of black limbs and gray trunks, though now and again a cedar was
green. Woodpeckers were in the bare trees and the sound of their work
drummed through the limbs and echoed across valleys of brown stickers
and black creeks.

Blackie had spent almost a week in bed. During that time his face
lost the black color and the swelling from the poison of the rattlesnake.
The two fang marks in the side of his neck were almost healed. Still he
had told no one about his vision. In fact, for the first three days after he
got out of the hospital the vision was disturbing, not comforting. As he
lay in bed convalescing, he argued with himself. Was it the poison of
the snake? Was it a hallucination rather than a vision? Maybe it was the

result of a drug, the antivenin. Then he remembered that the voice told him to say it was a drug if he wanted. When Blackie remembered the sound of the voice, he became calm and the debating ceased.

During this week of convalescence he was fussed over by nearly everyone. Harper had been the first one to nurse him and he felt bad about lashing out at her, but there were things he had felt for years and they had to be said before the situation could improve between them as somehow he felt it would. Hannah was in and out of the room every hour and Bub would often come in and just stand in the corner, saying nothing, simply standing. Even Tadpole made periodic visits. On one occasion she brought a jar of newly caught spring lizards for a present. She had caught the lizards in a mineral spring near the house and had put them in a wide-mouthed mason jar. The spring lizards were two inches long and had red gills and big black eyes and skin which was golden and covered with black dots.

"They your friends," Tadpole said. "They your friends who don't talk and who won't make you talk." Her black hair was still arranged in pigtails which stood straight up from her scalp and she wore a blue print dress.

"They're pretty," Blackie said.

"Don't you eat them though. I know folks who grab them lizards and fix them right up lickety split. You're not going to do that, are you?"

Blackie laughed for the first time in a long while.

There were two others who were spending a lot of time in Blackie's presence—Cat and Carol. The bad blood between them was getting worse as they vied to see who could take better care of him, while Blackie for the first time in his life was beginning to feel a sense of guilt and remorse.

One afternoon about three o'clock, Carol came into Blackie's room. Her blond hair was freshly washed and her blue eyes were shining. She was wearing a pair of blue jeans and a blue sweater.

"Sure do look blue," Blackie said.

"I feel blue."

"No. Why?"

"Well, there's something I have to say. I don't like saying it, but I have to."

Blackie brushed his hands through his hair, rubbed his eyes and sat up in bed. "Sounds serious."

"Blackie, I'm thirty-two years old. I'm not a kid anymore and I've got to decide what I'm going to do with my life. You and I have been playing around for years now and for a while it was fun and all, but now I've—or we've got to make some decisions. Look, I'll just come straight out and say it: Will you marry me?"

Blackie felt his heart speed.

"I know this is awful sudden, but I think the decision has to be made."

"Carol—I don't know what to say, I . . ."

"Like I said, I know this is sudden but I know that I've been thinking about it for the last year or so, and if I've been thinking about it, I think you have too, right?"

Blackie pulled the bedcovers up and folded his hands. He couldn't look at her.

"If you don't answer today that's all right. I know I'm coming on strong and you may have to think about it, but at least I want you to say you will stop going out with Cat. Can you do that at least? Can you promise me you'll stop seeing Cat?"

"She lives in this house, Carol. How can I stop seeing her?"

"I mean going out with her. I know you'll run into her, but I want you to promise me you'll not go out with her."

Blackie felt awful. It was a new feeling for him. In the old days he would have smiled and laughed and said sure, babe, and then seen Cat on the sly. He decided to face it head on.

"I can't."

"What do you mean you can't?"

"I like Cat. I didn't mean to like her—or maybe I did mean to, it's hard to say, but the main thing is—I didn't mean to hurt you. I really didn't."

"Do you love Cat? Is that what you're saying? Come on, damn it. Try to answer honestly for one time in your spoiled, bratty life. Do you love her or not? Yes or no?"

At that moment Cat walked into the room. Her blond hair—much whiter and thicker in texture than Carol's—had been combed and braided into one long plait which lay over her left shoulder and the very end of the plait secured with a tortoiseshell barrette. She was wearing a black wool skirt and a salmon blouse. Her heart fell when she saw

Carol. Cat was able to deal with Carol from afar, but to run into her face-to-face in Blackie's room was extremely difficult.

She was carrying a small tray which held two silver wine cups and a silver pitcher containing orange juice. "Well, I'm sorry. I guess I should have knocked," she said, and sat the tray down on a small mahogany table beside Blackie's bed.

"Oh, not at all," Carol said. "We were just discussing you."

"Me?"

"You sound so surprised."

"Well, I am a little surprised," Cat said, and blushed.

The blush made Carol furious. "Isn't that cute. Where did you learn to do that? It's just darling, and it adds so much color to your face."

"Carol, why don't you just take it easy," Blackie said.

"I was just admiring a blush on command. It must be hard to do. Do you practice blushing?"

Cat crossed her arms and lifted her face. Her small golden eyebrows rose. "Carol, may I be forthright?"

"I doubt it."

"I don't like you very much. Frankly, I don't like you at all. You are a pernicious influence in this house."

"Well, honesty at last. I admire honesty, and I'll be honest with you. For six months you've done everything you can to finagle your way into this family, but I've got news for you, little girl—everybody's seen through it. Everybody knows you want just one thing—Blackie. You think if you can get Blackie you'll never have to leave. But you don't have him, and you're never going to have him—is she, Blackie?"

Blackie sank down into the covers and pulled the sheet over his head.

Growling, Carol reached out and grabbed the bed covers and jerked them away. "Get out of there, you little bastard."

As soon as Carol started yanking one side of the blankets, Cat yanked the other. "He's sick," she said. "Don't you touch him."

"Get your hands off!" Carol yelled, and jerked violently with both hands and the pull was so great that Cat sprawled across the foot of the bed and tumbled toward Carol's feet and Carol grabbed the long plait of hair and began slapping her.

"Knock it off," Blackie said. "Hey!" He tried to separate the women, who rolled away from the bed growling and scratching and crying. Carol hissed things like "You little twat."

And for a few moments, Blackie's old self lay back in bed and enjoyed it all. He had never seen two girls fighting. It was funny and somehow sexy. Finally, when Carol had pinned Cat to the floor and wrapped the girl's blond plait around her throat, Blackie walked over and poured the entire pitcher of orange juice over their heads.

They contracted, spasmed, made awful faces and then fell apart, gasping.

Carol was the first one up. The orange juice had plastered the top of her skull and trickled down her face, making her mascara run in black rivulets from her eyes.

"All right, damn it. I want this thing decided right now. Right this minute. It's her or me. Come on. You think you're so tough, you're such a man. Decide right now. Her or me."

"Her," Blackie said.

"Why, you sonofabitch. Why, you little creep. How dare you joke around. You can't joke your way out of this."

"I'm not joking."

"Yes, you are—with your smug little face. Now her or me?"

"Her."

Carol's face changed from bared teeth anger to dismay.

Cat, who had gotten less of the orange juice, stood up. "We need to clean this place up. Someone's coming down the hall."

"Blackie," Carol said, and her stained face was open and vulnerable, the blue eyes wide beneath crinkled eyebrows. "You don't mean it."

"Yes, I do."

"You love me."

"Yes, I do. But you wanted an answer and there it is. You wanted a choice."

"Fine," Carol said. "If that's the way it is, then that's the way it is. But I'll tell you something, Blackie Longstreet—you will rue the day that you did this to me. You will rue the day."

Carol stormed from the room just as Hannah was coming in.

"What's all the ruckus about?" Hannah asked. She was wearing her long white apron and her black half boots and her white hat. She was very thin and her big hands hung beside her thighs.

"We'll take care of it, Hannah," Cat said.

"You'll take care of what?"

"I dropped some orange juice, but it's okay. Everything's okay."

And for Cat McGregor everything was more than okay for the next few days. She had vanquished her only competitor and had Blackie completely to herself. How she loved to take care of him. She came into his bedroom every morning around eight o'clock bringing a copy of the *Southern Chronicle* and the glass of pineapple juice. He was usually still asleep and she would stand and look at him. His black hair all mussed, cheekbones a little flushed, his naked chest still with a hint of summer's tan and smooth and without a flaw. She waked him by putting a palm to his head.

29

CAT SPENT THREE OR four hours a day with Blackie. She took him on his first outing since the accident. It was a blue day in mid-February. The sun was bright and the blue jays were crying from the walnut and pecan trees. Cat and Blackie walked into the grove. The leaves beneath the pecans were lavender and black and the bark of the trees was dark green and gray with a little light tan coming through where some bark had fallen away and the limbs of the pecan trees were light green on the bellies and black on the tops. Cat took off a black sable hat which she had gotten for Christmas. Blackie walked ahead of her and stooped to pick up the pecans. He grabbed a handful and dropped them into the black hat. There were a lot of pecans this year and they were long and slender and more rounded at the base than at the tip, their shells a light mocha with strips of dark brown running through the lighter color.

Blackie was filling the sable hat to the brim with the pecans. She loved to watch his big hands pile them in. His hands were turning red in the cold and the skin looked so smooth and clean and she could see the half moons of his thumbs shining, each one the size of half a quarter, and she loved the long points of his fingers, which were red and sensitive.

I wish I had a hundred hats, Cat was thinking. So we could stay out here all day, picking up pecans, bumping into one another and laughing. I wonder if he feels that way? Do men like to do things like this too? Just silly, no-nothing little things.

"Will you bake me a pecan pie?" Blackie asked. His black hair ruffled and blew in the wind and his blue eyes were shining.

"Yes."

"Do you know how?"

"I will learn."

"Hell, you don't have to learn for me."

Oh yes I do, she thought. I have to learn everything for you.

In a while they went back into the house and took the sable hat full of pecans into the kitchen. Never had a kitchen seemed so incredibly bright to Cat. Everything looked as if it was shining. The copper pots were gleaming and so was the big worktable which lay beneath the pots and so were the white tiles of the walls. Even the taps in the three big sinks seemed to shine.

"I feel so incredibly light," Cat said. "I feel like I could float."

"Me, too," Blackie said.

"You too?"

He smiled.

Hannah was stirring a black pot on the gas stove and Tee Tat was rolling out dough with a wooden pin near the stove and Bub was standing in his frayed red jacket and dark blue pants drinking a cup of coffee, his hair white and smooth and shining.

"Tee Tat, will you teach me to bake a pecan pie?"

Tee Tat looked up and grinned. She was chubbier than ever and today wore her hair in plaits and the light-colored skin of her scalp was shining between the kinky plaits of hair.

"Not today, missy."

"Why not today?"

"Too busy. You come tomorrow."

"Tee Tat, I think you're wonderful," Cat said, and hugged the little fat woman as hard as she could. She grabbed Blackie's hand and pulled him from the kitchen.

"Those younguns seem awful happy," Bub said.

"Uh-huh," Tee Tat said. "Too happy. I worry about little ole Cat. You know about that Blackie now."

"What about Blackie?" Hannah said, her face hard and very black and scowling.

"You know what I'm saying, woman. That boy's got rooster blood in him."

Hannah squinted her big eyes and turned around in a huff to stir the pot of pinto beans.

Later in the night, after everyone had gone to bed, Blackie and Cat sat together on one of the long leather couches in the library. A fire popped and sizzled in the stone fireplace and the flames danced across the rosewood paneling in the big room. The thousands of books which filled three walls of the room from floor to ceiling were lit by a number of small spotlights. Upon the mantlepiece sat a spray of new holly. The leaves were green and the berries red and plump.

Blackie had brought a bottle of chilled champagne and two glasses to the library. They were on their second glass now and he was holding Cat's hand and feeling things he had never felt for a girl before. Lightness, he thought. That's the right word. I feel like I could float right off this couch and bump the ceiling like a helium balloon. His heart felt funny, too. It felt big and soft and mushy in a way. It felt like it was full of something, some kind of liquid, something that was ready to pour over the brim.

"It's scary in a way," Blackie said.

"What's scary?" Cat was wearing a white wool dress and pale yellow slippers. She had pinned her blond hair into a stylish chignon.

"The way I feel."

"You mean all floaty?"

"Yeah, kinda."

"Maybe we're in love. Is this the way people feel when they're in love?"

"It reminds me a little bit of the way I felt on the operating table. The weirdest thing happened to me. I haven't told anybody it's so weird."

Cat's blue eyes opened and she grabbed his big thumb with her whole hand. "Tell me."

"I don't know," Blackie said. "I don't know if I want to tell anyone."

"Please."

Blackie looked at her and then looked at the yellow and red fire and then carefully told her the story.

When he finished, Cat's eyes were full of tears. She had always known that Blackie had this kind of depth to him. Others had not seen it, certainly not Carol, but she had always believed that Blackie had a deep and profound heart.

"We are one," Cat said. "What a wonderful thought. What a wonderful vision. Do you believe it was a vision? Did you think that God was speaking to you?"

"I don't know. To be real honest, I don't know if I believe in God any more than I did before, but I do believe there's something else. Some other kind of life. Some other kind of beings who have a lot more knowledge than we do."

"Could be angels."

"I don't think I can quite buy angels."

"Not at all?"

"Well, maybe a little. For instance, I believe you're a kind of angel."

Cat blushed and Blackie leaned over and kissed her. They held one another and then Blackie kissed her cheek and her chin and neck and pulled her on top of him.

He made love to Cat more carefully and gently than he had to any other woman in his life.

The next morning Ford was sitting in the little dining room, drinking coffee and reading the paper. On the table before him sat a bowl of yellow grits and a platter with six fried bream and several pieces of toast. The bream had been caught in the early morning by Tee Tat. She had cleaned them and coated them with flour and salt and black pepper and then fried them until they were crisp and brown, knowing that fried bream and grits was Ford's favorite breakfast.

He had arrived from Washington the night before. Two days earlier Johnson had secured him a place on the House Foreign Relations Committee. The day Ford had received the appointment he had spent the entire afternoon with the President. Johnson was still upset about the attack in Saigon. Several Vietcong clad in black pajamas had permeated the defenses around an American officers' billet in the downtown area and thrown several hand grenades. Two Americans were killed and sixty-three were wounded. The Joint Chiefs of Staff and Ambassador Taylor had argued for an immediate strike against North Vietnam, but the President had backed off. Ford had been surprised by the President's response. He thought that Johnson was aching for the slightest provocation so that he could open the war up "and teach those little yella bastards a lesson." But Johnson's attitude had changed. He seemed anxious, careful. He said the time was not right to respond. Then he had turned to Ford and said:

"I'm going to need you, son. I'm going to need your brains and your backbone. Don't you get all tangled up with your committee work. I'm going to be calling on you a lot."

Cat walked into the room rather slowly. She looked a little pale to Ford, but he smiled when he saw her. She always made him smile, and then he forced himself to retract the smile, remembering the other young girl who had so devastated his heart, thinking, I will never again allow anyone to do that to me, and if you're serious about this, Ford, you must start by not allowing yourself to feel that warmth for a girl that makes you smile at her. You must stop the feeling at its onset.

Cat said good morning and then sat down in a chair. She hurt a lot and her stomach felt upset. Blackie had made love to her twice. The first time had not been so bad, but the second time had come much too quickly and this was the one that did hurt and this morning she resented him for it. Why do men have to have it, she thought. And the expression he wore on his face. It could have been anyone. He was so lost in his own pleasure he didn't see me at all. Well, if he thinks that this is going to continue he can think again. I will not do this again with him or anyone else. I can't believe he was grinding his teeth, making that awful face and grinding his teeth.

"How's Washington?" Cat asked. For some reason she was rather drawn to Ford this morning. He had always seemed the gentlest of the Longstreets and his mind was keen and she felt quite sure that such a gentle person would never do to a woman what Blackie had done to her last night.

"Busy, busy, busy. Why, the place is always in an uproar and guess what?"

"What?"

"The President put me on the Foreign Relations Committee."

"Good for you." And he wasn't that bad looking. Since he had gone to Washington he seemed to have lost a few pounds. He had the black hair and blue eyes of the rest of the boys and she absolutely loved the lavender scar in his right cheek. She thought it made him look like a rogue. When you combined it with his gentleness, it gave him a special appeal. "Do you see President Johnson often?"

"I see him a good bit, yes."

"What's he like?"

Ford pushed his glasses against the bridge of his nose with his middle finger, which was plump and red. He left his hand there, middle finger pressing the glasses into his flesh, his head cast down and eyes squinting and lips pooched out as he considered his answer. "It's a profound question. A profound, profound question. Well he's a . . . a chameleon. Yes, exactly. Lyndon Johnson is a chameleon who takes on whatever color he needs to. If he's with military men he affects a military manner and if he's with clergymen he becomes like a simple country preacher. Lyndon Johnson is a man of many colors."

Blackie walked into the room in the middle of Ford's appraisal of the President. He looked at his brother's downcast face and his squinting eyes and knew that he was thinking carefully about whatever he was saying. He also knew that Ford was trying to impress Cat. He had known for some time that Ford liked her very much. Once he would have thought Ford's crush was funny and he would have engineered trouble between the two of them. Now he thought it was sad. He knew that his brother needed a woman in his life, but he also knew that Cat was not the one for him.

"Congressman!" Blackie boomed.

Ford rose and shook his brother's hand.

"Let's see where he got you," Ford said.

Blackie turned his head and revealed the two black fang marks.

They talked about the snake bite and Ford did not mention the housebreaking. He excused himself then, saying that Harper was having some business problems and that she needed to talk to him.

Blackie sat down across the table from Cat. She looked beautiful this morning. He reached out to take her hand, but she withdrew it.

"Ford's a great guy, isn't he?" Blackie said.

"He's very nice. He's—considerate."

"You won't find anybody with a better heart."

Cat raised her golden eyebrows and her pink chin and looked into a corner of the room.

"What's the matter?"

"You know very well what's the matter. Don't you ask me that."

Blackie sat back in his chair and smiled. "You're a mad little chick today, aren't you?"

"Don't call me a chick. I don't like it."

"You used to like it."

"There are several things that I thought I liked which I don't like anymore."

"Name one."

"Don't play with me."

"Go ahead."

"I don't like chick. I don't like to be called chick."

"Name another."

"You. I don't like you."

"Well, that's too bad. I was getting ready to go into town and I needed a driver, but I guess I'll just drive myself."

Blackie left the table and walked toward the door.

"You're not supposed to drive for two more days."

"I've got to buy some wrapping paper and bows."

"For what?"

"Christmas presents."

"Christmas has been over for two months, Blackie."

"Well, for some people it's over and for others it's just starting."

On the way to town Blackie told Cat about his career as a burglar. He told her about how he had started, how he picked his victims and how he had never even come close to being caught until the last two or three attempts, which had gone badly. He even told her about his secret room.

"You mean you keep the loot there?"

"The loot? That's a funny word."

"It is loot. You've been looting people's homes."

"Would you like to see the loot?"

"Not at all. I'm not even vaguely interested. How much do you have?"

Blackie laughed.

30

THEY DROVE THROUGH THE coun-
tryside toward town. It was fifty-five degrees and the sky was a light
blue and without a cloud. The land was mostly pasture. Barbed wire
fences sat on either side of the road. The posts were old and had turned
white in the sun and the wire which was strung between the posts was
rusty and red and beyond the wire lay hills and valleys of pasture which
the frosts had changed from green to gray and tan and dark yellow.
Sometimes on top of the hills stood five or six salt licks. They were gray
posts holding a block of white salt for cattle and the sunlight striking
the salt made it glisten and sparkle on the hilltop. In the valleys between the hills there was often a pond and most of the time the color of
the water was brown, though sometimes the ponds were black, and
around the edge were stands of cattails with trim, brown stalks and tops
of fluffy whiteness which broke apart in the wind, scattering themselves
across the surface of the black water.

Main Street was like most of the other main streets in Southern

towns. There was a wide asphalt road, on either side of which laid gray
sidewalks and then a line of stores and shops, most of them two stories,
some of them with green canvas awnings and all of them made from red
brick. There were no trees or gardens on Main Street, just brown telephone poles and endless strands of black power lines and on the poles
were nailed posters advertising MASKED BOLO MEETS GORGEOUS GEORGE or
revivals and healing services.

Cat and Blackie walked hand in hand down Main Street. He told her
what he had in mind—he wanted to give back everything he had stolen.
He said that it would be dangerous perhaps, but that he was determined
that everyone would get back their jewels. Cat squeezed his hand a little
harder as he was talking. She had never imagined he could have the
courage to be so honest. It gave a whole new side to him and, if it was
possible, made her love him even more.

"But how will you do it?" she asked.

"Through the mail. Or at least I'll start through the mail. This
sounds really crazy, but what I want to do is wrap up the jewels in nice
paper and bows and then put all that in a brown box and mail it to
them."

"It's a wonderful idea," Cat said.

"You think so?"

"It's just splendid."

"Well, I thought I would start this way and see what happens. I'll
have to be real careful with the first few though. I'll need to mail them
from a post office which is distant from Waverly and then wait and see
what happens. If these people start sending out postal inspectors and
cops to find out who stole the goodies, then I'll have to find another
way."

"Can I help?"

"Sure."

They kissed one another lightly and then went into a Woolworth's
dime store. In half an hour, they bought two hundred dollars' worth of
ribbons and boxes and wrapping paper, tape and seals and even a host
of Christmas cards.

When they returned to Waverly, Blackie took Cat to the secret room
and showed her the treasure. She was aghast.

"How long have you been—doing this?"

"Awhile."

"There must be a fortune here. You never tried to sell it?"

"Didn't want to."

Cat stood before the tables which held neat piles of shimmering earbobs and necklaces, blue diamond rings and red sapphire brooches, stacks of silver forks and golden spoons.

"You'll never be able to send all of this back. Never."

"Well, maybe I can send some of it, then you can give me a few ideas about what to do with the rest."

"How do you know what belongs to who?"

"I kept all the piles separate. Each pile represents a break-in. I remember every one. I want to give it back. Every bit of it and you know something? I think it can be just as much fun giving it back as it was taking it. We'll have to be clever and smart. We may even have to do some sneaking around, but we'll have a ball, an absolute blast."

Suddenly Cat turned and kissed him. "I love you," she said.

"I love you, too."

"Do you, Blackie?"

"I don't say it a whole lot, so when I say it I mean it."

Blackie put his arms around her and pulled her close and rocked her back and forth.

The next few days with him were some of the happiest in her life. They spent almost all their time with one another and Cat was completely amazed at how gentle and light and sweet life could be. She had never felt so sure about the inherent goodness of life as she did now. For years, every day had been a struggle for her: working for her father, sneaking time to read and study with her mother. Even when she had come to Waverly, those first days—though filled with wonder—were very hard. Now everything seemed easy and good and she knew that it was because of love. It makes everything bearable, she thought. If you are loved, everything bad is less bad and everything good is better. Living without love, without loving, is like being ill—everything irritates, everything discourages and tears and rends. You are cold in the morning and flushed at night and there is always about you a sense of uneasiness, as if something ghastly is about to happen. As if just around the corner there waits the last blow to finish off your miserable existence. Without love there is no hope and no health. Without love there is only malaise.

Blackie began mailing off the packages late at night. He and Cat drove to a post office some twenty-five miles from Waverly. Blackie sent the first brown box which contained two emerald necklaces and four gold rings to Mrs. Abigail White. It was the first house he had robbed three years earlier. He waited and watched for ten days and when no sheriff showed up at the door, he began sending out the other jewels, following the exact order of the robberies.

Three weeks later at 2 A.M., Blackie was lying in bed and wondering how he was going to get General and Mrs. John Stanton's things back to them. It was a lot: a complete silver service, several gold goblets and five pounds of jewelry. He was about to go downstairs and get a glass of milk when he heard the wind across the yard pushing through the evergreens and blowing leaves and then thundering through the bare branches of the oak trees beside the house. It was a big wind and it pushed against the side of the house making the timbers pop, rattling the windowpanes. The rain came after the wind. The drops were light and soft except when the wind caught them and then they hit the house hard.

Blackie smiled, thinking, Why not? There's nothing wrong with it at all and it would be much more fun. Who cares about mailing the stuff back? That's boring. Boring! Taking it back the way I got it is what I need to do. What a thrill that would be. What an absolute thrill.

Thirty minutes later he had found his black bag and checked his tools and donned his black nylon jumpsuit. He went up into the attic and got the Stanton's jewels and then went back to his room for a pair of needle nose pliers. He poked his head out his bedroom door to make sure the way was clear and when he turned back to look at his room the thought shot through him, You will never see this place again. He dismissed it and cut off the light.

General Stanton's house was the seventh one he had robbed and it was only sixty miles north of Waverly. He got there in less than an hour. He parked the car in the same tunnel of holly trees that he had used the first time two years ago. Carefully he rubbed the black grease-paint over his face and neck and hands.

He stepped into the night woods. The rain was falling through the winter limbs of pecan and mulberry trees, and since there were no leaves to slow the rain, it was noisy and completely covered the sound of his movement. He stopped for a moment and turned his face to the black sky. The rain stung his forehead and cheeks. He smiled and took in the night woods. The sound of the rain pinging through the bare limbs and striking the dry leaves of the floor. The wind rascaling the trees and making them creak and sigh, making them drop the parts of themselves that were no good, the rotted bough and branch, thousands of these things falling to the bottom of the dark. He held out his hands beside him and balanced in the falling: leaves and limbs and scales of bark and old fruit that was no good and the rain, the sweet, black rain, he balanced in the falling of all things and felt as if he would never die.

It took him ten minutes to make his way through the woods to the edge of the Stanton's back yard. He carried the silver and jewels in a black knapsack. He set it down and studied the house. No lights were burning. He looked at his luminous watch—four-fifteen.

Quickly he ran across the open yard and pressed himself against the wet side of the brick house. He listened. There was no sound except the rain.

Within the house, General Charles Stanton was loading his pistol. He had not been able to sleep and had been standing in front of his bedroom window when he saw the figure clad in black running across the yard. He had been robbed twice in the last couple of years. Neither time was the intruder caught. He was determined to make a lesson of the next robber. He finished loading five shells into the .45 caliber service revolver. Quietly he left his bedroom and stepped through the dark house.

Blackie pulled off the screen and pushed the small window. It was locked. He found his glass cutter and cut a circle, put his hand through and opened the lock. He climbed in the window and then leaned halfway out and grabbed the heavy knapsack.

General Stanton was a tall man who had shaved his head. He wore a black mustache. Dressed in a blue robe and red slippers, he stepped quietly toward the back of the house. He could hear a noise and it made him furious to think that he was being robbed again.

Blackie put his glass cutter back into the black bag, caught his knapsack and moved from the small laundry room into a long hall. He remembered that he had taken the jewels from General Stanton's bedroom, but decided he wouldn't risk returning them there. He walked to the edge of the carpeted hall.

The general was standing in the shadows. He couldn't tell exactly what the black figure was doing. He cocked the .45.

Blackie heard the noise. He stopped and looked up and listened, then decided it was his imagination.

"All right," General Stanton said. "You hold it right there."

Blackie jumped and sprang toward the hall and he heard an explosion and felt something strike the back of his head and he hit the floor and tried to raise his hand to his head to see what had happened, but he couldn't.

The general stuck his foot under the intruder's belly and turned him halfway over. He studied the face covered with black greasepaint and blood.

"You won't do it again, will you?" the general said. "You won't steal from me again, will you?"

31

CAT HAD GONE INTO the newspaper a little earlier than usual. She worked hard from seven-thirty until ten-thirty and then took a coffee break. Her work had been very good this morning. She had written ten obituaries in three hours. She liked writing much more than she liked throwing the newspapers. She was sitting in the new canteen drinking her coffee black when two reporters walked in, two women. One was a tall redhead, the other a short blond. "What in the world was he doing there?" the redhead asked.

"That's what I've been trying to tell you, Gladice, he was stealing."

"Oh, come on."

"Stanton found him with a knapsack full of stuff. Pretty professional job, too. He was wearing black camouflage and black makeup on his face."

Cat set her coffee cup down.

"Was there any kind of struggle?"

"Looks like Stanton just blew him away. One shot right to the back of the head. It was a real mess."

"Excuse me," Cat said. She had left her booth and walked behind the two women, who were standing before a red vending machine. "Who are you talking about?"

"I beg your pardon," the blond said.

"You were just talking about someone who was shot. Who was it?"

"Do I know you?"

"Please."

"It was Blackie Longstreet. Do you work here or something?"

Cat looked at her. She crossed her arms over her chest and felt her mouth open a bit. She stood and stared and then walked out of the building to her car.

When she arrived at Waverly, she found Bub and Jebodiah sitting on the back steps of the house crying.

There were a thousand people at the funeral. The eulogy was given in three parts. Wick spoke first, then Ford and finally Harper. Cat sat in the front row of the First Presbyterian Church. She had not cried at all in the past three days. She busied herself with greeting guests and answering the phone.

Harper had cried only once. When she discovered that her youngest son was dead, she immediately went to her safe and opened a black box. Inside lay four black envelopes. Each envelope was printed in white ink with one of her sons' names. She picked out Blackie's and opened it and began following the instructions which she and Blackie had put together on his eighteenth birthday. She started with his wardrobe for death and was surprised to see that the typed description of his clothes had been marked out with a red pen. A note was scribbled at the bottom of the page—See other side.

When Harper turned the page, she found the following:

Dear Harper,

Well if you're reading this I guess I'm dead, huh? Wonder how it feels? Oh well, hope I wasn't doing anything too bad when it happened. Listen, I know we decided that I was supposed to wear a pinstripe suit and red silk tie and all that stuff, but that ain't me. You know that. Do you think I could wear my bluejeans and my tennis shoes instead? I'd like to have on my leather jacket, too. I know you don't like this idea a whole lot, but I'd just feel better wearing what I usually wear. Thanks.

Oh yea—I guess we never got along real good, but I just want you to know that it wasn't your fault. I think I was bad from the start.

Love—and I mean it now—Blackie.

Harper read the note and laughed a little and then cried. The crying lasted ten minutes or so and then she willed herself to stop, thinking, If I keep this up, my eyes will be puffy and red and my whole face will swell. Everyone will stare and point and I will not have it. I will not look stricken and helpless, because I'm not helpless, not in the least bit, no ma'am.

After Blackie was buried, the family came home and gathered in the den. The rival newspaper and the television stations were carrying stories about "the rich boy, cat burglar." Cat told the family all that Blackie had told her about his career, then she and the two brothers went to the attic and Cat showed them Blackie's treasure room. Three quarters of the stolen goods were still there. They marveled that he could have taken so much.

Harper did not go with them. She sat alone in the den, stunned by the revelation of the secret room and stung by the fact that Cat had known about everything and had not told her. It was like a dream. It was like Blackie was a completely different person than she knew, living a different life. For a while she simply sat and her mind wandered over everything: the phone call from the sheriff and the scores of robbed houses and the secret room in her own house and Blackie's face, white and dead in the coffin. Her mind saw it all.

In a while, the others returned from the attic and Harper coolly recited her plan for dealing with the press.

"We will call a news conference next week and we will tell everything that Blackie did and how he did it and that will be that. The sheriff's coming over tomorrow. I'll give him the property that Blackie took and let him distribute it to the proper owners. Does anyone have any questions?"

"Are you okay?" Ford asked.

"I'm rather tired so I'm going up to my room. There's plenty of food that people have brought so don't bother Hannah. She's upset and probably will be for a while."

She went upstairs, directly to Blackie's room. When she walked in, the smell of him encompassed her. They had separate smells, each of her sons. She wondered if that was an odd thing to notice about them, but their aromas were quite distinct. Ford's was sour, Wick's aromatic, Starkey's sharp and Blackie's—sweet.

Who would ever think that you would have a sweet smell, Harper said to herself. Why, your smell should have been wild and sassy, something like lemons and incense. Who in the world would ever have thought that you would smell sweet? She glanced about the room and then focused on the large bookcase that took up one whole wall: helmets and baseballs, cap guns and fishing bobbers, red shotgun shells and black dumbbells and a tall stack of dusty *Playboy*s. There were four shelves which held nothing but model airplanes. When he was ten they had been the passion of his life. She went over to the bookcase and picked up the B-29 Strato Fortress. She remembered it as being one of his favorites because of all the gun turrets. She held the plane to her chest and looked around the room and then went to her own room, setting the gray model plane with the small bubbles of glass and machine guns on her bedside table.

Two sleeping pills later, she saw him sitting on the edge of her bed as he had done when he was a boy—his black hair cut in a flat top and his impossibly big blue eyes shining and his hands holding the B-29 Strato Fortress and saying, Harper, she's just the best wings in the sky, just the best ever. Look at these gun turrets, ain't they something? I worked all afternoon on them, all afternoon and part of the evening, too. Do you think I could fly one of these one day? Do you, Harper?

Around five in the morning, she awoke. She was sweating and shaking. She had seen Blackie in her dream, sneaking toward the window of a house, trying to climb in, but the window was too high until Cat appeared and gave him a boost and he scrambled inside and there was the loud blast of a pistol.

She probably did help him, Harper thought. She was probably part of the whole thing. She certainly knew all about it. If she had told me I could have stopped this, I could have saved him if she just had told me what was going on. Why didn't she tell me? It would have been so easy, why?

The day following Blackie's funeral, Cat went into the newspaper and worked her regular day. She wrote her obituaries and did the best job she could. She was numb and she had not slept for some days now. At four o'clock she left the paper and came back to Waverly and went to her room. The books stood waist deep about her bed, five or six stacks of them. She had given a list to Bub and asked him to bring them to her room. After everyone else had gone to sleep, she read all night, losing herself in *A Farewell to Arms* or *The Count of Monte Cristo* or others.

It's the one thing I've done in my life that has never hurt me, Cat thought. Books have never let me down, never hurt me, never left me. Books succeed where everything else fails. They're like pets in a way. Always there, always happy to see you and holding for you in themselves the purest kind of devotion, hoping only that they will make you happy and that you will stay with them as long as you can.

Someone knocked on her door. She looked at her clock. It was seven-thirty. Hannah came into the room wearing her white apron and the white hat with the embroidered border of yellow daisies. She looked even thinner and blacker than ever. She was carrying a tray of food.

"Child, you better eat you some supper now. I brung you my fried chicken and rice and gravy and biscuit and I ain't gonna make you eat no vegetables either."

"I'm still not very hungry, Hannah."

"Well, you eat anyway, else you're gonna dry up and blow away."

Hannah sat down on the young woman's bed and patted her hand. "You got to let that boy go. He's in a better place than you and me. You can't keep on grieving about him, chile. You a young thing and got lots of beaus out there waiting on you. I know something about grief—it's a hungry thing and the more you feed it the bigger and the hungrier it gets and the only way you can stop it from growing is to stop feeding it."

"How do you stop feeding it?"

"Well, you start by feeding yourself," Hannah said, and picked up a chicken wing, poking it toward Cat's mouth.

Cat wanted to take a bite of it just to make Hannah feel better, but the sight of the chicken made her stomach turn.

Ford stepped into the bedroom. Cat looked exhausted. Her hair was blond and sunny, but there were blue circles under her eyes and crow's feet etched into the corners of her face. Even so, he thought her as beautiful as ever and the grief that she felt called to his own as if to say, Now there is something for us to share, now there is a way to begin.

"The chicken really is superb," he said.

"Please make this child take some nourishment, Mr. Ford. She getting skinny as a broomstick."

"Maybe she'll eat something in a while, Hannah."

"She need something now."

"Well, let me give her a try," Ford said.

Hannah got up and Ford sat down in her place.

"I'll be back in a few minutes and I want half that plate gone."

Cat said nothing.

"I don't think I've ever seen so many books by one bed in my life," Ford said. "Have you read all of these?"

"Most of them."

"Which one's your favorite?"

"Ford, I know you're trying to make me feel better but I just don't feel like talking right now."

He looked at her and brushed back a stray hair from her face. "You know, I used to think about this. It probably sounds crazy, but years ago, even when I was a boy, I used to sit around and wonder who would be the first of us to die. How would it happen, when would it happen and how the survivors would look at each other after it was over. I said to myself how could we ever look at each other honestly again. Before, we thought or at least felt that we were immortal, but when the first one of us died, then that illusion would be finished and I knew that we could never look at each other without a certain distance. I knew that after the first death, we could never be as close to one another as we had been because we could not allow ourselves to love each other deeply when we knew that sooner or later someone else would die."

Cat looked at his chubby face. Behind the wire-rim glasses, she could see that his eyes were red. He's been crying, she thought. He must have a tender heart. She knew that Wick had not shed a tear, and though Starkey had not been able to come home, she somehow doubted that he had cried either. Ford was the heart of the four brothers, and as she looked at him now, she could tell that the heart was broken. Cat reached out and touched the lavender mark in his cheek.

"Blackie used to tease me about it," he said.

"I know."

Gingerly, Ford touched her hand. She opened it and he laced his big fingers into her small ones.

Cat started to cry then. It was the first time she had cried and the tears hurt. They felt as if they were cracking open her eyes and they ached and stung so much that they felt like blood. She held Ford's hand and cried a long time.

32

AT SIX O'CLOCK IN the morning in
Saigon, three Vietnamese boys were sprawled together in a brown,
smelly pile. They were sleeping in a cardboard hovel which sat in the
small garden of a villa. The small structure lay beneath the window of
the room in which Starkey and Tim Ferguson slept so when the first
beer can went off, Bin heard it and sprang awake. He rubbed his face
and yawned and shook his two brothers. He had red bumps across his
arms and legs where the mosquitos had bitten him.

"Menu! Menu!" Lieutenant Tim Ferguson called from his room.

"Oui, monsieur," Bin called back. He shook his brothers again, then
sorted through a pile of rubble, found the card and raced to the window
of the villa.

Starkey had heard the beer can go off, too. It was the way Ferguson
had been waking up for the past couple of weeks. Though both of them
were first lieutenants, Ferguson had date of rank on Starkey. It was only
two weeks, but it was enough so that Ferguson was the CO.

"Mon capitain, are you big hungary?" Bin asked.

"Big, very big hungary. Starkey, are you awake?"

Starkey turned over in his bunk.

"Bin—my little lad—I think I'll have joudza this morning."

"Ah, Chinese food not good for Americans. Make you fart."

"No, that's Lieutenant Longstreet."

"You—Ferguson. You fart. Chinese food not good for you."

"I'll just have some hot tea," Starkey said.

"Come on, Starkey, at least get an egg roll."

"How can you eat that stuff for breakfast? Just some tea, Bin. And get something for you and your brothers."

"Shrimp?"

"No, that's too expensive," Ferguson said. "Eat chicken."

"Oh, for God's sake, Tim. Hey Bin, you get whatever you want," Starkey said. He got up, found some money and went to the window.

"I want shrimp too much maybe."

"You get shrimp. Get all you want."

The Vietnamese boy hollered and squealed and leapt down into the garden.

"You give those kids a lot of grief, you know?" Starkey said. He put on a pair of blue jeans and a Hawaiian shirt and thongs.

"How about going down to check the wires," Ferguson said. He ran a hand through his red hair and belched and took another slurp of beer.

Starkey gave a mock salute. He left the room and walked down the long hall which ran through the center of the villa. The floor was made up of squares of white marble and the walls were yellow plaster. The four enlisted men were up and answering phones and writing reports in their various offices. There was no air-conditioning in the villa. Only overhead fans stirred the thick, hot air of the city. Starkey nodded good morning to his men and went to the wire room. A calendar read March nineteenth, nineteen sixty-five. Starkey looked at the date and felt guilty. It was three weeks since Blackie had been killed. He felt guilty because he had not been crushed by his brother's death. It had not even surprised him really. He had thought that if Blackie continued breaking into houses, sooner or later this could happen. So when he got the phone call, he had not been surprised at all.

He grabbed a handful of messages and poured a cup of coffee and sat down at a desk. The teletype machine was clattering. Above his head on the wall was a dart board with a picture of Ho Chi Minh in the center of it. He set his coffee down and went to the double window and pushed open a tall shutter. In the papaya bush beside the house sat a black monkey. It had green eyes and yellow tufts of hair on its ears. It was eating a green papaya with the right paw while the left inserted a small, purple finger into its ear and wildly jiggled.

It wasn't that Blackie's death had not saddened him—it had. But it was the kind of sadness that one human being feels at the early death of another and this was why he felt guilty. You should have been grief-stricken, Starkey thought. You should have felt it deeply and not been able to sleep or not been able to eat or not been able to do something. You were able to do everything. When your brother dies, you should hurt and you didn't. Why not? That's an awful way to be. Why didn't you hurt? At least I'm thinking about it, he answered. At least I'm trying to understand why I didn't feel more. Isn't that good?

Starkey went through the ten or twelve wires which had come in during the night. There was nothing interesting, nothing exciting: a village chieftain had been kidnapped at An Loc, three ARVNs had been blown away in the delta, there were some strange troop movements north of Da Nang. He threw the wires back into the tray. I'm dying, he thought. I'm sitting here in this paper factory and I'm dying.

Corporal Vachel Fox stepped into the room. He was shirtless and barefoot, wearing only a pair of blue jeans. Across his bare chest he wore a bandoleer of shiny shells.

"Well, you don't look any too happy," Fox said.

Starkey looked at him. "Don't you think you could put on a shirt at least?"

Fox smiled and smoothed a hand over the bandoleer and the large blue skull which was tattooed in the center of his chest. "I reckon I could. What's eating you?"

"I'm spinning my wheels. I'm just sitting here day after day and I'm spinning my wheels."

"Well, I think things'll heat up pretty soon."

"Right."

"Johnson's sending in two more Marine battalions. Heard it at Command Headquarters last night. Two battalions and another twenty thousand in support."

"Are you serious?"

"Oh, yes sir. We're getting ready to kick ole Charlie's butt."

"Twenty thousand troops? Johnson's sending twenty thousand?"

"Well now, look at that face. I ain't seen such a happy face in a while."

Starkey picked up the phone. "I need to call Major Brown and tell him now is the time. Hell, everybody in Saigon will want in on this."

"Somehow I don't think so, Lieutenant. I really don't."

At five-thirty in the afternoon, Starkey was talking to Eugénie in the bar of the Continental.

"So what did he say?"

"Said I'm the only one who asked for a camp. Can you believe that? The only one."

"What will you do if you get one?"

"I'll do a good job."

"You think America can win the war, don't you?"

"I think we can win the war—if we get in it."

"You think you're not in it now?"

"I know we're not."

Eugénie shook her head slightly. Her dark hair had just been dried and it was light and puffy. She wore a yellow suit with cream trim and light yellow spike heels. Eugénie loved Starkey, but she could never allow herself to go out with him unless she had another relationship. She was afraid that if she went out with Starkey without being involved with someone else that she might lose herself completely to him. She had someone now and they had been going out for two weeks and she felt safe about seeing Starkey again and more than that she loved seeing him.

"René wants us to meet him for a drink at the track," Eugénie said. "He's bought a new horse—*C'est un bel animal, vraiment, et très rapide.*"

"Oh, I can't wait to see René again."

"He adores you."

"Oh wonderful."

"Why are you so cross?"

"I don't like him."

"Then why don't you just say so?"

"I did."

"You were trying to be ironic. You were using my irony. It's not good for you. You're not made for it. You're made to be straightforward. Apple pie and all that."

"If the son of a bitch is wearing mascara, I'm not sticking around."

The Phu Tho Racetrack was crowded. There were probably two thousand people there when Starkey and Eugénie arrived. The track was built by the French in the early twenties, and though it was somewhat rundown, many of the French planters and businessmen still came to the track every day to drink and bet on their Arabians. Most of the crowd at the track was Chinese or Vietnamese while only seventy or eighty spectators were French. The French always stayed to themselves toward the center of the track, sitting in a collection of wooden boxes which were busy with Vietnamese waiters in white jackets.

By the time Starkey and Eugénie made their way to René Couvier's box, the twilight was down on the racetrack. The light in Saigon in the evening was not like the light Starkey had seen anyplace else. It was a kind of soft lavender which faded to purple at the edges of anything in the distance and it was always humid and did not carry sound well and to Starkey it often felt dangerous. René Couvier sat in his wooden box surrounded by his friends. Most of his friends were French colons with the exception of a few Chinese and one American who had blond hair and a big neck.

When the American saw Starkey, he jumped up and threw out his hand. "Starkey, thank God you're here. These guys don't believe me. Geannie, how are you? God, you look gorgeous. Hey René, get us some booze, man. Everybody's gone dry here."

"Well, your wish is my command," René said.

"Aw gimme a break, will ya."

René smiled at Eugénie. "Don't you adore him when he gets butch. How've you been, my dear?" René Couvier was wearing a white cotton suit with a pink orchid in his lapel. His hair was brown and swept back in slick streaks from his forehead. He was puffing from an ivory cigarette holder.

Starkey was introduced to the others, some of whom he had not met before. Champagne and hors d'oeuvres were ordered and Starkey sat on the other side of Eugénie so he would not be close to René. The American's name was Bob Jenkins and he was drunk with bourbon and his face was red and sweating and he was sitting beside Starkey and talking loudly.

"It's the damnedest thing, Stark, it's just the damnedest thing in the whole damn world."

René leaned across Eugénie. His eyelashes were heavy with mascara. "He's been going on about this all evening."

"Well, hell, nobody would know about it if I hadn't told you."

"No one believes you, dear."

"Don't call me that shit."

"Oh, pardon, alors. Mais tu es si mignon."

"Yeah, same to ya, buddy—now look, Stark. You see Number Six out there. You see that black Arabian. Yea, that one. Name's Papillon and you know who owns him? You won't believe this. You know who owns that big stud? The Cong."

A waiter set down a tray with three bottles of champagne, a dish of white biscuits and a red bowl of caviar. The caviar was heaped into a black mound and in the center of the mound sat a well of cream cheese dressed up with a dozen green olives. Bob grabbed a bottle of the champagne by the neck and slunk down in his chair and began filling his glass. René's friends began scooping up the caviar with silver spoons embossed with gold dragons. In the beginning they heaped spoonfuls of the caviar and cream cheese onto the white biscuits, but soon they were just eating mouthfuls of black caviar and drinking champagne.

René and Eugénie talked about the new Paris fashions and René asked if Eugénie had run into Bao Dai in Paris and she said that she had spent several evenings with the Emperor and that he had a lot of money and was doing very well, retaining a chateau in Provence as well as a suite of rooms at the Cay u Lite.

"He's a great celebrity in Paris," Eugénie said.

"I think it is one of the problems we have in Saigon," René said. "We have no celebrities."

The talk about celebrities animated one of René's friends, who held a biscuit spread with black caviar in each hand. He wore an obvious and synthetic red hairpiece which was slightly askew. His name was Dupré Pearon. He was a colon whose family had lived in Hanoi until Ho Chi Minh had driven the Catholics south.

"Oh, but we do have celebrities," Dupré said.

"No, I don't think we have any at all," René said. "And it's a serious state for us. Human beings must have someone to—admire. In the North they have, of course, and they have had for years—Ho Chi Minh."

"We have two such people," Dupré said. "We have the Ambassador Henry Lodge and the General Westmoremand."

"Land," said René. "Westmoreland."

"Ah, wonderful—West More Land. Don't you think it sums up the whole American attitude—West: More Land. Isn't it why they are here really and truly? Everyone is a colon, no?"

Starkey ate two biscuits with caviar and drank citron presse soda and it suddenly occurred to him what Bob Jenkins had meant.

"Hey, Bob. What did you say about Number Six?"

Jenkins was sunk down in his chair. He had already drunk half the bottle of champagne. His blond hair disheveled in the warm breeze. "It's only the most interesting thing going on at the track. It's only the bestest thing, you know. The only thing that's worth a damn so why are you asking? Why don't you just talk about ole Bao Dai. That's really, really, really interesting more, don't you think?"

"His name's Papillon, right? Now what did you say?" Starkey asked.

"The Vietcong own him."

"Come on."

"Apparently he's run three or four times. An Arvin guy told me. The Cong are cleaning house with him. They've been winning five or six million piasters a race."

"Would they allow that here? Would they allow the Vietcong to race a horse in Saigon?"

"How they gonna stop it?"

An announcement was made over the track loudspeakers that the final race was ready to be run. René and Eugénie were arguing about the best restaurant in Bali when Bob jumped up and shouted, "Shut the hell up. Just shut the hell up. Who cares about Bali."

René reached out and patted the big American's thigh and gently coaxed him back into his chair. He fixed Jenkins a caviar biscuit, then leaned over and whispered something into his ear which made Jenkins scowl and squirm.

33

EIGHT HORSES LINED UP at the
starting gate. The conversation among René's friends ended. It was
supposed to be the best race of the day. The pistol was fired and the
gate crashed open and the black and brown horses dashed onto the red
dirt track. There were six laps in the race and by the end of the fifth
Papillon was running a close second to the favorite of the race—a horse
called La Marshall. René and his friends stood up at the last lap and
cheered and waved lavender handkerchiefs to encourage La Marshall.
Bob Jenkins watched them and then he stood and took a long drink of
champagne and then began yelling, "Come on, Papillon. Come on,
baby. Let's go, go, go!"

Coming down the final stretch, Papillon pulled even with La Marshall
and began to nose ahead for the lead. The jockey for La Marshall
slapped his horse with the riding stick and jerked the reins and the
black Arabian swerved to the left and collided with Papillon, forcing
him into the rail. La Marshall stretched and sprinted, winning by three

lengths. René and his friends tittered and screamed and ordered more champagne and Bob Jenkins was the first one to see the two small men wearing black pajamas. They jumped onto the track and walked into the winner's circle and a few people yelled and then the two men leveled the black machine guns which they had been carrying close to their bodies. The first bursts of the machine guns were short and abrupt and the big black horse seemed only to flinch and jerk as if the shots were blanks, but when the Vietcong let the bullets fly long, the horse shivered and jumped, then dropped onto its front legs and threw its bleeding head backwards, almost parallel with its bloody back and the head rolled to the left until La Marshall collapsed, pinning the jockey beneath it.

The stands around the winners' circle had completely emptied and people were scrambling over seats and screaming and from the main gate several National Police were running up the track toward the Vietcong, who seemed cool and almost careless, one of them pulling a grenade from his pocket and walking over to the thrashing jockey. The Vietcong struck the jockey several times in the head with the butt of his rifle and then opened the jockey's mouth and knocked out his teeth and hammered in the grenade. The two little men wearing sandals and black pajamas then walked into the stands, and when they saw the police running toward them, they fired the machine guns into the air and the cops hit the dirt and did not return the fire. The grenade exploded and blew part of the jockey's head into the air and it thudded onto the stands. The Vietcong laughed and walked into a wooden tunnel that led to the outside.

From somewhere beyond the track sirens began blasting and the National Police finally made their way to the dead horse and headless jockey and they ran around brandishing pistols and blowing silver whistles. René and the others had fallen onto the floor, a mound of silk and gabardine, hiding beneath several white parasols. Jenkins bounded down onto the track and, hands on hips, walked toward the slaughter. Starkey got Eugénie out of the track and into a cab just as jeep loads of ARVNs arrived.

"Where do you want to go?"

"I need a drink."

"Just tell me."

"I can't think."

"Cercle Sportif," Starkey said to the driver.

It was one of the oldest and most traditional of the colon's clubs in Saigon. Americans and Vietnamese were not admitted to the club until 1963. It was an old and elegant house with a long front porch, twenty large rooms, several tennis courts and a rectangular swimming pool set in a palm tree garden holding banks of pink and blue frangipanis and clusters of yellow orchids set in black pots. Most of the Americans stayed in the bar, which was loaded with bright bottles of American liquor and tall racks of French wine. There were leather chairs and wicker chairs and an ancient teak floor covered by Oriental rugs. By the time Starkey and Eugénie arrived, most of the people in the bar had heard of the attack. They were laughing and joking and terribly agitated. There had not been an attack in Saigon in a while and they were giddy with the excitement of it. Above the mirrors of the bar sat an RCA stereo system. The Armed Forces Radio Network was playing a collection of the Beach Boys' greatest hits. At the end of one song there was a commercial. Several men were moving through brush. There was the sound of crunching twigs and the whistle of branches against fatigues and hard breathing, then a voice:

"All right, hold up. Fan out and make camp. No fires. Charlie don't need a beacon."

Then another voice, soft, almost tender, but still masculine:

"It was a hundred and six today. You hiked ten miles through the worst the Ashau could give. Now you're tired. There will be no hot food, no hot shower, but still you're warm. You're okay because you've got Him, and you know He's all you'll ever need—now or any other time. God—the best buddy a soldier can have. This is Reverend Billy Jackson. Remember the unit that prays together, stays together. Go to church. You won't regret it."

When the commercial finished, a broadcaster read a letter from General Westmoreland which said very subtly that VC prisoners must never be killed and that every soldier should do his best to support the Chieu Hoi program for defectors because each defector "means one more soldier for the GVN and one less for Uncle Ho."

Starkey ordered a double vodka martini and a soda. Eugénie lit a cigarette. She was shaking.

"I haven't seen it before," she said.

"It happens fast."

"I mean someone being murdered. I haven't seen it."

"It happens real quick."

"I don't think so. I think it's slow. Everything's slow. I thought they'd never finish."

"Took maybe fifteen seconds."

"It had to be longer than that."

"Twenty-five maybe. No more."

"And it was like it wasn't real. Did you feel that way? Of course you've seen lots of this, but—it seemed to me that they weren't real. Neither the Vietcong nor the jockey nor the horse. Not even the police. None of it was real."

"It was real."

"Did you hear the jockey's head when it hit the stands? It sounded like a cabbage. It made a kind of—thunk. It didn't sound real either."

"You want to go back and have a look?"

"I understand why you want that camp now. I want it for you."

"You want it for me? Wait a minute. You want me to get the camp assignment?"

"It makes life interesting. No—not interesting. It makes life thrilling —death does. I can see that now. How wise you are. I had never felt it before, but it's perfectly true that death livens life up a bit, don't you think?"

"No, I don't think so."

"Oh, of course you do. That's why you want to command the camp. You're bored with life. You want the sound of explosions and the rat-tat-tat of machine guns and the possibility of death. Listen, I'm with you, I'm for you, after this afternoon I understand completely." Eugénie stuck her fingers between his own. "Let's go to the Continental. They've ballroom dancing on the terrace this evening. We can dance until dawn." She reached out and touched his jaw.

Starkey knew then. The kindness and warmth were always the keys. If she became sweet like this, it meant she had found somebody else, it meant she was seeing somebody else. He felt a sense of panic and pain, wondering why she always had to do this. Why couldn't she just allow herself to love him without having someone on the side.

"Do you know you have a striking jaw?" she said.

"Uh-huh."

"Terribly striking. Sometimes when I see it just right, it makes me shiver. I shouldn't tell you, of course."

"I know why you're telling me."

"Look." She rolled up her sleeve and showed him her forearm. "Look at the gooseflesh."

"You're just cold."

"It's that jaw. It's that angular, striking jaw."

"Put on a sweater."

"Why are you being so cross?"

"Because I know what's going on and I don't like it. Why can't you understand that? Why can't you see that you're telegraphing everything?"

"You're being silly."

"I know what you're doing."

"I'm shivering."

"Yeah, you're shivering. I'd like to kill the sonofabitch."

René and Bob Jenkins walked into the bar. The colons smiled at them. René's white suit was dirty from lying on the floor of Phu Tho. His orchid was smashed and tattered in the lapel. Bob Jenkins seemed more sober, though his face was still flushed.

"On fait la bombe ici, non?" René asked.

Several glasses were raised.

"I want a party. I want a wonderful party."

The bartender cut off the radio and put on a Supremes record. As soon as the music started, René began to dance and pantomime his way into the bar. Several colons got off their bar stools and danced singly. The music was loud:

> *Baby, baby*
> *Whenever you're near*
> *I hear a symphony*
> *Each time you speak to me*

René danced into the heart of the colons, who wore the latest Paris suits and shoes and scents. Most of them were very thin and their apparel was composed of the subtlest color: lavender and dove gray sportcoats, light tangerine trousers and burnt saffron shirts. They drank

small amounts of the worst liquor; Pernod and Absinthe in the beginning, then moving to Wild Turkey or tequila and the weaker of them
sliding to gin and lime mixed with fresh pineapple and coconut juice.

The whole bar of the Cercle Sportif was dancing now, including
Eugénie, who insinuated herself into the colons and did a kind of modi-
fied Bugaloo. Starkey was not dancing. He sat at the table drinking his
Bireley's orange drink. He thought about Eugénie and who she was
seeing now and what were they doing together and the thought nearly
made him sick, so he forced himself to think about something else,
something he had noticed at the Phu Tho Racetrack. It was the manner
of the Vietcong. They were utterly confident, completely sure of themselves. He had not seen this confidence in the ARVN forces at all, even
the Vietnamese Rangers and Marines did not have it. He had seen it in
some American troops when they were first in-country, but it always
vanished after a couple combat patrols or when a platoon had to dig
some dinks out of a tunnel. Surely those two Vietcong had been through
similar experiences. Why weren't they gun-shy? Why weren't they
beaten down? It troubled him and right now it felt good to be troubled
because he didn't have to think about Eugénie.

When the song finished, René and Eugénie sat down at his table.
René was very loud and very arch and Starkey noticed for the first time
that he had plucked his eyebrows. He was talking about the wife of
Nguyen Cao Ky.

"My dear, she's had everything done to her that she can. Her boobs
have been lifted, her butt tucked and her teeth capped. Not only that—
she's going to get round eyes."

"What do you mean—round eyes?" Eugénie asked.

"I mean that she's trying her best to look Western and she's going to
Hong Kong and have her slits made round."

"Can they do that, Starkey?"

She squeezed his hand and stuck out her bottom lip. Starkey looked
at her and then looked away and did not squeeze her hand in return.
How he wished it was an honest pout, an honest flirtation. If it were
honest, he knew it would have the power to make him dizzy and warm,
but it was not honest. She flirted with him because she had someone
else, because she felt safe.

"Of course they can," René said. "It costs so very much money but

Madame Ky does not care about money. She thinks she is headed for big things. They say Nguyen Cao Ky may be the next head of state."

"Who says?"

"Oh my dear, everyone says. He is doing all the right things: tiger hunts with General Thieu in Boloven, bird hunts with Westmoreland in Camou. Leisurely weekends deciding the rise and fall of nations with Lodge in Dalat. Yes, the Air Marshal is a young man the American's wish to aggrandize."

Bob Jenkins came over from the bar. He polished off a red, white and blue shot glass and set it on the table. "Are we going to get some chink food?"

"Why don't you sit down and have a drink," René said.

A lot of fire had gone out of Jenkins. He was like a big blond boy. "I'm really hungry."

"Are you that hungry?"

"My stomach hurts it's so hungry."

René turned to Eugénie. *"Voudriez-vous dîner avec nous, tous les deux?"*

34

THE TRAFFIC IN CHOLON was terrible, so they got out of the cab two blocks from the Arc En Ciel restaurant. Starkey had been in Cholon six or seven times, but the place still fascinated him. Most of the people were Chinese. The air was wet and thick with many smells: the odor of sewage which ran through the stone gutters on either side of the dark streets and the smell of gray mold which crept up the sides of buildings, and ginger from small restaurants and a sweet aroma from a tiny garden of camellias and jasmine. The streets were jammed with Chinese, and Starkey and the others had to fight their way through. The shops were open and busy and all of them were lit by neon signs and flashing Chinese script. Almost every shop was selling food of some kind. Eugénie stopped at a large store. She grabbed Starkey's hand.

"Have you been here?" she asked.

"No." He let her hold his hand.

"You've got to see it. It's so macabre."

Eugénie pulled him. René and Bob followed.

The place was a kind of butcher shop. It was dark and smelled like blood. They walked down a narrow and twisting path lit by kerosene lanterns, many of which were marked U.S. Army. Hanging on either side of the aisle were the disemboweled bodies of pink pigs and several carcasses of oxen and farther into the dark hung hundreds of ducks and chickens and peacocks, all of them plucked, the skin yellow and white and the heads still connected to the bare bodies and beyond these hung the skinned bodies of dogs and puppies, monkeys and snakes, each of them retaining its ghastly head and the shocked eyes of sudden death. All along the path there were cubbyholes where the Chinese worked on something dead lying on a bloody table, their black eyes and yellow skin glimmering in the dark.

René put a hand in the small of Starkey's back. "Isn't this place gorgeous?"

"Oh, it's beautiful," Starkey said. "How did Eugénie find it?"

"We became bored one evening and decided to do the town and among other places we did this one. It is a truly terrible place, is it not?"

Eugénie was about ten feet ahead of them. She waved them forward.

"This is my favorite spot," she said. "I've tried one of everything in this room."

"What do you mean you've tried it?" Starkey asked.

"I think she means she ate it," Bob said.

Light bulbs dangled on thin cords from the ceiling and revealed wire cages holding hundreds of green toads with black spots. There were four or five wooden tubs holding black eels with yellow fins and long, meaty, pink mustaches and beside the tubs sat wooden boxes which contained a pulsating mass of something that looked like grubs, fat things with blue flesh and orange heads. Beside the door which led to the outside stood stacks of eggs which were covered with a kind of black, fuzzy mold and behind the eggs hanging from the wall was a poster of Uncle Sam all dressed in red, white and blue, saying, "I want you."

Eugénie paused at the door. "See anything you like?"

"Not really," Starkey said.

"How about just a sliver of dog."

"I don't think so."

"A sliver of dog, a chunk of cat and a smidgeon of eel."

"Sounds like something out of Macbeth."

"How witty you are."

When they arrived at the Arc En Ciel restaurant, a long line went out into the street. They had been waiting about ten minutes when they saw Monsieur Villeneuve leaving the restaurant. He was with a lovely Vietnamese woman dressed in an ao dai.

"It will take you forever, my friends," Villeneuve said. His face was red and his eyes blue and his white mustache neat and sharp. "Come to my house. We'll have the restaurant send a selection of its best food."

The food was delivered an hour later, after several rounds of gin and pineapple juice had gone down and washed away the smell and the memory of the Chinese butcher shop. Everyone ate greedily except for Eugénie, who only nibbled at ginger shrimp. When the coffee was served, Monsieur Villeneuve said that the next morning he was going to his land in Kontum for his yearly tiger hunt. He invited everyone to join him.

René traced a limp finger over a plucked brow. "Do you know I've lived here all my life and never been on a tiger hunt. *Ça doit être passionnant, vraiment.*"

"*Oui, une expérience primordiale, le péril passionnant du tueur qui court le risque de se faire tuer,*" the old man said.

"*C'est-à-dire que le tigre chasse le chasseur?*"

"Papa," Eugénie said.

"I'm sorry—pardon me, Starkey."

"Good God, I'd love to go," Bob Jenkins said. "I didn't know you people still hunted tigers. How do you do it? I mean, do you sit up in trees or shoot from trucks? How does it work?"

"We usually hunt from the back of elephant."

"An elephant! That's the way the Brits used to do it in India. I've read all about it in Jim Corbett's books. Have you heard of him?"

Monsieur Villeneuve nodded. "I knew him."

"Jim Corbett? You knew Jim Corbett? Jesus, Mary and Joseph."

Starkey smiled at Jenkins. He had felt the same kind of astonishment when he had discovered that the colons still hunted tiger. He had been on three hunts with Monsieur Villeneuve. He had killed only one tiger and he still felt guilty about it. He had shot the tiger from the back of an elephant while the cat was drinking at a stream. It had been a long shot, three hundred yards, but he still felt bad about it because the tiger never had a chance really and he decided if he hunted tiger again he would do it by foot.

Monsieur Villeneuve's hunting land lay one hundred and seventy miles north of Saigon. He owned twenty-five thousand acres of jungle and grassy plateau, deep in the country of the Montagnard. Most of his land was concentrated around a villa which sat on an old tea plantation. He did not use the land to grow tea or coffee, although it would have supported both. The Rhade tribe lived in the very center of his land in an ancient village called Bak Jin.

The party of hunters arrived at Bak Jin in the early afternoon of the next day. Starkey had been to the village twice before, but he was still amazed at its primitiveness. Bak Jin was a slash of brown mud in a jungle valley beside a river. It was composed of forty longhouses which were built in parallel rows and made of wood and bamboo and each house was built on six-foot-high stilts. Notched logs served as stairways into the houses. Bak Jin was the home of Monsieur Villeneuve's Rhade guide. His name was Me.

As the two Buick station wagons slushed through the brown mud of the Rhade village, the whole place came to life. Orange jungle cats scattered and muddy dogs howled and hosts of green parakeets streamed from house to house while monkeys screeched and threw leaves from the trees. Halfway into the village, Rhade children began following the cars, laughing and singing a song of welcome. They were dark brown with long dark hair. The girls wore ankle-length black skirts and their breasts were bare. The boys wore gray loin cloths and sometimes a green GI T-shirt. When the children smiled, they gave Starkey the creeps because like all good Rhade they had filed their teeth into white triangles.

"My God, look at those teeth," Bob Jenkins said.

"I think they are elegant," said René.

"You wouldn't think they were so elegant if you knew why they filed them," Starkey said.

"Well, why do they?"

"To break through bones."

"It sounds like a good idea."

"Human bones."

René pressed four scented fingers against his lips and his eyes went wide.

"Are you saying these guys are cannibals?" asked Jenkins.

"Some of them are. Some of them aren't."

"How do you know which is which?"

"Get an invitation to dinner."

Villeneuve and Eugénie rode in the first car. They pulled beside a longhouse and the children swirled around the car and the twenty Rhade who lived in the longhouse walked out onto the porch waving, smiling their teeth. Me sidestepped his way down the notched log and jumped calf deep into the brown mud. He was barefoot, his skin sooty and dark. He wore a loincloth and a white T-shirt with red lettering which said MARINES! On his back, tied by a leather strap, he carried a crossbow.

When Villeneuve got out of his car, Me ran up to him, grabbed his hand and said, "Let's get drunk together."

Coming from behind, Bob Jenkins heard the greeting. "Now that's my kind of man."

"It's their usual way of greeting each other," Starkey said.

"Me, you look well," Villeneuve said. "How is hunting?"

"The monkeys are good and the pig, but the lizard is best."

"Do you still make the lizard salad?"

"I make," Me said, smiling his set of white triangles.

"Let's get drunk," Bob Jenkins said, extending his hand.

Me grabbed it. "Get drunk! Yes, yes. Let us get very, very drunk together."

"We will hunt Bo-Kla tomorrow?" Villeneuve asked.

"He has killed."

"Bo-Kla?"

"Near the river. A woman with her clothes. She is in Bo-Kla."

"Well, that ought to make it a little easier," Starkey said.

"What's happened?" Jenkins asked.

"A tiger has killed someone."

Jenkins clapped his hands. "God, that's exciting. I can't believe it. I just can't believe it. A man-eater. We're going to hunt a man-eater."

* * *

Starkey understood Jenkins' incredulity. It was difficult to believe that in 1965, only a hundred and seventy miles from Saigon, in the middle of a modern war which made use of laser-guided bombs and computerized Gatling guns—it was hard to accept that men in loincloths were hunting man-eating tigers, but they were.

The hunting party reached the villa later in the afternoon. It was two stories with pink stucco walls and bright blue shutters. Jasmine covered most of the walls and camellia bushes sat in the front yard. Villeneuve had not been to the villa in months. Once he came three or four times a year to hunt, but that was before the Vietcong had made their presence known by beheading two Baptist missionaries. The villa had ten rooms, but little furniture and most of it bamboo. Several of Me's family dusted and cleaned and prepared dinner.

They sat on a stone patio in front of the villa. Long grass stood seven feet high between the camellia bushes. The smell of tea was in the air, a rich, brown smell just like the smell of tea steeping in a pot. The tea fields lay below the villa and ran to the edge of the jungle. They ate chunks of pork wrapped in blue orchid leaves and cooked in rice wine. Served with the pork was a big bowl of rice and bamboo shoots and steaming bowls of green tea. Me's lizard salad was saved for last by direction of Monsieur Villeneuve.

It was served in a large orange pot. As soon as it was set on the table René took a peek, then left, heading for the house.

"Come back here," Jenkins yelled.

"It's too ghastly."

"Oh, it can't be that bad," Jenkins said. He pulled the bowl toward him and looked inside.

There were about two hundred dead lizards in a mound in the center of the bowl. They were a light green color except for the tails, which were purple. The legs of the lizards had been gnawed off by Me, but the heads were still intact.

Jenkins pushed the bowl toward Villeneuve. "They're not even cooked."

"Of course they are."

"They don't look cooked."

"It is a subtle dish. The haute cuisine of the jungle. They put a little pork fat in a wok, gently sauté the lizards, then add a little plum brandy and toss in some red cabbage and ginger. It's really very tasty," Villeneuve said. He took a pair of chopsticks and filled a small bowl with the soft green lizards.

"I pretend that they're green beans," Eugénie said. Her black hair was blowing in the breeze. She wore a khaki blouse and skirt. She wore a little rouge on her cheeks and her eyes were hazel and shining with the last light of the sun. She filled a bowl and started to eat.

Starkey felt uncomfortable sitting out on the patio. They were perfect targets for snipers. He had brought along his .357 again, though he did not bring a grenade this time. He carried the pistol in the water buffalo hide holster and strapped it to his waist. Villeneuve had not protested, perhaps remembering the two missionaries who had been beheaded. Starkey remembered them, too. Whenever he doubted whether or not the United States should be in Vietnam, he thought about things like the murder of the missionaries.

"I don't think we should stay out here much longer," Starkey said.

"Why not?" Villeneuve asked.

"Snipers."

"Oh, you worry about silly things."

Starkey didn't want another argument with the old man, so he changed the subject. "How will we hunt tomorrow?"

"You want to hunt on foot, don't you?"

"I think it would be more fair."

"Why?" asked Eugénie. "You're still using a huge rifle. Go after him with a knife—that would be fair."

Both of them seemed edgy, so Starkey excused himself and went to his room.

It was on the second story. The floor was blue tile and the three big windows were covered by white curtains. He lay down in his narrow camp bed and pulled the yellow mosquito net tight. There was a flash and rumble in the distance and the white curtains filled with the wind and floated into the room and it reminded Starkey of Waverly, the curtains filling the room and the thunder and the smell of rain and he remembered Blackie and how he seemed to love the rain, how the rain made him so bright and happy and for the first time Starkey missed him the way he should have missed him all along.

To stop hurting, he tried to think of something else. When there was a thought troubling him, a thought or feeling which was particularly bad, he tried to make himself think about sex and so tonight while the distant thunder rumbled and the jungle cried with the creatures of the night and the smell of the tea fields flowed into the room, he thought about making love with Eugénie and for a while it was good, until he started wondering if she had made love with the other guy she was seeing. Starkey wanted to think the best about other people and when he was younger he did, but in recent years he had found that if he suspected something about a person it was more than likely true. She's sleeping with him, he thought. I might as well face it. There's nothing I can do about it so I'm going to just accept the situation as it is and get just as tough and hard as she is and have sex with her, have fun with the whole thing and not be so serious about it and maybe I'll get somebody on the side, too and then I'll stop hurting about it.

35

DOWNSTAIRS, EUGÉNIE HAD JUST gotten out of a tub of cold water. There was no hot water in the villa now. She looked into a mirror at her makeupless face and frowned at the several acne scars which always appeared on her cheeks without the compound. She flipped her damp hair and then walked out onto the balcony. She was naked and the air from the jungle felt moist and warm. She looked up at Starkey's room. His light was on and for some reason she thought about his hands, seeing the blue veins running beneath the red flesh and dusting of brown hair and she thought of his hands and the way that something so big could be so delicate. She loved Starkey more now than she had ever loved him and she knew it was because she was seeing someone, which meant that she was still free, still not committed to Starkey completely and so she could love him much more deeply, and she hoped that Starkey understood that she was doing this as much for him as for her, because she knew that he needed to love her and the only way she could get close enough to him to let

him love her was if she had someone else. Some men needed to be
loved and this was the majority of them, but others, the best ones,
needed to love someone else and Starkey was one of these and he
should be happy now.

Eugénie went back inside and put on a robe and went up to Starkey's
room. She tapped on his door.

"Yeah."

She came into the room and opened his mosquito net and lay down
beside him.

"I was thinking about you," she said.

"I was thinking about you, too."

"What were you thinking?"

"What's going on with you and that other guy."

"Nothing's going on."

"And then I decided I'm not going to worry about it. Isn't that
good?"

"It's all right if you still love me. Do you still love me?"

"I'm trying to love you less."

"Well, that's okay. You love me less and I'll love you more and we'll
be happy." She took one of his hands and put his thumb into her
mouth.

Everyone had finished breakfast by five-thirty in the morning. The light
was just beginning and it was a dark pink color and the long grass and
camellia bushes in the front yard were glistening with the dew of the
jungle. Starkey stuck a Purdey rifle into his shoulder and sighted down
the barrel. It was one of Monsieur Villeneuve's best guns and Starkey
had wanted to shoot it as soon as he saw it. The Purdey was a double
barrel, weighed thirteen pounds and shot a two-and-a-half-ounce ball.

Me trotted up the mud road which led to the house. The elephants
were behind him. They moved over the mud so quietly that the only
sound was the sound of their feet sucking and hissing as they pulled
them from the mud. Starkey thought that the elephants looked beautiful
in the early morning. They were three different colors. Their legs were a
dark gray, almost black, stained with the dew of the long grass, and
their chests and sides were a dusty brown color and the higher part of
their backs, just below the orange blankets and wicker riding platforms,
was a light lavender.

René was drinking a brandy and soda. He had not put on mascara or blush this morning, though he had penciled his plucked brows. He pointed at the platforms on the backs of the elephants. "Do I have to get up there?"

"No," Eugénie said. "You don't have to get up there. You can walk behind the elephant."

"I could probably get more exercise."

"Oh, you could get lots. They say the tiger always attacks from the rear."

"Really?"

"But you could get lots of exercise."

"How do I get up there?"

"Like this."

Eugénie hit the nearest elephant in the center of the trunk and then lightly kicked his front leg and leaned herself against it. The big animal went down on one knee and dropped his head and trunk and Eugénie stepped into the curl of the trunk and the elephant stood and tilted his head backward and she jumped and straddled his neck. "Ta-da," she said.

It took René several attempts to get on the elephant and by the time he finally made it everyone was ready. Me rode the lead elephant. Monsieur Villeneuve sat immediately behind him on a wooden bench which was attached to the wicker platform. Eugénie and Starkey and the handler sat on the second elephant and René and Jenkins on the third. Five Rhade followed the string of elephants, the last one of them pulling a white kid goat.

For two miles the wide tea fields were flat and held long grass and a few pine trees and growing in the brown long grass were the tea bushes with their shining green leaves and white blossoms and the whole valley shimmered beneath the white sun and the tea bushes filled the air with sweetness. The caravan covered this space quickly and then came to the tall jungle. It was green and dark and the trees formed three separate canopies so that when the elephants disappeared into the green, the air became cool and wet and the white sun was left behind.

They traveled through the jungle until it was almost dark and then made camp. After the tents were put up and supper was broiling over the fire, Monsieur Villeneuve explained the way the hunt would go. Me would leave immediately after supper and take the white kid and tie it at a stake about a mile from the camp at the end of a steep valley. A half a mile beyond the valley was a plateau of long grass and it was broad and deep and held a number of marshes and according to Me it was where the man-eater retreated after he had killed. The kid would bleat all night long and hopefully pull the man-eater in from the long grass and then Me and the Rhade would circle around and move through the grass on the elephants and drive the tiger down into the valley, where the hunters would be waiting on foot just behind the kid.

"Do we have to be on foot?" René asked.

"Well, I think Starkey wants to be on foot and I haven't tried it in a few years," Monsieur Villeneuve said.

"I'm not shooting, though."

"Couldn't we put him in a tree?" Jenkins asked.

"Oh for God's sake, René, you're such a chicken," Eugénie said.

"Yes, I'm a chicken. I admit it."

"Put him in a tree." Jenkins popped a Budweiser beer.

When the beer can popped, several white pheasants thundered from a big fern and everyone jumped and then laughed and Starkey was amazed at the incongruity of it all. Here he was a lieutenant in the army, eating Iowa corn-fed beef from the PX, drinking a Coca-Cola, preparing to hunt a tiger in 1965 in the middle of a guerilla war.

After supper everyone played a few hands of poker and drank port and ternum, which was a special rice alcohol that the Rhade fermented for three years and served only on real occasions. Monsieur Villeneuve and René went to their tents early and Eugénie and Starkey and Bob Jenkins sat in camp chairs beside the fire.

"I think this is probably one of the last times we're going to be able to do this," Starkey said.

"Don't be such a pessimist," said Eugénie. "It could all blow over."

"Rumor has it that Johnson's putting a hundred and fifty thousand men in here by next December."

"You're kidding," Jenkins said.

"MACV's even talking of bringing in B-52s from Guam."

"Well, they're not going to bomb the jungle, are they?" Jenkins asked. "I mean if they bring in B-52s to bomb Hanoi, you know that makes sense, but not to bomb the jungle, unless it's the Ho Chi Minh Trail."

"If Johnson brings them in, he'll bomb everything."

"How do you know?" Eugénie asked.

"Because I know him. It's the way he looks at everything. If he has a problem he solves it fast and quick using as much power as he can bring to bear. He's not a subtle man. The more power, the better. It makes him look good or so he thinks."

"You know the President personally?" Jenkins asked.

"My family knows him."

"I hope it doesn't happen," Eugénie said.

"It's gonna happen."

"Why are you such a damn know-it-all?"

"Everything is about to change, Eugénie. Your life here, your father's life, nothing will be the same. The war's going to get big, bigger than anybody knows, except Johnson. He knows how big it's going to get because he wants it big and I'll make you a little prediction. I predict that in two years' time we'll have three hundred thousand troops in Vietnam and Johnson will be bombing everything. Every village, every town, everything that can hide the Vietcong North and South, and in the fourth year Ho Chi Minh will pull out his boys and try to make peace and Lyndon Johnson will be called the greatest wartime President since FDR."

"Is that what you want? You want Lyndon Johnson to be called a great President?"

"I don't give a damn about Lyndon Johnson."

"Then why are you here?"

"I'm here to win."

"Oh that's great, that's just great, Starkey. You're here to win. What an enlightened attitude!"

I am a soldier and it is not only my duty, it is not only my obligation, it is my delight to win, it is my craving. So next you will say why, and the only answer I can give is that I am afraid to lose again, because I am a Southerner and all of my life I have carried the thought that I was defeated before I was born, and the pain of that defeat, the pain of Gettysburg and Shiloh and Appomattox, has afflicted me and fired me with one single idea: in war, I will never lose again, no matter what the cost, no matter if I and my kind must rain bloody hell upon the face of the earth.

Starkey thought these things an hour later, lying in his tent. He was never able to be so elegant in an actual argument, but somehow just thinking them was good enough.

The next morning he and the others rose at five o'clock. The pink light of the sky shined the top of the jungle, but had not sifted down into it and so the air in the camp was black and green and soggy with the night sweat of many trees. The hunters drank their coffee and listened to the young kid bleating a mile away. Me had taken the elephants around the plateau of long grass. At six o'clock he and the other Rhade would begin the drive, hoping that the tiger had been drawn closer by the noise of the kid.

By six-fifteen Villeneuve and Jenkins and Starkey had positioned themselves at the end of a narrow valley whose other end opened onto the plateau of long grass. The three men stood fifty feet apart. Two miles away they heard the opening din of the Rhade as they shouted and beat metal pots and clapped their hands.

And he heard them, too, having been drawn toward the place where they slept, he much closer than any of them had suspected, not in the long grass, but waiting now in the green jungle, the soft, quiet ferns and living leaves that never betrayed his steps, and if these white men thought that he had come so close to them because of the kid, they were wrong because he came not for the kid and not for the brown men, but rather he came for the white men and the smell of them which was different from any other smell in the jungle, a smell so sweet and so rich that he had never been able to resist it since he had taken the first one of them as he slept on the green machine with its long gun a year ago.

"Try not to hit him in the head," Villeneuve said.

"Why not?" asked Jenkins.

"It will ruin the trophy."

"I think I'll just take him where I can get him."

Starkey was looking into the curling green jungle when he saw the first movement. The beaters were still a good mile and a half away and it was too early for anything to be coming out, even game, and yet he saw something.

Jenkins was nervous. He had hunted bear when he was a young man in Ohio and he had killed several boar since he had been in Vietnam, but he had never hunted anything as smart as a tiger.

"If we had any guts we'd be using bows," he said.

"You Americans. You have such guilt," Villeneuve said.

He had learned to smell fear. It changed their sweet, fat smell and made it sour and sharp, and of the three, the one who was most sour was the one with the bright, shining hair and so he moved to take him.

Starkey saw part of him then. He was red in the jungle, a red smear gliding through the green leaves. "Bob," he said, quietly.

"I think we should give them a chance is all," Jenkins said.

"They have chance enough."

"Bob?"

"Yes sir."

"He's thirty yards away on your left moving straight for you."

"Very funny."

"Goddamnit Bob, listen to me."

Bob Jenkins turned to look at Starkey. He saw his face and clicked off his safety and turned and saw the tiger as it left the green cover and he saw the amber eyes and thought that he had never seen eyes so big, so pretty. The tiger jumped for him and he fired.

The tiger grabbed him by the throat, jerked his blond head to the right until there was a crack and the body went limp. He stopped and looked at the two white men with the raised rifles and then he sank his teeth into the body and tucked it under him and sprang into the green.

Starkey ran after the tiger hoping to get a shot, but a wall of vines and thorns stopped him in ten feet. Villeneuve was behind him. Starkey turned and looked at the old man.

"Jesus," he said.

Villeneuve's face was without blood.

"We can go straight up the valley," Starkey said, and the old man grabbed him.

"It's no use."

"No, he could be alive."

"He's dead. He was dead in a second."

"We could radio in choppers."

"There will not be anything left."

Starkey was shaking. He squatted down.

Villeneuve knelt beside him and handed him Jenkins' gun.

"What happened?" Starkey said. "He had another shot. What the hell happened?"

Villeneuve handed him Jenkins' rifle. "He only loaded one barrel," he said. "The other's empty."

Far away, almost a mile, they heard the tiger roar once and then another time and then the jungle covered everything with green silence.

36

DURING THE WEEKS FOLLOWING
Blackie's death, Cat felt as if there were a hole in the center of her chest
and in the center of the hole beat a pulse of pain. She missed him all
day long, from the moment when she first saw the light until she finally
went to sleep. There were only a few minutes when she did not think
about him. When one of these times occurred, she felt guilty about it.
"If you really loved him you would never let him out of your mind, and
if you did forget him for a second, the pain of not thinking about him
should be greater than the memory of his loss."

In addition to her grief, Cat had to endure something else. It came at
night. It was something she had never thought of. Just as she began to
fall asleep, just at the moment when reason and reasonable thoughts
begin to break apart and dissolve, a startling illumination, almost like a
voice, said, You're going to die. This head, which rests on this pillow,
which holds this brain, will one day rot down to the skull, nothing but

yellow bone and rattling teeth and there will be no thoughts, no feelings, and what are you going to do about it? What are you going to do?

It made her jump and half rise from bed, and she sat in the darkness and shivered until the questions stopped and her eyes closed. Sometimes this process would occur two or three times a night until exhaustion brought her a smooth, dark sleep.

After a whole month of this torture, Cat went to Harper and tried to tell her what she was going through, but the old lady dismissed her and said that everybody would adjust in time. It made Cat even more uneasy. Harper seemed cooler and more distant than she had in a while. One afternoon she found Hannah in the kitchen and told her about the spells.

"I guess I sound crazy, don't I?" Cat said.

"A little bit."

"Do I really?"

Hannah looked at the young woman. Over the past few weeks she had lost weight, blue circles glared beneath her eyes and even her blond hair did not hold its usual freshness.

"What's making me have these thoughts?"

"The devil."

"Oh, Hannah."

"You don't believe in the devil?"

"I just want to go to sleep. I just want to stop thinking these things."

"Then you talk to that voice you hear. Square your chin and squint your eyes and call it a liar. Do you believe in heaven?"

"Well, I guess so. I mean, I believe that when we die we go to be with God."

"Then call that voice a liar. When it wakes you up the next time, you just say, Baloney, you're a liar. I ain't gonna die. Not ever. I ain't gonna die and I ain't gonna rot and I will go on and on and on as long and as far as I want to and if you say anything other than that you are a liar."

Cat tried it that very night. When the voice spoke to her, she squared her chin and gritted her teeth and said out loud everything that Hannah had told her, and as soon as she did, she felt as if she had spoken the truth and the voice did not trouble her again that night, though it came the next and she was even more forceful this time and the voice grew weaker, and by the end of the week she was having a night or two when she was not awakened at all.

The next week Cat was offered a new job at the *Southern Chronicle*. The managing editor came by one day and asked her if she would like to be a regular reporter covering local politics. She accepted and was given her own office on the third floor with a window that let in the blue sky and the shaggy tops of the green live oaks.

Ford was coming home from Washington almost every weekend. He was spending a lot of time with Cat and she knew that he liked her and she liked him somewhat, though her conscience said you shouldn't be seeing him so often, you should be loyal to Blackie, so that once or twice she did not go out with Ford when he asked her because of these thoughts, and then she got fed up with them the way she had the night voice and she determined that she would go out with Ford whenever she wanted to.

Waverly was becoming a part of her. During the weekdays after work, she took long walks through the woods, which shimmered with the tall trunks of poplars and oaks, cedars and sycamores. The crepe myrtle was her favorite tree. The fields of Waverly were dotted with them and for some reason they reminded her of Blackie, for they were sensual trees. The old ones had trunks which came straight out of the ground and the skin of the trunks was smooth and brown and lavender, but incredibly smooth like the tanned back of a boy who worked out hard, the skin of the crepe myrtles even having ripples and twists of flesh which asked you to reach out and let your fingers stroke a smooth dip or a long cord.

The black people at Waverly had taken Cat completely into themselves. Hannah and Bub had brought her to their pine house for Sunday dinner and Fuzz and Tee Tat had invited her to the Tiger River for the baptism of their youngest child. Bub made sure that the pink rosebud he brought to her room every morning was the prettiest one and he always sprayed it with an extra bit of lilac water. When Cat told Vic and Hattie Cash that she had never seen a healing service, they asked her to come to the next one which was held at their small white church. On that day Leroy Smith was healed of the Saint Vitus' dance and Tom Young was made to hear. Vic and Hattie even took Cat into their confidence and told her how upset they were that Nathaniel had left Waverly and joined the NAACP.

Two months after Blackie's death, Cat was feeling better, though she

still missed him. It was then that something else occurred—something
to do with her health. Spells of weakness and dizziness and lethargy.
She forced it from her mind. She willed it to go away, and for a week or
so the symptoms stopped, and she convinced herself that it was only her
imagination.

One weekend, Wick and Alice came for a visit. Alice was always
introduced as a friend but Cat and the servants knew that there was
much more to it than that, though they accepted her gracefully.

Ford did not arrive home until late Sunday afternoon. He had a drink
with everyone in the den and told them some Washington gossip and
that he had been seeing a good bit of the President, who was relishing
his job and was convinced that he could win the war in Vietnam in one
more year.

Two drinks later, Ford and Wick were able to steal away for a walk in
the pecan orchard. The trees were gray and black, but the first green
leaves were showing. The brothers had gotten through all the small talk
and now spoke about deeper things.

". . . rather, I know I love her. In the beginning, I think it was just
sex and infatuation, but now it's something completely different," Wick
said.

"It's just a very odd predicament."

"You haven't heard the worst of it. Alice is pregnant."

"Oh, Wick."

"Pretty bad, huh? I was terribly upset about it, couldn't sleep,
couldn't think right, but Alice just turned everything around. I mean
she's so cheerful and hopeful and bright. She's amazing."

"I guess you're leaving the Church then."

"No."

"No?"

"She's going to have the baby."

"Are you serious, Wick?"

"Very."

"And then what?"

"Well, I haven't thought that far ahead. She's just going to have it
and live in Charleston and I'll see her often and give them everything
they need. I mean—they're mine, both of them, and I'll never let them
go."

They talked for another few minutes and Wick said that he knew he was acting selfishly and that for Alice's sake he should leave the priesthood, but he couldn't do it because he loved his vocation and right now he was beginning to make real progress, having been made monsignor and chancellor of the Diocese, and more and more he began to believe that God had never wanted him to be a simple parish priest but rather had destined him to be a bishop.

Near dark, Ford walked the couple down the front steps to their car. He waved goodbye and watched them drive down the dirt road which ran between the green gingkos. Ford loved his younger brother. He loved his passion and he envied his ambition, which was the family trait valued above all others. His other brother had certainly retained his ambition. In their last phone conversation, Starkey had told Ford that he was still working very hard at becoming a camp commander. When Ford asked if he wanted him to speak to the President, Starkey had said no, he had to do it on his own, and Ford had admired the purity of that answer as much as he admired the ambition. As for his own desire to cut out a notch in the world—well, it was running down again. He was getting bored with his job. He had been a congressman for three months and already he was getting tired of it. It was disgraceful of him. He felt ashamed, but the fact was that after a month he could see all the ramifications: what there was to do, how to do it and what would be the outcome. He was disgusted with himself and disgusted with his life. There was only one brightness on the horizon—Cat—and later in the evening when he asked her to go to Washington with him for a few days, her complete elation lifted him out of his doldrums.

"Do you think I could interview some people? I think it would help me a lot in my new job."

"I can get you a couple of very good interviews."

"How about one with the President?"

Ford looked at her. "Are you sure your last name's not Longstreet?"

Cat first saw the Capitol from a taxi. The building was so white and so shining that she could not look at it with her eyes wide open.

"What kind of stone is it made out of?"

"Marble, I think."

"All of it?"

"Yes, I think so."

"It's more beautiful than Waverly."

Though the House Dining Room was not. The place was rundown and badly in need of repair. The white walls were peeling paint and the gray drapes were dusty and filled with moth holes. The silverware was scratched stainless steel and the dishes and bowls were stained and chipped and slightly greasy and the paint on the ceiling was falling in such profusion that Cat found some chips in her red Jell-O salad. She and Ford had just been served creamed chicken on toast when a waiter appeared and handed Ford a note. He read it, then stuck it in his pocket.

"Well, I think you said you wanted an interview with the President, didn't you?"

"And you said it would be very difficult."

"Not anymore. Come on."

Riding to the White House, Cat was breathless. "What's happened?"

"I'm not sure."

"Well, what did the note say?"

Ford reached into his pocket.

"You know one of your ears is bigger than the other one."

"What?"

"I noticed it when you got your haircut. Your right ear's bigger than the left one—the dingle down part. It's cute." She took the piece of paper from his hand and read:

> Ford, another disaster over there. What the hell's the matter with them chinks? Come see me right now.
>
> *L.B.J.* Commander In Chief.
> P.S. Burn this note cause the grammar's bad.

In the White House, a butler escorted the couple from an elevator down the hall to the President's bedroom. Lyndon Johnson had a cold and was conducting business out of his bed. As usual, everything in Johnson's reach fed by electricity was running. The three television sets which hung from the wall were running, as well as a stereo radio by his bed and a pocket-sized transistor radio emblazoned with the presidential seal which sat on a nightstand. A fan blew air toward the President and a humidifier wheezed steam in his direction as he sat on the edge of his bed wrapped in an electric blanket with his feet in an electric foot massager, a thermometer in his mouth and a phone in each hand.

When Ford and Cat were conducted into the room, Johnson turned the phones away from his mouth and bellowed, "God almighty damn, Ford, it's about time you got here. Hell, I'm trying to prevent the fall of the Asian continent. Sit down. Who you got with you?"

"This is Catherine McGregor, Mr. President."

"Hey, honey. How do you like all this power? Hell, you'll probably never see this much power in your life again. Ford, check my temperature." He lowered the phones to his mouth. "Horace, you get those five thousand acres by the ranch and if that little chicken shit greaser says no, audit his ass . . . hold on . . . yea, General, you're a hard sonofabitch to find. Now how many are dead and wounded? Wait, hold it, just wait." He lifted the phones again. "What's it read, Ford?"

"A hundred and one."

He dropped the phones to his mouth. "Good God, I'm burning up. The Commander in Chief of the Free World is burning up . . . goodbye Horace, get the land any way you have to. . . . General, now how many of my boys are dead and wounded, goddamnit answer me . . . uh-huh, twenty-three dead, all right, and wounded . . . well, find out and call me back as soon as you know."

Johnson slammed down the phones. He was wearing his black-rimmed eyeglasses and a pair of white silk pajamas with the presidential seal on the pocket. "He killed twenty-three of my boys, the little slant-eyed bastard. Can y'all believe that? I'm trying to make peace, I'm trying to bring about an honorable way out, and ole Ho is killing my young men, lord God get me some air, Ford, get me some fresh air in here, I'm smothering."

Ford went to one of the large windows and opened it up.

Johnson scooted through scores of maps and charts and propped himself against the headboard. A faint veil of sweat gleamed on his brown forehead. He threw some aspirin into his hand and chewed them up and made an awful face.

"Young lady, can you swallow pills?"

"Yes sir."

"Well, you're a better man than me, I'm always scared to death they're going to choke the life out of me," Johnson said, and slugged down a swallow of water, then squirted nasal spray into each nostril and finally took two shots from a metal inhaler.

"Lordy, Lordy, Lordy—what I want is peace. Just simple, straightforward peace, but how can I not respond when ole Ho is killing my young men in Qui Nhon?"

"How did it happen?"

"Y'all eat fried chicken? Little lady, do you like real good fried chicken?"

"Yes sir."

"Well, you're about to eat some of the best fried chicken north of the Mason-Dixon line and you know why it's so good? 'Cause a nigger cooked it in a black iron frying pan. There's some things that God ordained to always go together—and niggers and chicken and black iron frying pans is one of them."

A butler knocked on the door and Lyndon Johnson hollered him in. The butler was carrying a silver platter piled a foot high with fried chicken. "How many you got there, chief?"

"Sir?"

"How many chickens did you bring me?"

"I think there's two, sir."

"Two? Goddamnit, we've got guests here. Y'all knew we're having guests, I need four at least. Go tell them to fry me up two more and I want some milk gravy with lots of hot sauce and pepper in it."

Johnson grabbed a piece of chicken in each hand and looked at Ford. "He blew them up, that's how it happened. The little sonofabitch sent in some sappers and they blew them boys up in their barracks. Now what do you think I ought to do? Rusk wants to bomb them and so does Westmoreland."

"What do they want us to bomb?"

"It's not us. It's me, Ford. I'm the one who's doing the bombing. It's me that has to bear this. They want me to bomb a barracks in the North and a bridge."

"What will it accomplish?"

"It'll show those little chinks that Lyndon Johnson will not be pushed around. It'll demonstrate that the United States of America will not be terrorized."

Ford folded an arm across his stomach, fitted the elbow of his other arm into an open palm and with his fingers stroked the purple birthmark in his right cheek. He looked at the platter of fried chicken. "Is there a wing in there?"

"You want a wing, boy?" Johnson began fishing through the chicken. "You want you an ole wing—here you go."

"I love wings," Ford said, pulling it apart and holding the round, plump piece in his right hand and the flat piece in his left. He began to slowly pace around the room.

"Wings are good, but the sweetest meat's in the back," Johnson said.

"I don't think so."

"Are you disagreeing with me?"

"I don't think we should bomb them. I think we should do what they don't expect." Ford stuck the round part in his mouth and cleaned it with a twisting, tearing motion. "You see, they expect us to bomb them. That's precisely what they think we'll do, so we don't do that. What we do is—we offer them peace. We say all right, gentlemen, you've snuck in and you've killed a lot of our troops and we could have taken revenge for that and killed a lot of your troops, but we didn't. It's time to talk. It's time to find an avenue toward peace: come, let us reason together."

Johnson's black hair gleamed. He laid four fingers on his mouth and tilted back his head and his brown eyelids fell and hooded the brown eyes and he pulled down on the corners of his mouth, thinking.

Ford stuck the flat part of the chicken wing into his mouth, then pulled off his wire-rim glasses and using his little finger rubbed the bridge of his nose where the glasses had depressed the flesh and then he put the glasses back on and cleaned the flat part of the chicken wing.

Johnson patted the bed beside him and Ford came over and sat down and the President threw a long arm around his shoulders and set a big hand on Ford's thigh and pulled him close and whispered, "It's what I want more than anything in the whole wide world, Ford—peace. I want peace for my country and peace for their country and peace for the whole world. Why, I want peace so bad I can taste it. But you see ole Ho knows that, Ford. Ole Ho knows how much I want it so he's going to hold back on it 'til he thinks I'll give him anything for it. So, I've got to turn over a new leaf. I've been showing too much restraint and if I want ole Ho to do business with me I've got to make him think I've changed my mind. I've got to make him think I don't give a shit about peace and what I really want, what I really desire with all my heart, is to cut his ass, to beat the dog shit out of him no matter what the cost, and once ole Ho sees that, then he's going to come to me, Ford. Yes-sir-ree-bob, he's going to come to me."

37

WHEN CAT RETURNED TO Waverly
she wrote for two days straight without sleeping. She read it to Ford,
who thought it was good writing, but rather inflated. He suggested
several revisions.

"I want to show it to Harper the way it is," Cat said.

"I think it's great to show it to Harper, but you've got to get rid of all
the poetry."

"It's my style. It's what makes my writing different."

"It's what makes your writing sophomoric."

Cat was so angry with Ford that she almost hit him. She went back to
her room and resolved not to omit one of her poetic images and that if
anything she would increase the number of metaphors and what did
Ford know about writing anyway? As a matter of fact, what did he know
about anything? He was a spoiled aristocrat who had failed at everything including his meeting with President Johnson. He could have
scored a major success by agreeing with the President and supporting

the bombing and then he would have been made a real advisor of the
President's as opposed to a glorified confidant.

At three in the morning, Cat still could not sleep so she got up and
made some of the revisions which Ford had suggested. Around six-
thirty she was just finishing her work when she felt her stomach grab
and she became sick. In the last two weeks, this event was getting worse
and not better and so late in the afternoon she went to Hannah, who
was fixing supper in the kitchen. She was making a dough for dumplings and whistling silently to herself and her blue-black skin was shining with perspiration.

Cat picked up a stool and sat near Hannah, who did not look up from
her work.

"Do you know how to cook chicken and dumplings?" Hannah asked.

I hate chicken and dumplings, Cat thought.

"It's something every nice young lady need to know so to make her
husband happy. There's some things Southern gentlemens have to eat
or else they won't be right and they are grits and fried chicken and
chicken-and-dumplings. Watch what I'm doing now."

A large ball of white dough sat in a mixing bowl. Hannah took a little
flour and threw it on a wooden board and then set the ball of white
dough on the board. She rubbed some flour on a rolling pin and then
rolled the dough out and this took her five or six minutes until the
dough was flat and smooth. She took a knife and cut the dough into thin
rectangles and put them into a bowl and went to the stove and took a lid
off a steaming pot. A deboned chicken was bubbling in the pot and the
liquid was yellow and rich and filled with pink and white chunks of
chicken. With a slotted spoon, Hannah took out every piece of chicken
and set them in a bowl and then turned up the heat. The yellow broth
began to boil and she dropped the dumplings in one by one and the
white dumplings boiled and tumbled in the yellow broth.

"You watching me, girl? You got to feed these dumplings in real slow
on account of if you don't they'll stick together. You understand what
I'm saying?"

"I don't feel too good, Hannah."

The old woman looked at the white girl. She seemed pale and her
eyes were dim.

"The last two or three weeks I haven't felt well at all," Cat said, and
then described her symptoms, after which Hannah grabbed her by the

arm and told her she had to go to the doctor right away. Bub was found and Cat was taken to Doctor Calhoun. Two days later she found out that she was pregnant and told Tee Tat (who nearly fainted) and then the two of them told Hannah and so all three of them were sitting in the trunk room and Hannah was proposing solutions.

". . . but I wouldn't want to send you to Dr. Calhoun for it, because he's the biggest gossip in town and if you think women is bad about gossiping you oughta just hear the men."

"I don't think we should send her to no doctor, no way," Tee Tat said. "The root worker who she need to see. The root worker can do things a white doctor ain't even thought of."

"Don't you want to know whose it is?" Cat asked.

"Honey, ain't nobody saying a young woman have to tell all her secrets," Hannah said.

"It was Blackie," Cat said.

Hannah rolled her big hands in her apron and looked down at the floor and began whistling, almost silently, Go Down, Moses. Tee Tat was shaking her head.

"I'm not going to have an abortion," Cat said. "I appreciate all of your thoughts and your counsel, but I'm going to have this baby and I'm going to name it Blackstone after it's daddy and I'm going straight to Harper Longstreet and tell her so."

"Don't do that," Hannah said. "Miss Harper ain't quite right yet. She still grieving for that boy. She won't be understanding."

"Well, she's going to have to understand this. I'm carrying her grandson and I will not abort him and she needs to face up to it just as I have to."

Cat went to see her in the morning. She was in the greenhouse, working with several pots of impatiens. The green leaves were slender and a light green and the blossoms of the impatiens were young and white and the heart of them was a trumpet of green.

Harper was wearing an old housecoat and her tattered slippers. She had not been to a stylist in weeks and her black hair was stringy and lifeless. She had been working at the Greek and Latin, playing her guitar, walking and keeping all the usual commitments of her daily routine, as well as writing blistering editorials and supervising the harried minutiae of the paper. To her own mind, Blackie's death had not forced her to give one inch. Others, however, saw the change. She was jumpy, indecisive, her thoughts sometimes disconnected and her physical person neglected: makeup badly applied, hair forgotten, apparel often covered with dandruff and lint, and to the shock of all, sometimes the stench of body odor radiated from her.

Lately, she had begun to communicate with the servants again, but she had become more and more distant from Cat, seeing her as seditious and conniving, thinking, She could have told me about him. The only reason she didn't was because it gave her an edge over me. She had more knowledge than I did. That's right. I see it now. She made the great discovery with Blackie. She found out that if you know someone deeply, you have control, and if you have control, you have power.

Occasionally, Harper thought of confronting Cat, but she pulled herself back, thinking that this would look plaintive and weak. She decided to wait for that special moment when Cat would make herself vulnerable, and then she would show her what power was all about.

"I've brought you the story, Miss Harper," Cat said, holding the four sheets of paper.

"My name is Harper. H-A-R-P-E-R. Not Miss Harper or Miz Harper, just plain Harper." She glanced up at Cat and her black eyes were shining. "What story? Oh, the thing you wrote about Lyndon. Is it any good?"

"I think it's good."

"If you think it's good, then you need to go back and rewrite it until you know it's good."

"Well I—I know it's good."

"I guess you just happen to have it with you?"

Cat handed her the pieces of paper and Harper sighed, dramatically took out her reading glasses and began reading.

Beyond Cat's fear of Harper Longstreet, there was indignation. Why did she have to treat everyone with such disdain? Why did she have to seem so vexed over the smallest request? It's childish, Cat thought. She just likes acting that way—as if her life is the most important thing in the world. If I am successful one day and attain some kind of fame, I will not act the way she does. I will not be haughty and puffed up. I will be the exact opposite. I will be kind and patient and encouraging to others.

"Did someone help you with this?" Harper asked.

"Ford read a—"

"Ah-hah—Ford. He has a good editorial eye."

"He just made a few suggestions."

"Well, I think the editing is brilliant."

"What about the writing?"

"The writing is—not without promise."

Harper handed her the sheets of paper and Cat held them against her chest and looked at Harper's feet, feeling all her courage leaking away.

"Is there anything else?"

"Yes."

"Yes—well, what is it?"

"I'm pregnant."

Harper looked at her with unblinking eyes, and then pulled off her left glove and stuck it in her left hand and set her bare index finger into her chin. "And so?"

"How could you say something like that to me? How could anybody be so cruel?"

"I don't think I'm the one who's warranted chastisement."

"You know, I've got something to tell you that you're not going to like very much, but before I do tell you there's something I want to say. You are the most conceited, self-centered person I have ever met in my life. You're haughty and cold and mean, and if you think people love you, you're wrong. Nobody loves you, not even your own grandsons— that's right, your grandsons because they are not your sons and you are not forty years old, you're seventy and you're mean and everybody at Waverly is scared to death of you including me, and if you weren't worth a zillion dollars nobody would put up with your shenanigans at all."

"Is that the best you can do?"

"I think this baby is a boy and if it is, I will name it after its father— Blackstone Longstreet."

Harper's smile was cold and slow. "How clever you are. How very, very clever."

"You don't think I'm pregnant?"

"Oh, I'm certain you're pregnant. I've no doubt about that at all. I'm also certain it's not Blackie's."

"You're wrong."

"No, I'm not wrong. I'm not wrong about the father and I'm not wrong about you. I never should have allowed you into this family. I knew from the beginning that it was a mistake. It cost me my son. It cost me Blackie."

"What in the world are you talking about?"

"You knew what he was doing and you didn't tell me."

"I couldn't tell you."

"Why not?"

"Because I, I didn't know much about it, I mean, I just found out myself, I—"

"You didn't want to tell me because you thought you could use it against me somehow. Because you thought you could blackmail me, pressure me to let you stay here permanently. Well, you're not going to stay here, not at all. I want you out of this family and out of this house. Go back to the coal mine, little girl, go back where you belong."

By twelve o'clock in the afternoon, Cat's clothes and few possessions had been thrown into cardboard boxes and sat at the bottom of the dirt road which led to Waverly. Bub and Jebodiah had so infuriated Harper by their tardiness in collecting the clothes that she brought in two white men from the dairy to clean out Cat's room.

She stood at the bottom of the dirt road, surrounded by cardboard boxes and two leather suitcases. She looked up through the row of gingko trees toward the twelve white columns of Waverly. Never in all of her life had she felt so alone, so empty. She had lost everything—Blackie and Boykin and Hannah and Bub and, the most important thing of all, perhaps more important to her than even Blackie—she had lost the sense of home, lost the place where she felt she could do no wrong and the place where every wound would heal and every pain would mend, and as she stood now waiting on the taxi which Harper had ordered that would take her to town and then she did not know where, as she stood she stared as intensely as she could at Waverly, she strained to fix in her mind every detail of the big house and everything that had been hers there. She cut the memories into her mind so that no matter what awaited her down the road, she would have these memories of home, these last sweet details to keep her from despair.

38

NATHANIEL CASH STOOD outside the bishop's residence in Charleston. The house was four stories of red brick with mortar the color of mustard. He rang the doorbell for the second time. He had just gotten a haircut. There was only a thin stubble on his black, gourd head, though a perfect part ran down the left side of his skull. He had not slept well the night before and the whites of his eyes had an orange tinge.

He had come to ask Wick Longstreet to help him. He knew that Wick probably would not, and in a way, Nathaniel wanted him not to help. It would finally put an end to things, he thought. Then I would know that it was oppression, pure and simple, that binds my family to the Longstreets. If he turns me down, then I'll be able to clearly see the truth and then I can be done with all of them.

A maid answered the door and Nathaniel told her that he had an appointment with Monsignor Longstreet.

He had never been in a rectory before and the place made him uneasy. The hall had several statues of saints whom he had never heard of: St. Charles Borromayo and St. John Vianni. These statues were painted and the eyes of the saints looked like the eyes of women who wore too much makeup. He sat down in a small waiting room that had purple curtains and a bronze crucifix on the mantle with the body of Jesus still hanging on the cross. On a table in the corner lay several black rosaries and a black-framed picture of President Kennedy. Printed on the top of the photograph was the inscription PLEASE PRAY FOR THE DEPARTED SOUL OF JOHN FITZGERALD KENNEDY. On another dark table sat a bell jar in which stood a baby who wore a gold cloak and a gold crown and who held a gold orb in his right hand. A small sign read SUBMIT YOURSELVES TO THE INFANT OF PRAGUE. A baby king in a jar—it gave him the creeps.

Monsignor Longstreet came into the room with his hand extended and his smile blazing. They exchanged greetings and talked about Waverly and Wick asked Nathaniel if he had heard that Cat had left and Nathaniel said yes that he had heard it and that he felt sorry for her and Wick said that so did he and that he was trying to find out where she had moved.

They sat down on a leather couch and the polite talk continued until Wick glanced down at his watch. It was the cold gesture of all white men, Nathaniel thought. It was their ubiquitous sign of impatience.

"I know you must be busy," Nathaniel said.

"Oh no, not at all."

"Yes you are. Why don't you just go ahead and say it?" Wick smiled.

"I told you there's something I want you to help me with."

"I'd be happy to help in any way."

"Goddamnit don't talk to me like that, Wick. You're beginning to sound like all the rest of them. At least at home you were honest— arrogant and patronizing, but honest. There's going to be a sit-in at Woolworth's in Pipestown. They've still got a white-only lunch counter there. Still got colored water fountains and colored rest rooms. It's like the Civil Rights Bill was never passed. We're gonna break them open and we need some responsible white leaders with us. Will you come?"

It was the question Wick was afraid he was going to ask. He had known for some time that Nathaniel was organizing for the NAACP and Wick certainly believed in that organization, but he did not see himself as a crusader. In addition, the bishop was completely opposed to his priests joining any kind of a demonstration and he had sent a letter to all of the priests in the Diocese saying that anyone who joined a social protest would be sent to pastor a missionary church.

"I need time to think it over, Nathaniel."

"Why?"

"Well—look, I want to be honest with you. I don't want to blame this on anyone or anything else. I just don't know if I'm cut out to carry signs and lay down in front of buses. I just don't think I've got what it takes."

"Do you know a guy named Bear Lawson? He's the sheriff in Pipestown. He says if the NAACP tries to integrate, he'll shoot us down in the streets. This is America, man, and this guy's talking about killing colored people because they want to sit down next to white people and eat a hot dog. Do you think that's right?"

"Of course not."

"We're meeting outside the city limits on May the second and we're marching down Main Street. We're going to eat at the Woolworth's lunch counter. Come with us."

Nathaniel got up and moved to the door of the sitting room.

"Nathaniel, I just don't think . . ."

"Look, Wick, don't give me any of your bullshit, man. I know you. My family has been wiping the noses of Longstreets for a hundred years. We cut your grass and sweep your house and fix your meals and we all done it with the goddamn biggest smile you've ever seen. I know you, Wick. I know you like one man rarely knows another, like one people rarely knows another—I know you from serving you, man, so don't try to lie to me. Just don't."

Wick had rented a small house on the Isle of Palms a few miles outside of Charleston. He had told the bishop that sometimes he needed to spend the night away from the rectory and the bishop had agreed. He had moved Alice into the small house with its long screened porch which faced the sea.

Alice had not liked the house when she'd first moved in. In fact, she had not liked anything that was happening to her. The reality of her condition had changed things. What am I doing, she thought. I can't go through with having this baby. How did I end up like this? The only thing I can do is go home, find a doctor to give me an abortion, and forget about this thing.

After several terrible fights with Wick, she made plane reservations several times, and once actually flew home to New York. Her third day there, she realized how much she loved him and it amazed her. She had never in her life loved anyone like this. It would be a priest, she thought. Of all the people in the world, I would fall for a priest.

When it was clear to Alice that she really did love Wick, she decided that he would have to leave the church. Sooner or later, he would have to. She did not know whether or not she could convince him to do this, but she did know someone who could. Alice sat down and carefully wrote Harper a long letter, telling her about the pregnancy, confessing to the old lady that she desperately needed help.

After his conversation with Nathaniel, Wick worked until nine o'clock assisting the bishop at confirmation in the cathedral. When he arrived at the white house beside the sea, he was exhausted and troubled by Nathaniel's visit.

Alice had fixed him pot roast and baked potatoes and after supper they sat in front of a fire and looked out at the white moonlight on the black ocean. During dinner, Wick had told her everything that Nathaniel had said and that he felt like a coward and more than that he felt immoral.

"I should be there," Wick said. "On May the second, I should be right there, right at the head of the line." He was still wearing his black vest and collar and the long-sleeved white shirt. His face was thin and gray with fatigue and his hair was black and thick. He was smoking a cigarette.

"Darling, you need a shearing," Alice said, and ran a hand through his hair. "Someone in the Lady's Altar Society said that you looked woolly."

"The Lady's Altar Society thinks everyone looks woolly."

"I was thinking of joining up."

"Please don't do that."

"Just teasing."

"I don't know what to do."

"What would you like to do?"

"Frankly, I'd like to stay out of it, have nothing to do with it."

"Could it be dangerous?"

"Of course it'll be dangerous. Bear Lawson's a criminal wearing a badge."

"Maybe now is the time for you to leave. We don't need the money. You could work for civil rights and not have to worry about the repercussions."

"I can't even talk about that now, Alice."

"When can you talk about it?"

During the next few days, he worked harder than usual at the Chancellory, filling every minute with chatter and superficial thought so as to avoid the beating of his conscience. One night, after a dinner of roast leg of lamb that he had prepared for the bishop, he took a cup of coffee into his study to look over a list of candidates for elevation to deacon. The bishop followed him in.

"It's almost ten o'clock, Father. Go to bed," the bishop said.

"Oh, I just wanted to glance over these candidates."

The bishop was wearing a long-sleeved, thermal undershirt and black pants and a pair of boots still sloppy with black mud. He had spent the day fishing and his face was red beneath his white hair. He was drinking a tiny glass of B & B. The smell of the swamp mud was sour and sharp and filled the room.

"What do you think about that kid Tom Lowery?" the bishop asked.

"I like him. He's got a lot of spirit."

"I don't know. He's involved in this civil rights stuff. I haven't said anything to him directly, but if he goes in for it in a highly public way, I'll turn him down for deacon. I don't know who came up with this follow your conscience crap. Probably Augustine, but it's caused the Church nothing but trouble. Obedience should be the number one rule, Wick. Obedience before everything else. To trust in conscience is to trust in anarchy. You'd think we'd know that by now." The bishop sipped his brandy. "Keep an eye on Lowery. Let me know if he steps out of line."

Whether Tom Lowery stepped out of line, Wick didn't know, but the bishop's attitude and his attempt to suppress a primary doctrine of freedom made Wick step *into* line—the mile-long line which waited outside the city limits of Pipestown. He had come to the march unofficially. He wore faded galluses and work boots and an old Carolina baseball hat. He wanted to see what this thing was all about—this thing called the Movement.

There were two thousand people assembled for the march. Three quarters of them were black and the other white. They seemed to come from every part of society: some of them were beatniks with longish hair and goatees, wearing blue jeans and red bandannas tied around their heads, while others wore black three-piece suits and others blue print dresses or pink and yellow bermuda shorts or greasy jump suits which said Gulf or Smith's Car Repair or just plain Joe. They were different ages: an old man and an old woman barely creeping along, holding a trembling banner between them which read LET MY PEOPLE GO, and a young blond woman whose seven-year-old child waved a sign on which was painted ONE NATION INDIVISIBLE. They were crew-cut teenage boys and middle-aged women who sat in lawn chairs and ate ham and cheese sandwiches while their beer-bellied husbands read the sports page for the third time wondering, When will they get the show on the road.

Wick walked the length of the line, from the back to the head of it and on every face he saw something different: I'm so happy to be here or I'm mad or I'm not quite sure what to do or I'm never going to do this again, I'm prayerful, I'm sad, I'm proud as hell of this country, I'm proud of me, I'm bored, I'm hungry, I'd love to screw her eyes out. I'd give anything to see his chest, her legs, his ass, their boobs, amen.

The leaders of the march were at the front. There were ten or twelve black preachers and several white ones. All of these men wore dark suits and white shirts and black, narrow ties and their faces did not have the variety of expressions which belonged to the crowd. The faces of the leaders were all the same—determined, anxious, thoughtful. Wick stepped behind the leaders and listened to a quiet, but anguished debate.

"Do they have them or not? That's what I'm asking you. Do they have them or not?"

"Just hold it, Bob, I'm trying to find out." The black man then shouted into a walkie-talkie. "Ed, do they have them? Ed? We got to make a decision here, man. Has Bear Lawson got dobermans?"

"I'll tell you one thing," said another man. "These people didn't bargain for no dogs. If they got dogs, we should cancel this march right now, I'm telling you."

The decision was made to go forward. The word was passed from the head of the line that Bear Lawson might have dogs. The leaders began linking arms. Two nuns wearing black habits and a rabbi with a red yarmulke on his head jumped out of a car and joined arms with the leaders. Nathaniel Cash ran up from the ranks and stepped in the line.

In front of the marchers was the black road. On either side of it stood a host of white dogwoods. The trunks and limbs of the trees were gray, and since the trees were all very old, the trunks were thick and twisted and sometimes the scales of the gray bark had fallen away and the skin beneath was pink. The blooms of the dogwoods were white. The wind blew the white blossoms and they filled the air and blew across the black road and made the road look as if a sudden snow had fallen.

Beyond the dogwood trees lay a bridge which forded a brown river. On the other side of the bridge stood Bear Lawson. He had a hundred and fifty policemen and state troopers. The policemen wore white helmets and the troopers wore straw hats and all of them had on sunglasses and pistols and most carried brown night sticks. The American flag was flying and so was the blue and white state flag and Bear Lawson stood in between the two flags, wearing a blue suit, his empty hands stuck into his pockets, thinking:

"I got to stop their asses this side of the bridge, otherwise they'll just flood me over. My Lord, how many of them are they? Five thousand? Where do all these niggers come from anyway? Probably New York and New Jersey and such as that and I just hope they ain't got no kids. Men I don't mind and women I don't mind, cause nigger women if anything got harder heads than nigger men, but dear Lord I hope they didn't bring no kids, cause I just can't take it if something happens to them."

The marchers moved down the black road through the stand of dogwoods. The leaders started singing "We Shall Overcome" and the rest of the line picked it up. Wick took a few quick steps and moved behind Nathaniel. He reached out and touched his shoulder. Nathaniel turned. He saw Wick and grabbed him.

"You're here, man. You actually came. I didn't think you would."

"Neither did I."

"Come on up front."

"I don't know, I think I need to stay right . . ."

"Aw come on," Nathaniel said, and pulled Wick to the front line where he joined arms with an old woman. She had false teeth which had been tinted a believable yellow, and brown, mottled skin, and she wore a straw hat on which she had painted in red JUSTICE SHALL FLOUR-ISH.

"Isn't it just wonderful," she said.

"Yes ma'am."

"Do you know I've got seven grandchildren and all of them is piss-ants. Don't do a damn thing but go to college."

"Well, it's probably good that they're getting an education."

"Hell, they don't do anything there but eat, sleep and cheat. They ought to be out here. They could learn more about life right here, than they ever could in college."

39

THE MARCHERS STEPPED ONTO
the bridge and saw Bear Lawson standing about midway with a bullhorn
at his mouth. He was bald-headed and his pink skin gleamed in the sun.

"A permit has not been licensed to you. If you cross this bridge you
will be in violation of the city ordinances of Pipestown, South Carolina.
Halt and desist."

The leaders gripped arms a little tighter and moved forward.

"You know it takes a certain amount of courage to stand in the
middle of this bridge by yourself and yell at two thousand people,"
Nathaniel said.

"I am ordering you," Bear Lawson said in a bureaucratic voice, "as
the chief law enforcement officer of Pipestown and vicinity to disperse
as you do not have a license nor a permit to parade around and act
foolish."

"I know you, Bear Lawson," yelled the old woman on Wick's right.

"I am asking you to turn around immediately . . . ."

"I worked with your sister at Shealy Mills."

The marchers now were only twenty feet from Lawson, who had not moved. "Why don't y'all just stop this. Why don't y'all just go back to New Jersey or wherever and stop this 'fore you get hurt."

Bear Lawson dropped the bullhorn to his side, shook his head and walked toward his troops. He said to his second in command, "Jack, go get them dogs."

Jack Wills saluted and grinned, revealing a mouthful of black and brown teeth. "Niggers can't stand dogs, can they, Bear? Niggers is just scared shitless of dogs."

"Are you having fun, Jack?"

"Oh yes sir. I ain't had this much fun in a while."

"Let me tell you something—this ain't no fun. It's what we have to do, but it ain't no fun. Now get that goddamned smile off your face and go get them dogs, and if one chile gets bit, I'm holding you responsible."

Nathaniel and the other leaders were the first ones to see the dogs.

"Oh, Lord, Jesus," said a black minister on Nathaniel's right.

"The Lord ain't going to let them dogs bite us," said another black man.

The front line suddenly slowed down. Some of the leaders had completely stopped. There were fifteen dobermans waiting at the other end of the bridge. They were black and tan and their muscles quivered and not one of them barked, though all of them had bared their teeth and the white fangs were shining.

Nathaniel grabbed Wick's arm and the black minister's arm more tightly and he sped up.

"Should you be leading them into this?" Wick asked.

"No," Nathaniel said, "I shouldn't." Then he began singing in a loud voice. "I'm gonna lay down my sword and shield, down by the riverside, down by the riverside, down by the riverside, I'm gonna . . ."

The others sang along and the line began to move again.

Thirty feet from the end of the bridge and forty feet from the black dobermans, Nathaniel said, "Take off your coats and wrap them around one arm. Keep tight now. Keep together. Don't let them splinter us, just keep real tight, that's it, you're doing good now, just hold each other, just stay real close, uh-huh, keep on holding now, yes, oh yes."

And listening to Nathaniel's deep, steady voice, Wick discovered his own voice again, and though he was shaking and felt as if he was going to throw up, he thought this is the way to die, or no—this is the way to live. Not hiding in paneled offices, not placating aging prelates, but risking everything for what you believe. Risking your life for the truth. And at that moment, Wick Longstreet admired Nathaniel more than he did any other man in the world.

As soon as Nathaniel and Wick and the others left the bridge, the handlers and the dogs were ready.

The dogs were dripping saliva and snarling and their teeth were bared all the way to the pink gums, and the handlers gave them enough room on the leashes so that one grabbed Nathaniel by the leg and the other by the arm and he struggled not to lose his balance.

The old lady screamed and prayers were shouted and the white law officers were laughing and encouraging the dogs and Wick grabbed the doberman that had Nathaniel by the arm and looked into the animal's dark eyes which were filled with cold light, animal light, and when he broke the dog's grip, he saw the handler's face and it was the same as the dog's—snarling, filled full of saliva and teeth and the eyes of the handler cold and unblinking and shining with animal light.

The crowd behind the leaders kept pushing forward and singing and the words now were black and white together, black and white together, black and white together some d-ay-ay-ay.

The white-helmeted policemen and the state troopers rushed forward then, and as they did, dust swirled around them, brown dust boiled with them and they made a sound, a hiss and growl, and when they collided with the marchers, the marchers gasped, groaned as one body and then began to collapse and fall, while the white men shouted and screamed and beat everything before them, even the dogs, even their own kind, pounded the brown night sticks against any flesh that was near, their mouths wide open, spit running down their chins and their eyes wide and distended and ruthlessly white.

The policemen and troopers beat their way through the marchers on the bridge, pounding everyone who stood to bloody stumps. Three policemen had singled out Nathaniel and all of them were beating him, and when Wick tried to interfere, one of them turned and rapped him right between the eyes and he fell backward and collapsed into a sitting position, hands upon his knees, blood running from between his eyes, and all around him he could hear the curses of the white men and the prayers and gasps of the marchers and the sound of the night sticks as they slapped and broke open human flesh and bone. He saw the old lady with the straw hat still standing and pointing a finger at the huge form of Bear Lawson, who had shed his coat, his white shirt spattered with blood and yellow mucous and the old lady screaming at Lawson, "You sonofabitch! Look at what you're doing. Just look." Lawson punched her in the mouth, then swept her aside as he worked his way across the bridge.

Wick crawled over to the old woman. She was lying on her back. Her false teeth had been broken and knocked out of her mouth and they lay scattered on her chest and her mouth was a well of bright blood.

"Wha ha-pen?" she said. "Wha ha-pen?"

Wick held her hands. "It's okay. It's okay now."

The old lady put her trembling hands to the sides of her face and then her mouth, and she discovered the broken teeth on her chest and picked them up, one by one, and began to cry.

Paddy wagons pulled up to the edge of the bridge and the marchers were thrown into them. Nathaniel was bleeding from two head wounds. The policemen grabbed him and pushed him into a squad car. Two state troopers caught Wick by the arms and one of them said, "Father Longstreet?"

The blood was still running down Wick's forehead and his left eye was blinded by it and he wasn't thinking right.

"Are you Father Longstreet?"

"Can we get some help for this lady? She's hurt. She's terribly, terribly," Wick said.

The young state trooper told the other one he'd catch up to him. He put his arm around Wick and guided him out of the bloody marchers and took him beside a large tree.

The trooper took out a handkerchief and began wiping the blood out of Wick's left eye. "Name's Bob Williams, Father. I go to your Sunday Mass. How in hell did you get involved in this mess?"

Wick sat under the oak tree and leaned back against the trunk. He was still dizzy and he looked up at the new green leaves of the old oak and then down at the swirling bodies before him. The police cars and paddy wagons were flashing their red, white and blue lights, though

their sirens were silent while the police loaded the cars and trucks with
the limp and blood-soaked bodies of the marchers. The middle of the
bridge was empty, and below the bridge the brown river was smooth
and silent, and beyond the river ran the black road which held a few
stragglers and then there were the dogwood trees and their white
blooms shining and blown by the invisible wind and the rest of the
marchers stood beyond this, silent and wavering and breaking apart.

For some reason an old theological doctrine crept into Wick's mind,
something he had not thought about since he had studied sacred theology in the monastery. It was the distinction between God's active will
and his permissive will. The violence he witnessed today would be
termed God's permissive will, meaning that God did not want all these
people to be hurt but had permitted it. But why? Why did the old lady
have to have her teeth knocked out? Surely God with a blink of the eye
could have stopped it. Let everyone else, all the young and strong be
beaten and subdued, but why did the old lady have to be wounded so
badly? He knew the rational answers. The old woman had placed herself in danger. It was her own choice. God could not be expected to save
men from their own folly. If she had stayed at home, she would have
been safe.

Does that mean that when we make foolish decisions that God just
throws up his hands and says, Okay he or she or they just made another
stupid move, so go get them, tear them up, slash and beat and burn
them. I will not save stupid people.

Yes, it was a foolish action, but it was also a courageous one. She had
risked herself for the good of others, so that others could have a better
life and many courageous actions were often foolish ones, ones in which
a person placed himself in danger and does that mean that you will not
protect us, you will not save us, even when our foolish actions are
courageous? If that is so, maybe it is because you do not care and what
happens, happens and you are the God of watching and not the God of
doing, or maybe you are not God, nothing is God and we have to
understand that when we stand up for the truth, we stand alone and
there is nothing to save us, nothing to block the many blows that are
waiting.

Wick had a headache for two days after the march. There was a purple
knot in the middle of his forehead and a red split in the center of it.

Everyone at the Chancellory wanted to know what had happened and he told them that he had been riding in a friend's car and there had been a screeching stop and he hit the mirror.

At ten-fifteen one morning, he was putting the finishing touches on a speech for Bishop O'Hara when the housekeeper told him that he had a visitor. He went into the parlor and found Harper sitting on the couch.

She was wearing a dark gray suit and black blouse. She was thin and still did not completely look herself. Her earrings were dark rubies set in gold scallops.

Wick tried to act surprised and happy, though in fact he was exasperated that she had not called first. She was shocked by the wound between his eyes and he told her the lie and she fussed over him until he finally changed the subject and gave her a brief tour of the mansion. They talked a bit about Cat, Harper saying that perhaps she had been too hasty in asking Cat to leave, but the truth of the matter was that the girl had deceived her and not only her, but the rest of the family as well. This reminded her to ask him if he had been keeping up with his brothers, writing or calling, and Wick said not as much as he should and Harper gave him a small lecture on the importance of family ties.

Mrs. Callahan came into the room and asked if they would like tea and Wick said yes, and while the two of them politely argued about Irish soda bread or biscuits, Harper studied his wound.

She didn't for one minute believe that it had come from a car accident. It bothered her that he was lying. She could always tell: he dropped his head and looked to the left. She hoped that he would tell her the truth, but presently she wanted to concentrate on the main problem.

"I received a letter last week from Alice Grooms," Harper said.

"Oh?"

"I think you can probably guess what she confided."

Wick leaned forward, set his elbows on his knees and his face in his hands. His black hair was cut short. The purple knot was shining. He shut his eyes.

"I don't think it's a catastrophe," Harper said. "Do you?"

Wick opened his eyes and sighed and looked at her.

"I think it's a perfect time for you to forget the Catholic Church and settle down. I like Alice a lot. I think she's bright and warm and—"

"Conniving."

"Every woman is conniving."

"God, I can't believe she wrote you about it," Wick said. He got up and swept his hands through his hair.

"So, what now?"

"I'm not sure."

"Good, I am." She opened her briefcase. Mrs. Callahan came in and served the tea. Harper set three folders on the coffee table and waited for her to leave the room.

"Naturally, I would like for you to forget this ecclesiastical business altogether. I think you would do well in politics—much better than Ford. He just doesn't fit in that world at all—but I realize that you probably aren't interested, even though I could get you an administrative position in the governor's office. So I've brought along two other alternatives." Harper opened the first folder.

Wick shook his head. "Harper, look . . ."

"Just let me make my case. Since you seem determined to muck about with the Church, I put a little pressure here and there and found out that they are looking for a new rector at the Episcopal Cathedral. It would take some doing, instruction, maybe a recantation or two, but I think you could have the job, then marry Alice and raise your children. Now—here's a picture of the rector's office, the plans for the new rennovation, the proposed—"

"Harper, just stop it, just stop it, okay? I'm not going to become an Episcopal priest."

"Fine. Second alternative."

"I don't want the second alternative."

"You've got to do something."

"That's right, I've got to do something—me, not you. Just let me make my own decisions. You're always hovering over me, over all of us. We have to live. We have to decide what's right and what's wrong. Not you. It is my life, not your life. My child, not your child. Why can't you see that?"

"I do see that."

"No, you don't, no you don't."

"Will you just consider the second alternative . . ."

"No, goddamnit I won't. Why do you relentlessly keep pushing? I will not consider it. No, I will not. No. No, no, no."

"Don't speak to me like—"

"You force me to. You keep pushing and you keep pushing until I lose my temper."

Harper stood up. She looked at him and smiled bitterly and almost said something, but then dropped her eyes and left.

They did not speak again for a long time.

40

FROM MAY UNTIL NOVEMBER,
Wick worked hard in the Movement and took a few more blows: a
punch in the mouth while he and Nathaniel and a thousand others
walked up the steps of Day Cross College in Alabama, a kick in the side
ordering a hot dog in Calhoun, Georgia, and a broken nose when he and
Nathaniel attempted to wash clothes in an-all white launderette in
southern Mississippi.

In the beginning, Wick had limited his involvement in the Movement
to once or twice a month and even then, he joined his brothers only
when the bishop was out of town. By November, however, he was more
obvious. At least once a week, he was addressing a local rally or partici-
pating in a local sit-in. Finally, the bishop confronted him.

Wick had finished the early Mass in the cathedral. He had shaken
the hands of the parishioners and then gone back to the altar to pray.
The air was smoky with incense and the candles of the altar were still

burning and everything smelled holy and pure and Wick had gone back to pray because he wanted to feel holy and pure too, but he did not.

Lord, do you know the real reason I'm doing this? Do you know the real reason I'm involved with Nathaniel and the others? It's because I love speaking to the crowds, because I love walking on the front line and having people ask my advice and defer to my admonitions. It's just ambition again, isn't it, Lord? I'm doing this because it is an opportunity to take command, to aggrandize myself in the eyes of others. Isn't that my real motive?

Bishop O'Hara walked out on the altar. He looked powerful and shining and bright in his scarlet chasuble and skullcap and his purple and scarlet stole. Wick was wearing only a white alb.

"I want this to stop," the Bishop said.

Wick kept kneeling.

"I've been aware of it for some weeks now and I want it to stop. I will not have one of my priests, particularly my chancellor, involved in this Communist conspiracy and that's what it is, Monsignor. It is a plot by the Communists to suborn this country. If you have anything else to do with this Movement, I will remove you as chancellor and send you to the most barren parish in the state. Do you understand?"

Wick did not answer.

The bishop stared at him and then disappeared into the sacristy.

Two days later, Wick was giving a sermon in a black church on the outskirts of Charleston. His subject was the necessity of nonviolence. It was nine o'clock at night and the windows of the church were open to let in the cool air. The sanctuary was jammed and most of the congregation was black and they wore dark suits and dresses and their faces were sweating and smiling and they shouted Amen and Go on now and Tell it brother, and then suddenly there was an explosion.

The air was unbearably white and thunderous, and then it was dark and people were screaming and Wick found himself lying on his side ten feet from where he had been speaking. He couldn't see and the smoke was choking him, and without thinking, he scrambled over several people toward a smoldering hole in the wall.

He made his way outside and it seemed impossibly dark and cool and he looked back at the church. Orange and white flames were leaping out of the windows. People were crying and cursing and some were praying or reading their Bibles aloud. One purple-robed black woman dashed from the church and her hair was burning and several men tackled her and put a coat over her head. A child held smoldering hands into the air and screamed. A young black man with a zigzag wound in his jaw held the hands of a white man, who shivered and coughed and then went still, his brown eyes wide and flashing with the flames of the church.

From somewhere in the church Wick heard a voice, a scream, or at least he thought he did. He ran behind the church. The wood was hissing and spitting and the fire roared. He listened and decided that it was only the sound of something burning and then he heard it again and ran to a window and saw a black boy who had fallen into the floor. He was waist deep and the yellow flames behind him were twelve feet high.

Wick jumped into the open window and scrambled inside. The air was so hot that he could not breathe standing up, so he crawled toward the boy. The floor was scalding and covered with glass and raw splinters of wood, but he could breathe and he moved quickly.

The boy was screaming. His eyes were black and wide and running tears and he was struggling to push himself out of the floor. The fire made so much noise that as Wick put his arms around the boy, he had the most peculiar thought—that the fire sounded like a waterfall, crashing and spewing, thundering across the dry pine floor. He tried to lift the boy from the hole, but he couldn't. The fire was bubbling the varnish on the floor and then exploding the bubbles into flames, and it was so close now that Wick felt the hairs on the back of his hands wither. He leaned his mouth close to the boy's ear and said, "Can you scoot down, son?"

The boy cried and his bottom jaw shivered.

Wick shook him. "Listen to me now. It's going to be all right. Can you just scoot down, go under?"

The boy twisted a little and then wailed, "It's cutting me."

"You have to go ahead. Go on now."

He twisted and turned again, and this time he went down three or four inches and then disappeared.

The fire was upon Wick. Several embers were smoldering on his sleeve and he could not see a way out. He grabbed an edge of the hole in the floor and ripped away some planks and descended into the hot smoke.

Underneath the floor, he grabbed the boy. He couldn't see anything except the yellow flames that were burning overhead and the smoke was sharp and sour and smothering and just as he was beginning to pass out he prayed, "Oh Lord of light, lead us from this darkness, lead us out." And he grabbed the boy and moved without thinking, without any indication that it was right, moved straight ahead into a gray wall of impenetrable smoke.

He broke out into the cool night with the boy tucked under his arm. He stumbled ten or twenty yards from the church and then collapsed, and several people rushed over to him and beat out his smoldering jacket and someone took the coughing boy from his arms and he looked up at the black sky and saw the white and blue stars and the glittering powder of smaller stars beyond these and he thought about Hannah's gingerbread, how smooth and dark it was, how sweet.

When he came back to, a fireman was giving him oxygen and someone had put bandages on his right arm. There was another priest kneeling near him. Wick did not know him.

"Well, that took a lot of guts, young man," the priest said.

Wick breathed in the oxygen. He had an awful taste of smoke in his mouth and throat.

"The little boy's all right. A few cuts here and there, but sound enough. Aren't you Longstreet?"

Wick kept the oxygen mask over his mouth thinking, He's probably some friend of the bishop's.

"Name's Jim Dunlap, from New Orleans. I heard your talk tonight. It was damn good—bright, tough, made a hell of a lot of sense. The Church needs your kind of spunk. You ever want to move to another Diocese, you let me know. I'm at the Chancellory Office in New Orleans. Give me a call. Just say Dunlap. People know me there."

It was several days later before Wick learned that Dunlap was the archbishop of New Orleans.

The television stations and newspapers were full of stories about the bombing of the black church and the heroism of Monsignor Longstreet. The mayor of Charleston gave Wick a medal and the Knights of Columbus gave him a party and the Legion of Mary said two rosaries a day for him for a week, which was about the amount of time that had to pass before Bishop O'Hara could transfer him to Corn, South Carolina, population sixty-six with a Catholic congregation of nine.

There wasn't a Catholic church in Corn, South Carolina, and Mass had to be said in the green dining room of a red brick hotel named Purity. Wick and Alice drove into town and asked directions to the rectory. It sat two streets behind Main, beside a junkyard where hundreds of wrecked cars rusted in the sun. Wick and Alice drove down the weedy driveway and stopped.

It was a pink mobile home with plastic blue shutters and a porch made of plywood and cement block.

"Here it is," Wick said, extending his hands. "Here it finally is. My worst nightmare. You know everybody else in my family had reasonable nightmares—people running after them with axes or coming down with a rare disease or the trust funds going bust. Harper was afraid all her life that one morning she would wake up bald. But not me, oh no. No, I had to have a nightmare that's much more common, much more possible. All my life I have been afraid that somehow I would end up in a mobile home with fishbowl windows and plastic shutters—and here it is."

"Oh, Wick," Alice said, and touched his shoulder.

"It looks like where one of those fortune-tellers live. Well, maybe I could make a little extra money. Father Longstreet: Palm Reader and Personal Advisor."

"I don't think you'll be here long."

"How does three years sound?"

"No."

"Might as well get started." Wick took her hand and studied it. "I see a gift in the near future—a healthy nine-pound baby boy with blue eyes."

In fact there were two gifts in the near future—two baby boys—but they were not healthy. It happened just after Alice had rented the entire first floor of the Purity Hotel. Wick had spent the day trying to find food and lodging for a band of migrant workers and he had not returned to the rectory until after eleven o'clock at night. He was exhausted. He poured himself half a glass of bourbon and put in three ice cubes and drew a tub of hot water. The small trailer had been mildewed and rusty when he first moved in, but Alice and he had worked on it hard and now it was not so bad. He took two swallows of bourbon and lit a cigarette and got in the tub.

He sank down in the hot water slowly and he was thinking, What if there finally isn't a God at all. What if we have created him ourselves because we're afraid to die. Let's say you become certain of it. What would you do? If you suddenly became convinced that there was no God, how would you change your life?

I wouldn't change it at all, he thought. I would still be a priest and still say Mass and still want a role of responsibility. In the first flush of the bourbon when his eyes warmed and his muscles relaxed, he remembered Voltaire: if there were no God it would be necessary to invent one. It seemed so clear to him at the moment. Whether God actually existed or not was not as important as whether we thought he existed. By merely thinking that God exists, our lives take on meaning, and meaning shields us from despair. To believe in God is good, whether He exists or not.

The phone rang several times and he sipped his bourbon and sat in the hot water and waited for the phone to stop but it didn't. Finally, he got up.

"Sacred Heart."

"Wick, please come quickly. I'm bleeding, I can't stop and I have a terrible pain."

Two hours later the surgeon was going over an X ray with Wick. The doctor was dressed in his white surgical suit. Wick wore his black clericals.

"So if we take the fetuses now, I'm reasonably certain that Alice will be all right."

"What do you mean by taking them?"

"Cesarean."

"What will it do to them?"

"They're a little early, seem to be low in body weight, so I think their survival will be questionable."

"In other words if you perform the cesarean, Alice will live but the babies may die."

"I believe that is an accurate assessment."

"And if you don't do the cesarean?"

"We might lose all of them, but—we might not. We've stopped the bleeding. The pregnancy could possibly go to term."

Wick went into the chapel and prayed with all his might and there was no questioning, no conditional clauses—if You are there, if You care, if You really exist. His prayers were hot and pure and simple to the God he could not see and could not doubt.

"Just let me know what is the right thing to do, just let me know what is the right answer, somehow say it deep in me and let it be You, really You, because I don't know the right way here at all. . . ."

Wick walked back into the X-ray room. "Go ahead and take them," he said.

"We'll need to contact the next of kin. There are some forms to sign."

"I'll sign them."

"Well, thank you, Father, but we need—"

"I'm her husband. I'll sign them."

The operation took three hours. For the first time in a long time, Wick began praying the rosary. He had found the beads in the inside pocket of his coat and he took them out and began saying the joyful mysteries. He said the joyful mysteries because he hoped God would see it as a sign of faith. The Our Fathers and Hail Marys and Glory Be's came simply and naturally and with each decat, he felt as if he was filling up, as if something was running down into him and collecting and filling him and his panic began to subside and disappear, though the dark little voice that was never far from him managed to whisper, It's not Him, it's just the placebo effect, it's hypnotism.

The tiny boys were put in an incubator and hooked up to various machines. Doctor Talmadge said that if they made it through the first two weeks, their chances of survival would be good. During these days of waiting, Wick spent four or five hours each day with Alice. Her spirits were strong and she seemed to be handling things much better than Wick. Finally at the end of two weeks, the children had each gained a pound and the doctor said he thought things were going to be fine and it was then that Wick went into the small room where his sons lay alone.

He asked the nurse if she could leave a moment and then he knelt down by the glass incubator and put his hands through the examining door and took the right hand of each of his sons. How incredible these tiny hands felt. How warm and soft, and when each of them moved in his own hand, when the small fingers gripped his own, he wept. He was kneeling beside the bed holding the hands of his sons and the tears ran from his eyes and dripped from his chin and he prayed:

"Thank you, thank you, thank you for letting them live, for letting Alice live and I give them back to You now, even though You've just given them to me, I give these little ones back and hope that You will let them be Yours, let them become the apple of Your eye and I promise with all my heart never to doubt again, or at least I promise to try never to doubt again, oh Lord of Light, oh You who hear our prayers and keep them at the doors of Your heart."

41

CAT'S CHILD HAD BEEN born a month earlier. She had spent the next three weeks at home with the seven-pound boy she had named Blackstone, but home was a grim place. It was a three-room apartment on the poor side of town. As soon as Ford found out that she had left Waverly, he tried to get her a nice place, but she had insisted on not accepting his help in any way. For the first week she had breast-fed the baby, but then had stopped because it was too painful. Ford found a black wet nurse for the child and Cat felt more kindly toward it, though the love and devotion and wonder she thought she would feel for the baby had never really materialized and she was horribly guilty. In fact, when she was being completely honest with herself, she recognized that the baby depressed her.

"How am I supposed to support it? How am I going to support me?" And for the first time in almost two years, she thought about going back to her father, then dismissed the idea. It was at this time that she completely lost touch with her family. Ford and Hannah and Bub and even Tadpole came over every day or two. They brought her food and supplies and Tee Tat even brought some curtains and several pieces of furniture: a small card table inlaid with rosewood butterflies, two oak chairs, a full-length mirror gilded with gold.

When the baby was four weeks old, Cat started back to work. She was surprised that Harper had not fired her from the paper and even more surprised when she learned that her salary was increased by 20 percent. Her job was her salvation. She loved writing articles about local politicians and statewide races and simmering scandals. The mail that came into the *Southern Chronicle* was wildly in favor of her work and by the winter of 1965 she was considered to be one of the best writers at the paper.

Ford continued to see Cat on the weekends, and six weeks after the birth of the child, he proposed to her. She turned him down gently. Hannah was exasperated with her.

"Why didn't you accept?" Hannah asked. "It would be the end to all your problems."

"I don't love him."

"Oh, chile."

"You don't believe in love?"

"You can learn to love somebody."

"Well, I think that's all wrong. I think you should love someone when you marry them. I think that when you walk down that aisle you should feel like the luckiest woman in the world. Besides I'm seeing someone else."

"Don't you be teasing me."

"We had supper last week—twice."

"Who is it?"

"A boy who works for the newspaper. The police reporter—Bucky Cates."

"Cat, you gonna struggle for the rest of your life you marry somebody like that."

"Who says I want to be married? I'm doing all right. I'm standing on my own. Besides, sometimes I think marriage is an institution that men use to suppress women—and I will not be suppressed by anyone, Hannah, man or woman. I will not."

* * *

Bucky Cates was tall with brown eyes and soft ringlets of brown hair, wide shoulders and a narrow waist. Cat liked him because he was fun and funny and he made her forget her problems. They never planned anything, which meant that Cat was leaving the child more and more with the wet nurse. He would just show up at her apartment and say, Let's drive to the beach or I want to get falling down drunk with you, and once he came over late at night and began undressing at the door saying, I've got to have you right now, right this very minute, and they made love in the hall of the apartment house. It was the first time that Cat had sex in such an uninhibited way, and she liked it.

Sometimes Cat went so far as to spend the night at his house. She knew it was irresponsible, but it got her away from everything. They had little time for sleep because Bucky's police band radio was always on and reports were constantly pinpointing a robbery or a rape or some kind of accident. In a second, they were up and gone, half dressed, beer in one hand and cigarette in the other, tearing off in pursuit of the story.

One night the radio popped and whined with the news that there was a potential suicide at the Rembert Bridge. It was only two miles from Bucky's apartment and they were there in ten minutes.

The Rembert Bridge went across the Catawba River. It was one of the tallest bridges in the state, at its highest point being two hundred feet above the brown water and gray boulders. At night, the huge silver beams and bolted columns of the bridge were lit by floodlights. Cat and Bucky arrived to find that a policeman had walked up an access stairway to within twenty-five feet of the summit where a person was sitting on a ledge, teetering back and forth. Flashlights in hand, they followed the route of the cop.

"I can't get to them," the cop said.

"We work for the *Southern Chronicle*," said Bucky.

"Listen, it's just too dangerous. We need a ladder and a net. You stay with them while I go back to the car and radio for a truck. Keep them talking."

"You keep saying *them*," Cat said.

"He's got a little boy on the other side of him."

Cat and Bucky moved closer. The man was wearing a red scarf and a black overcoat and sat about twenty-five feet above them on a long beam. The wind was blowing the scarf about his head and he was drinking from a small bottle.

"How do you talk to somebody like this?" Cat asked. "What do you say?"

"You got me."

"Bucky, you're supposed to keep him talking."

"Where'd that cop go?" asked the man in the red scarf.

Bucky crossed his arms and looked down at the dark river.

"He went to get some help," Cat said.

"What kind of help?"

"Well, I don't know, just some help."

"If they try to put me in the State Hospital again, I'll jump and take this kid with me." The man reached beside him and suddenly set the small boy on his lap and he nearly lost his balance.

"Be careful," Cat yelled.

"Don't you holler at me like that," the man said. "I'm sick and tired of people hollering at me and ordering me around."

"Bucky," Cat said. "Don't you want to take over?"

"I can't," he said, and in the floodlights of the bridge, he looked frightened and weak.

"All right, all right," Cat said to the man. "What's your name?"

"Why you want my name?"

"So I can talk to you."

The man hugged the child to his chest and settled his face against the small head. "Call me Ishmael."

"What's the child's name?"

"I don't know. I picked him up at the drugstore. What's your name, little boy?"

The boy said nothing.

"Are you going to answer me?" Ishmael said. "Huh? Are you going to answer me?" He grabbed the boy by the shoulders and dangled him over the abyss.

The child screamed.

"What's your stinking little name?" Ishmael asked.

"Don't hurt him," Cat yelled.

The boy was screaming.

Ishmael grabbed the boy's right arm and then dropped him below the beam and dangled him in the dark, swinging the boy back and forth.

"Take it easy, just take it easy," Cat was saying.

"Tick-tock, goes the clock . . ." Ishmael was singing in a childlike voice and swinging the boy ". . . see how it runs, now and then it chimes again and makes the hours fun . . ."

"Billy," the boy screamed. "My name's Billy."

Ishmael jerked Billy back into his lap. "Now see there, Billy, if you had done that sooner, you wouldn't have a problem."

In the distance, there was a siren.

"Who's that?" Ishmael asked. "Is that somebody coming for me? If that's the goddamned fuzz I'm leaving, I'm going on down to the dark."

"It's the fire department," Cat said. "They just want to help you."

"They want to put me in the booby hatch."

The truck was closer and the cop returned to the bridge. He stood behind Cat.

"What's he doing?" the cop asked.

"What do you think I'm doing?" Ishmael said. "God, what a stupid question. I'm contemplating the light and the dark and right now the dark looks pretty good."

"Why don't you let us have the boy," the cop said.

" 'Cause I'm crazy as hell and I'm going to take him with me."

"Oh come on, fella," the cop said in a soothing voice. "You're not crazy. You're just a little out of sorts. Why don't you let us have the little fellar?"

"Out of sorts!" Ishmael shrieked. "Out of sorts! You call this out of sorts? Why hell, you're crazier than I am."

The firetruck pulled up at the bottom of the bridge with red and blue lights flashing.

"Keep him talking," the cop said. "I'll direct them boys up here."

"Where's he going?" Ishmael asked.

"He's going to get the firemen."

"They ain't firemen, sweetheart. Do you really believe that? Shit, they ain't firemen—they're shrinks dressed up like firemen. Got a bunch of hypodermics on them and straitjackets and what are them little ole things called they put on your thumbs—screws or something? Yeah, they got them, too. I can't abide it any longer. I'm just going on."

"Let me have Billy. Can I just have Billy?"

Ishmael looked at her and grinned and his eyes were showing all of their whites. "Yeah, you can have him—if you come get him."

Cat sank back against the bridge. "Oh, God," she whispered. "Bucky, please go up there."

Bucky was squatting down, shivering, arms wrapped around himself. "I can't."

"Please, Bucky, come on."

"I can't, can't, can't. Don't ask me to. Please don't."

The firemen clambered up the access walk.

Ishmael stood up and held the boy against his side. "Well, looks like nobody loves you, Billy boy. Guess me and you have to take a little walk."

"I'm coming," Cat said.

"Better hurry up."

She was shaking and her hands felt limp, but she climbed the narrow ladder until she reached the iron beam on which they stood.

"I can't go any higher. I just can't. Let me have him. Billy, come here."

The wind was blowing hard and Ishmael's overcoat billowed and the red scarf streamed about his face, which was full of his white eyes. "You know there's madness in the world, honey. Just unprovoked, unreasonable madness. It ain't from disease and it ain't from want and it ain't even from religion, it's just madness for the sake of madness and there ain't nothing we can do to stop it." He looked at her and smiled. "Come a little bit closer now."

"I can't."

"Yeah, you can. Come on, now."

Cat pushed herself up onto the beam and sat down. The wind was blowing tears in her eyes.

"It's one good thing I done tonight. One good thing. Go on, boy."

Billy squatted down and scooted across the beam and Cat grabbed him.

"There now," Ishmael said. "Ain't it good to be loved."

He brought his arms high over his head as if to dive, and jumped.

He hit the boulders and not the water and there was the sound of meat and bones and a scream.

* * *

Cat dreamed about Ishmael for several nights, always waking up as he hurled himself from the bridge. Bucky was with her most of the time. He held her and tried to comfort her, but she felt that he should have been the one to deal with the madman and she resented him for his cowardice.

42

BUCKY STARTED BORROWING money from her two months into the romance. Not much at first, twenty-five or thirty dollars.

"What's this for?" she asked.

"I'm not going to tell you."

"What if I don't give it to you?"

"I'll be sad," he said, and poked out his bottom lip, his soft, shining brown eyes opening so wide that they made her heart hurt.

It went on and on, the crazy hours and the crazy sex and Bucky borrowing more and more money, so that Cat was beginning to bounce checks, particularly at the grocery store. One morning when she stood at the register having just filled a shopping cart with a week's supply of baby food, the cashier wouldn't accept her check.

"Ma'am, you'll have to see the manager."

Cat blushed. There was a line of people behind her. "I know there have been some problems, but I assure you this check is good."

"No ma'am, I can't accept it. You'll have to speak to Mr. Huggins."

Mr. Huggins heard the conversation and walked over. He was thin and small and had a gold front tooth. He took the check from the cashier, looked at it and then at Cat.

"You Miss McGregor?"

"Yes. I'm sorry about—"

"I ain't going to take this check. I'm fed up with them, just fed up with it. Now if you want to come back and get this food, we'll keep it for you, but you'll have to bring cash 'cause I ain't accepting your checks no more."

It was the first real fight between them.

"Where is the money going?" Cat asked.

"That's my business."

"No, it's not. It's my business because it's my money. Now what are you doing with it?"

"I don't have to tell you a damn thing, Cat. I don't have to account to you for diddly squat."

She didn't see him for ten days. The first three or four were easy, but the rest were hard. Ford called her in the middle of things.

"Honey, I've got some bad news," Ford said.

"Oh, great."

"Harper's had a stroke. It happened last night right after supper. She couldn't seem to get her breath and then she fainted."

"How is she now?"

"Well, they're using that word *stable*. She's stable. I've never understood what it means really, but I think she's going to be all right. I hope you'll go see her."

"Well, I'll—I'll try to go this afternoon."

But Cat didn't go to the hospital that afternoon, nor that week; in fact, she didn't go at all. For the next few weeks, she felt happier and stronger than she had in a while. She turned out bright, sassy stories at the newspaper and pulled the reins in on Bucky and went about her life in a buzz of new energy, only now and again stopping to think, I never knew that someone's misfortune could bring such joy, such optimism into your life. I never knew such a thing was possible.

* * *

Harper slowly began to recover. Ford kept Cat informed about the recovery process: hours in the whirlpool, hours in traction, injections and painful exercises and endless bottles of pills. Cat felt guilty for enjoying the old lady's misfortune. What's happened to me, she thought. How could I have acted that way?

"It's natural," Bucky said as they lay in bed drinking a glass of wine.

"But it's not good."

"Well, it was good for a while, wasn't it? I mean you were happy and got a lot of zip out of it and probably got rid of a bunch of hatefulness, and now you'll probably end up giving her a call, and then go to see her. She'll feel better, you'll feel better, so the whole thing was good. There's no real evil in the world, just varying degrees of goodness."

"I'm shocked."

"At what?"

"Those are pretty good ideas."

"Yeah, well, once in a while even I think about it all."

He wanted to make love to her then, but she stopped him and just held him. His ideas made her feel tender, made her feel closer to him than she ever had and she thought for the first time that maybe she wanted there to be a chance for them.

And then there was the night when she came to understand him, completely.

She had stopped at a downtown liquor store to get a bottle of wine for supper. She was running short of money again. Earlier in the day she had lent Bucky fifty dollars. Just as she walked out of the store, she saw him and a young man enter a bar across the street. A small sign above the door read ARROWS. It was a place she had never heard of. She decided to go over and surprise him.

She walked into the bar and it was so dark that she had to stand for a few seconds so that she could see. There was yellow sawdust on the floor and it was fresh and she could smell the sharp resin of pine. The place was nearly empty. It had a wooden bar and a brass footrail and there were several young men standing at the bar, but she did not see Bucky. Above the bar was a picture of a boy in blue jeans, wearing no shirt, and he was built well and had a good suntan. She walked around the other side of the bar and several of the men turned to look at her and then she saw Bucky and the blond young man standing at a separate bar and she felt relieved and started to move toward them when she saw the young man laugh and reach out and touch Bucky's face, and they kissed lightly and looked at one another and then kissed again and this time not so lightly.

She turned away and backed into the shadows and did not look at anything but the yellow sawdust.

All the way home her heart was beating so fast that she thought she was going to faint. As soon as she got in the door, the maid said that she had to go downtown a minute and she left and the baby started crying and her heart was beating hard. She made herself a drink, bourbon and water, and drank it down fast and it burned and she picked up the child and walked the floors, thinking as the baby screamed, This is hell, this is hell, this is hell.

Bucky came home a half an hour later. He walked in the door and she saw his beautiful eyes and curly hair and she felt sick. The baby was shrieking and he laughed and took it from her arms and almost like a charm the shrieking stopped and the child went silent and began to coo and she hated him for it, she hated the child for it, just as she hated herself.

Cat made herself another drink, though the first one had been enough, and watched Bucky put the child in the white wicker bassinet.

He walked toward her and opened his arms.

"I went into that bar today," she said. "What's it called, Arrows? I saw you go in and I went in and saw you there with that blond boy."

Bucky stiffened up a bit then sighed, and his hands fell and slapped his jeans and he said, "I hope you have a whole bottle of that stuff."

"Are you queer?" she asked.

He didn't answer.

"I saw you kiss that guy."

"I didn't kiss him."

"Yes, you did—oh, okay, you didn't kiss him, he kissed you."

Bucky poured himself a drink and then opened the refrigerator and looked around. "Do we have anything to mix this with?"

"Why don't you take it straight."

"Any juice or anything?"

"You can't take it straight, can you?"

"Goddamnit, quit pushing me, Cat."

"Pushing you! Pushing you! What's been going on with you and him? I want to know. I want to know right now."

Bucky closed the door to the refrigerator and walked over to the counter and leaned against it and took a drink of the brown bourbon. "His name's Jack Thomas. I went to high school with him. He played first base on the team. Look, he's got some problems. I've been trying to help him. He's hooked on heroin."

"I see. He's hooked on heroin. What are you hooked on?"

"I'm not hooked on anything. I'm just trying to help out an old friend."

"Oh, okay, I see now. Gosh, what a nice person you are. What a— what a good friend you are. You've probably been helping him with my money, haven't you?"

"I'm not going to lie about that."

"Well, thank God you're not going to lie about it. I feel so much better knowing that you're not going to lie."

"I've been trying to get him off for a month."

"I bet you have. Is it real hard?"

"It's the hardest thing I've ever done."

"I'm sure it is, but keep on working on it, Bucky, just keep giving it all you got."

"I understand what you're saying to me, Cat. You're not as smart as you think you are."

"No, I'm not. You're quite right about that. I missed all of this. You would think I wouldn't have, but I did, so for you to say I'm not smart is probably the only truthful thing you've said today."

"I am not a homosexual."

"Did you kiss him at that bar—or excuse me—did he kiss you—in fact, did he kiss you twice at that bar today or not?"

"What do you mean?"

"Oh God, Bucky."

"I don't know what you're trying to prove."

"No, I don't think you do. I really don't."

"I think you need to calm down, take a bath or something."

He moved toward her as if to kiss her, but she held up her hands.

"Okay," he said. "I'll call you tomorrow. You know we have that party tomorrow night, that beer bust. It'll be a blast. I think we both need it, you know?" He stuck his hands into his jeans and started to say something else, but then just smiled and left.

She spent the night questioning herself, and the questions at first were things like how could he lie so brazenly and how could he take her money to support a junkie, money that had to feed a baby, and why was she always attracted to men who were rotten, and there were many more questions which went on and on and on, though the image of Bucky kissing the young blond began to come more often and she asked herself, How could he lie about that? All the other things I could understand him lying about and hoping to get away with because I wasn't there, but I was there when he kissed him and I saw them and how on earth could he lie about it?

And then finally around five-thirty in the morning, when the first birds began to sing heartless notes, the thought came to her that maybe he wasn't lying. Maybe he hadn't kissed the boy. He had always been so honest before. In fact, the boy did kiss him and it could be that Bucky was completely surprised by this, completely caught off guard, and so he let the boy kiss him and did not really respond because he was his friend and he wanted to help him get off the heroin, and so he just put up with the kiss and it meant nothing.

Just before she left for work that morning, a delivery man brought over a brown box. It contained a white cashmere baby blanket, cashmere booties and a blue wool skirt that was her size. She opened a note:

> The cashmere is not terribly practical I realize, but it is soft. The skirt, I think, makes a bit more sense.
> I hope things fit.
>
> *Harper.*

By lunchtime, she was feeling better about Bucky and realized that she had been rash. She was ready to call him and try to work this out. She decided to take him out to dinner at the nicest place in town and so she went by the bank to take some money out of the savings account.

"Fifty dollars out of savings, please," she said to the teller.

"Yes, ma'am." The young girl flipped through a thick book, read something and then frowned. She picked up the phone.

Cat was feeling better, the knots let loose in her stomach. She looked at the girl's skin. It was pink and smooth and without a wrinkle or blemish. She was going to compliment her when she said, "I'm sorry, ma'am. That account is not negotiable."

"Um—I just need fifty dollars. There's three hundred in it."

"No ma'am, it's not negotiable."

"I don't know what you mean. Have you got the right account? It's Catherine McGregor . . ."

"Yes, ma'am, or Mr. Buckland Cates, and it's completely empty."

"Not . . . not anything at all?"

"Nothing."

The pain was the hardest and the deepest and the longest pain she had ever felt, and sometimes at night when it was very bad, she tried to make it worse by remembering a happy time with him. When she had made herself hurt as badly as she could, she would say, "There—now never let it happen to you again, never ever let yourself be hurt like this again."

It was the middle of the month and she was broke. Most of her salary from the newspaper was going to pick up checks she had bounced at a convenience store. Ford had once again offered to help her out, but she had refused. Hannah and Bub started bringing over masses of supplies until she told them to hold off and that she could get out of this herself. One morning another box arrived. There were more baby clothes and a blue silk blouse.

Everyone is arriving at Waverly next Sunday for dinner, except Starkey, of course. He's doing very well, by the way. He signed for a third tour and recently they put him in charge of a camp—as a captain.

Dinner is at two o'clock. If you come, everyone will be happy to see you.

Harper.

Harper had started writing the notes for one simple reason: she wanted Blackie's son. In the beginning, during Cat's pregnancy, she had convinced herself that she did not care about the child one bit, but after it was born, she found herself thinking about it all the time. What color were his eyes, his skin and hair? Did he have all his fingers and did he have dimples? Wick's two boys she could attain easily. She had already seen them, having visited Alice and Wick for a weekend. It was Blackie's son that seemed out of her grasp and it made her want him desperately.

During the worst part of her illness, during that muddle of days when she wasn't sure if she would survive, Harper kept thinking about the boy. The image of the child helped her to pull through. As soon as she was able to think clearly again, she decided she would approach Cat, bring her back to Waverly. It was the only way she could have the child.

Her newest regret was that she had started writing notes before Ford had told her that he was quite serious about asking Cat to marry him. She had agreed to the marriage because she saw that he was determined to do it, but if she had only waited with her notes, it would appear that she was writing because the situation forced her to, rather than out of need. Still, she would make the best of it. The most important thing was to get the child. She would make do with Cat—for a while.

43

IT WAS SIX-FIFTEEN IN the morning at the Special Forces Camp called Bak-Ti. Like most camps, it was built in a valley near a river. The river was black and shallow and along the sides of it there were green vines and thick ivies and walls of briars and ferns and everything was green, but not a single color of green, a hundred different colors, and then farther up the sides of the mountains the vines gave way to stands of bamboo and the triple canopy began— mahogany trees and teak and pepper trees and the color beneath the canopy was brown and the land was open and at the top of the mountains there stood green elephant grass and brown boulders and the elephant grass was filled with crickets which were singing.

Starkey was awake. It had become his custom to wake an hour before the rest of the men. He lay in his concrete hooch and looked at the pink light coming in through the gun apertures. He could hear dogs barking in the village and a rooster crowing and he was waiting for a very specific sound, thinking it was late and feeling himself tense up, wondering why it was late and then he heard it—three beats, brassy and sharp, the Buddhist priest striking his gong. He relaxed.

He looked at a picture of Harper which sat beside his cot. He hoped he had her kind of guts, her strength. It had only been two months ago when the doctors had said that she wouldn't recover from the stroke. Ford had called him in Saigon on a diplomatic line as soon as it had happened. Starkey had been badly shaken. It was then that he realized he had never thought of her becoming sick, of her death. It was not normal. She was over seventy and he should have been preparing himself for her death for years.

When Harper had been at her weakest, Starkey had spoken to Ford at four o'clock every day and then gone to a church and prayed. He worried himself to sleep. Almost every night, he awoke in a kind of panic. It had never happened to him before, even when his parents were killed, but he would awake in a panic, saying to himself, What will I do? When she's gone, what will I do? It would take another hour for him to get back to sleep.

The crisis had lasted three days. A week later, he went to the embassy for his usual four o'clock call. The phone rang and he heard the voice, weak, faintly slurred, but still with the chipperness.

"Well, they tried to put the old girl away, but she held on."

"Harper?"

"It's me—still."

"God, I can't believe you're calling."

"Neither can the doctors—wupps, hold on a second, I've got to shoo this damn preacher out of here. If I hear the Twenty-third Psalm one more time, I think I will croak."

Starkey laughed for the first time in days. That night, he finally rested. The very next morning, he forced himself to start preparing for the time when she would not call, when he would never hear from her again.

Soft Touch banged on his door. "Wake up, Dai-wi. Time to rise and shine."

"Okay."

"You up?"

"I'm up, I'm up."

The team called each other by their personal call signs. There was Soft Touch and Sugar, Dink Killer and Zorrow, Meat, Shit Head and other names. Some of the team were called by their last names, none by their first. The men called Starkey Dai-wi, which was captain in Vietnamese.

Today would be a quiet day. The heavy weapons man was training some strikers in 81mm mortar firing and the medics were scheduled to teach the Montagnards how to tie off severed arteries. Starkey had some paperwork and he had to talk to the engineers about laying concrete on some mud paths in the camp, but other than that the day was easy. He lay on his cot a minute longer, thinking that there was a part to it that was beautiful. People didn't like for you to say that, but it was true. There was a part of war that was beautiful and exotic and fun, but you could not say it because people would think you were crazy. Maybe the beautiful part was why there were so many wars. Maybe cutting through jungles and fording black rivers and laying strange women who knew different kinds of sex and counting on your buddies in desperate situations, sweating with them, tying knots, breaking down guns with them and hacking through the green with them and finally going home at night and talking about it all around a fire and drinking booze with them—maybe this beautiful part of it was why there was war as much as anything else.

Starkey ducked out of his hooch and stretched and took a look at the camp. The red dust was everywhere. It rose from the bare ground and covered the TOC building and the team house and the armory and the thatched roofs of the strikers quarters. It blew in the air and lay on your skin and got in your ears and nose. There were big squares of earth in the camp which were marked by off-limits signs and long lines of string. The Americans had been trying to grow grass here for three years, but the best they could get was a few patches.

In the middle of a nearby patch of grass stood a white duck which wore a pair of dog tags. Starkey went over to the duck and waved his arms. "Get off there, Colonel," he said.

The duck looked at him, turned its head at an angle.

"Go on!" Starkey said.

The duck had been a pet of the last camp commander. It was named Colonel Custer. The camp commander had had the dog tags made for the duck.

A small boy ran to the edge of the grass. He was a Montagnard and had mahogany skin and black wavy hair and white teeth. There were three Montagnard boys in the camp and the Americans called them the three stooges: Curly, Larry and Moe. This was Moe.

"Dai-wi, you outranked. This one higher than you. He a colonel."

"Yeah, well, the colonel better get off that grass," Starkey said. He clapped his hands.

The duck quacked and lifted its yellow head.

"You must salute first," the boy said.

"How do you know?"

"He my friend."

"Go ahead. You salute."

The brown boy walked to the edge of the grass, pulled himself to an impeccable attention and saluted.

"Please to go, Colonel Custer," he said.

The white duck quacked and waddled away.

"See, Dai-wi?"

"Yeah, I see. You two make a good team."

"A-team stuff, Dai-wi?"

"A-team stuff, all the way. Is my shower ready?"

Moe and the other boys performed a lot of personal tasks around the camp like filling the fifty-five-gallon drum with water for showers. The drum sat in a rusted frame beside the team house which was a long building with a thatch roof. It was buried three feet in the earth so it would stay cool.

Starkey stepped into the shower. Green ponchos had been draped over the frame to give a little privacy. Moe was standing on a ladder behind the frame. Starkey gave the order and pulled a chain and the cold water ran down and Starkey yelled like an Indian and then scrubbed himself for a good five minutes.

Back in his hooch, he dressed in baggy green fatigues and jungle boots and drank a cup of instant coffee that Moe brought him. The commo man walked over and brought two radio messages which had come in the night. They were Blackbird intelligence reports which stated that there was troop movement in the free fire zone located about twenty-five kilometers from the camp. Starkey went looking for Dink Killer. He was the intelligence man of the team. Maybe he could figure out what this meant.

Walking down through the red dust of the camp, Starkey jumped off the concrete path and landed in a parallel trench. It was muddy and wet and three feet deep. The trenches connected all the buildings of the camp and ran out to the periphery. A swarm of black gnats zoomed up from the stagnant water and went straight for his eyes and face. He batted them away and squished through the mud. Sergeant Vachel Fox walked up beside him on a path.

"Jesus, these things are awful," Starkey said.

"Well, what you doing in there, Dai-wi?"

"You seen Dink?"

"You better say Dink Killer. He don't like just Dink."

"Listen, I want you to get Jones over here and ask him if he can lay some concrete in the bottom of these things. Where'd you say Dink was?"

"He's down there behind the Strikers' mess. I think he's got him another cobra."

"Oh hell. He didn't get Patton, did he?"

" 'Fraid so."

Patton was the pet mongoose. He was long, dark brown speed with gray eyes and red whiskers and yellow teeth. He was the best rat killer in the camp and Dink Killer liked to bring him cobras and watch the fight.

Starkey jumped back up onto the pathway and hurried down through the dusty camp. On the left was a concrete building with a metal door and a tin roof. A sign above the door read LBJ MEAT MEMORIAL. Two yellow dogs lay against the metal door. The building was a freezer. It had been built to house the three hundred pounds of USDA choice Texan beef which came every month to the camp. The word was that President Johnson had got the Pentagon to buy all the beef that Texas could produce and now there was so much of it that the steaks were stacked to the ceiling.

He went by the TOC building with its sandbag walls and thatch roof. Ten or twelve Strikers wearing tiger fatigues and blue flip-flops stood in a semicircle around a young medic who held up a piece of transparent filament, saying, ". . . it is called a suture. Not a line, not a—a gossamer or a piece of string, but a suture . . ."

Below the TOC building was lockup. Outside of it two Americans stood above a VC prisoner who had been taken the day before. The VC was squatting on the ground. He was shirtless and wore black pants and his hands were tied behind his back. The Americans were smoking cigarettes and one of them leaned down to the VC and made a gun with his thumb and finger and put it to the VC's head and said "boom" and then he blew cigarette smoke from the barrel of his finger.

"Smith, let's get this guy's hands untied," Starkey said.

"Why do you want to do that?"

Smith was thin and bony. His face and long forearms were dark brown from the sun and the fingers and thumb of his right hand had been tattooed with the word DEATH.

Starkey traded stares with him, then reached over and took a hunting knife out of his web gear and bent down and cut the rope around the VC's hands. "Get him to the medic. His hands are cut."

"All right."

Starkey moved very close to him. "Say again?"

"Yes sir."

Starkey looked into his eyes a moment and felt his muscles tense. He turned and started again for the Strikers' mess, thinking that one day he would have to fight him.

It was a rectangular building. The walls were three feet high and then open all the way around and the roof was rusted tin. The green sandbags which formed the walls had been filled with mud and the sun had dried them hard. Only half of the Strikers were eating breakfast this morning—two hundred or so. Starkey knew where the others were. He went past the mess and then up a red dust hill and looked down the other side. The rest of the Strikers had formed a circle around Dink Killer and Patton and a black cobra.

Starkey moved through the crowd of Strikers. They were Vietnamese and wore tiger fatigues and flip-flops, and as he moved through them, he could smell the Vitalis which they got on R & R and smeared on first thing in the morning, streaking it through their black hair. He could smell the fried fish they had eaten for breakfast and the sour, spicy, fermented smell of Nouc-mam sauce, which they dumped on everything, even the stone-ground grits which they had started eating because Central Supply had sent Starkey a ton instead of a case.

Dink Killer was on his knees in the red dirt. He was a big man with a shaven head and a black mole the size of a dime in his right temple. He was speaking to the mongoose in a soft voice. "Take it easy now. You got him once, just take it easy. Finish him off, baby."

The cobra was bleeding from the mouth and the mongoose was making a noise that sounded something like "Riki-tiki-tiki. Riki-tiki-tiki-tiki-tiki."

Patton's brown body was flat against the dirt, his gray eyes were fastened on the cobra and his long, fur tail was twitching from side to side, his red whiskers vibrating so that if he had a mind he might be thinking, Big cobra, you are very big, but you are very heavy too because the morning is cool and you haven't been in the sun and so you are slow, big hood, way too slow for warm blood, for mongoose blood.

The Cobra's back was black skin and its eyes dark red. It was already tired and so lay close to the earth, the small mouth half open and the black tongue licking the air.

Patton made a feint to the left and the cobra flinched and heaved its long body into the air three feet high, the light, yellow underbelly going flat and then the hood opened, widened and expanded even more, almost a foot across and so broad now that it made a shadow over the small mongoose, who bared his dark, yellow teeth, the small jaw shuddering uncontrollably. He darted at the snake's underbelly.

The cobra struck the earth beside Patton and the mongoose leapt on the broad hood and bit the snake just behind the head so that the huge creature let out a loud hiss and threw eight feet of black coils around the mongoose, but they would do no good. Patton bit four more times and slithered from the coils crying out "Riki-tiki-tiki. Riki-tiki-tiki."

The Strikers applauded and cheered and D.K. grabbed the mongoose and stroked him.

Starkey waited for D.K. to collect and pay off bets. Several Strikers stretched out the snake and beheaded it. They began to strip off the skin. They would cut the snake up and mix it with bamboo shoots and Nouc-mam sauce for supper.

D.K. saw Starkey. "Oh Lord, I guess you're ready to throw me into the brig."

"You can't keep doing this."

"It's the last time, Dai-wi."

"We need him."

"Want to hold him?"

Starkey took the warm mongoose, which immediately crawled onto his shoulder and lay around his neck. He wanted to reprimand D.K. but as usual found it difficult because he was so friendly. It was D.K.'s way. While he was in camp he was warm and friendly, but in the bush he changed. Some said he had killed over twenty VC. There was a rumor that after he shot a man he would rush to him and try to suck the last breath that came from his mouth.

"I think we may have some problems in the free fire zone," Starkey said. "A Blackbird snapped a few pictures. MACV says trucks are moving through there."

"How?"

"The old French bridge, I forget the name. The one that goes across the border."

"Champion Bridge?"

"Champion, yea. They say trucks are moving across it."

"Hell, Dai-wi, that bridge was blown two years ago."

"MACV's got the pictures."

"They're smart little fuckers. I've always said that. They're smart as hell. I think we ought to do a little recon and see what we can see."

"It'll be me, you and four Strikers."

"Ought to take Fox. We'll need a good light weapons man."

"Nope. Just two of us. I don't want to risk any more. We'll go right after I get back."

"Oh, yeah. Saigon. You going to see your little honey?"

44

STARKEY HOPED HE WOULD see her. It had been three months since they had been together. She had written him four letters, each one cooler than the others. He knew she was seeing the other guy. When he was with her it didn't bother him so much, but when he was away it bothered him a lot.

As he was walking back to his hooch, a jeep skidded to a stop beside him. The driver was from the 101st Airborne. He said he had come to pick up some of the surplus steaks. Starkey signed a requisition form and looked toward the back of the jeep and saw them. There must have been fifty hanging on a wire that was strung across the frame. They were dark red and black and dried, though some of them were softer, fresher than the others and these new ones had attracted the black gnats of the camp and as Starkey looked at them he was not quite sure at first and then he was sure, more by the smell than the sight of them, more by the rotting odor.

"Is that what I think it is?" Starkey asked.

"Yes sir. Sixty-four. All from my company, too. We got four of them yesterday. Zapped them in a little place called Lon Tai. You know how it got started, don't you?"

Starkey looked at the gnats eating them.

"The Dinks think if you don't have all your body parts on you when you die, you can't get into heaven. So shit, I don't know, a hundred years ago or something like that they started cutting off ears so their enemies couldn't make paradise. We're just keeping up the tradition, you know? So far we got sixty-four that ain't going to see them pearly gates. Not bad, huh, Captain?"

Starkey looked into the brown eyes of the young second lieutenant, wondering, How did this happen to you, young man? How did you come to be so much without feeling, without even simple disgust? You probably went to college and drank beer with your friends and studied a little history, remembering a bit about the Romans and a tad about the Greeks. You studied sociology and read about how the human being coalesces into groups and you studied psychology, the methods and intricacies of the human mind, and you had to study biology, you had to see the miraculous union of the mind to flesh and bone and sinew. Did you forget all you were, when you came here? Did you forget it all?

"Captain, are you all right?"

"Are you, Lieutenant? Are you all right?

It bothered Starkey for the rest of the day, so much so that at five-thirty he went back to his hooch and drank a beer, something he had not done in a long time. The alcohol relaxed him and he thought about Eugénie and that he was going to be glad to see her.

Around six-thirty, Vachel Fox ducked into the hooch. "Hey, Dai-wi want to wet a line?"

"You know, I've been to that river five times and I still haven't had a bite."

"I got three big ones last week."

"What? You didn't tell me that."

"You didn't ask."

"What'd you use for bait?"

"I ain't going to tell you what I use for bait."

"Aw come on, Fox."

"Leeches."

"Leeches? You're catching trout with leeches?"

"My own, too. Found all three of them on my bod last week."

Starkey laughed. "Maybe that's the secret."

"I'll tell you what, leeches'll get you a lot more fish than those damn dried flies ever will."

"All right," Starkey said. "Saddle up. We'll just see."

Starkey opened his dufflebag and found his fishing vest which was wrapped in plastic. He pulled out the vest and with it came the smell of Waverly, the smell of his room, books and leather boots and linseed oil and the smell of the house itself, sweet and damp, holding the scent of pines and jasmine and the long green grass of the fields. It stopped him for a moment and made him see Blackie and Ford and Wick and they were all sitting in the big kitchen and Hannah was frying bream and hush puppies and everything was all right, everything was safe and slow as a long summer evening, when the wind was gone and the katydids were quiet and he could hear the rockers of Boykin and Harper creaking on the long front porch.

The river was a hundred yards from the camp. It was narrow and the water was black and clear. Big green and brown boulders sat in the water, and ferns and briars and bamboo hugged the banks so that it was hard to fish unless you walked out into the center of the river and stood on one of the flat rocks. There were a few palm trees on the bank. Tiny blue and yellow parrots sat in the top of them. Fox and Starkey shared the same flat rock.

Starkey pulled a fly off his vest. It was a black gnat and he looked at it, just to enjoy the tiny hook and the black thread wrapped around the shank of it, and then the swirl of black feathers and the yellow knot at the eye of the hook. He had started making himself stop to look at his lures when he had first come to Vietnam. He had told himself that he must learn to enjoy the little things, and that if he took time to be happy with the little things, then he would not be so unhappy with the big ones.

Vachel Fox pulled a skinny leech out of an M16 shell. He had six shells and each one held a leech which had been sealed inside with a daub of white wax. The leech was black and slimy and it was tapered at both ends.

"Is it yours?" Starkey asked.

"Naw, it's wild."

Fox set a hook into the back of the leech. It curled into a black loop and he cast it into the shallows of the river. Starkey fished the white water just below the rocks. The two men worked the river quietly for a half an hour, neither one of them getting any bites. The sun began to set, blazing behind the teak trees in the distance, and below the teak trees the jungle was deep green and throwing shadows which reached the river and turned the black water even blacker.

"Fox, if you could be anyplace in the world right now, anyplace at all, where would it be?"

Vachel Fox wiped sweat from his skinny neck and then rubbed it on the seat of his green fatigues.

"Dewey's Cue and Cushion, I reckon."

"A bar?"

"Nope. Pool hall. Real good slaw dogs. Big tables."

"You a good pool player?"

"Fair to middling."

"I'd be right here, you know? I wouldn't want to be anyplace but right here. I know it sounds crazy."

"That's 'cause you ain't seen the worst of it yet," Fox said, and turned to look at the officer. He had grown to like Starkey, though there were times when he still resented him, resented the way he never lost his temper when somebody sassed him, just lifted his chin and raised his eyebrows, resented the fact that he always used a fork and knife, even with Spam, always a cloth napkin. Still he was open and friendly and he had balls, and even though you could see the silver spoon sticking in his mouth, you felt like he'd give it to you if you ever asked him.

Starkey reeled in his line slowly. "God. If I can just stop this infiltration, Fox. If I can knock the VC out of this sector, man, oh man."

"And what if you don't stop them? What happens then?"

The question rang in Starkey's head all night. Not because he had not thought of it, but because someone else had asked it. The answer he wanted to give was simple: if I fail at this I should put a gun to my mouth and blow my head off. I will deserve it because anybody could win here, anybody could beat the hell out of these guys, and if I don't, if I blow this chance, then I deserve the worst damn thing that can happen to me.

At 6 A.M., Starkey gave his second in command some final instructions and then he left for Saigon.

Eugénie met him at eleven-thirty on the patio of the Continental Hotel. He didn't know how much he had missed her until he saw her. She was wearing a white pleated dress and mauve high heels and her short black hair and hazel eyes were shining. He wanted to jump up from the table and hug her, but he knew she would hate it, so he just smiled and gave a little wave as if he were cool. He noticed his hand was shaking.

"Well, don't I get a hug?"

He started to rise.

"Oh, forget it."

She had this way of keeping him off balance.

A waiter came over and she ordered a vodka on the rocks and Starkey ordered a Coke and some pâté. He tried his best not to look at her greedily, but now and again he did and she saw him and he could tell it irritated her. They talked about her father and that the rubber plantation was doing well, though he did not feel safe hunting anymore. She said that René had asked about him and wanted all of them to get together tonight for supper at the floating Chinese restaurant, the name of which she couldn't remember, and oh yes she had been to Hong Kong twice and of course had bought far too many clothes, mainly silks, though the real reason she had gone was to get wallpaper for her father's house, though she didn't know when in the world she'd have time to get it up, since she was leaving for Switzerland next week.

Starkey looked away from her beautiful eyes and looked down at the table and felt his heart catch. He knew what this meant.

The waiter brought the drinks and the pâté. The Coke was in a frosted glass and the vodka in a martini glass. Eugénie drank the vodka in three swallows and ordered another with some water. The waiter sat the pâté between them. The plate was a rose color and the pâté was black and round and the center of it was made of ginger and shaped like a lotus blossom.

Starkey looked up from the table and tried not to show anything. He took a knife and spread some pâté on a sliver of white bread and handed it to her.

"So how do you like it?" Eugénie asked.

"Bak-Ti?"

"Are you out there defending freedom?"

He took a sip of Coke.

"Or are you just playing soldier? Crawling around with a knife in your teeth."

"Why are you doing this to me? Why are you going at me like this?"

"To break through. To establish contact. Every time you go away for a while, it comes back again. Everytime I think I've seen the last of it, it crops up again and usually just as strong as ever."

"What?"

"Your goddamned superiority. I mean, I come to meet you for a drink having not laid eyes on you in three months and you don't even get up from the table."

"I thought you wouldn't like it."

"Oh, bullshit. Don't try that kind of legerdemain with me. You thought I wouldn't like it. Yea, right—what I like is someone acting superior and distant and like they own the world and everything that's in it. I love it, I love that kind of superiority."

"You're not reading me right."

"Oh, I'm not?"

"No."

"Well, how should I read you, Captain?"

He sat back in his chair and folded his hands over his stomach. He didn't want this. He didn't want to fight. How had it started?

"You see there—look at that posture." She mocked him, letting her eyes widen and her face go slack. She slumped and folded her hands and raised her chin.

He tried a different tack. "I think you look pretty good. You look in charge."

"That's exactly what I mean, damn you." She slammed the table with the flat of her hand. "You're not in charge. You are not in charge of me and I want it stopped. This damned superior attitude. I want it ended. I will do whatever I want, whenever I want, and I don't have to answer to you or anyone else, you sonofabitch."

Starkey reached across the table and grabbed her right hand and twisted it back hard and she gave a little scream and the blood left her face.

"I need to go up and take a shower. I'm in room 232. If you want to see me, come on up there. I love you, Eugénie, but I won't put up with this."

He signaled a waiter. "Give her some coffee."

Starkey went upstairs and took a long shower and felt sick. Was he acting superior? He tried to think back on his actions. He had been reserved, but he had done this because she seemed to hate it when he was obvious in his affection.

There was a knock at the door and he put on a robe and opened it.

"Are you Starkey?" the young woman asked.

"Yes."

"Um, hey, listen, this is kind of embarrassing, but I'm a friend of Eugénie's—uh, could I come in a minute?"

She was a thin redhead. She wore a pair of blue jeans and a black pullover sweater. "I was supposed to meet you two for a drink."

Starkey could not remember having met her.

"She's just a mess. She hasn't been herself at all lately. We're all kind of worried about her."

"I'm sorry, I don't think I know you."

"Oh, jeez, I'm sorry, I'm Linda Barns. I work at the embassy. Eugénie's told me all about you, of course. She worships you, I guess you know."

"You could have fooled me," Starkey said.

Linda sat on the couch. A frilly collar peeked out of her sweater. She wore brown oxfords and pink socks, the tops of which had been turned down and each had a pink hem. Over her right bosom was an antique pin with sequins.

"I think it all started when she didn't get this part she wanted really bad. It was some Indian movie. I read the script—I don't know anything about movies, but I thought it sounded awful."

"When did this happen?"

"Let's see—last week? Yeah, I think it was last week. She started doing white dogs right after that."

"Does Papa know?"

"Papa?"

"Mr. Villeneuve. Have you met him?"

"No, I don't think he knows, or at least—actually I don't know if he knows or not. You mean that she's doing white dogs, right?"

"Yeah."

"I know it's not a good sign."

"It's a disastrous sign."

"She told me a little bit about her past, her drug problem."

A white dog was a mixture of opium, kahlua and cream topped off with crème de cacao. It was one of the things Eugénie did when she was on her way back to her habit. Starkey was almost happy about it. He knew it was an awful way to feel, but the truth was when she was doing drugs, he knew how to deal with her. He knew he could deal with her. Her habit gave him an edge.

"She said to give you this." Linda handed him a note.

Starkey,

I'm sorry. I didn't know I was going at you until it was too late. Let's just have fun. I just want to have fun, okay?

> Wicked witch of the East.
> *Eugénie.*
> XXXXXXXXXXXXXX
> These are kisses.

Starkey went down into the lobby and Eugénie ran up to him and hugged him.

"Are we copacetic?" Eugénie asked.

"We're copacetic."

"I think you need me now."

"I know I do."

"No, I mean like this." She touched him.

"I know what you mean."

She grabbed his hand and pulled him toward the elevator. Her hazel eyes were big and shining. "Linda will be furious."

"Why?"

"Jealous. Just jealous, jealous, jealous. Why shouldn't she be?"

45

EUGENIE WAS WILD. THIS was an-
other reason Starkey liked it when she was going back to her habit, and
though he liked her wild, he knew it was wrong, but he couldn't let go
of the edge.

"You know what I want to do? I want to stay up the whole three days
you're here. I don't want to get a wink of sleep, just go, go, go."

"I'm sorry about your part."

"Don't talk about it."

"You're a good actress."

"You're prejudiced."

"Yes I am, but you're still a good actress."

"I don't care anymore. It doesn't matter."

He took her hand and kissed the pink faces of all five fingers. "One
day you'll be in Hollywood."

"Do you think so?"

"Will you take me with you?"

"I never travel alone."

"I know. So I guess you're going to Switzerland with what's his name."

"I don't believe you. Are you worried about that?"

"Yep."

"How long have you been thinking about that?"

"Soon as you mentioned it."

"Oh Starkey."

"Why do you keep seeing him then?"

"Let's not get into all that again. I'm going to Switzerland with Linda."

"Are you really?"

"Feel better?"

He felt great.

They met René and his new friend Vincent down in the lobby and then the five of them went to the Cercle Sportif for a drink and Eugénie slipped her vial of cocaine to the bartender and he made her a white dog. It made her crazy and she jumped up on the bar and started dancing to "Let's Go Surfin' Now" and Linda got up with her and they danced together hard. Several of the French colons were wearing white jackets and they got angry and left. Eugénie and the others had another round of drinks and then walked out into the sweltering afternoon. The streets were jammed with tiny white-and-blue taxicabs and old Peugeots and ancient Citroens and red Honda motorbikes. The air was blue and gassy and the sidewalks were crowded with Vietnamese and Americans. Eugénie stopped and looked at the Americans. They towered above the Chinese and the Vietnamese and Eugénie had never seen this many of them in Saigon. She caught Starkey by the arm.

"Look at all of them," she said.

"All of who?"

"Americans."

"Oh—yeah."

"I've never seen so many."

"You ain't seen nothing yet."

They made their way through the crowds to the Rue Catinat. Things were impassable here, a logjam of bodies. The smell of ginger and sweat and gas fumes and sewage and frying foods. Beggars and cripples and bar girls crammed the corners of the streets. Off-duty American soldiers and on-duty ARVN infantrymen and Vietnamese businessmen in blue suits squirmed and crabbed, and nobody looked anybody in the eyes unless they were up to no good. Eugénie directed everyone into Roy Rodgers' Bar and they stayed and drank.

It was after dark when they left and everyone was a little drunk except for Starkey, who had nursed two beers. Eugénie wanted to eat at the floating Chinese restaurant and she led the way past the Marie Curie Lycée, where she had gone to school as a girl, past the sandbagged villa which housed MACV headquarters, past yellow and pink villas and green yards filled with jasmine and sleek tamarind trees. Finally, away from the crush of the crowd, they got a cab.

The restaurant was situated on a large raft which bobbed in the middle of the Saigon River. Starkey ordered the most exotic meal on the menu. It was called Squab in Nest with Three Eggs. Vincent made a face.

"God, it sounds awful." He looked at the waiter. "Do you have spaghetti and meatballs?"

Starkey thought that Vincent looked very much like Bob Jenkins. He was surprised that René had found someone else so fast. He felt badly about Bob. He felt that it was his fault that the tiger had gotten him. He sort of missed Bob Jenkins. He was a decent guy in his own way.

"Please have some taste, Vincent," René said.

"Try the eel," Linda said.

"I don't want the eel. I want spaghetti and meatballs."

"We have," the waiter said.

"You have spaghetti and meatballs?" asked Eugénie.

"We have."

"And a cheeseburger," Vincent said.

"No cheeseburger," René said. "Just bring him the spaghetti."

"Hey, this is America," Vincent said. "I can have what I want. Bring me a cheeseburger and spaghetti and meatballs."

"We have," said the waiter.

"See, he has," Vincent said. He had a new haircut and his blond hair was short and it made his face look round and boyish.

"I think he's right," Linda said. "I think it is America."

"It is the way you will win," René said to Starkey. "Not by bombs, but by buying."

"Wonderful alliteration," Eugénie said.

"What do you mean?" Starkey asked.

"You cannot beat them on the field. It will never happen."

Starkey looked at the mascara on his long lashes.

"If you buy them, if you turn Vietnam into Missouri, then you will win."

"Oh, I think we'll win," Starkey said.

"By buying, yes?"

"No, the right way."

"Which is what?"

"Fighting them. Taking them on."

"Don't get him started," Eugénie said.

"You think war is the right way?"

"I don't know if it's the right way or the wrong way. I didn't ask for it, I'm just in it and since I'm in it I want to win and I don't see anything wrong with that. I mean, I think war should be outlawed and I hope I see that day, but until then if we have to fight then we should fight to win."

"Boring, boring, boring," Eugénie said.

"He is cute," René said.

"Very," said Vincent.

Starkey held up his hands. "Okay, okay."

The waiter came over and there was another round of drinks and the food came out quickly.

Eugénie was determined to stay up all night. She made a list of ten bars and by dawn they had been to nine and everyone was very drunk except for Starkey. They had made a circle around the city and now were sitting in the bar at Ton Son Nhut Airport. Vincent was facedown on the table and René's mascara had leaked from his watery brown eyes and smeared his cheeks. Linda was groggy, but Eugénie was vivacious. Starkey was looking out the window and watching C130 transports arriving every fifty seconds.

"I've got it," Eugénie said. "We're going to Suloi."

"Not I," René said.

"Sure you are."

"Honey, that's eighty miles away," Starkey said.

"But only sixty by air," Eugénie said. "Come on. It's my treat. Everybody's fading. We can't fade. I'll pay for the whole adventure."

"What's so adventurous about Suloi?" Starkey asked.

"Shark hunting."

"What?"

"You can do it from a helicopter. Kill them with rockets. We must try it. We just must."

Four hours later, Starkey and Linda and Eugénie were walking down Qui-Lan Street in Suloi. René and Vincent had declined the invitation. The air here was clean. It was soft and filled with the smell of the sea. It was a white city. The roads were made of crushed white shells and the walls of the city were white stucco and the wooden houses which sat behind the walls were painted white except for the shutters, which were blue or yellow. There were many sugar palm trees and stands of green bamboo and small red-and-blue birds singing from the shaggy tops of ferns.

Starkey had not heard about hunting sharks from helicopters and he did not have the vaguest idea of how to arrange it.

"Suloi is famous for it," Eugénie said.

It was almost twelve o'clock and the sun was white and strong and so hot that Starkey could feel the sweat roll from the back of his scalp down his neck.

"Famous for shark hunting?" Starkey asked.

"I've heard about it, too," Linda said.

"It's obviously black market," Starkey said. "I have no idea of how to make contact with whoever runs it."

"You could probably ask in any bar in town," Eugénie said.

"I doubt it."

She gave him a hard look and then walked across the white street and into a bar.

There were three or four Vietnamese officers and one American sitting on stools. There was no air-conditioning. Four overhead fans turned at a high speed. Everything in the bar was fluttering: the officers' hair and shirt collars and potted ferns and the white napkins under drinks. The place stank like a urinal.

Starkey ordered three Chinese beers. He took a sip of the beer and it was hot and Eugénie was looking at him.

"Guess it's up to me, huh?" Starkey asked.

"Don't you think it should be?"

"No."

He took another sip of the beer and then walked over to an American.

"Excuse me, I know this must sound a little crazy, but I'm looking for a contact to do some shark fishing from a—"

"Two streets down, take a left."

"Uh—is this with a—"

"Chopper. Yep."

Starkey turned around to see Eugénie smiling.

Two Huey gunships gleamed at the end of a wooden pier. A plywood office sat between Starkey and the helicopters. He pushed a bell and an American answered the door. He told them that it would be a hundred dollars for a two-hour run and twenty dollars for each rocket fired. Starkey said no, and Eugénie said it was fine and paid the money.

It was almost an hour before the young pilot arrived. He was wearing a flight suit and tennis shoes. He said that the chopper would hold only three people. Linda said that she would be very happy not to go.

Starkey walked around to the left of the Huey and saw a host of red sharks tattooed beneath the door. There were also two elephants.

They got in and buckled themselves into the seats. "Are those your kills?" Starkey asked.

"Some of them I zapped and some of them my customers zapped."

"How about the elephants?" asked Eugenie.

"Yea, I got two."

"You killed two elephants?"

"They were Commie elephants." The young man smiled, and stuck out his hand. "My name's Bobby Smith." He wore his hair in a brown flattop. There was a pink scar at the point in his chin. The flesh around the scar was puckered and blue.

"Hold on," Smith said. "We're flying didi mow."

The Huey lurched into the air and they reached thirty-five hundred feet very quickly. The South China Sea was blue and even. They flew down the length of the coast. The sand was white and the palm trees were tall and dark green and the water was a light blue and clear and the long sand bars were shining through the water. They flew above the white sand and over the mouth of a brown river. Several motorboats cut white wakes in the river.

Smith pointed down at the boats. He was wearing a copper friendship bracelet on his right wrist. "PBRs," he said.

Eugénie looked at Starkey.

"River patrol boat," Starkey said.

"Listen, you guys want to go for the big ones or the little ones?"

"Sharks?" Starkey yelled.

"The big sharks or the baby ones?"

"Why not try the big ones?"

"It's a little hairy."

"How come?"

"They hang out at the Chou-Li sandbars. Takes a lot of petro. Had to ditch a bird last year. Sharks almost got me."

"Why don't we just try the little ones," Starkey said.

"No, let's go for the big ones," said Eugénie.

Smith grinned and saluted.

It took forty-five minutes to fly to the Chou-Li sandbars. The color of the sea turned from light blue to dark blue and there were some white caps. The sandbars were very close to the surface and the water was clear and there were many sandbars and several palm trees were sticking out of them.

"You need to wear these," Smith said. He handed them two pairs of polarized sunglasses. "Just look straight into the sandbars. Sharks are easy to see. Look like shadows."

They flew along for about ten minutes. There were hundreds of sandbars and most of them were long and narrow and white, and in between the sandbars were flats of light blue water and occasionally a hole of dark blue. Starkey saw the first one. It was long and black. Even at a thousand feet, it seemed very big.

46

SMITH CIRCLED THE SHARK.

"What kind is it?" Eugénie asked.

"Hammerhead," Smith said. "Man-eaters, some of them. Haven't seen one in a while. Last year I killed boo koo." He pushed a button and armed his HEAP missiles. "Who wants the first shot?"

"I do," Eugénie said.

"All right. Now listen, I'm going to set us on a straight trajectory. You got a stick and I got a stick. All you have to do is ease forward when I tell you and then push this little red button."

"It fires the rocket?"

"Roger. You ready?"

She looked at Starkey. "Am I ready?"

"You're ready."

Smith brought the Huey down low—fifty feet above the blue surface. He swung out to sea and made a long loop. "Okay. The shark's going to be straight ahead of us, but we need to be a little lower so push forward on the stick just a touch."

Eugénie pushed the stick and nothing happened, then she flinched and the stick jerked and the Huey bolted and jumped down ten feet.

"Damn," Starkey said.

"It's okay," Smith said. "I got dual controls. You have to move it smoothly, just push even. Come on. We need to be down another twenty feet."

This time Eugénie didn't flinch and the helicopter slid through the air.

Smith pulled down the sight from the windshield. "Now look right through here. When the shark gets between these two crosshairs, fire away. You okay?"

"Think so."

"Be looking through the sight now. Yeah. See him? He's coming up. You looking?"

Eugénie saw the black form at the top of the sight. It quickly dropped toward the crosshairs and she pushed the button and there was a bang and the Huey shook and bounced in the air.

Smith banked a hard right just in time to see the explosion.

It missed and the big shark darted into one of the blue holes.

It took them fifteen minutes to find another one. Smith set up the same course, went through the same instructions, only this time he told Eugénie that he thought the sight was a little high and he wanted her to wait until the target fell an inch below the crosshairs.

She saw the form dropping down through the sight and just below the crosshairs. She pulled the trigger. The Huey jolted and Smith swung them around to see the explosion. Half of the shark blew into the air. The water churned and whirled in a bloody froth.

"Good shot," Smith said.

"Did I do that?" asked Eugénie.

"You did it," said Starkey.

Smith reached into a small cooler beside him and handed out some beers. They drank a toast to Eugénie's kill and then Smith asked if Starkey wanted a try.

"Nope, I'm fine," Starkey said.

"You sure?"

"I think we need to get on back," Starkey said. "We look low on petro."

"I want to show you a little flying though," Smith said.

"Sure," Starkey said. "What outfit you with?"

"First Air Cav." He pulled a jungle hat out from under his seat and put it on his head. On the brim, he had written in black magic marker DEATH FROM ABOVE.

"I like to use the thirty-cals. It's real shooting when you're using them."

Smith pulled the Cobra two thousand feet into the air. He found a pair of binoculars and scanned the blue sea. They flew for twenty minutes until he spotted what he wanted. "Yeah, I see them. Hold on, we're going down."

The Huey swooped down low and Smith made a pass across a number of small black shadows. He drove the helicopter straight up past forty-five hundred feet and then let her fall in a swift spiral and he began firing the twin thirty-calibers, swooping so close to the surface of the sea that spray hit the windshield and he was yelling, "One, two, three, four, kill a gook and kill some more!"

The Huey came back around. Smith had hit three or four sharks and they were thrashing on the surface of the sea, and then suddenly he let go two of the HEAPs at once, and the sea exploded with fire and black smoke and Smith was yelling, "Ain't it great! Ain't this machine great! It's what America can do. Death. We do it bigger and better than anybody else. Fucking-A, man, nobody can kill like a white, male, native-born American. Nobody in the whole fucking world."

They didn't think about the heat and the smell of the hot bar in Suloi, they just went to it. Starkey ordered three double martinis and he and Eugénie drank them down fast.

"Geez—was it that bad?" Linda asked.

"I think I left part of my stomach in the seat," Eugénie said.

They drank two more rounds and then found another bar with air-conditioning. It was almost nine o'clock at night and Starkey was exhausted. Eugénie and Linda had been sneaking away to the rest room and doing lines of coke and they were full of energy. Starkey had drunk two martinis and a beer and he was bombed and needed something to eat.

"They have superb pheasant at La Savoisienne," Eugénie said.

"A couple hot dogs would be fine," said Starkey.

"I don't eat hot dogs."

"A steak then. Surely you can get a steak around here."

"This is our problem," Eugénie said. She was looking at Linda, but she was talking to Starkey. "It's hot dogs and steak-and-potatoes and big he-man stuff, you know? Why can't we do something different once in a while? Why can't we do something exotic?"

"Fine," Starkey said. "What do you want?"

"I want the pheasant at La Savoisienne in Dalat."

"Be nice now, sweetie," Linda said. She reached out and took Eugénie's little finger and shook it, looking at her deeply.

Starkey noticed this, but did not think about it much, until later.

When they touched down at Dalat, a full moon was shining. They took a bus from the airport to the Lang-Biang Palace. It had been one of the great hotels of Vietnam, having been built by the French in the green days of colonialism. Linda and Eugénie sat together. Starkey sat alone.

The bus chugged up the winding mountain roads. In the moonlight, the pine trees were silver with dew and the red blooms of rhododendron were shining. In the bottom of the forest, white moths fluttered through the dark trunks of the pine trees and left the woods, turning silver as they flew across the road, disappearing into the darkness of a ravine.

The Lang-Biang Palace sat on top of a mountain. Below the hotel was a small lake, several pink and white chateaux, a canopy of pine trees on the far side of a mountain and then the yellow walls of a convent and the black spires of a church.

They went into the pine bar of the hotel and Eugénie ordered three dry martinis and then disappeared into the bathroom with Linda. Starkey was so tired that his vision was blurry. The bartender set the martinis down and Starkey asked him to take his back and give him a glass of mineral water with lemon. The bar was falling into ruin. It had once been beautiful with pine wainscoting and molding around the ceiling and big pine planks for the floors, but now it was rundown. The paint was fading and several pieces of molding hung from the frieze. The big leather couches and wingback chairs were losing stuffing from holes. Even the hotel servants looked shabby and ill humored, wearing soiled white uniforms, cigarettes hanging from their lips, smelling of body odor and fish.

Starkey sipped his mineral water and wondered why Eugénie was starting to go after him again. Usually when she was taking drugs she was warm and playful, the way she had been in the afternoon on the helicopter. Why couldn't she stay that way? He remembered how her hazel eyes flashed with the light of the sea and how she laughed and how she had held his hand and leaned against him when the helicopter bumped and rolled. It had been one of the happiest times between them. She seemed so fun and full of life and he had thought about asking her to marry him, right there, right then, high above the blue South China Sea, he had thought about whispering the proposal in her ear.

Eugénie tapped him on the shoulder and he turned around. She was smiling. Both women had redone their faces, adding blush and eye liner and frizzing out their hair. They were gaudy with makeup.

"Hi sailor, new in town?" Eugénie asked, and kissed him voluptuously.

He handed them their drinks and felt relieved because everything seemed all right again.

The women drank the two martinis and then around 2 A.M. asked the bartender if he would bring a pitcher of margaritas out on the terrace.

It was chilly there and there was a wind blowing the black pine trees. Yellow orchids grew in stone boxes around the terrace. The white moon was fading. Across the mountains there was a flash.

"What was that?" Linda asked. She was slurry drunk.

"Lightning. Had to be lightning, huh, Starkey?"

"Maybe."

"Maybe. Listen to him. The ole military commander. Gotta be cautious. Don't want to commit myself 'til I got the facts, ma'am."

There was another flash, this one brighter, and then a series of others, closer and brighter still, and the sky thundered, rattling windowpanes in the hotel.

"God, what is it?" Eugénie asked.

Starkey got up and walked to the edge of the terrace. The booms made long patterns now. "Mortars."

"Mortars? Are you sure?"

"Eighty-twos. The VC's best."

Eugénie put her arms around him. "Not up here, Starkey. They couldn't be up here."

"They're here."

"Let's go to bed," she whispered.

Starkey stood and looked at the rounds going off in the distance. "Probably fifteen, eighteen clicks away."

"Let's go to bed. Right now. Don't you want to?"

It was a big room with twenty-foot ceilings and three big windows which opened into a stand of pine. The scent of pine straw and wild strawberries filled the room. They were lying naked on the white sheets and the last of the moonlight was shining through the windows and the mortars were booming.

"They scare me," Eugénie said.

"Pretend they're something else."

"Like what?"

"Like thunder."

"Oh, that's crazy. They don't sound like thunder at all."

"Do you think he'll buy this?"

"He's got to. It's the way things are."

Starkey dried off and wrapped himself in a towel. He opened the bathroom door and saw them lying on the bed. He thought it was a joke.

Eugénie held out her hand to him. "It's okay," she said.

He walked toward the bed and then Linda held out her hand, too. He stopped. "What do you mean?"

"She means it's okay," Linda said. "We want you with us."

"Y'all are kidding, right?"

"It's all right, baby," Eugénie said. "Everything's all right. It's just a part of me that you didn't know about."

Linda ran her hand along Eugénie's long leg and began to kiss her shoulder.

The mortars were booming hard now and Starkey looked at Eugénie and he could feel the mortars in his heart.

47

FORD SAT IN HIS congressional office
in the Capitol. His desk was littered and piled with letters and com-
plaints from his constituents and he had already missed two votes this
morning because he had spent three hours trying to get one of his
constituents into a state old folks' home. It was the way almost all of his
days had gone as a congressman. He always became deeply involved
with the plight of two or three people and ended up neglecting a hundred others. But now it was over. Ever since Cat had said yes, he had
decided to leave Washington. He planned to serve out his term and then
go home and be the very best husband and father that he could be. He
had also decided that today was the day to tell the President.

At eleven o'clock, he went over to the White House and a secretary
directed him to the small sitting room which lay just off the Oval Office.
He sat down on a beige couch. There were two red leather chairs and a
coffee table with a white cloth. On the table sat a piece of square plastic
inside of which was a handwritten note. It read:

Lyndon,

I couldn't have done it without you. Thanks.

Jack

P.S. I love your beanless chili—and that's hard for a Bostonian to say.

Lyndon Johnson loped into the office with a small, bald-headed man tucked under his right arm and two blond secretaries following. He was speaking in soft tones and his big head was so close to the little man's ear that it looked as if he were nuzzling him. The President saw Ford and stretched out the hand of the arm which cradled the small man.

"Congressman, how are you? Do you know Senator Daniels? He's essential to our plans for Vietnam."

Ford did not know the senator and as usual answered in complete honesty. "I don't know him."

"He's Tom Daniels," Johnson said, leaning toward Ford a little, the black bags of his eyes squinting, holding Ford's hand, crushing the senator into his armpit.

"Doesn't ring a bell."

Johnson squeezed Ford's hand a little more tightly and pulled him closer. "I'm sure you've seen him around the hill. He's very, very, very important to the plans of your President."

"Hi," Daniels said. "I'm sure we've met."

Ford was going to say that he was certain they had not, but the President fixed him with a brown eye.

The President turned to Daniels and laid his long arms on the small shoulders. Johnson's black hair was slicked back and the smell of Brill cream began to permeate the room. His huge brown ears jiggled as he nodded for emphasis.

"Tom, I need you. I need you now, I need you tomorrow and I'm going to keep on needing you and your wisdom and your guts until we beat the hell out of those little slant-eyed chinks."

"Gooks, sir."

"Huh?"

"You call them gooks."

Johnson shook the senator's shoulders and grinned and turned to Ford. "Ain't he great. Ain't he precious. Gooks, not chinks. And to think I've been calling them chinks all these years. You're right about that, Senator, and you're right about a lot of other things. I need bombs. I need planes. I need the wherewithal to support my boys in Vietnam. And more than anything else, Tom . . ." Johnson bent his knees and stared straight into his eyes. ". . . I need men like you, with vision like yours. Will you help me?"

"I'm your man, Mr. President."

"Will you support me?"

"I will, Mr. President."

"Someday, somehow, someplace, sometime in some way you are going to change the destiny of the Free World, Tom. I know it. I can see it in your eyes and I wouldn't be surprised at all if it was from this very office."

The senator's bald head and brown eyes gleamed. He seemed to shiver.

Johnson snapped a finger at one of the blond secretaries. "Now I want you to take this gold tie clip, which is just like my own"—he snapped at the other blond—"and this vial of earth from my ranch, and I want you to keep them close, just as I do. Remember me, Tom, and I will remember you."

The President hugged him and then turned him around, gave him a little shove and slapped him on the butt.

The secretaries closed the door to the small sitting room.

Johnson collapsed on the couch, picked up the end of the white table cloth, blew his nose and then wiped his dripping lip on the border. "How'd I do?"

"Mr. President, I need to tell you something."

"Shoot."

"After this year, I'm going to retire from the Congress. I don't plan to run again."

The President asked why and Ford told him that the girl whom he loved had accepted his proposal, that he was never made for politics, that he missed hunting and fishing and Waverly and that he had growing doubts about the war.

"What kind of doubts?" Johnson asked.

"It doesn't make a lot of sense to me. It's so far away. There's so much destruction."

The President sighed and pulled a globe from beside the couch. He put on a pair of glasses and lifted his head and turned the globe to

Southeast Asia. The backs of his big hands were red and swollen and there were small, black scabs of blood on them.

Ford touched the President's wrist. "That looks painful."

"I bear it on my body—this war. Everytime I lose a plane, everytime I hear about some of my boys getting blowed up, even when I hear that we've hit the wrong target and killed enemy civilians—my body stings and burns and bleeds, so don't you talk to me about doubts." The President put a finger on Vietnam and squinted and stuck out his jaw. "Look where I'm pointing to."

Ford did as he was told.

"What do you see?"

"Vietnam."

"No, you don't. What you see is the Alamo." He spoke very quietly. "What you see is a place where an army of young Americans are taking a stand and they are surrounded. The enemy encamps around about them. They are asking, they are pleading, they are praying for my help. I cannot let them down. I dare not. Can you?"

"I don't think it's that way, Mr. President."

"You don't think it's what way?"

"I don't think it's the Alamo."

Johnson set his hands on his jowls and pulled the flesh down. "I've been there all my life, Ford. I've been surrounded all my life. Outgunned, outclassed, outnumbered, and I've always won. I was made for this battle. I was fashioned for it from the beginning, and whatever I have to do to win I will do."

The President slapped his knees and rose with a groan and a sigh. He took off his glasses and stuck them into the pocket of his pin-striped coat and folded his long arms behind his back. He seemed suddenly tired and his great shoulders sagged. "You know I keep having this dream. I'm in this fort, behind this big ole concrete wall, and I'm looking out on the flat plains of Texas and I see them, way off yonder in the distance. At first only three or four and then a hundred and then a thousand and a hundred thousand and they're marching straight toward me. More than the eye can see or the mind can count, and when I look back behind me, I can't see any of my friends. It's deserted. I'm all alone. And so I turn around to face the enemy, and then I do see my friends or I see part of them. Their heads are stuck on pikes and lifted toward the wall and I can see their blue brains dangling out of their mouths and their bloody eyes and the blood pouring down the stump of their necks, and I suddenly wake up, the sweat standing out on me. And you know what my first feeling is? Do you know my very first feeling when I wake up out of that dream? Disappointment. Horrible, horrible disappointment. 'Cause I know I could win. I know I could take on that vast black crowd and I could win and win and go on winning, until the plains were pure and the fort was safe and the world was not a place of enemies anymore."

Arms still folded behind his back, brown eyes dry, shining, he said to Ford, "I'll miss you, boy. I'll miss you a lot."

For the next couple of days Ford felt terrible. How could he leave the President in his time of need? How could he just run home and marry and enjoy the life of a country squire when Lyndon Johnson was trying to defend liberty in a desolate place? Several times he had actually picked up the phone, but a flurry of thoughts had made him put it back down. The fact was he didn't believe in the Alamo theory or the domino theory or any other kind of theory whose end result was war and death and destruction. His mind assailed him then. Well, what is the logical extension of this? Does it mean that if the Russians invaded West Germany you would not fight? Yes, I probably would not. How about England? Would you fight for England? Not if it meant using nuclear weapons. How about Florida?

Lost in his usual maze of questions, Ford did not rescind his decision. He flew down to Waverly on the day that Cat returned.

It was a late afternoon in March 1966 and Cat was riding with Bub and Hannah in a pickup. Hannah was talking about how everyone was excited that she was coming home and excited about the marriage and excited about having another Longstreet baby in the house. Cat made Bub stop at the beginning of the red dirt road and she looked at the gingkos that grew on either side. The leaves were light green and small and the grass beneath the limbs of the trees was a darker green and blazing with clusters of yellow daffodils. Moving up the road, she saw the twelve white columns and the two magnolias and the high roof.

Cat got out of the car and Hannah got the baby, and for a second, Cat just looked at the great house, soaking in the presence of it, the whiteness, the coolness, the stillness of it.

Jebodiah and Tee Tat and Tadpole all ran out to see her and she spent the next half hour hugging and kissing and answering questions.

While her things were brought in and everyone fretted over the baby, she went up to her room, opened the door and closed it behind her. Here was her canopy bed and her cherry wood furniture. She closed her eyes and felt the soundness, the safeness of the place reach out and embrace her in a hug that was as real as any hug a human being could give and she promised herself that no matter what happened, no matter how bad things became in the future, she would never leave Waverly again.

There was a tap at her door. She opened it and Ford was standing there and she smiled, though her heart fell, seeing the dark green circles beneath his eyes and the pink jowls and the huge stomach pushing black hairs through his white shirt.

"It's so wonderful to have you home," he said.

He hugged her and she tried not to tense and tried to give herself to him. "Harper is waiting to see you in the library."

"I need to freshen up just a bit."

"Of course, of course, take your time," he said.

The birthmark in his right cheek was dark lavender. She could smell his deodorant and the golden tongue of his belt was poked through a new hole toward the tip.

48

CAT PUT ON A pink linen dress and white pumps. She parted her blond hair on the right and fastened it with an ivory barrette and put on a pair of pearl earrings. She left her room and walked down the familiar hall and the floor cracked and popped in all the familiar places. At the landing of the double staircase she stopped. The teakwood steps and railings were polished and the wine-colored carpet was dustless, descending to the marble foyer. She stepped down the stairs slowly and stopped once again when she reached the marble floor. She remembered the evening when she first saw the bright squares of marble. She remembered how she knelt down to touch them and how wonderful it seemed to have a floor of marble in a house. She knelt down and touched the floor again. It was so cool and smooth and it was still wonderful.

She paused at the great wooden door which led to the library, thinking, How shall I be? The answer came back easily. Be yourself. But what was that now? After all I've been through, what exactly am I now? Just open the door and go in and see.

The smell of leather and dust and books. There was the stone fireplace and the leather chairs and couches and the thousands of books gleaming from the tall shelves. In the middle of the room, Harper Longstreet sat in her stainless steel wheelchair.

Cat was shocked at her appearance. She had lost a great deal of weight and her black hair was now streaked with white.

"How was your trip?" Harper asked. She held out her hand.

Cat took it. The hand was small and bony and cold. She noticed that the fingernails were shorter and without polish.

"Did Bub get you situated?"

"I think so. Did you see the baby?"

"I did. Very handsome, like all the Longstreets. Blue eyes, a dimple. All in all—a good job."

For the first time, Cat looked her fully in the face. Harper Longstreet was not the same. She was an old woman. When Cat had left, Harper was strong and vibrant and commanding. Now there were hollows in her face and two round spheres of rouge and her temples were pale and deep and there were blue veins in them.

As for Harper, she had seldom seen a girl so healthy. The blond hair and the wide blue eyes, even the color of her skin, seemed unpardonably fresh and unspeakably new. It made her almost sick to look at Cat, but she forced herself to do it. She commanded herself to behold the girl.

Goddamnit, how I wish it were not you, she thought. It should have been someone else. One of the great families. An Elliott or a Smythe or Guignard, but it is not them, it is you, and I will have to do the best that I can.

The silence broke with both of them speaking at once.

"I want to—" Cat said.

"You must—"

"I'm sorry, go on."

"Not at all. After you."

"I just wanted to say that I want to help you in any way that I can."

"Oh, do I need help?"

"I'm sorry, I didn't mean it like that."

"Do I look infirm?"

"I know you haven't been well."

"I repeat—do I look infirm?"

"Yes, you look infirm."

They glared at one another. Cat crossed her arms over her stomach and put down her head. "I need to go check on the baby."

"May I be very honest with you?" Harper said. "I don't like you very much. I'm not sure why. You seem to be smart, you're obviously attractive, but for some reason you simply get under my skin. I grit my teeth when I see you. Maybe it was the way you came into this family. I don't know, but I do know this. I don't have a lot of time left to live. A few months, maybe a year, and in that time I would like to try to like you. You're marrying my son. It will place you in a position of responsibility. If we work together, I can help you make the transition, but before I can work with somebody, I have to like them. So, I'm going to treat it like a campaign. I'm going to work at trying to like you. Will you help me?"

"I don't know how to help you."

"Well, you can start by not wearing all that mascara and eye shadow. What color is that anyway?"

"Twilight in Paris."

"God. And stop slumping. A young woman who is as pretty as you should not be a slumper."

"I don't know how to stop it."

"Think more of yourself. Slumping starts on the inside. You have a good mind, an attractive appearance, so be proud of them and stand up and show yourself off. Now, I think we should begin by spending an hour with one another in the morning, an hour in the afternoon and a half an hour in the evening. Do you think you can do it?"

Cat didn't know if she could do it or not. She didn't know if she could do any of it—marry Ford, raise Blackie, put up with the harangues of Harper. She lay in her canopy bed and looked out the window at the stars shining in the black sky. The hardest part of the whole thing was Ford. Oh she liked him. He was sensitive and smart and kind, and sometimes she even had fun with him. But she felt about him the way you feel about a good friend. The very idea of going to bed with him horrified her. She looked at her bedroom door and had the sudden compulsion to throw on some clothes and run out and never look back.

After all, you are supposed to be in love with someone when you marry them, aren't you? Oh, right. You were in love with Bucky and look how that turned out. Make this thing work, Cat. You will never have to leave again, if you are just determined to make this work. How many times do you have to have sex with your husband anyway? Once a month? Twice maybe. Come on now. Come on.

The next morning, Cat arrived at the table in the small dining room about six-fifteen, ten minutes before Harper was wheeled in by Jebodiah. She wanted to arrive early so that she could put herself in the right state of mind and also to show Harper that she was trying her best.

The mahogany table was laid in white linen mats and big white plates and simple silver. An arrangement of flowers sat in the center of the table, daffodils, silver bells, jonquils and flowering mint. Jebodiah pushed Harper into the dining room at exactly six-thirty. She was reading the *Southern Chronicle*. As soon as she was in place at the table, she pushed a buzzer and Hannah came in.

"Yes, ma'am?"

"Oatmeal and dry whole wheat toast and Postum. Do we have any fresh skim milk?"

"We sure do, Miss Harper."

"Good, I'll have just a little then for the oatmeal."

"Miss Cat?"

"I'll have a waffle with strawberry preserves and syrup and sour cream and a Coke."

"Oh nonsense," Harper said. "She'll have the same breakfast as I. You need to eat a good breakfast. It's the basis for the entire day."

"I don't think I like oatmeal."

"Have you ever eaten oatmeal?"

"Not in a while."

"Oatmeal and dry toast and Postum for two, Hannah."

Harper had pulled her black and white hair into a severe bun. Her spheres of rouge were less today. Her black eyes were round and imperious. "If you're going to be a Longstreet, you have to eat like one."

There was no more conversation between them at breakfast, and afterward, Cat went to the newspaper to finish a story about alleged payoffs to the County Council. At three o'clock, she arrived back at Waverly, dreading the next meeting with Harper. Hannah brought little

Blackie up to Cat's room and she held the baby for a while and nuzzled his nose and felt loving toward him, until she felt the warm, wet current in the palm of her hand. She handed him to Hannah.

"You gonna see Miss Harper this afternoon?" Hannah asked. She was wearing her white apron and the white hat with the daisies. She was thin and very black and smelled of collard greens and fatback.

"Hannah, how in the world am I going to get along with her?"

"A little at a time."

"What's that mean?"

"It means that sometimes you lay down a little and sometimes you stands up a little and sometimes you don't do nothing a little."

"Why is she so hard to deal with?"

"That's what you have to find out. That's the secret to the whole thing."

At four-fifteen, Bub knocked on Cat's door and said that Harper was waiting to have tea with her in the music room. She put on a yellow cotton dress with a green satin belt and green pumps. She combed her hair and used only a touch of mascara and no eye shadow.

In the middle of the music room sat a black, grand piano. On either side of it were two small sofas covered in red damask and two Queen Anne end tables holding brass lamps. A golden harp sat in one corner of the room. The paint was peeling off the frame and the chips glittered on the floor. Harper sat in her wheelchair before a small tea table. There was a Victorian tea service, silverware and rolled napkins. A silver plate held cucumber sandwiches. They were small, crustless, white squares with a wafer of green cucumber and a yellow edge of mayonnaise.

Cat came in and sat down at the small table. She was determined to be cheerful.

"Well, how was your day?" Cat asked.

"Better."

"Better? You mean you weren't feeling well?"

"I've had two heart attacks and a stroke."

Cat took a breath. "Could I pour you some tea?"

"We don't have tea. We have Postum."

"Oh. What's in Postum anyway?"

"Oats."

Cat looked at the beautiful silver teapot and sighed. She poured a cup of the black Postum. Harper erected the evening edition of the *Southern Chronicle* and Cat did not see her face again until Jebodiah came to roll her away.

At supper, Cat sat across from Ford. Harper talked about a new offensive that the Vietcong had undertaken in the Delta region and was worried that Starkey might somehow get involved, although he was far to the north. She asked Ford if he had heard from Wick and he said that he had and that Wick had called him to say that he was going to spend a week at the monastery.

"Why does he keep going back to that place?" Harper asked.

"I think that in his heart of hearts, he's still a monk."

"Ridiculous. In his heart of hearts, he's a cardinal, or at least he should want to be a cardinal. The only men who go into monastaries are saints or misfits. Wick is neither."

Cat was completely left out of the conversation, except during the dessert of blackberry cobbler and whipped cream when Harper turned to her and said, "I will see you on the upstairs balcony at ten-fifteen."

She got there early and sat down in one of the green cane rockers. She felt something on her hand and rubbed her fingers together and held them up into the light which was coming from the hallway. It was pollen—gold and shining and smooth. As her eyes adjusted to the darkness of the balcony, she saw it gleaming upon everything. It glittered on the rockers and the white rope hammock between the columns and glittered on the gray floor, the pollen even shining on the ferns set out to catch the first of spring, gleaming on the outside of the white stone columns and the red pansies rising from the earth of flower boxes. She got up and walked to the railing of the balcony. There was half of a moon and the pecan and walnut trees were black trunks and a spray of green leaves, and on the leaves was a dusting of gold, shining in the moonlight of March.

Suddenly Harper was behind her, giving an order.

"You can set the tray right there," Harper said.

Hannah put a tray on a small table. It held a pitcher of milk and a saucer of graham crackers. After the black woman had set the tray down, she walked behind Harper and looked at Cat. She lifted her thin black arms beside her head and crossed both fingers in each hand.

"I've brought us a little something to make us sleep," Harper said.

Cat was relieved. At least Harper was talking to her. "What's that?"

"Buttermilk and graham crackers."

The thought of it made Cat's stomach turn.

"Don't you like buttermilk?"

"I like it all right I guess."

"Well, you should like it more," Harper said. She spread part of her newspaper on her lap, pulled a small flashlight from her pocket, snapped it on and started to read.

"Please don't do that," Cat said.

"I beg your pardon?"

"Please don't start reading again. What's the point of us getting together if you're just going to read. We need to talk. We need to, to engage one another, to exchange ideas."

"What ideas would you like to exchange?"

"Oh, I don't know, anything. Let's talk about anything . . ."

"What do you think is the solution to the Vietnam problem?"

"What?"

"You wanted to exchange ideas—all right, what do we do about Vietnam?"

"I don't believe you. I really don't."

"Now there's an astute answer."

"All right—withdraw. That's what we should do. Withdraw and get the hell out of there."

"You're wrong, of course. We should blow them up. All of them."

"And another thing, I hate buttermilk. I hate it, positively, absolutely. And I hate graham crackers and oatmeal and I positively despise Postum. God, who ever came up with that idea anyway. You've got to let me be myself. I want to learn things from you. I want to fit in here more than anything in the world, but you've got to give me a little room."

Cat waited for a response. When there was none, she ran from the balcony and locked herself in her bedroom. She tried her best not to cry, but it happened anyway, and she cried a long time until she went to sleep.

The next morning, she thought about leaving again, just giving up. Then she said to herself, Not yet. Not yet. I'm going to give her the best I have, so that twenty years from now, I won't look back and say, You had a chance to have a home, but you blew it because you didn't try hard enough. She scrubbed her face, put on a touch of mascara, then wiped it off and scrubbed her face again. She looked in the mirror.

"There," she said. "Plain Jane. I hope it makes you happy, Harper."

At the breakfast table, things were silent between them. Hannah came in and asked for their orders.

Harper looked up from the paper. "I'll have oatmeal, dry whole wheat toast and . . . a Coke."

"Ma'am?"

"A Coke."

"A co-cola?"

"Yes, a Coke, a Coke. Don't make such a big fuss about it. It is important to try something new once in a while."

Harper glanced at Cat.

She was smiling.

49

IT WAS 4:30 A.M. at the Monastery of Peace. Wick was in the kitchen making a kettle of potato soup. The overhead lights were burning, but the kitchen was still dark and shadows fluttered behind the four standing fireplaces and the long, overhead racks of pots and black pans and deep boilers and scores of baking sheets and bread pans. A candle was burning on a small stone shelf. It was beeswax and the sweetness of it filled the kitchen. Behind the candle an inscription had been laid into the wall in blue tile: SWEETER THAN THE HONEYCOMB. Wick had been at the monastery three days now. The old cook had taken sick and Wick had been fixing the meals. This morning he was also trying to teach young Brother Boniface how to make potato soup. They had been working together since three-thirty. Brother Boniface had chopped twenty pounds of potatoes, two pounds of celery. The potatoes sat in a big stone bowl. They were white and faint yellow and they were mounded high in the bowl, and beside them was a much smaller bowl of green celery, and then a stone pitcher of milk, a smaller bowl of cream, a block of yellow butter and a red bowl holding bay leaves.

Boniface threw some salt into the boiling kettle. He was talking nonstop as he had been since he first woke Wick. There had been a manifestation at the monastery and the whole place was bubbling with the news.

"Of course, I'm trying very hard not to believe that it was a miracle. I think it's important to be skeptical."

"Put in the potatoes and the celery," Wick said.

Boniface dumped them into the pot. "I think we have to doubt with every ounce of our reason, and then if it still holds up, we just fall down and say, My Lord and my God. Isn't that right, Brother?"

Everyone still called him Brother here. It made him feel a little happy, a little sad, a little regretful that he had left this simple, good, deep place.

"I mean, I mean it just seems to me that we all can't just up and call every healing a miracle—of course, we're not doing that. This is not an average healing at all—at least I don't think it is, do you?"

Boniface was twenty-two years old. He was a handsome young man with black eyes and a long jaw and brown hair. This morning he was wearing his habit.

"Do you, Brother?"

"I don't know enough about it to say."

"Well, it was the size of a baseball and the doctors in Atlanta said it was spread throughout his whole body and he had maybe a couple months and then Brother Gregory touched him and prayed for him and it disappeared within the hour. I know. I was working in the infirmary and I saw Brother John about two hours later and the tumor was gone."

"You need to let this boil twenty minutes and then drain it. I'll be in the chapel. Come get me before you add anything else."

"You don't think I'm being hysterical, do you, Brother?"

"No, I don't think you're being hysterical."

"I mean, hysteria can be as much of a sin as anything else, can't it?"

"I guess it could be."

"Oh Lord."

"What?"

"Sometimes I don't think I'll ever get into heaven."

"Sure you will."

"Do you think heaven's a real city? I mean with gold streets and things like that?"

"Twenty minutes," Wick said.

The chapel was dark. The only light was the light of the tabernacle. The golden rectangle was shining and sat in the middle of the white marble altar. Wick walked down between the tall columns. Near the altar, he saw Brother Peter sitting in his wheelchair. The old monk waved at him and Wick waved back and Brother Peter asked with sign language what was for lunch and Wick signaled back soup and the brother signed good for my stomach.

Wick eased down into one of the old wooden chairs which sat beside an enormous column. He took the letter out of his pocket. It was the reason he was here. He opened it and turned to the last paragraph of the second page.

As Vicar General of the Archdiocese, you would be second in command to my auxillary bishop, John Lazak. I know you probably have lots of ties to the Diocese of Charleston, but if you could just take the job for a year until I could get someone else, it would help me. I left New Orleans and accepted the red hat in St. Louis because I wanted to make a difference in the Church. We must become more involved with the Civil Rights Movement. I need your courage and your experience and your vision.

> Please consider the offer.
> Yours in the Lord +
> James Cardinal Dunlap
> Archbishop of St. Louis

Wick had told Alice about the job and they had had another dreadful fight. At first, she had said she would not allow him to go to St. Louis, and then later she told him that he had to make up his own mind, but whatever his decision she was not going to drag the children around the country following his career. In his heart, Wick knew the decision he should make. He should stop agonizing and simply leave the Church and take care of Alice and Tommy and Tim (who were doing fine). It was the right decision, the moral answer to the problem.

Sitting in the darkness of the Trappist chapel, he sensed the presence of God. He knew it was bad theology. He intellectually understood that God was everywhere present, that He was being itself, but still here he felt as if he were in a dark corner of God's mysterious and infinite heart and he felt that his prayers were not prayers at all, but really just simple conversation, so he said, Please help me to want to leave the Church, because I still don't want to, even though I know I should. Please help Alice to live with things until I have the courage to do something, and please don't in any way blame her because this is my fault, my continuing fault, and you know, I just love them both. I love Alice and my boys, and I love being a priest. Do you know how much—of course you do, I guess, though frankly I don't think you understand us as much as people say, I really don't. Please help Brother Boniface with his worries about heaven and let him learn to make good potato soup because it will help him here as much as anything else, and bless Brother Peter's stomach and bless Brother John that his miracle may be a real miracle and bless Brother Alered that he may have the wisdom to get me to do what I should. In Jesus' name I ask these things, the firstborn of the dead, the first light of the long, cold dark. Amen.

He sat in the darkness and felt hidden, safe, secret, protected, special. He sat in the deep, deep darkness and suddenly understood the meaning of the Scripture—*Hide me beneath the shadow of your wings.*

Brother Boniface found him and they went back to the kitchen and finished making the potato soup.

Around nine o'clock, Wick went to the greenhouse to do some work for Brother Alered. The old man was sitting very straight on his work stool, before his workbench, his long shoulders level and his big hands black with topsoil, working at a small maple tree.

Alered saw Wick and continued working. His bald head was shining in the sun and his glasses had slipped to the edge of his long, patrician nose.

"This darn tree," he said. "I can't get it to do what I want. I've been working on it for six months and it just refuses to help."

"What do you want it to do?"

"Well, see this limb? Come over here. See this limb? I want it to turn up and then down like this, just a little, just like that, but it won't."

"What did you want me to do today?"

"Oh, nothing really. You can shovel some topsoil if you like, but I really just wanted to see you. Heard anything else about the miracle?"

"Do you think it is a miracle?"

"I just don't want John to be disappointed. He's such a dear, good boy. I would hate for him to believe that God had intervened and then six months down the road find that the cancer was back."

Alered looked at the young man. His face was strained and twitchy. He thought he detected a few silver follicles in his head of black hair. He could see muscles tensing beneath the surface of his face and he noticed that since Wick had left the monastery, he had developed a slight stoop, as if everything was far heavier than it seemed. Alered had prayed very hard that he would know the right thing to say. He still wasn't sure. He was sure only of love. That he loved Wick very much and that God loved Wick very much and that somehow he felt that everything was going to work out. Suddenly he said something he had never even thought.

"You could come back here, you know?"

"Back to the monastery?"

"Well, yes."

"Oh, Brother." Wick laughed. "I've got a mistress and two kids." The old man blushed.

"I can see me walking into Father Abbot's office. 'Father, I think I've learned all the lessons that the world can teach and I'm ready to come home. By the way, do you think you could work out a stipend for Alice and the kids?' "

"I know it would take time. I know you would have to make decisions."

Wick sat down on a stool near the old monk. "Brother, can I be absolutely honest with you? I don't want you to think less of me, but I have to tell you this: sometimes I wonder why I'm staying in the Church. Is it because I love being a priest or because I want to be a bishop?"

"It's an honest question."

"Yes, and the honest answer is—I want to be more than a bishop. I want to be a cardinal. I know it's outrageous to say it, but I want the red hat. I think I've always wanted it. Ever since I walked through the doors of the seminary."

"Well, let me ask you a question. Let's say the job with Cardinal

Dunlap did not work out and you had to spend your days as a priest in that little town you're in now. Could you do it? Could you help colored people with their civil rights and marry and bury and be happy as a country priest?"

Driving back to Corn, Wick wished that he had not answered Alered so quickly. The disappointment in the old man's face hurt him, but he had told him the truth. If things didn't work out with Dunlap, he didn't know if he could keep working as a parish priest, though now as he went over it, he thought he could return to the monastery. Why was that? How could someone who wanted to be a quiet, faceless monk also want to be a cardinal? It didn't make sense to him, not at all.

Wick drove into the driveway of the rectory. He stopped the car and looked at the rusting trailer with fishbowl windows and the cement block foundation and rotting wooden steps. If there was any doubt about his decision to take the job, it vanished.

Alice came over in the evening. She left the two babies with the full-time maid. She was getting trim again. She had recently restyled her hair. It was short and parted on the left side, an auburn wing of it falling just across the top of her yellow eyes. Wick fixed her steak and onions for supper and they drank a bottle of French wine from the case that Harper had sent. They were sitting in the cramped front room of the small trailer drinking a second bottle of wine. Wick had his arm around her. Across from them in a corner of the room sat an entire manger scene. The figures were three feet high—Joseph and Mary, the baby Jesus and cows and donkeys. The three wise men were in Wick's bedroom. The figures had been sitting behind the trailer exposed to the elements and Wick had felt guilty about it, and before he left for the monastery, he had put them in the church secretary's office. He returned to find them stuffed in his trailer with a note: There's not enough room.

"She's a bitch," Alice said.

"She's not a bitch."

"Well, I think she's a bitch. You have little enough room as it is. Oh, and Cat McGregor called. The wedding has been set for July tenth. You'll be in St. Louis then. Do you think you can come down for it?"

Wick squeezed her.

"I know you have to go. How could you turn it down?"

"St. Louis's a pretty city. You'll like it. When will you come up?" She poured them each a little more wine.

"I spoke to Harper yesterday. She sounds a lot stronger. She must have an incredible will to live."

"Hello? We were talking about St. Louis?"

"No, you were talking about St. Louis, I wasn't. I'm not talking about it because I'm not going. Look, I understand what your career means to you, your vocation, but I just can't deal with it anymore."

"I don't want to fight."

"I don't either. We have fought and fought and fought and I think we both understand each other so let's not fight. You go to St. Louis and I'll go to New York. That's where we can start with things. I don't know what happens after that. I really don't know. Do you?"

50

IT TOOK STARKEY TWO weeks to get another flyover by a Blackbird. He got the pictures late one afternoon as he sat in the steamy kitchen of the team house. Sergeant Vachel Fox had brought them over.

"I couldn't believe it, Dai-wi. Look at those headlights."

"How many would you say?"

"Shit, I'd say thirty, forty trucks there. Big ones too. Two or three tons."

"It's great," Starkey said, and laughed and kissed the pictures.

Fox looked perplexed.

"Don't you know what this means?"

"It means we're in the middle of a hornet's nest."

"It means we've finally found the source of all the supplies coming into this sector. It means we can stop them, Fox. We can stop them dead. Go get me Dink. We need to have a little powpow. We need to figure out what we're going to do."

Starkey and D.K. and Fox stayed up late that night. They pulled out maps and carefully located the Champion Bridge. Fox would be in charge of demolitions and D.K. would handle the mortar. They would take eight Strikers and two Montagnards and leave at five-thirty the next morning.

Starkey went back to his hooch at ten o'clock. He checked his gear and laid it out carefully. He cleaned his shotgun and then his .357. He wrapped the automatic shotgun in plastic to keep the night moisture off it and tucked his pistol into the water buffalo hide holster. He stripped to his green boxers and smeared on insect repellent and got under his mosquito net and started thinking about her again. During the daytime, he was able not to think about her, but at night he thought about Eugénie a lot. The night he had found the two women lying in bed was horrible. He had gone back to his room and Eugénie had come screaming after him. He had lost his patience and screamed back and then Linda came in and took Eugénie away and then returned to say that Starkey had to understand that this was the way Eugénie was now and that probably it had been the way she had always been and that he should just accept it. The next morning, they met for breakfast and Starkey said, as he had a dozen times before, that he thought they had to break things off, and Eugénie said, as she had a dozen times before, Sure if that's the way you want it, and then she left with Linda. The girl was the only new part to things, but he asked himself what did it matter if it was a girl or a boy, she always had someone else and he couldn't stand it anymore, it made him sick and he felt like this time was the last time.

He didn't go to sleep until late and so the brass gong woke him at five-thirty. He dressed and got his gear together and made sure the strikers were up. He went to the kitchen in the team house. D.K. and Fox were already there. They ate a bowl of Cheerios with chunks of fresh pineapple and goat milk from the hamlet.

"The Montagnards want to take their damn crossbows," Fox said.

"What's wrong with that?" D.K. asked.

"I just don't like it. It's less firepower. They ought to take BARs. That's what they're trained in."

"I think it's neat."

"You think what's neat, D.K.?"

"Crossbows. I want to take one home as a souvenir."

"We'll see how neat you think they are when a hundred and fifty gooks come running at us head on and we got two of our guys shooting arrows at them. Oh, it'll be real fuckin' neat then."

Starkey took his cup of coffee and walked outside the team house. The air was sticky and warm. He could smell fish being fried down in the Strikers' mess. He looked at the concrete walls of the TOC building and saw a brown rat race down the spine of the yellow thatch roof. He told himself to remember to put out more D-CON when he got back, which reminded him that he needed to get Patton vaccinated for rabies.

Big Tom and Little Tom walked up to him. They were the Montagnards. They wore flip-flops and loincloths and green army undershirts. They had wavy hair and dark skin and both of them were chewing betel nuts and their thin lips were red and so were their teeth. They were carrying crossbows. Each weapon had a teakwood stock at the end of which lay the steel bow. A piece of wire was the string for the bow and it was made taut by turning a hand crank on the bottom of the weapon. On the knob at the end of Big Tom's handgrip was a white daub of beeswax and sticking out of the wax was a host of fine black and gold bristles. These were hairs plucked from the beards of Vietcong whom Big Tom had killed recently.

"Dai-wi, we need titi beeswax," Big Tom said.

"Titi? You need more than titi. You'll get a lot of VC, won't you, Big Tom?"

"Some, yes, I think so. But titi beeswax."

"Sure," Starkey said.

He got the Montagnards the beeswax, gave a few last orders and instructions and they left at six.

They walked in a single line, following the ox cart road which led from the camp to the hamlet. It smelled of sour, wet straw and Noucmam sauce and buffalo manure and they passed by it and went into the jungle.

D.K. took point. Then came Fox and the Strikers and Starkey and the Montagnards were last. At the end of the first five miles, Starkey called for a rest. The jungle so far was easy. It was not thick. There were mahogany trees and some ferns and brown jungle floor. Starkey knew the land descended in the next few miles and the going would be hard because the jungle was wet and green and thick and dangerous because you could not see in front of you on either side.

"Hey, D.K.?" Starkey said.

"Yo."

"I go point for five clicks."

"Roger. Want a Milky Way?"

"Nope."

"Lots of energy, Dai-wi. Lots of get-up-and-go."

Starkey went to the head of the column. He was already starting to shake. He chambered a round in his shotgun and made sure the safety was on and took his .357 out and flipped open the cylinder. He was shocked. It was empty. Not one round. He squatted down, shaking his head, looking at the empty chambers. Jesus, what are you doing, he thought. What the hell are you thinking about? He took five shells from a bandoleer around his waist and loaded the .357 and stuck it into his holster and did not fasten the catch. He felt it coming from his stomach then. He stepped away from the column into the wetness of a fern and tried to throw up quietly so the men could not hear. He tried to make as much come up as he could, using his finger at the end so his stomach would be clear for the march. This always happened when he took point.

The first two miles were easy and then the jungle was real jungle. The ground was wet and soft. It was ferns and vines and mushrooms, millions of them, some of them black and some yellow with red stalks and some the lightest color of purple, and there was green moss and dark brown moss and then beneath everything there was rot, just plain old stinking rot, which was everything that had once been alive. Hanging in front of him were banyan trees and neem trees and clusters of green bananas. He could not see more than three feet into the jungle and he used his ears as much as he could, but it was difficult to hear because the jungle was always humming, murmuring as if it were talking about you, about how tired you looked and how nervous you were and what could it do to get at you just a little more.

Starkey did his five clicks and pushed on for another two and it was four o'clock in the afternoon and the jungle was turning to night. It was funny darkness in the jungle, because it did not start at the top of the green, but rather at the bottom, the darkness growing from the black sludge and going to blue and black mushrooms and the ferns and trees, and suddenly the air was purple and the voice of the jungle was stronger, bolder, somehow knowing that this was your weakest hour, so that in the late afternoon the jungle was very dark and very strong and it knew it was and so did you.

Starkey had Fox set out five tripflares and five claymores around the perimeter of the camp. The men wanted a fire but Starkey said no. They were only ten kilometers away from the free fire zone and Starkey didn't want to let the VC know that he was here.

By six o'clock the jungle was night. One lantern hissed in the middle of camp. The air was noisy with the sounds of crickets and tree frogs and mosquitoes. Before Starkey turned in, he went to every man in the platoon and spoke to him. This had been his custom since he had taken his first patrol out three years ago. He spoke to them because he was concerned about them, because he wanted to let them know he was in command, and also because he wanted to know everyone's exact position if something went wrong. Starkey went to the Strikers first. They slept in the center of the perimeter on brown bamboo mats which they carried on their packs. Their blue and white thongs sat in a communal pile. One of them had set a small, ivory elephant-god near his head. Another had stabbed his red-handled knife into a log beside him. A third was already asleep. He lay on his back and sitting on his chest was a Bulova travel clock, the numbers glowing in the dark. Starkey called each Striker by name, asked if he was all right, joked a little and then said that reveille was at 5 A.M.

The Montagnards slept in hammocks that they had stretched between two trees. They had hung their crossbows on the trunks near them. The slender arrows with white duck feathers, they cradled in their arms. Each Montagnard had cut down green ferns and lay the cool leaves on top of their bodies. In the lantern light, they were almost impossible to see. The cut ferns smelled sweet and fresh and green.

"Big Tom, you okay?" Starkey asked.

"Okay."

"You need anything?"

"Fire."

"We'll have a fire tomorrow. How's Little Tom?"

"He sleeping. You sleep too, Dai-wi?"

D.K. and Fox were lying near the lantern. Insects were swirling around the light, black gnats and orange-eyed mosquitoes. A black flying roach banged into the lantern, then fell into the moss and buzzed black and green wings until Starkey stepped on it. Fox had pulled his green beret to the tops of his eyebrows. His poncho came up to his chin and he had smeared white insect repellent over the rest of his face.

"Damn, Dai-wi, I'm getting eat up. Let's get this light out."

"Hold it a second," D.K. said. He was sitting on his poncho, stripped down to his green boxer shorts. He held a bottle of rubbing alcohol in his left hand and, using the right, slapped it all over his body. His pink flesh reddened and the smell of alcohol was sharp.

"I don't believe you," Fox said.

"It's my one luxury."

"Charlie don't need a fire to find us. He can just follow the scent of alcohol."

"I'll be ten feet straight ahead by that big banyan," Starkey said. "Relieve me at twelve."

"I'll probably be Swiss cheese by then," Fox said. "Damn D.K. . . ."

The light was extinguished.

Starkey sat down by the banyan tree. He propped his shotgun beside him and clicked on the safety. He was hurting everywhere, but mostly the small of his back and his feet. He took off his right boot and pulled away the sock. He could feel the blister. It was an inch wide. He found his med kit in his webbing gear, opened a bottle of Merthiolate and poured it and gritted his teeth until the pain was less. He put a clean gauze on the blister and pulled off the other sock and boot. This foot was wet and stank, but it didn't have a blister. He rocked back on his butt and put his hands under his thighs and kicked his feet until both of them were dry. He took a pair of fresh socks from his pack, smelled them—the smell of soap and cleanliness. He put them on and set his feet on top of his boots and there was a hole in the canopy of the jungle and through the hole he could see the new moon shining. He opened his pack and found a Milky Way and bit into it and looked up at the clean light of the moon and wiggled his toes in the dry socks and felt like a king.

This was one of the reasons he did it. This was one of the reasons why he was a combat soldier. He loved these moments. He loved being tired and dirty and stinking, and then finding one good thing like the clean socks, one small good thing that made all the other bad things less, and he loved the feeling of command, the feeling that his men were sleeping just beyond him, depending on him, trusting him. He knew that there were plenty of the other times, too. The times when men were killed or horribly wounded, the times when he hurt so bad or was so tired that he couldn't think, the times when he could not find one good thing, but these times were not tonight.

He felt a motion near his right foot and jerked it away. There was a buzzing sound. He found his penlight, cupped a hand over it. The narrow beam revealed a struggle between a centipede and a wasp. The centipede was black and three inches long. Its scales were black rectangles and the outer edge of the scales was outlined in red. The tiny feet of the centipede were yellow and almost all of them were wrapped around the big wasp, which was dark red with a green, triangular head and a huge pair of black pincers. The two creatures squirmed and rolled, neither one seeming to have the advantage. Starkey watched them for a long time. The fight went on and on. He wondered how many other death struggles like this were going on in the jungle, and if there was a God, did God know about these mortal struggles, did he care? Or did God, if there was a God, did God simply sit high in the dark, watching this centipede and this wasp, completely unbothered as Starkey was unbothered. And then it occurred to him that this was the essence of things, and if there was a God, he was the God of war, not the God of peace. Starkey watched the battle until Fox relieved him at twelve.

51

HE WAS THE FIRST one up at 5 A.M. He woke D.K. and the others and they were marching by five-twenty.

They arrived at the free fire zone late in the afternoon. They did not need the maps. They could see it for themselves. They were standing on a small hill which overlooked a valley and other hills in the distance. It was a place of black destruction. The jungle was burned out. The trees were shattered black and brown sticks, and the earth was scorched and littered with ashes and jagged stumps and there were craters everywhere. Now and again, there was a stand of green bamboo or an expanse of brown elephant grass, but mostly this was a place of black stubble and muddy craters and stumps and bombs. You did not see them at first. You did not see them easily, but after you saw the first one, you began to see the others. They looked just like bombs ought to look—long and eliptical with tailfins. They were black or gray or green and some had turned to red rust. Some of them lay on smooth beds of gray ash and some stood straight up in a hill of red mud showing only their fins and some had split a tree stump in half and sat perfectly balanced between two fingers of wood.

They stood and looked at the place and then Starkey pulled the men around him and gave them some final instructions before they went in: travel single file, only walk behind swept earth, if a plane is heard, immediately fall and cover, touch no discovered ordnance.

Starkey took a mine sweeper and went to the head of the column. A Striker with a second mine sweeper followed him. The column started out and it was hard and slow. It took Starkey three hours to cover two clicks, but it was good enough. In the distance, he could see the Champion Bridge—or what was left of it. The cratered earth ran to the edge of a bluff where the bridge began. There was thirty good feet of the bridge on this side. Below the bluff was the Long Ly River. It was muddy and brown and two hundred feet wide. Bare piling rose out of the river every ten feet, leading to the center of the bridge, which was still intact—probably forty feet of boards and railings sitting on the concrete pilings, then another row of pilings leading to the second bluff and the green jungles of Cambodia.

There was a small bamboo grove about a quarter of a mile downriver of the bridge. Starkey led his patrol there, posted his lookouts and waited for the dark.

The men sat in the green bamboo. It was dark and green and alive. It was a relief from the miles of ash and burned trees. D.K. and Fox and Starkey sat together on the edge of the bamboo and looked at the bridge. The mosquitoes were big and hungry and the conversation was punctuated by slaps and cursing.

"Well, I think the Air Farce is nuts," D.K. said. "There's no way Charlie can be using that bridge. Sixty percent of it's gone."

"They got pictures," Fox said.

"So?"

"What do you mean so? I'm telling you they got fucking photos of trucks going across that bridge."

"Not across that bridge they don't. Maybe across another bridge, but not that one." He slapped his neck. "Damn it."

"You get him?"

"Damn that hurts." He held the mosquito up. "Look at the size of that bastard."

Fox tore up some tissue and stuck it into his ears.

"Good idea," D.K. said. He grabbed some of Fox's tissue and did the same thing. "You ought to put some in your ears, Dai-wi. It makes it a lot better if you don't hear them."

Starkey said nothing.

D.K. watched the captain. He was studying the bridge with binoculars. D.K. could see his lips moving, saw him saying—damn, damn, damn. It made D.K. smile. The captain wanted a fight, a kill. Some of the guys said that the captain was ambitious, brass happy, but D.K. didn't believe it. He likes to fight. He's a pisser just like me. To him there ain't nothing better than shooting them little bastards, than going against them one on one. God bless you, Dai-wi. Kill them all and the ones you don't get, I will.

Starkey pulled a plug of Brown Mule tobacco from his hip pocket. He took out his pocket knife, cut a sliver and stuck it into his mouth. He chewed tobacco only in combat.

D.K. pulled his own plug of Brown Mule out. He bit off a corner. He liked the way the captain cut his with a pocket knife. It was a fine way to do it and D.K. wished it was his way too, but it wasn't. He watched the captain chew, ball the plug in his cheek and then spit. It's a hell of a good spit, D.K. thought. It ain't a stagey or a show-off spit. He just drops it down in his jaw and shoots it out the corner of his mouth straight as an arrow. Not a lot of noise, not a lot of show. D.K. spit this way too. So did the other guys on the team. D.K. smiled again. That's when I knew you were a good soldier, when everybody started spitting like you. That's when I was sure.

Starkey waited for three days and nights and there was no movement on the bridge. The men had not eaten hot food in almost five days and he knew he needed to get them back. He had almost given up, thinking the intelligence was wrong, when he heard the sound around nine o'clock at night. It was faint at first and then grew stronger. It was a rumbling sound. All his men heard it. They crept to the edge of the bamboo and watched the bridge.

Lanterns appeared on either side of the bluff. The rumbling sound grew louder. Starkey took Fox's Lee Enfield with the starlight scope and sighted it on the nearest gate of the bridge. Through the lens, the forms were green. He saw fifty or sixty men wearing peasant hats. They had ropes over their shoulders and were pulling something very heavy until they got to the gate of the bridge. There they stopped, squatted down

and picked up the long platform. They walked to the end of the first
section of bridge, dropped the front edge of the platform and slid it
forward until it connected to the first bare pilings. Others had already
dragged another section to the gate and the men picked this up and
walked out, dropped it and slid it to the next pilings.

Within forty minutes, the two gangs of men connected the bridge.
Ten minutes later the first trucks started rolling across. Starkey was
happy.

"Can you believe that?" Starkey said. "Can you believe those guys?"

"It's pretty smart," D.K. said.

"Pretty smart?" said Fox. "It's fucking Einstein stuff."

"It ain't that smart," D.K. said.

"No," said Starkey. "But it's real good. It shows a lot about them."

"What's it show?" D.K. asked.

"They got guts and lots of will and that's good for us."

"Why in the world is that good for us?" Fox asked.

"Because when we beat them, when we blow this bridge and shut
down this infiltration route, it means we've really done something. We
need for them to be good. We need for them to be the best there is."

Just at dawn the peasants, wearing yellow hats and sandals, pulled
the last platforms from the bridge and slipped into the jungle, a host of
small children using shovelfuls of dirt to cover the gouges of the platforms and a last group of them sweeping the filled ruts with green palm
fronds.

Starkey and Fox studied the bridge for the rest of the day. They
decided they would place a charge on each piling. It would be hard and
difficult work, but Starkey wanted the bridge completely destroyed. By
eleven o'clock that night the peasants had not brought out the platforms
and Starkey decided they had to move. The three Americans took an
inflatable raft and carefully made their way down to the river and the
base of the pilings. They worked with plastic explosives and army green
tape and penlights until four o'clock in the morning and then returned
to the grove of bamboo. They slept for four hours and then fidgeted and
worried until nine o'clock that evening when they heard the rumbling
sound again. The bridge was connected and the trucks started to roll
across.

Starkey held the wireless detonator. He had pulled all of the patrol, except for two lookouts, in a tight circle around him. "When she blows, everybody follows Fox. Remember—single line. No cigarettes. No light of any kind and no noise. We got to get out of here quick. Any questions?"

"Can I push the button?" D.K. asked.

"What?"

"I just want to make it go boom."

"Yea, sure." Starkey handed him the radio detonator. "On my order."

D.K. was grinning.

Starkey looked at the men and the campsite to make sure that everything was ready, then he watched the trucks going across the bridge. He waited for six trucks to get in the center of the bridge.

He looked at D.K. "Do it."

The first charges went off and the others followed in three-second intervals. They were not loud explosions, they were dull pops and muffled cracks and small plumes of fire, but the pilings started to give way, breaking in half at the waterline, starting beneath the near gate of the bridge then shearing off across the river. The bridge did not begin collapsing until the first eight pilings had gone down. Suddenly there was a big explosion in the center of the bridge, an orange and white blast of light and flame. Two trucks flipped into the air, tossing out bodies. Several of the men cheered.

"God Almighty, what was that?" Starkey asked.

"A little surprise," Fox said. "I just wanted them to know we'd been there."

The charges continued exploding, marching across the river, breaking the concrete pilings neatly in half at the water line, and the big central part of the bridge that was burning fell into the river, taking with it five trucks.

"Let's move it," Starkey said.

"Hey, we still got charges," D.K. said.

"Right now. Let's go."

Fox led the way with a mine sweeper. The moon gave enough light. The patrol moved quickly, hearing the final charges popping behind them.

They marched eight hours without a rest. They were well away from the free fire zone when Starkey let them take a break.

"Dai-wi, how about some hot chow? I feel like my gizzard's froze," Fox said.

Starkey looked at the ground and considered.

"Oh, come on," D.K. said. "What you think them gooks gonna do— track us down? Hell, we won, man. We zapped their asses."

Starkey allowed the fire and the hot food. He gave the men forty-five minutes and then moved on. He pushed them for ten solid hours and gave them no breaks and he knew they were angry with him, but he wanted a great distance between the free fire zone and the patrol. Finally, at four-thirty in the afternoon, he stopped and set up camp. They were exhausted. In the last steaming light of the day, the Montagnards went hunting.

"Get us a pig!" D.K. yelled.

The temperature was almost a hundred and the humidity was so heavy that it was hard to breathe. The men were beneath three green canopies of jungle, and so there was shade, but it was hot darkness and there were green gnats coming up from the muddy river which lay below them. The Strikers sat together. They took off their blue flip-flops and threw them in a pile, then rolled up their trouser legs, exposing yellow calves. Two of them went straight to sleep. Another lit a black joss stick before his ivory elephant-god. A third, whose right arm was tattooed with a skinny orange tiger running from elbow to wrist, pulled out a set of worn cards from his pack and told the fortune of a friend.

D.K. was sitting on a rotten log. His face was dirty, his shaven head growing five days of black stubble. He was so tired that he just sat for a few minutes, his filthy right hand playing with the large black mole on his temple. After a while, he took out his hatchet with the red-and-white peppermint stick handle. He found his whetstone and began sharpening the edge.

Starkey and Fox were sitting on a rock covered with green moss. Fox had pulled off his webbing and gear and his camouflage shirt. His face and neck and hands were dirty and streaked with sweat. His chest and waist were white and clean and glistening.

"I think I'm going to take a dip," Fox said.

"I think I'll go with you," said Starkey.

Just as Starkey stood up, he heard a thump and looked down at his feet. It was a Russian hand grenade. He couldn't do anything. He just looked at the grenade and said, "Jesus."

Fox followed his eyes. He sprang and grabbed the grenade and threw it into the jungle, and as soon as he did, a machine gun started firing at them from the hill above.

52

FOX CLIPPED STARKEY IN the knees and knocked him to the ground. The grenade exploded in the jungle. Two more were thrown. One of them landed in the middle of the Strikers, who were struggling to put on their flip-flops. It exploded and several of the men screamed. D.K. had grabbed his rifle and hatchet and climbed a nearby tree. He was hiding behind several limbs, screaming, "Sonofabitch! Sonofabitch!"

Starkey and Fox were behind the larger rock.

"D.K.? D.K.?" Starkey yelled. "Do you see them? Where are they?"

"Up the fucking hill. Right on top of us."

"We got to flank them."

The machine gun was blasting. It was tearing up the campsite, blowing around pieces of leaves and bark and rock. The air was full of debris and dust.

"Go to the right," Starkey yelled.

D.K. jumped out of the tree.

"I'm going left," Starkey said.

"No, I'm going," Fox said.

"Look . . ."

"Look, shit. You stay here. I'm swinging up left."

Suddenly three Vietcong ran straight into the camp. They wore black pajamas and black headbands and they were screaming. The Strikers opened fire, but missed the lead VC, who dove at them and exploded. His body blew apart. The arms and legs were cut into pieces and the severed head splattered against the rock where Fox and Starkey lay. Brains and entrails and blood were everywhere and the other VC were firing, standing straight up and laughing and firing and D.K. ran straight for them, leveling one of them with several blasts from his shotgun. The other VC fired point blank and one round hit D.K., spun him around, flung the shotgun from his hands, but he whirled and threw himself on the VC, taking out his hatchet and hammering the screaming head until the VC went down and he kept hitting him until he stopped struggling, then dropped his face to what remained of the VCs and put his lips on the bloody mouth and sucked.

"D.K.!" Starkey yelled.

The machine gun was still firing, still exploding the camp.

D.K. covered the shredded mouth of the VC with his own and sucked loudly.

"Get off him, D.K. Get off him!"

Suddenly the machine gun went silent. Starkey waited a second and then ran to D.K. and pulled him off the bludgeoned VC.

"Y-e-e-e-e-ow-ow-ow," D.K. yelled. "Y-e-e-e-e-ow-ow-ow!"

"Shut up," Starkey said.

D.K. kept screaming. Starkey slapped him, but D.K. kept screaming and finally Starkey punched him and knocked him back and saw the big hole in his chest.

"Get us a dust-off," Starkey said.

"Is he bad?" Fox asked.

"Where's the Demerol? Where the hell is it?"

"I got it. I got it."

"Here, give it to me. Get on the horn."

Fox found the radio and started calling in their position. D.K. was lying on his back. His bald head was covered with dirt and scratches.

His brown eyes were wide and round and dazed. Starkey broke open a
new hypodermic and jammed it into a bottle of clear Demerol. D.K.
blocked Starkey when he tried to shoot him up.

"I'm not that bad, am I?" D.K. asked.

"Aren't you hurting?"

"It went right through, didn't it? Didn't it go right through?"

"Yeah. It went right through."

D.K. coughed and blood spurted from his mouth. He put a hand to
his chin and saw the red blood and his eyes got bigger and rounder and
he began breathing very fast.

"Oh shit, Dai-wi. It's a lung shot. Oh shit, man."

"Let me give you some Demerol."

"No, no. I don't want it. I can't see good, Dai-wi. Oh damn, damn. Is
he got a chopper?"

"It's coming." Starkey glanced at the Strikers. One of them was
tending to the wounded.

D.K. coughed again and there was even more blood and his hands
were clamping and twitching at his side.

"I don't want that Demerol. Don't you give it to me."

"I won't give it to you."

"You're just talking to me, Dai-wi, 'cause you think I'm dying. I
know that's why you're talking to me."

"We got a chopper coming."

"Oh man, oh man. I can't see good. Oh God. Can you hold my
hand?"

Starkey locked his fingers through D.K.'s.

"Please, can you hold my hand?"

"I got it," Starkey said, and held it up for him to see.

"I can't feel it. I can't feel you."

"I'm right here."

"Am I dying? Don't keep it from me. Am I dying?"

"I'm with you, D.K."

D.K. shuddered and a big bubble of blood came from his mouth.
Starkey wiped it away.

"Don't give me no Demerol."

"I won't."

"Dai-wi . . ."

His head dropped to the left and the brown eyes blinked twice.

The choppers arrived twenty minutes later. Four Strikers were dead, two were untouched. The Montagnards were the last to climb aboard. The white daubs of wax on their crossbows were bristly with new whiskers. They told Starkey they had come up on the VC from the rear. On the way back to the camp, Starkey shot himself up with Demerol.

For the next few days, he kept himself as busy as he could. He did all the things in the camp he had been putting off. He laid concrete in the bottom of the trenches and set out small tins of D-CON and taped new thermite grenades to the safes and tied down an extra twenty yards of concertina wire around the camp. Night was his worst time. He hung out at the bar in the team house as long as he could. He wasn't drinking. He just stayed and listened to the Beatles and played cards and pickup sticks. Around twelve o'clock, he went to his hootch, took out the hypo and shot himself to sleep with the Demerol, thinking, I didn't even get to see him again. I worked with the guy for months, I held his hand while he was dying and I didn't get to see him the right way—all decked out in his uniform, with his green beret. I should have seen him one more time. He was a soldier. It's not right. The Demerol hit then. He felt his flesh rush with the warmth of it and his tongue went numb and his fingers and he was out.

The next week Starkey received a letter of commendation. Colonel Roberts said that the infiltration of supplies through his sector had dropped by almost 90 percent. He told Starkey to pack his gear, that there was another route near the DMZ that needed to be capped. He said that he had personally requested that Starkey be promoted to Major and he was sure that Westmoreland would approve it.

A few days later there was a letter from Wick and one from Eugénie. Starkey read Wick's first. It was the happiest letter that Starkey had ever gotten from his brother, full of details about life in the cardinal's palace full of plans and expectations. Toward the end of the letter Wick wrote that his sons were well and then asked Starkey how it felt to be an uncle. Starkey stuck the stationery back into the envelope. He was still amazed at his brother, amazed about Alice and the two boys. He never would have imagined that Wick could have ended up in a situation like this. He always seemed too good, too pure, too devoted to his career. Eugénie's note was short and funny and oblivious to the harm she had done him. She said that she was returning to Saigon in a month and that they had to get together and work things out, that she was finally ready to and that she had gotten rid of Linda two weeks earlier and that she had done this because she realized that the girl had deep psychological problems.

Late in the afternoon, Colonel Roberts arrived unannounced. He asked to speak with Starkey alone and they went to the kitchen in the team house and sat down. There was a plywood floor and cement walls. Red ants were streaming across the brown thatch of the ceiling and several green chameleons were stuffing themselves with them. The kitchen was damp and smelled of mildew.

Colonel Roberts threw down a manila envelope. "You better have a look. We got these two days ago. All hell's breaking loose sixty miles south of here."

Starkey looked at four night photographs. Each one revealed a line of truck headlights. "Where is this?"

"Where do you think?"

"DMZ?"

"Champion Bridge."

Starkey studied the pictures. "No way."

"They were taken two days ago."

"I blew everything. There wasn't one piling left."

"I'll tell you something, Captain. You took a very high-profile job when you took this sector. A lot of people knew about it. Westmoreland himself knows about it. Your majority has been put on the back burner until this—setback—is taken care of. When can you do it?"

"I'll leave tomorrow morning."

"Leave tonight."

Starkey took Sargeant Fox and three Montagnards. He wanted to travel light and fast so he didn't carry the radio. Fox chose the ordnance: three hundred pounds of plastique, a sixty-millimeter mortar, three BARs, one bazooka, one flame thrower, thirty hand grenades and fifteen claymores.

They marched eighteen hours without a break and the entire time Starkey was thinking, It has to be a mistake. Those couldn't be pictures of Champion Bridge. I did everything right. I know there wasn't one piling left. I know I did it right, damn it.

By eight o'clock the next night, the heat was still simmering. It was one hundred and three degrees below a starry sky. Starkey had not stopped once. Finally Fox grabbed him.

"You need to rest them, Dai-wi. You're pushing too hard."

"We got to keep moving."

"We ain't going to be worth a shit."

"No."

"Look, goddamnit, we've got to stop. Now you either order them to do it or they will break ranks."

"I want another hour."

"I'm telling you, man."

"One hour."

When the break came, the Montagnards threw themselves into a muddy river.

"Build a fire," Starkey said.

"Are you serious?"

"Let them brew some tea, eat some good chow. We probably won't eat again for two days."

"The fire will give us away."

"I hope it does give us away. I hope those fuckers see us coming fifty miles away. Let them dig in, let them line up. I want them to be as ready as they can get. We can take them. There's nobody in the world that we can't beat. Don't you believe that?"

Fox glanced at Starkey's round blue eyes and the hollows that had developed in his cheeks. The officer had not been the same since the firefight, since D.K.'s death. He seemed like a man who had lost something.

"Sure I believe it."

"I mean, what happened to your palaver about technology, how American technology can whip anybody, anything. What happened to all that?"

"We got the technology."

"We got more than that. Everything's with us. Technology's with us, skill, professionalism, history. Did you ever think of that? History. History is on our side as much as anything. We've never lost a war, Fox. Never. We've never lost one and you know why, because we're better, smarter, tougher than everybody else. We're going to shut down the infiltration route and then we're going to the DMZ and kick some more VC ass there and we'll move on and on until we've beat them all and there's nothing and no one who can stop us."

They rested for three hours and then marched on, entering the free fire zone around 1 A.M.

It was moonlit dark when Starkey drew near the bluff of the Long Ly River. He bivouacked his column in a newly exploded crater and then went on without a mine sweeper, walking toward the bluff. A hundred feet from where the gate to Champion Bridge once stood, there was nothing but rubble. It made him smile. Damn right, he said. He dropped down low and made his way through the rubble to the very edge of the cliff and looked out over the still river. There was nothing. The center section was gone and the section on the other side and all the pilings. The river was smooth. There was nothing across it. Just to make sure, he slipped down the side of the muddy bank. Mosquitoes were buzzing him. They hit him in the eyes and zoomed into his ears, but he didn't care. Halfway down the bank, he heard a noise behind him.

"It's me, Dai-wi," Fox said.

Starkey moved on until he got down to the edge of the river. He was up to his calves in mud. It was stinking and the mosquitoes were singing in his ears and the heat was thick. He looked across the river, squinting his eyes, and it was clean and clear. Fox walked up beside him.

"What do you think?" Starkey asked.

"Think we did a pretty good job."

"This is why we're going to win. 'Cause we do things right and we do things smart and we don't make mistakes."

There was a sound then, the sound of a motor, across the river. The two men ducked down behind blocks of concrete. Starkey took Fox's Lee Enfield with the starlight scope. Through the lens he could see that a gully had been cut down through the bluff, just beside where the bridge had been. A truck with headlights burning rumbled through the gully and toward the river. Starkey handed the rifle back.

The truck stopped at the edge of the river.

"What you gonna do now?" Starkey said.

Another truck rumbled down through the gully and then several more and they formed a line at the water's edge. Several peasants jumped out of the trucks. They lit torches and their numbers grew until there were twenty or thirty. Slowly the peasants began to wade out.

"They're in for a big surprise," Starkey said.

"Why?"

"Engineers surveyed the bridge in 1961. It's forty feet deep right there."

The peasants were wearing their yellow straw hats and holding torches above their heads. The water came up to their calves and they kept moving out, kept walking forward.

"How are they doing it?" Starkey said. "It's deep there. It's real deep."

The trucks began to move then. The gears grated in the night and slowly the trucks followed the peasants.

Starkey was so incredulous that he stood up. The peasants were walking across the middle of the river now. He saw them, scores of their torches waving over their straw hats, walking across the water, now not even calf deep, only ankle deep. The long line of peasants stepping lightly across the black expanse of the river and the trucks following and Starkey couldn't believe it.

He slogged downstream.

"Dai-wi!" Fox whispered.

"They can't do this. They can't," Starkey said.

He worked his way through the mud and stood exactly in front of the advancing column and then got down on hands and knees and moved out into the stinking water and it quickly rose to his eyes, but he kept pushing out, feeling nothing but mud and reeds and then he felt something else. It made him stop, dig his fingers, his knees deeper and then he moved again toward the peasants and the trucks and he began to rise out of the water on stones. He could feel them, there were flat stones beneath the surface of the river.

Crouched down low, Fox caught him by the neck. "Come on, man."

Starkey turned and grabbed Fox's rifle and stood up, yelling, "You can't beat me goddammit. You can't beat me."

He opened fire walking straight for them. Fox reached for him and fell and there was a fullisade of shots from the lead truck and Starkey was knocked backward, feeling something burning through his chest, feeling all his air suck out and the water rushing in, thinking, No way, there's no way they can be doing this, just squeeze the trigger, come on, come on, just do it right . . .

53

IT WAS SUMMER AT Waverly. The fields of green grass surrounding the house were filled with yellow daisies and the bright faces of wild violets. The ginko trees bordering the dirt road were dressed out with new leaves and the magnolias which stood above the front steps were ripe with hundreds of green bulbs.

Cat McGregor wasted no time in returning to the routine of Waverly. She rose at five-thirty every morning to greet Hannah and Bub and Jebodiah and the others as they entered the back of the house. She had been disappointed to learn that during her absence they had stopped using the wagons and now arrived in pickup trucks with WAVERLY printed in white letters on the doors. Around six-thirty she had her coffee with Hannah and Bub and learned what was happening in the house and across the estate for the day: sometimes all the curtains were to be washed, sometimes moldings were to be painted or leaks fixed or the chandelier in the ballroom taken down and each crystal cleaned by hand, and in addition to the house, Bub had a list of things to be done on the grounds: azalea and camelia beds weeded, pine straw laid on the interior roads, new blocks of salt set out in the pastures, sparrow nests swept out from the gutters.

At seven o'clock Harper was rolled into the little dining room and she and Cat discussed local political races or scandals, Harper carefully pointing out which ones Cat should investigate and write about. Afterward Cat went to the newspaper. She had been given a new office. It had two large windows and oak paneling. A smaller office sat as an entrance to her own. She wanted to get herself a secretary. She knew she didn't need one really, but she wanted one. Late in the afternoon, she left the paper, came home for a cup of tea. When she had first come to Waverly, she liked to drink cold iced tea and sit with Hannah and Tee Tat in the kitchen, listening to stories about voodoo and haunts and miraculous trees which sat in the secret places of the woods and could heal any illness, unless it was sexual. Now, however, she liked to drink hot tea from a silver service while sitting in the music room.

She had a nap before supper, and if Ford was back from Washington, she managed to spend an hour with him. It was not that she didn't like her fiancé, she did like him. She thought he was reasonably smart and often funny. The only thing which she could not abide was touching. If Ford patted her on the back or tried to hold her hand, it made her uncomfortable and the same question always arose: How in the world will you ever go to bed with him? How will you do it?

One evening she decided to address the question head-on. She and Ford were having Hannah's homemade peach ice cream and sitting at the long table in the big dining room. The chandelier was burning and the lights flashed across scores of silver bowls and trays and serving dishes which sat on the rosewood sideboards and inside the china cabinets. Ford was beginning his second bowl of peach ice cream. He had gained even more weight in the last month and his face had two pockets of red, jiggling flesh which could only be called jowls. He had recently let his black hair grow longer and had bought a new pair of wire-rim glasses with rounder and smaller frames.

"You know I feel guilty. I guess that is the word—maybe it isn't the word, in fact, maybe it's not the word at all . . . ."

Cat silently tapped her foot under the table. "Go ahead, go ahead. You feel guilty about what?"

"You're right, my dear. I'm always debating with myself. I wonder why I do it?"

"Go ahead."

"Oh well, I feel guilty—if that is the word—about leaving the President all alone with—"

"I need to talk with you about something," Cat said.

Ford stopped, looked at her. The birthmark in his left cheek was a pale lavender.

"If things work out, if we do go ahead and get married, I may have a problem with some things."

Ford nodded, touched a napkin to his lips, put his hands in his lap and sat up straight.

"I'm not very interested in sex. I never have been. There's something about it that I find offensive. I suppose it's important to marriage, but it's not important to me. I'm telling you this, just so you know from the beginning."

Blood rushed through the skin of Ford's face and his scar became a deep purple. "Of course—well, not of course, that's a stupid response but, I mean, well, I certainly understand what you're saying . . ."

"Do you understand?"

"I think so."

"I just don't like it."

"I don't blame you. Sex is, uh . . . ." Ford stumbled and stuttered and turned even a deeper shade of red, his scar a deeper purple. "Sex is just, well, in a certain kind of way, sex is barbaric, completely and utterly barbaric, and if I were a woman, I wouldn't like it either."

"Besides, the most important part of marriage is friendship, companionship, and I think we can be good friends, don't you?"

"Oh, the best of friends."

"Now the other thing is weight. I think you need to take some off."

"You're definitely right about that."

"Can you lose thirty pounds?"

"Thirty?"

Cat reached out and touched his hand lightly. "And I'd like you to do it by the time we get married. It's not so much for me—it's for you. Can you imagine looking back at the wedding pictures two years from now and seeing this obese, bespectacled thing in a tuxedo? You would hate it. You would think how could I have allowed myself to look like that."

She's exactly right, Ford thought some hours later. He was lying in his bed. Sex is not so important. All my friends say it is the first thing to go stale in a marriage, and since many marriages are based on desire first and compatibility second, the whole marriage comes to an end when sex loses its luster. Who knows? After the first few months of marriage, as the friendship deepens, maybe the sex will get better. Wouldn't that be marvelous? A good, deep friendship, a sensitive compatibility, and then gorgeous sex. Fiesty sex, the kind of sex . . . Now, now, let's wait and see . . .

At seven the next morning, Harper had Bub roll her out onto the front veranda. She drank a cup of tea and looked out at the green fields and the long row of gingkos. The dew was heavy and she could see it sparkling on the blue and yellow morning glories beside the gravel driveway. Lately, she had started letting go of some of her discipline, not all of it, but some. She stopped forcing herself to translate Greek and Latin. Her guitar playing was weak, but she kept it up and she was doing exercises that the doctor assigned and she stayed on the phone for hours each day with editors and reporters, but she let go of the Greek and Latin.

For the first couple of days, she felt awful. It was the same old thought: you have been given a good mind for languages and you're not using it, it's going fallow. What is wrong with you? You're wasting what you've been given, just like your father did. Wasting, wasting, wasting. She fought the impulse to pick up the books and after a few days the most amazing thing began to happen—as the compulsion to study lessened, she began to remember things, all kinds of things that she had not thought about in years. She remembered lines of poetry, paragraphs from famous speeches, old bits of gossip, even part of an Ira Gerschwin song which she had not thought of in years:

> *I've been around the world in a plane*
> *I've settled revolutions in Spain*
> *The North Pole I've charted*
> *But still I can't get started*
> *With you.*

And she remembered so many other things: what it was like to catch her first bream. How red its breast was and how blue its scales and she remembered how hot Antonia felt the first time she held her and she remembered seeing the blue eyes, the incredible blue light of her first grandchild, and she recalled her husband, Anthony, how good and gentle he was and how he always wore a red silk tie on Friday nights and the taste of his Old Fashions, which he filled with chunks of pineapple and red cherries and green mint. She recalled cubbyholes where she had hidden old love letters bound with blue ribbon and remembered old boxes holding golden needlework she'd done as a girl and she remembered that toads always have rough bellies and that the fire of fireflies will stick to your fingers and the feel of a full, smooth tick and she remembered the first words of her first suitor—Hey, I ain't never been out with a girl yet—and the first words of Blackie—Mama, say shit—and she remembered her father's last words: Take time to do the good things, take time to do them.

And she was stunned that it had done this, that letting go had done this, because she thought that it would bring chaos and it was a kind of chaos, but it was good, most of it, though there were some of the sad and painful things too and she took them with all the others, she accepted them all, so that after three or four days of these memories, she sat out on the veranda and asked herself, What good did it do? All the discipline, all the ambition.

It made her laugh. She sat in her wheelchair on the front porch of the great house and laughed until the tears ran down from her eyes.

Cat was standing in the foyer and looking out the window at the old lady. How much she had changed. Her black hair was white, there were hollows in her cheeks and her body had shriveled in the wheelchair—still Cat envied her. She must be so content, she thought, sitting there, surveying her kingdom, laughing at some past victory. It's exactly the way I want to be. When I get her age, I want to have done so much, to have succeeded so brilliantly at so many things and then I can sit on the veranda filled with memories and laugh and laugh and laugh.

Cat walked outside just in time to see Harper crumple the front page of the *Southern Chronicle* and hurl it into the yard.

"Damn those idiots," Harper said.

She sat down in a green rocker beside the old woman.

"Mayor Williams has run the gamut of political experience. *Gamut*—

spelled by my illustrious editors *gambit*. It's that Charlie Woods. He's an idiot. An utter idiot. Do you realize he only has a high school degree?"

"How in the world did he get the job?"

"Oh, God. I don't know. His father worked for my father and in he waddled. He's simply awful. I'm so sick of it. I'm so sick of them, maybe I'll just go ahead and do it and be done with it."

"Fire Charlie?"

"Sell the newspaper. The Hearst Corporation has been after me to do it for years. They called again last week. Maybe I should take the offer. I could divide it up between the boys. If it was managed right, the silver spoon could be passed down to their great-grandchildren. What do you think?"

Cat was startled. She had never thought of this possibility. She had thought that there would always be a paper.

"Well, I guess it would depend on how much money they were offering you."

"It is a great deal. Would you like to know how much?"

"Not really. It's none of my business," Cat said, though she wanted to know desperately.

"Tommy Hearst wants to have lunch next week. I hate that expression—have lunch. It's such a Yankee way of saying things."

"You could do that."

"What—sell the paper?"

"Well, go see Mr. Hearst."

"Don't you think little Blackie might like to work for it one day?"

"I think you should do what you want to. It's your paper. You made it what it is. You should do whatever you feel like." Cat forced herself to say this, but in reality, she was terrified of the paper's being sold. It was her niche in the world.

Down at the road, a Western Union truck turned into the driveway and sped forward, leaving a trail of red dust whirling behind it.

Harper saw it immediately, and knew what it could mean.

"Cat, would you fix me a cup of tea?"

"Sure. Honey or sugar?"

"Honey. Orange blossom."

Cat saw the truck. "I wonder what that's about?"

"Oh, I've been expecting a wire. Make sure it's orange blossom."

Harper didn't want her there when she read the telegram. She didn't want anyone to see her face.

The young man ran up the stairs. "I have a—"

"Yes, yes. I'm Harper Longstreet."

She took the warm envelope and waited for the boy to climb back into the truck. She put her left hand to her face and set the telegram on her knee. The tears were already in her eyes and she was shaking. She opened the envelope and closed her eyes for a moment and then pulled out the wire and opened it.

Dear Mrs. Longstreet,

It is with the deepest of regret that I inform you that your son Captain Starfield Longstreet is currently listed as missing in action.

Harper breathed and made a little sound.

It is not certain whether Captain Longstreet is living or deceased at the present time, but I will try to determine this as quickly as possible. He is a fine soldier and I am hopeful.

Sincerely,
Gen. Richard Atkins

54

THE WORD SPREAD QUICKLY and soon the whole house knew. Harper called both of the state's senators and Ford put in a call to the White House. The most important thing was to find out the truth, even if it was crushing.

Around 11 P.M., after many more phone calls, an Equinil, and two Scotches, Harper was lying in her four-poster teak bed, thinking, He is not dead. I know he is not. He's too skilled and he has my instinct for life and he is someplace—a hut, a cave, a ravine, he is someplace in that jungle waiting to be found. I know it. But what if he is dead? The question made her stomach hurt and she shivered. Well, if he is, then he is. I will not let it ruin me, what of me is left. I'll grieve and hurt, and feel that god-awful hole that comes with grieving and I will endure it for a while and then I will banish it. I will stop it. And Harper thought back to all the others she had lost: her husband and her daughter and Boykin and her very own sweet Blackie and that was enough suffering for any life. So if Starkey is dead, then he is dead and I'll feel it for a while and then I will bury it because I have suffered enough.

She felt the pain in the center of her chest. It was sharp and pulsating. She sat up in the bed and felt her heart begin to race. Damn it, I'm not going to let this happen to me. Not now. Not until I know. The pain became worse and she felt the tingling in the tips of her fingers and her breathing was picking up. Stop it now. She reached over for the nitroglycerin tablets and stuck one under her tongue. She tried to make herself relax. The pill helped a little, but soon the pain grew sharper and she felt the steel band around her chest and it was squeezing her so she could hardly breathe.

"Damn it, stop doing this," she said aloud. "Stop it right now."

But she was seeing bright spots and the pain was so bad that she was grinding her teeth. Suddenly she sat up in bed and said, "All right."

She threw two pillows on the floor beside the bed and started to pull back the covers when everything went black.

It was ten-thirty in St. Louis and Wick was still working in the cardinal's palace. Cat had called him earlier in the day to tell him about Starkey and he had sent a wire to the archbishop of Saigon asking him to do all that he could. The news had upset Wick. He was surprised by his response. He knew he respected his brother, but he did not know that he loved him and besides he thought he had prepared himself for this eventuality. He remembered Starkey at his evening Mass and said to God, I know I have no right to ask you for anything really, because even if it doesn't feel sinful I know that I'm breaking my vow, but look out for Starkey. Hold him, keep him, bring him back safe.

After Mass, he went to see Cardinal Dunlap and told him what had happened. The cardinal seemed oddly distant, but he said that he would call the Vatican to see if the Church had any links to the Vietcong in Starkey's area. Wick couldn't eat supper so he went into his office.

Wick's departure from South Carolina had been difficult. Despite all of their attempts, Alice and he had had one fight after another. Two days before he left, Alice had packed up and taken the boys to New York. From St. Louis, Wick had called her several times a day, but she would not speak to him. Eventually they did speak and Alice told him she was living with her parents and that the children were fine, but that things had to change.

"Look, you've got to make up your mind."

"I know."

"I know," she mimicked. "That's what you always say in that soft little voice, I know, then you don't do a damned thing. I'm sick of it."

Alice slammed down the phone and told herself that that was it, it was over, and for several days she went to one party after another and drank and saw old friends and each day she felt sicker and sicker and she couldn't believe it. She couldn't believe that she could love anyone this much.

One evening after five Scotches, she couldn't bear the pain of it anymore and she flew to St. Louis and went to the cardinal's palace and rang the doorbell, having had four more drinks on the plane. A sleepy little nun answered the door and Alice demanded to see Wick, who had just come down the stairs, and they embraced and kissed in the front door of the cardinal's palace and the little nun almost fainted.

They went to a hotel and made the best love they had made in a while, and the next morning, they fought bitterly and Alice was determined to leave.

Several days later, she rented a suite of rooms in the Drake Hotel. She saw Wick every evening. She felt defeated and weary and in love. She started smoking cigarettes.

Wick had buried himself in his new work. Living on the fourth floor of the cardinal's palace, he rose at 4:30 A.M., had half an hour of reflection, then met with the cardinal at five and went over the calendar for the day. At five-thirty the cardinal, Wick, old Bishop Lazak, and two young monsignors ate breakfast in a large dining room. They were served by three nuns from the Little Sisters of Charity. The cardinal insisted that everyone be in their offices at seven o'clock.

As vicar general of the Archdiocese, Wick settled disputes between pastors and their priests, sat on the board of two seminaries, rotated priests among the two hundred churches and worked as a kind of ecclesiastical press agent for the cardinal and the Chancellory Office. In addition to all of these duties, he had opened a civil rights office in the Chancellory and had hired Nathaniel Cash as a consultant. When Bishop Lazak died suddenly, Wick took on his duties as well, while the cardinal searched for a replacement.

So now at ten-thirty at night and even though he was worried about his brother, he was working and enjoying everything about it: the contacts, the prestige, the ability to affect the lives of millions of Catholics.

The phone rang and Wick answered it and Ford told him that Harper had had another attack and that she was not expected to live. Wick told him that he would be down early the next morning. He hung up and sat back in his chair. He saw her sitting in her bed, grabbing her chest, her face going white. He made himself stop seeing it and suddenly thought, Is that what we have to look forward to? If we're lucky enough to make it into old age—is that the payoff?

He got up from his desk and took the small elevator up to the cardinal's bedroom. He knocked on the door.

It was a large room. The walls were paneled in dark oak and the floor was an oak and white spruce parkay. There were two chests of drawers, a leather sofa and two Edwardian leather chairs which sat by the fireplace. The room was freezing and gold curtains billowed from the tall windows. The cardinal lay under a stack of covers in an oak bed. On the headboard was carved a large crown. Cardinal Dunlap was a thin man. He wore white pajamas, a purple robe and a purple shawl across his shoulders. On his head sat a red skullcap. He held in his lap and on his chest a pile of papers and documents.

Wick explained about Harper and Cardinal Dunlap gave him permission to leave and then asked him to sit down for a moment.

He pulled a straightback chair to the edge of the cardinal's bed. He was wearing a black cassock with red piping and his black hair was a bit longer than usual. He was tired and the exhaustion showed in his eyes, the blue one and the brown one. The wind was whipping the gold curtains into the room.

"Is it too chilly for you?" Cardinal Dunlap asked.

"I'm fine."

The cardinal lifted a handful of papers. "Do you know what this is? It's a list of all the Catholics who died this month in the area. Almost nine hundred. It's an average number. In a year it adds up to around ten or eleven thousand bodies that the Church has to bury. It's one of the biggest problems I have. When I became archbishop, I thought my greatest challenge would be how to keep the soup kitchens going or finding enough money to fully fund the seminaries, but I was wrong. My biggest problem is where to bury all these people."

"You should build a high-rise mausoleum. Go up, not down."

The cardinal laughed. "I know you're joking, but—it might work."

"It would work," Wick said.

The cardinal pushed stacks of paper from his stomach onto the bed. "It's that kind of quickness, that kind of creativeness, that makes you such a valuable man. It's why I want to offer you John Lazak's job. Wick, I'd like you to be my auxillary bishop."

Wick looked at the cardinal, then looked away.

"Well, are you interested? And don't start saying you're not worthy and all that crap. Nobody's worthy, but somebody's got to do the job. It would make you the youngest bishop in the United States. Probably raise a few ecclesiastical eyebrows, but it's time for them to be raised. Things are changing. Do you want the job?"

"Yes."

"There's only one problem that I can see." The cardinal sighed and clasped his pink hands over his stomach. "This is not easy to say, but it has to be said. Two days ago, I was made aware of the presence of a young woman in your life—Alice Grooms. Do you know her?"

"I know her."

"Are you seeing her?"

"Yes."

"I want to tell you something, young man. I'm sixty-one years old. I've seen a lot of things in the Church, good things and bad. Good men and bad. You're a good man. You're also a smart man. It's a rare combination in the Church. Most of the good men are dullards or round-eyed fanatics, and most of the smart men are crooks or politicians. So you are a rare and special commodity. I need you. The Church needs you. But you've got to make a decision. It will be a very hard decision for you—or at least I hope it will. If it isn't, then I've overestimated you. The hard decisions are the best decisions, the ones that cut you up inside and make you bleed. Take a couple weeks off. Think, pray. If you have to spend a few days at that godforsaken Trappist monastery—what's its name?"

"Monastery of Peace."

"It still amazes me that you were ever there. Did you really want to be a monk?"

Wick looked at the floor.

"Well, do whatever it takes. If you need money to help you out of this situation, I can give you a hand."

The cardinal leaned forward, opened a drawer in his bedside table and pulled out a red zucchetto. "Take this with you. It's yours if you want it, and I'll tell you something—it's only the beginning for you, just the first step. I've never met a young man with more talent or a brighter future. Think hard."

55

CAT MCGREGOR WAS ALONE at Waverly when the call came in. Harper had been in the hospital for two days and Ford was spending most of his time with her.

"He's all right," the general said.

"Are you sure?"

"He took two rounds. One in the upper chest and one in the leg. The doctors are more worried about the leg than the chest wound. We flew him to Subic Bay this morning. The doctors tell me we should have him home in a week."

It took ten days for Starkey to get home and Cat was the first one to see him walk through the door. He was not expected to arrive until one o'clock in the afternoon, but he climbed up the front steps at eight-thirty in the morning. Cat was walking across the white marble of the foyer when she saw the door open. Starkey stood there, leaning on a black cane. He was wearing his uniform, green beret cocked on his head. He looked so much like Blackie: the blue eyes, the long jaw and ruddy, thick neck and the blue-blackness of his hair. She wanted to rush up and hug him, but she felt self-conscious because she did not know him, so she just went to the door.

"You must be Cat," Starkey said.

"I saw you at Harper's birthday party, but you didn't see me, I don't think."

"I've heard a lot about you though. Got a hug for an old soldier?"

Cat threw her arms around his shoulders and her cheek touched his own. She held him and noticed that he even smelled like Blackie and she said to herself at that very moment, in the long, warm reach of his arms, that she did not have to do anything in the future that she did not want to do and that her life was her own and if people didn't understand that, then too bad because she would do what she pleased.

A few days later Harper came back home. The heart attack had weakened her even more and she spent most of her days in her bed or on the front porch. Though her body was deteriorating, her mind was still quick and she was beginning to notice something between Starkey and Cat. Sometimes they sat together on the front porch or sometimes took long drives together and there was that long look between them and the smile that went with it which always seemed so silly to Harper, making her feel a little angry, a little cynical, and if she was honest, just a little envious.

Wick had spent his first few days at home walking through the woods which surrounded the house. The summer was young, but already the temperature was rising to ninety-three and ninety-four degrees. The magnolia trees beside the front steps of the house were white with soft blossoms and the air was sweet and heavy and drowsy with the aroma. He spent as much time outside as he could. It seemed to release him from the prison of himself, from the staleness of his mind and the argument and counterargument of his decision. Usually he took a walk early in the morning when everything was wet and shining.

He walked down the front steps and across the yard. The grass was a light green and beyond it the pine trees which stood on the outside of the forest were darker green, though the greenness was dull and tired and not at all like the wet and lush greenness that the English oaks held and the slender maples and the big American sycamores with their white trunks shining in the darkness of the woods. He walked on until he reached a valley where the blackberry bushes were six feet tall. A few of the blackberries had ripened and they were black beads drawn into a cluster. He ate a few and remembered when he and Blackie used to hunt king snakes here with forked sticks. He swung up then, through the part of the woods that was completely pine, and the floor of the woods was ankle deep in the brown straw and the crackling cones and the red and gray scales of the trees which had fallen into the dry straw, which here and there allowed a few blue morning glories to grow.

One day having finished his walk, Wick went into the kitchen and sat down at one of the pine worktables. Hannah brought him a cup of coffee and a fresh biscuit, in the center of which was a piece of ham. He looked at the biscuit and shook his head. Hannah put her hands on her hips.

"What's wrong with you? You been moping around here for more than a week."

"Trying to figure something out, I guess."

"What is it?"

Wick sipped his coffee.

"Now you look here. I ain't going to pull and fight this thing out of you. You come in here 'cause you wanted to talk to me about it or you wouldn't come in here, you would just kept to yourself like you have for the last week. Now you want to talk or not? I got other things to do."

"How'd you get so smart?"

"Must be from working for white folks."

Wick laughed and drank a little more coffee. It was the first time he had laughed since he had left St. Louis. He had eaten very little and slept very little.

"I don't know what to do, Hannah. I'm caught between two things. I don't know which one I want more. It's hard to decide. It's just not like me. I mean, I've always been able to make a clear decision."

"Who you talking about? You aren't talking about you. You talking about somebody else. You never been able to choose. Double-minded is what the Bible calls it. You have always been double-minded, which is just selfishness. Ever since you were small you wanted both. You wanted chocolate and vanilla or Pepsi and Orange Crush or lemon pie and banana pudding. You growed up now—least you supposed to be. Time to quit having everything. Time to put away childish things and act like a man. Life ain't both things or a bunch of things, it's one thing for most people and it's time you learned it."

The old black woman scowled, pushed her white hat down on her head and left the room. Wick was stinging. It wasn't that he had not seen his own duality; he had seen it. He had identified it, but he had never seen it quite so clearly, and he had not thought of it as selfishness. Was that the real problem? Was he just a small, selfish child who wanted everything? God have mercy on him if that was true. He had always thought it was his spirit battling against his flesh, but maybe that was self-delusion. Maybe it was just plain greed.

Late in the afternoon Starkey and Wick rolled out the old, rusted cooker under the pecan trees in the backyard. They wore madras Bermuda shorts and short-sleeve shirts. Starkey's thigh bore a thick bandage and he was still using his cane and limping. The two of them had cooked out many times together and each knew his duties. Starkey spread the charcoal and lit the fire; Wick made sure the chicken was soaked with red sauce.

Since he had arrived home, Starkey was having strange nights. He would fall asleep early and deeply and then the dreams would start, awful dreams about the bridge and the line of trucks which he could not stop, no matter what he did. Then at some point, he would hear a gurgling noise and behind a bush there was D.K. sucking the mouth of a dead body that was already stiff and blue, and when Starkey pulled D.K. off, he saw that the body was his own, but he could not wake up. This was what made the nightmares different. He was so tired, so exhausted, that he could not wake up and the dreams went on and on until it was light and then he would wake up gasping.

Even in the daylight, even as he lit the fire in the cooker, he had a terrible sense of guilt: that he had failed his men, that he had failed his country, that he had failed Harper.

He looked at Wick. His brother seemed so confident and so sure of himself. He stood with his big thumb white with pressure as it dug into his hipbone, the other hand pouring red sauce over the chicken. Wick put his tongue in front of his teeth and now and again popped it free, making a sucking noise, and Starkey knew that it meant he was feeling strong, tip-top. For the first time in his life, Starkey wanted to reach out to Wick, to approach him and say, I need a little help, I just need you to give me a little help. But when Wick turned and looked at him, hands on his hips, one leg slightly bent, his mouth slightly open and the teeth almost bared, somehow Starkey felt intimidated and he shuddered and looked away from his brother's awful confidence.

"Get a chill?" Wick asked.

"Oh—uh, no, well yeah, a little one, I guess."

"Did you want some garlic in the sauce? I went ahead and put a little bit in there."

"Yeah."

"How long you need the cane?"

Wick looked at his brother's eyes, then glanced down at the bandage on his leg. He was doing everything he could not to gloat—oh, not about the wound. The wound was terrible and he even felt sorry for him about the wound, but he loved the fact that his brother, his big, tough brother who always succeeded and who never made a mistake, his brother had finally failed. Starkey was going to be a camp commander, Starkey was going to be a big war hero, Starkey was going to be the youngest general in Vietnam, but Starkey had failed, just as he himself had failed so many times, and he wanted Starkey to taste it, to taste failure, to eat it for a while.

"Think you'll get a silver star or something?" Wick asked.

"No."

"Why not? Harper said you took on a column of troops."

"Not really."

Wick wanted to make him feel it, so he feigned concern. "Look, sometimes you just strike out, you know? You do your best and it all goes wrong. You just fall flat on your face. It's all right. It'll work out."

"I don't know," Starkey said. He glanced at Wick's eyes—the blue one and the brown one—and they seemed hard and flashing, and the blue one was cold as he had ever seen it. "I just don't know. Do you think it'll work out?"

"Oh sure, course it will. Look at my life. You know what I've gone through, lots of ups and downs. You just go on. You say to yourself: I blew it. I did everything that I could, I used every ounce of talent and I blew it. I failed. So? So what? You just move ahead."

"I don't know if—I can, Wick."

Wick heard the plea in his voice and he knew he was tasting it pretty good. "Sure you can." He clapped his brother's thin shoulders. "Hell, be a failure, be a grand failure. Be the best failure there ever was. We have too much success in this family anyway. Don't you think? Let's get these chickens on, I'm starving."

Cat McGregor was spending a lot of time with Harper. She was giving back rubs and leg rubs and fetching juice, pills, ointments and salves, and she was utterly sick of it. Still every morning she came into Harper's room smiling and cheerful and determined to dissuade her from selling the paper. One morning when she walked into the old lady's room carrying a silver tray with juice, she found Harper breathing hard and holding a hand on the center of her chest. Her pillows had been thrown on the floor beside the bed.

"Are you all right?"

"Juice."

"Do you need your medicine?"

Harper was white except for the black skin beneath her eyes. She was very thin and small, though her hands seemed larger, the veins black and thick. Her hair was white.

Cat gave her the juice and picked up the pillows and started to fluff them.

"Not yet," Harper said, breathing a little easier.

"You put those down there?"

"Do you know what happens to the body once its dead? It lets go of everything. It's a mess. It ruins everything beneath it. I'm not going to do that. I'm going to put myself right on the floor when the time comes so everything will be neat and simple. How are things between you and Ford?"

"Oh Harper, you're going to live for twenty years."

"You didn't answer my question."

"I like Ford."

"Well, that's good since the wedding is only a month away."

"I wanted to talk to you about that. So many things have been happening—your illness, Starkey—don't you think we ought to postpone things for a while?"

"Things?"

"The wedding."

"Are you in love with Starkey?"

Cat sighed, sat down in a chair and smoothed her small, red hands over her thighs. "I need to be very straightforward with you, Harper. I need to just come out and say it—I think I do love him."

"I thought so."

"You did?"

She nodded.

"I guess you think I'm a terrible person."

"Starkey is the best of the bunch. He always has been. He always will be."

"But Ford is a wonderful man. He is—I know he is—and I've tried to love him. I've worked at loving him, but I just can't, and it's sad because he's the kindest person I've ever met."

"Yes, he's too kind. A man shouldn't be that kind. A man should always have an edge to him, a coolness. Ford never had it. Do you want to break off the engagement?"

Cat was a little shocked and at the same time full of admiration for Harper. She loved her curtness, the way she approached problems. "I'm not sure. I'm really not. I don't want to cause trouble between them. What would they do to each other?"

Harper knew what Ford would do. He would become sputtering mad. He would confront Starkey and he would scream and yell a little, and then would somehow convince himself that after all, this was probably the best thing. His usual boundless optimism. She did not know how Starkey would react. She never had, but she did know this: Starkey was the one who should head the family. She had always believed that, but she'd never thought that he would do it because of his military career. Now that it was over, she thought that he might take charge of things— if he was properly enticed—and the way to do that was to give him a challenge, something that seemed almost undoable. She knew exactly what that challenge could be, but in order for it to work, she had to make some changes in her will.

She picked up the phone and dialed the lawyer's number.

While the phone was ringing, she smiled. It was a way of keeping Cat under a Longstreet thumb, and even though Harper felt closer to the girl than she ever had, still she did not trust her, nor did she want her sons to.

She laughed.

Jebodiah found Harper the next morning. She was lying beside her bed. Her head was propped on two saffron pillows. She had smoothed the wrinkles from her silk nightgown and tucked the hem of it under her legs and clipped her small ankles together. Her black eyes were open and fixed upon the photograph of her four sons which hung beside her bed.

Many people came to the funeral and Harper was buried beside Blackie and among the rest of the family in the Longstreet cemetery. The will was read one week after her death. Hannah and Bub and the other servants were left small pieces of land, their children and grand-children assured college educations. Money was left to several state institutions and museums and galleries. Several family friends were remembered with possessions and furniture. Cat was given the peach orchard, trucks and coolers. Each son and Harper's great-grandsons were left a substantial trust fund and then there was a surprise: it was discovered that the *Southern Chronicle* was nearly bankrupt. It had been losing money for six years. Harper left it, all of it, to Starkey. She had made this change on the evening of her death. It was her challenge to Starkey and it was the way that she could keep Cat McGregor from dominating the family. Harper had known that the girl would run right over Ford, but she could not run over Starkey. The marriage between them—and Harper had felt certain that it would happen—was to be her last laugh at Cat McGregor because more than any of her sons, it was Starkey who possessed her own stubbornness, her will, her refusal to be beaten by anyone or anything.

And eight days after Harper Longstreet's death, the three young men and Cat lay in their beds late at night in Waverly.

Ford was thinking how lucky he was to have Cat as his fiancée. He had feared Harper's death, and even when he was a teenager he had thought, Oh God, when Harper dies, please don't let me be alone. Please help me to have in my life a pretty girl, a kind girl, whom I love and who loves me, so I don't have to face the darkness alone. Not that he believed in the God of the Bible—the patient, loving father. He did not believe in that. That's foolishness, he thought, the hairs of your head being numbered and all that, but there is something else. I'm not sure—something like a vast, celestial kindness, an invisible smile that lies at the base of all that is. Yes, I believe in that—the smile beneath all things, the kindness we cannot ever know. It's why Buddha was smiling. Exactly, exactly. I believe in the inexplicable smile of Buddha, the inexplicable smile of the Universe, the smile that gave me Cat . . .

Starkey's thigh was throbbing as he lay in his bed. Beside his bed was a prescription for pain, but he did not take it. He had learned to sleep in a kind of fetal position which helped make the pain less. He had stuck his middle finger into the two-inch-deep hole in his thigh through which they had inserted the pin. This, too, seemed to make the pain less, though he could feel hair growing in the hole and it was soft and mushy with a kind of wax. He was afraid to go to sleep, afraid to see D.K. sucking blood from the corpse. He made himself get up. He was wearing green boxers and his leg was yellow and half as thick as his other leg and it had four long blue-and-red scars and the deep hole and he felt sorry for the leg, almost as if it belonged to someone else. He got his cane and limped to his desk. He picked up the balance sheets the lawyers had given him. It's almost impossible, he said to himself. How did she let it slip like this? It's just an impossible situation. Unless you came up with something like—cheaper ink. Yea, now cheaper ink would help a lot, then you could . . .

When the will was read and Cat found out that Harper had left her the peach orchard, she cried. It meant that no matter what happened with the Longstreets, she had a place to begin, that finally she was assured of an edge in life. Now as she sat in bed she looked back over the last years of her life: the tyranny and soot of her father's coal mine, the prison of her muteness and backwardness and naiveté, the first startling and wonderful weeks at Waverly and Blackie and Boykin—she saw all of it and she felt full of gratitude and remorse. Gratitude for all that Harper had done for her and remorse because she wanted to love her. Why wouldn't you let me do it? I just wanted to hug and thank you and you wouldn't let me get close, damn it. I wanted to be your shining star, the best Longstreet of them all. And I'll tell you something, old lady. I still may be the best, I still may do more than any of them and maybe somehow you will know, wherever you are, maybe somehow you will see me and you will know.

And the last waking thoughts of all of them belonged to Wick. He had made his decision, and if he was honest with himself, it had come as soon as the cardinal had offered him the episcopacy. He lay in the dark not believing in God anymore—what kind of God would place me in this position, would have me make this choice? He did not believe in anything but his own will and his own ambition. They were the only things that had not failed him and they were the only things to which he would be true, but somehow just before he went to sleep, from someplace in himself that had not yet been seduced by his will, there came an old contrition, one that he had learned as a novice in the monastery, one that even his will would not eradicate.

Oh my God, I am heartily sorry for having offended Thee, and I detest all my sins because I dread the loss of Heaven and the pains of Hell, but most of all because they offend Thee my God, who art all good and worthy of all my love. I firmly resolve with the help of Thy holy grace to confess my sins, to do penance and to amend my life, Amen.